From Finland with Love

ELLIE ALANKO

ISBN: 978-0989427210

For Mark

And in memory of my parents,
Kaarlo and Vivian, and my
brothers Lauri and Paul, Finns all

Contents

PART 1: ALINA ALONE

~Olen eksyksissa.~
~I am lost.~

~Ei ole koiraa karvoihin katsominen.~
~Judge not the dog by its hair.~

Panic! at the Salon

Chi-Chi and I stare at me in the mirror. I sit solemn as a priest, black-smocked and choked with a spongy white collar. Since childhood, I've been accused of the spurious offense of not smiling. The young stylist, Chi-Chi, stands behind me, hands on my shoulders. Her streaked hair is twisted conically atop her head. Loose sparkles from her metallic eye shadow shine on her cheek like happy freckles. Women bustle and chatter around us, blow-dryers roar, but we seem to be in a vacuum focused solely, alas, on me.

Chi-Chi swoops the sides of my long hair out in angel wings, then drops them to my shoulders. The bright, busy salon houses two dozen stations at odd angles. The odor of ammonia and fruity hair products permeate the air: orange, kiwi…grapefruit? I have a sudden craving for vitamin C.

"Alina, right?" Chi-Chi says, resting her hands on my cape. I nod. "So. Tell me." She pulls up some split ends for close inspection, smooching her mouth in a look I interpret as disapproving. "What's going on here?"

"Not much," I say, assessing my straight brown hair. I don't think she hears me. Hip-hop music pulses. Women with tinfoil in their hair shout over it, hyped up on lattes. Between the smells, noise, and blinding foil, the place is sensory overload. The dozens of females here on this Thursday morning confirm my opinion that women in this affluent California suburb don't work. I so do not belong here. Thank goodness I don't live here!

She plucks off my glasses and combs out my lank, washed-out mane, once blond, now darkened to a faded brown. "Ash-toned," she says, and I think yes, dusty, dust-colored, a waste of a color. I'm not one to dwell on my looks, but since Chi-Chi now holds my head in a vise-grip toward the mirror, I examine myself. My face had snubbed the peasant nose of my father in favor of my mother's longer, narrower version. A good nose. Like my straight back, which is the feature Mom often praised, scrubbing it hard with a rough loofah in the sauna. My seriously slanted eyes are grey, the bones beneath them high.

Chi-Chi releases my head and flips strands around dismissively. "And forget the color, there's no *style*." I look at her in the mirror behind me, hands now on hips. And everyone says I'm judgmental. "Right now your hair is making no statement."

It's quiet hair. I'm comfortable with that. We have a good relationship. I come from a quiet, Finnish-American family.

Chi-Chi's on a roll. "I mean, what is your hair saying? 'Don't look at me, don't notice me, I'm dull and uninteresting.'"

Wow, it's more talkative than I'd thought. Not to mention rude. "I'll try to be a better listener," I offer.

Puckering her mouth again, she rakes my hair back with her long nails. "One, we've got to cover this."

I bend toward the mirror, squinting at my temples. There's more ash-tone than I'd thought. I finger the hair above my ear. "Where'd all this come from?" The question's rhetorical.

"Your parents," she says. "One of them already grey?"

Both. "Yes," I say. Grey as ashes. Unfortunately, real ashes, as in cremains. But before my father died of cancer five years back, his hair was white and fluffy, like a bird's tuft. My Mom's silver hair turned a steely grey after her stroke, as if reflecting her resolve, her dogged determination against the odds to relearn walking, talking. That Finnish quality of fortitude called *sisu*. She's been gone almost a year now. I push stray hairs away from my eyes, now burning from the heat and chemicals in the air.

"It's hereditary. You're how old, forty?"

"I'm lonely—" A Freudian slip. I clear my throat. "I'm *only* thirty-three. So, can we just cover the grey and trim it? I'm going back to work after a couple of weeks off and I just want it to look normal. Natural."

She suggests highlights, and, detecting my consternation, says, "Highlights are natural." For emphasis she unpins her up-do and shakes it out for me. "Like this." I swallow. Her hair is a kaleidoscope: wide stripes of yellow and orange streaked over a purple base. "Sun-kissed," she says. That's the problem with beauty salons: these people lose all sense of perspective. They play Barbie too much, get lost in the dollhouse. There's nothing natural about Chi-Chi's hair. The sun has not kissed it—it's been plastered with psychedelic graffiti.

"Maybe not today," I say. "I'm sort of a casual person." One who does not like change. Whose whole family is gone, small as it was. Enough change for me.

She rifles through a drawer, "I have some magazines." I squirm in my hot vinyl smock. Why did I pick this random salon up here? I'm starting to think Chi-Chi's a mistake. The name disturbed me from the start. I'd asked for another hairdresser on the phone yesterday but when the girl asked "Who?" I couldn't bring myself to say *Someone not named Chi-Chi.*

Done flipping through magazines, she looks at my eyes as if noticing them for the first time, resting there under my hair. "Let me get our style books—they're better." She clicks off in her heels. What's she planning to do to me? I'm stuck in a rut, I know. My best friend Meredith and her little boy Lou will be coming back from Disneyland soon and surely she'll ask: *Did I hire a realtor to sell my parents' house up here? Bury Mom's ashes? Am I finally moving on?* I tug at the taut foam collar.

At least I can say I sent the letters. At Meredith's urging, I sent thin airmail letters, insubstantial and feathery light, like blowing wishes across the ocean, to two women in Finland whom my mother referred to as "aunts." I told them—quite belatedly, since Mom's been gone nearly a year—of my mother's death. I doubt I'll hear back, partly because I wrote in English, not knowing the arcane and difficult language of my forebears—except for *piru*, a mild epithet translating roughly to "devil," and the words for diamonds, hearts, clubs and spades, none of which I could gracefully work into my correspondence—but also because any aunt of my mother's would be easily ninety years old. Or worse.

Chi-Chi returns with a sizeable book. "What about this?"

My heart races at the picture of a bobbed red-head. That look would surely put me in the spotlight. "You're kidding, right?" When she doesn't answer, I stick my finger on the slick page. "That is *not* me."

Clearly annoyed and now sarcastic, she replies, "No, it's a model." She clutches the open book to her concave stomach. "This hairstyle would work on you, though."

"It looks a bit high maintenance, Chi-Chi." I'm thinking that inserting her name here is a good tactic.

"I mean, look at you, girl! I could make you fabulous." Around me swirls an astigmatic blur of glinting aluminum, fat, flashing wedding diamonds, and high-gloss ruby nails. I feel a sudden need to flee from all this loud fabulous. The scratchy collar, the noxious, infused air—my chest tightens, it's hard to breathe.

She slams the book shut and places forefinger to lips as if pondering the origins of the universe. "You've got a subtle beauty," she says, causing me to exhale a sigh of gratitude. Before turning away she puts that finger up to me, "But I think I can change that." When she calls that she'll be right back with the "mix," I panic, wanting out of this mix.

I half-rise in my cape, ready to escape, when I stop. At some point I need to change and this seems small enough. Trivial. It's only hair, right?

OK, Chi-Chi. Bring it on!

*

Cover it up! I need a hat, a paper bag, a burka. My hair is *orange.* I'm the bobbed redhead with bangs, but the vivid hue in the car mirror is distinctly clownish.

Back at my parents' house, my "home" for the past two weeks, I Google solutions for abused hair but by rote check my work email first. A message with a strange suffix catches my eye. Squinting, I read "Greetings From Espoo!" on the Subject line. The sender's address is from outside the company and judging from the ".fi" suffix, from outside the country. *From Finland?* My great-aunt is *online?* I'm aware that Finland is technically advanced, but my own mother considered computers, with their confusion of coiled cords and connections, to be mainly vexing dust attractors. She was always swiping Dad's PC cables out of their sockets.

When I click on the message, a large green marquee announces "JUKKA KOVANEN" over a full-screen picture of a smiling blond man astride a motorcycle—obviously not my great-aunt. The cheerful guy can't be more than twenty. He's wearing tight leather pants and a striped top that strikes me as French. "YOOK-ka KO-vanen," I mouth. The last name of my great aunt. But he looks so un-Finnish! I scroll down.

"Hei," the message begins. "My mummu has given me the letter you have been writing and we sees that you work for Data Repository Programs, Inc., which I have looked up on the internet."

Enterprising of him, but I wonder how he got my work email address at DRIP…

"I am visiting to America in this summer and would like to meet up with you. I am regretting if this happens too fast for you after your mother is died. We send condolences. But death is part of life and we all must go sometime. That is why we have children."

My stomach grumbles. Too much coffee, but I cannot give up my one comfort food.

"I am little bit late for asking but if you have something in your mind about visiting, please reply. I think it is a good idea and with Paavo and such we will all have good time. I will write little bit again soon."

He signs off with "*Terveisin.*" Best regards.

Family? Coming here? Soon! A jittery anxious feeling percolates up in me, like too much caffeine, causing me to flush and sweat. At the end he includes what I can definitely live without—yet another Internet joke:

"Three gentlemen are regarding an elephant," he writes. *"The one is German. The others is American and Finn. The German guy is thinking about how much is the money for such an animal to fill his pocket. The American is thinking it is good to be in a circous. The Finn guy is thinking, what is that elephant thinking about Me?"*

Beneath the silly but apt joke are more full-sized photos—three artfully posed pictures in front of a row of pointy pines—of the gleaming red and chrome bike. I scroll back up to the picture of the bike containing a human being, this Jukka, seeing little evidence that I'm related to the strapping leather-clad chap. Coming here this summer seems rather sudden. It's already late April! And who is Paavo? The phrases "*Paavo and such*" and "*We will all*" disturb me, as I'm not sure who all of them are. From the obvious affection displayed, the plural might include his motorbike.

I can't believe I have relatives coming! I am the only child of two only children, born late in my mother's life, her "evening star." The members of my family, all three, were congenitally shy and taciturn. My father, Aatos, true to his Finnish-American upbringing, was never one for the sort of frivolous speech others mistook as conversation. A math professor, he was content to lie belly-down on the floor in his boxers, a glass of vodka adjacent for inspiration, and scrawl equations on a yellow-lined pad until Mom roared near, vacuuming within an inch of his drink.

My mother, Lempi, though born and raised in Finland, was mildly more outgoing and on occasion could be uncannily bubbly—especially when the house was very, very clean. At such times, Dad could be counted on to mention her mongrel Swedish blood, as if to explain all the zaniness. Mom would wink at me and say, "Gypsy blood!" though I've never associated that particular group with undue tidiness.

Without them I've been lost. At times, I still expect to see them here when I walk in. They'll be greeting me for Sunday dinner, the smell of roast pork and apple cake wafting. Or the sweet, egg-y aroma of *pulla*, our everyday coffee bread, scented with pungent cardamom. Mom will put aside her dishrag to squeeze my hands in her damp, soft clasp; Dad will look up from his equations and his brooding brow will clear at the simple sight of me. "*Tytär*," they'd say. *Daughter*. Their voices come to me in waves, I hear them like random snippets of conversation on a beach, carried by a sea breeze, now here with me—now gone—swept away as quickly and ephemerally as they arrived.

I rise from my laptop, yanking off my Hello Kitty t-shirt, damp and clingy from the diabolical Mercury Valley heat. In my bra and pajama pants, I pour another cup of coffee and pace. Will I have time to entertain visitors working my sixty-hour weeks? And I'm wasting all my vacation time now in this rich backwater, achieving nothing.

Two weeks ago, I drove the hour northeast from my apartment in Silicon Valley on forced time off. Duncan, my manager, practically pushed me out the door insisting I use over-accumulated vacation time. The testing of software would go on without me, he claimed. I planned to finally clear out and start selling my parents' house here in Mercury. But with one free week left, I've done little except fill two garbage bags with clothing I'd never seen my folks wear and box a few textbooks. And write the letters to Finland.

I dial Meredith's cell number but there's no answer. She's down in southern California with her toddler visiting family and standing in long theme park lines. I try Cleo, a lesser friend but expert on all things beauty—my hair, *ugh*!—and leave another message. Desperate, I call my hometown friend April back East, whose husband answers in typical fashion by questioning me about all the nuts and "kooks" in California, all the divorcees. "Who wants to stay married to a kook?" I say, and since April's not there, we hang up.

Back at the kitchen table, I type: *"Paiva! How nice to hear from you. You are most welcome here."* So, like, when exactly are you coming? And how many are you? How long will you be in northern California? Instead I write:

"I hope to see you soon. My apartment is very small. But if you are many, I might still own my parents' house. Please write again soon with details. I look forward to meeting you all."

I attach one of the rare pictures I have of me with my parents, taken by a new colleague of Dad's when he transferred from MIT to Cal. In the picture, we're full of mirth. We'd started out staring solemnly—three Finns regarding a photographer. He pleaded, "*Smile*, will you?" and, looking at each other, we burst out laughing. After adding the photo, I type "*Best wishes,*" and hit Send.

Too keyed up to stay inside, I throw on my t-shirt and pocket an apple in my roomy pants for the neighborhood horse. I grab the house key from the console table, looking with chagrin at the golden pine box of ashes sitting there: my mother's unburied remains, the other matter I meant to finally deal with. Meredith, a therapist, says it's bad "*fung-shway*" to have ashes in the house. I'm not sure exactly what that is but think it has to do with candles and light, smoke and mirrors. Before walking out, I dial the number on my cell phone. Enough stalling.

~Niin metsä vastaa kuin sinne huudetaan.~
~The forest answers in the same way one shouts in it.~

Edna

Edna Smythe-Burr says I can Fed Ex my mother back East.

I stop walking. "*Fed Ex* her?" I say into my cell phone. Like something sold on E-Bay?

"Maybe not Fed Ex. Try UPS, US Mail. However you want to send the box." The box. What kind of person runs for Cemetery Commissioner? Are they appointed or actually elected? Do her campaign signs read got dead*?* Edna Smythe-Burr is the peevish cemetery official back in the Massachusetts mill town I hail from. Where Dad rests, still alone.

"I suppose I can use the mail…" I start striding again, the sweet, spring air in my face. Although, like my parents, I'm not impressed with the exclusive status of this moneyed community, the area is undeniably pretty. Oak branches twine overhead. Delicate pink and white blossoms spring out of plum and crabapple trees. Sun-facing magnolias are in full fuchsia bloom, while the petals of shaded trees remain cupped tight like Christmas bulbs. Rich, sheltered lawns spread a lush blanket over the land, which is currently wondrously hushed.

"I think we've been over this a few times. You're a hoot. Haven't I talked to you before?" She has. Probably a dozen times.

"I've just forgotten what to do."

"What's your name again?"

"Alina Eskala."

"Right. Finnish. Didn't you decide to fly the ashes out here yourself? Around now, if I'm not mistaken."

I pause. "Actually, the airline wouldn't let me take the sealed ashes onboard." And who wants their mom's remains battered about by those workers in neon vests you see chucking luggage into the bellies of airplanes?

"You're one for the books," Edna chokes out a laugh. "Listen, you're calling me at the wrong number. Cemetery Commissioner's just my night job. I work it from home. My graveyard shift," she chortles. *What she does for fun, obviously.* "Get a pen, honey. Write it down. Spacey Californians, must be all those earthquakes."

She's right. An earthquake has struck—a natural disaster—death. When my father died from liver cancer five years ago, the world as I'd always known it—the one with a solid steady earth and both my parents intact—was shaken forever. And then, over a year ago, a hurricane. "Wind in the body," Meredith, a therapist cum alternative healer, said. That's what Chinese medicine calls a stroke. That's what knocked my mother down.

Edna talks about packaging and mailing, slowly, as if I'm five. I reach the horse corral. Astro's the last horse in Mercury, a lonely chestnut, a vestige from the era when trains transported summer folk to Mercury's racetrack and gambling casino. Only the country club and golf course remain.

I slip the phone in my pants pocket, effectively muffling Edna's strident voice. The horse watches me sideways through long straight lashes. For some reason I think of Steffen, how he lowered his lashes and surveyed me after lovemaking, tracing his finger across my face, through the valley of my breasts to my stomach, connecting my scattered moles in a random constellation. His light touch making me want him again… I shake off these strange, disloyal thoughts. It's my loneliness talking. He's with Meredith and their toddler now.

Arching back my palm, I hold a green apple to Astro's star-stained face. He tilts his head and bares his yellow teeth to snatch it whole, crunching and drooling foam. Chunks of apple spew.

"What about a gravestone?" I hear Edna goad in her provincial Massachusetts accent: "I hope you finally got a marka."

A mocker? I have you. I pull the phone out of my pocket. "No, not yet."

"Didn't we talk about that, too? I remember you. You and your mother came out a few times to your father's grave. Somehow they got plots in Greenvale." She sniffs. "Most of the Finns are buried across town. Greenvale's pre-revolutionary, you know. A Yankee cemetery."

Yankees and Finns? It's 2007. Yankees are a baseball team. What is she, a DAR member? If my parents had associated the leafy green cemetery—or Mercury, for that matter—with snobbery, they would've snubbed them all to *Hel*sinki! Edna goes on to say that my parents must have bought the last two available plots back in the 1980's.

I say, "No room for me, then, I guess."

"What? You're young. Oh, you're pulling my leg," her jocular tone stubbed out. "Actually, you can fit two urns in one plot."

Oh! Good news—space for me! The issue actually came up with my parents. Planning ahead, my dad wanted to buy an extra plot for me. Mom scoffed, saying I'd want to be buried with my own husband. Unfortunately, the husband hasn't shown up yet. Maybe I should take my friend Cleo's advice and advertise for one online. "SWF, early 30s, Seeks Plot-Mate" my headline could read. Replies would come from the forward-thinking. Or the very old.

Edna brushes me off. "I'm going to try connect you to the town clerk. Maybe Bob can get through to you. Hang on."

I pat Astro's warm, solid flank. His head slants as I turn to head back. I don't want to mail Mom's ashes to this stolid woman, don't want her remains in Edna's fleshy, baubled fingers. I remember her wide pasty face, smeared red mouth, and thick baby wrists, banded with a line.

Meredith says I'm stuck in some phase of grief, denial, anger. But, like my mother before me, I won't cry, I'll stay stoic, have *sisu.* I know they're only ashes. Mom's soul has long since flown alight, aloft, up there dancing with the northern lights, with Dad. I start the short hike back. The phone clicks, then silence. Am I on hold or did she hang up on me? As I approach the house, an automated female voice comes on. "If you'd like to speak to an operator, say "operator."

I say "operator," and walk around back to sit on the redwood deck. The sauna my father built stands several feet away, under a shedding eucalyptus at the edge of the yard. The large property is secluded by a perimeter of trees. In the middle, a grand, ancient oak spreads its craggy, beseeching branches. When Dad first showed me this wooded expanse, he said with muted pride, "Finns are a forest people."

"If you'd like to speak to an operator, say "operator," the recording repeats. The connection cuts in and out. The trees and the nearby Mount Mercury make service here erratic.

"Operator!" I yell.

"I can't hear you. If you'd like to speak to an operator, say 'operator'," the tape says. I refuse to say 'operator' a third time. "Hello?" the voice asks. "Are you there?"

I say, "Yes." *I think so.* "Yes!" I muster all my lapsed vocal strength. I've hardly spoken in days.

"I can't hear you. If you'd like to speak to an operator, say 'operator.' Hello? Are you there?"

Am I here? Do I exist? If a tree fell in the forest…

"NO!" I shout to the machine. "No, I'm not here. I'm lost. Can you find me? If you're so freaking concerned, why don't you come find me?!" I snap the phone shut and hurl it flying wild into the weeds.

~Se koira älähtää, johon kalikka kalahtaa.~
~The dog will howl, which is hit by the stick.~
(The lady doth protest too much.)

Cleopatra

Meredith says ashes should be scattered, not buried. I find a ladder in the musty carriage house, carry it to the backyard, and lean it against the house.

With the cube containing my mother's remains, I climb the one story to the pitched roof and set the box on the narrow, leveled-off edge. Stepping one foot onto the roof, a splintered wood shingle tears loose in my hand. I gasp and clutch the ledge as the ladder shifts precariously, making me question the wisdom of climbing alone onto a crumbling roof. I take a breath, then swivel up to sit on the tight flat space, legs dangling over.

To my left lies a house whose owners spend much of the year in Tahoe. Their house replicates my parents'—a small 1920s, low-style English cottage with a steep roof, both sided with white shingles, windows trimmed in green. The short front yards and narrow spaces between the houses on this lane give no clue to the large expanses behind them—except for the gargantuan Italianate renovation on my other side, which swallows the whole length of its yard (and houses a boisterous new family who, judging from the quietude, must not be home).

Carefully, I stand. In the distance lie rolling hills, patches and strips of fluorescent yellow wildflowers streaked across their green canvas. A shimmer of water sparkles in a stretch of golf course.

When I first brought Meredith here to visit my parents, it was after a day kicking around Berkeley. Minutes through the tunnel, we found ourselves estranged in a totally different microclimate and *microcosm.* The bay-infused cool of Berkeley was replaced by the dry white heat of the Mercury Valley, with its SUV-clogged roads, gated communities, and new, homogenized strip malls. Driving through the bowered entrance of Mercury proper, we encountered our first alien life in the form of a middle-aged golfer—"accosted by a man in Lacoste!" I joked—at the helm of an oncoming cart. But I know my parents retired here for seclusion, not exclusion; nature, not nine holes.

I scoop a handful of soft, gritty ash, barring thoughts of what it once was. "Mom, I know you and Dad bought those plots back East, but." I clear my throat. "I haven't been back there once since you died. It's so far away. We swept the leaves off his grave. We left lilacs, roses. Anyway, I know you loved this, this…" I scan the park-like yard, "greenery. And since that creek out back is almost dry—" My parched voice cracks. I think of our family visit to Finland, the engulfing seas, lakes and rivers. More water than land. Maybe I should scatter my mother's remains in her homeland, her home *water.* But I can't delay this forever.

"Anyway, I hope this will be OK with you, Mom." I look up, wait for a breeze to hit the still air. A leaf blower starts its sudden, obnoxious buzzing. When I feel a draft stir, I fling my handful skyward, try to send the ashes flying to the heavens—then watch as they drop directly, unceremoniously, regrettably straight into the gutter and down to the yard below...

"Ouch!" Directly under me shines the brassy yellow hair of Cleopatra Crumm. She's bent over, rubbing her eye. "Shit!" Her voice booms through the still air.

Oh my God! No! "Cleo!" *Christ.* "Are you all right?" We were work colleagues for years, though sometimes I'm not sure if we're really *friends.* Our friendship is an accident of circumstance. Unlike Meredith, I don't collect friends; finding a good movie and dance partner isn't easy. People are married, home with small kids, crashing early into bed. And despite Cleo's aggressive dating strategies, she's often available.

She squints up at me one-eyed. "What the—?" she bellows—the volume of her voice perpetually stuck on loud—her bleached hair flashing in the noonday sun. I fumble the box lid on and scuttle down the ladder like a sorry hermit crab. I know that ashes that once made up a human body should return to the living earth, the wind, sky, water. But Cleopatra Crumm? No, no, *no*.

I lean toward her, "God, Cleo. I am so sorry! Is your eye hurt?"

"You dumped soot in it!" She removes her hand, revealing smeared mascara and an irritated, bloodshot eye the color of her skimpy halter dress.

"That was *not*—" I'm stopped by the approach of a strange thickset man with a beard. He meets up with us, glances at the ladder and roof where the pine box sits, then pulls Cleo's lower lids down.

Despite her unfortunate, bloodhound look, he pronounces, "She's good. What happened?"

"Alina was cleaning the chimney or something. Who knows?"

"Oh God, I feel awful. Let me take care of that." I reach out.

She puts up her hand. "I'll live." Her eye twitches, she swipes away mascara. "But look at you—your hair! I love it!" she cries.

I smooth my hand over my head. "I'm surprised to see you out here." I eye the guy with the wrestler's build, tighten the waist string on my pajama pants.

"You called me. Said you have some news. It's your hair, right? Why didn't you answer your cell?"

"I think I know why." The bearded man has walked a few feet away to stoop and pick my phone out of the grass.

"Oh." I say, taking it from him. "Thanks. I've been looking for that." When he says it was probably on *vibrate*, I take a step back.

Cleo says, "I finally found a house I can afford. In Folsom! We were headed there."

"It'll be a killer commute," I say. But Bay Area house prices are forcing people to move ever farther away. Recently I heard a radio ad for new housing in the *Far East Bay*—sounded exotic, but no doubt it was just some dismal suburb of Sacramento.

"Tell me about it. Anyways, you're sort of en route, so I thought I'd show Craig this ritzy area."

"Greg," he says. "It's Greg, not Craig."

"I said '*Greg*.'" They look away from each other to me. I've already sized up Greg, evidently Cleo's latest boyfriend, as her type: Neanderthal-like, muscular and stocky, with a working knowledge of tool use.

Below her irritated eye, Cleo's lips appear larger than usual, swollen. "Gee, did something hit your mouth too?"

"No, I had my lips plumped. You know, the 'bee-stung' look," she says, pressing them with her fingers, totally unabashed about confessing this in front of Greg. I flash on Chi-Chi and her "sun-kissed" look. Bee stung mouths, sun fried hair—why don't these women just go camping? She asks what I've been doing.

"I've just been taking some vacation time up here," I say, looking around the quiet yard in this nowhere place, seeing how feeble that must sound to Cleo, who likes cities, crowds, action. "You know, taking walks and—" I try to think of something. The letters to Finland. "Writing letters…" Four eyes blink at me simultaneously. Jesus, who am I, Emily frigging Dickinson? "I do have news. I have family coming! I thought you and Meredith would like to know."

"Who's Meredith?" Greg interjects.

"Our New-Agey therapist friend," Cleo says flippantly, though I appreciate her using the word "our." My two friends are such opposites. After Mom died, Meredith recommended yoga, Cleo dragged me to music clubs. Meredith drove me to Tahoe for a weekend, Cleo said I needed to get laid. One believes in the energizing powers of *chi*, while the other trusts the rejuvenating effects of Botox and sex. With Cleo, "natural" holds no sway.

I offer them something to drink. As we head inside, Greg says, "These houses out here are something."

"They're monstrous," I say, with my genetic distrust of wealth. *Happiness is a place between too little and too much*, my dad often said. I replay my parents' words in my head hoping I won't lose the sound, the true pitch and timbre, of their voices.

"They're fucking gorgeous," he says.

"Well, you might be disappointed by this one." Like my parents, I prefer the quaint old modest homes, increasingly disappearing, which served as summer cottages in this former watering hole for the Bay Area rich. Tiny Mercury, the bucolic enclave hidden at the base of the mountain, an unincorporated area of only a few hundred parcels, remains unknown to many even in the surrounding suburban Blaineville area.

I lead them into the little kitchen, where Cleo settles onto a chair. "I'm glad you're taking time off. You work like a dog and that company's a sinking ship." I don't remind her that she was the one who lured me there. No doubt it's why she recently bailed DRIP for a sales job in pharmaceuticals.

"Coffee OK?" I hand her a napkin-wrapped cube of ice.

"Don't touch the stuff," Greg says, so I pour him a glass of water. I boil water in Mom's dented metal coffee pot, then dump grounds directly into the water. As the grounds sink and stew, I tell them what little I know about my Finnish relative Jukka and his pending visit.

"You don't look Finnish," Greg tells me, rocking his short, burly body forward on his toes, as if to gain in stature, albeit temporarily.

I raise my eyebrows, thinking how little he knows, and throw a plate of stale egg bread—the last braid of my mother's *pulla* from the freezer—onto the table. "Well, my hair's really brown."

"I had a Finnish girlfriend once. Kirsti. She had this beautiful pale blond hair and huge blue eyes." He furrows his low brow, his skin tan and roughly-textured like putty, and looks off into the distance, "She looked like a fairy princess."

"Maybe she was Swedish," I say, as Finns, especially Eastern Karelians, tend to be darker, shorter, more Slavic or Asiatic than Scandinavians.

"Maybe she was *imaginary*," Cleo mutters. I stifle a laugh. In spite of our many differences, I enjoy her.

"Mind if I use the restroom?" I point Greg down the hall. I pour us steaming cups and fill mine with spoonfuls of sugar and milk, the way I've drunk it every morning since childhood. Sitting across the table from Cleo, I explain what I was doing on the roof. Sheepish, I raise my mug in a toast: "Here's Mom in your eye."

She spurts coffee. "Good thing your folks had a sense of humor." I drink to that. The liquid slides down my throat like warm, melted coffee ice cream. She peers at me for too long. "Not sure I would've done that."

"I already feel bad enough, Cleo. I just feel stuck about the ashes, the house…"

"No, I mean *gone red*. I'm not sure the shade suits you," she says with typical inconsistency.

"It's not like I asked for the *Ronald McDonald* look!" Then I soften up. After all, I almost blinded her. "Greg seems like a nice guy."

"You should try meeting one. Anyways, I'll never understand why you gave up Steffen."

"Why do you always bring up ancient history?"

"Because your recent history's boring. You make no effort."

"I *date*," I say. I lift my burnished bangs at her. "And I took a step."

"You're averaging one date a year. I'm just saying, Steffen's a hunk and you had all that great sex."

Irked, I say, "We were just way too different. You know that."

She shrugs. "Love's complicated."

"Lust is not love!" Did I just yell that?

Cleo throws her hands up. "Sorry."

I tromp to the sink and clatter my cup and saucer into it. What we had wasn't love. Love is quiet, love takes time. Sex, nudity was not what scared me about Steffen. We Finns know what's really scary—what lies beneath the skin. What Steffen tried too soon to penetrate. "We shouldn't even be talking about it. He's with Meredith. *And Lou.*" Artistic, rash, Steffen became too fervent too fast. He talked of love before I even got to know him!

What a *sense of pressure* I felt from the weight of his emotion. How suddenly I was the object of head-over-heels love! And our close call with pregnancy scared me off, made me realize I was not ready for his unbridled passion. Then my father was diagnosed with liver cancer…

Outside the window, the grand oak leaves bud into full glory. How to explain those hot, heady months with Steffen? I flush now at the thought, the second time today that I've stirred up memories of our infatuation. Maybe it's because we came up here once and, finding the doors locked and my parents away, made love under the sweeping canopy of that tree, the cool, rubbery grass tickling my back, the sky through the branches blue and endlessly clear.

When Dad fell ill, I withdrew and introduced him to Meredith, sure that he would appreciate her fine, pore-less skin, her beauty. She could be a muse for his painting. Or so I thought.

"He's with them—*sort of,*" Cleo insinuates.

I snap back, arms crossed. "Well he better come around. They have a son and it's time for him to get a fulltime job and marry Meredith. Commit." Lou should have a full-fledged family.

"Says Judge Alina."

"Meredith deserves better." I sigh. Poor Mere, a classic Northern California whole earth mother who got co-opted by motherhood. After several months alone with her baby, the dusty TV came out of the garage, and the home-pureed organic carrots were supplemented with trips to the drive-through. I think about the assortment of wholesome kid DVDs she started popping in early on; her chagrin that her son's first words were not "Ma-ma" or "Da-da," but "Bez-Bay"—"Press *Play*."

Cleo gulps the last of her coffee, then whips out a red pocket mirror and smiles a toothy monkey grin. She's older and younger than I—forty going on fourteen. We hear the toilet flush. "We should go. Craig—Greg—might want to get home. We got totally lost finding you out here." She leans in briefly with hot coffee breath, "Never date a Greg after a Craig." She grips her temples and purses her eyes shut, "Greg, Greg, Greg. I've got to get that right."

"A Gregorian chant," I say. The mantra over, Cleo opens her eyes to check her reflection once more, dipping her head to fluff the hair on top. Wiry greys spring out of the blond, as if electrified. She jumps up when Greg returns. I turn away when they kiss. After squeezing my arm, she taps out with her partner in tow. "Take it easy, kiddo." She winks. Or maybe it's a cinder in her eye.

*

That evening I resolve to go back to work early. The Payroll Department wants me to take my unused vacation time, but I'm getting nothing done. Besides, I might need the remaining week off when my visitors come. I'll call a realtor, deal with Mom's ashes later.

I grab a blanket and pillow and walk in the nighttime chill to the unheated sauna, the place I feel happiest. I've never lived in Mercury, save for caring for Mom during her final weeks. But here, in this sauna Dad built, I could just as easily be in our family sauna back East.

I sit on the cool cement floor, my spot as a child when we all *took sauna.* Until adolescence it was a family affair. Because my parents liked the hut scorching hot, I'd sit at the bottom while the steam clouded them above. I basked in the wet warmth, listening to their occasional talk, the sizzle and hiss from water splashed onto the hot rocks, the swish and slap of birch switches on flesh… Suddenly sleepy, I lie on a hard Aspen bench. Listening to the even metronome of chirping crickets, like sleigh bells chiming, I drift off in my dark womb.

~Ojasta allikkoon.~
~From the ditch to deep water.~

Exit Strategy

I'm out of here!

I was awakened by the neighborhood rooster, who began screeching around four a.m. My stays in Mercury have disabused me of two childhood notions: first, that a rooster's crowing is somehow associated with *dawn*, and second, that its crow sounds similar to "cock-a-doodle-doo." The banshee cry that wakes me repeatedly each night makes me conjecture that this rooster, who lives blocks away but sounds as if he could be in bed with me, is either a young cock much too eager or an old fowl who's hopelessly lost his timing.

Ignoring the rooster's nocturnal wake-up calls, I waited until rays of light shone through the sauna window before stirring. My hip and shoulder bones ached from the press of hard Aspen, and I was shivering under the thin blanket. Chill permeates the shadows of Mt. Mercury until the fiery sun blasts it away, temperatures altogether too extreme, too wildly extravagant.

After coffee, I shower and quickly dress for work—jeans, a strappy tee for outdoors, and a thick brown sweater for the office chill. My contact lenses grate after days of not wearing them. I dabble on lip-gloss and pull my loud hair into a tight short ponytail. When I check it in the mirror, I see a stubby orange tail like something out of a fantastical children's book, the kind I read to Lou. My look doesn't inspire me with confidence, but I'm dying to get back to work, to my friends. Dad often said, "*A man is valued by his work, not his words.*" Or her hair, right?

I hop into my car and curve along the busy country road that cuts through the valley, rushing past hills dotted with California scrub oak and groups of grazing cows; slowing past the Blaineville elementary school where a line of huge boxy cars idles like a stalled train.

Signs posted along the road announce "Happy 9th Birthday, Ashlee!" SUVs are plastered with student of the month stickers, adorned with vanity soccer-mom-type license plates. Such a loud, cheerleading culture, such open boasting and affection, everyone absorbed and consumed with *advertising* family life, as if "Family" is a brand, a commodity to be publicly promoted. Makes me glad my parents were less ostentatious in their love.

Racing onto the freeway toward Silicon Valley, leaving behind these suburban fanatics, my spirits lift. I drive up the Sunol grade, slowed up by an ancient, white-domed mini-bus sporting shredded, faded peace bumper stickers. My father, incongruously fast behind the wheel, taught me only two road rules: always look over your shoulder before changing lanes, and never get stuck behind a Volkswagen bus. Flying by the VW, like a large vintage toaster—and not moving much faster—I feel lighter, more buoyant. At the crest of the hill I see yellow smog nestled in the valley and smell its odor of home-baked bread through the vents.

I'm eager to see Ravi and Sri, my co-testers. They're like family to me. Who else am I with ten hours a day, six days a week? During our crunch weekends in the lab, the three of us run code till Sunday past midnight, repeating tests and eating vending machine food. Surrounded by the hum of machines in the darkened room, we develop that loopy, fatigued camaraderie borne from striving to finish the impossible by morning. Our late-night gatherings are cozy, with me blanketed in a sweater against the cool lab temperatures, and a sort of magic emanating from the blinking black screens and easy talk, like a tribe around a campfire.

Test engineering suits me well: ferreting out the broken pieces, flaws, inaccuracies, inconsistencies—the bugs. I enjoy my role in making the product run the way it should, being the arbiter of what's right and wrong, the judge of good and bad. I see my profession as righteous, part of a mission to produce software that's relatively pain-free for customers. One that ideally spares them the need to—God forbid—read the user manuals. After catching up with them today, I'll stop by Meredith's. With luck, she'll be home with Lou, and Steffen will be out.

When I arrive at work, the parking lot and office floor are oddly empty. But sitting in my cubicle, I'm quickly distracted by another email message. I gawk at a picture of Jukka squatting with his "friend Paavo." Both wear skimpy European swimsuits, white towels draped onto their hairless chests. They're surrounded by snow. A large rectangular hole cut into ice stretches behind them. This Paavo appears attractive. Despite the lunacy of swimming in icy tundra waters, my gut tells me he's normal and … *nice.*

The face that stares directly at me doesn't possess the ironic look so often seen on Steffen's, nor his flashy Hollywood blue eyes that, coupled with his sexy tousled hair, turn women's heads. Paavo's a quieter handsome: straight brown hair, a steady medium build, eyes, possibly, like Meredith's: hazel. Green with a burst of sunlight around the pupils. If Steffen is more like fun and flirty Cleo, instinct tells me this Paavo is closer to solid Meredith, who's genuine, the real thing.

The message, dated yesterday, says they leave "tonight on the red-eye." Aren't they flying back in time, into…today? Into SFO? *Now*??? Full of questions, hot and agitated, I flush. I jerk my sweater over my head when I hear Duncan say, "Alina, is that *you*?" *Shoot.* This hair has to go. I fumble to close the message, as if I've been caught viewing porn.

When I swivel about, my manager flashes a smile with a quick look at my tank top. I glance back to make sure the image of near-naked men is off my screen. Feeling exposed, I tighten my fiery ponytail and say, "It's hot in here."

"I guess so," he answers, following my glance. My eyes widen at this remark, but he says, "They shut off the A/C."

"Duncan, it's crazy. I have, like, relatives, well at least one, and I think they might actually be here!"

Arms folded and eyes on his feet, he says, "Alina, I am really, really sorry."

What's he talking about? My hair? The air? The heat must be getting to both of us, as he's dressed beyond casual, even for Friday. A forty-ish transplant from Massachusetts—the only thing we have in common—who pictures himself a California surfer dude, today below his t-shirt he's donned long board shorts and Tevas. He looks at me dead-on. "Something's going down."

Going down. My stomach sinks, heart speeds. I know this tone, that grave look. "What..." my voice creaks, stalls. He motions, and I trudge behind his squeaky sandals and jutting calves down the hall. One of the last of the lonely California smokers, Duncan leads me out to the balcony. He lights up and takes a long drag, holding in the smoke as if it's a joint.

Tight throated, I say, "What's *going down*?"

After a long and deliberate exhale he lets it out. "We are."

*

"I feel like such a shit," Duncan says, tossing his cigarette down to the parking lot below, where it lands in an unkempt little graveyard of toppled butts. "I told Lien that we couldn't just *let you go* the minute you got back from vacation." Lien being founder and CEO of DRIP; father-in-law of Duncan. He faces the uneventful lot dotted with cars, the squat white and glass office buildings beyond.

I stare speechless at his profile, his patch of freckles melding as his cheek turns red. *DRIP going under*? It feels like someone socked me in the gut. I lean forward to grip the cold metal rail. He turns to me and gropes for the delicate words that float beyond his thick fingers. "It doesn't seem like good timing for you."

I gasp, "Good timing? How could it be good timing for anyone!" My stomach churns.

When I ask about Sri and Ravi, he says everyone has to clear out within a couple of weeks. "Get this, they're making us cut back on electricity. No A/C! These guys are *cheap*."

"When did all this happen? I've only been gone two weeks!" Did they make me take my vacation days because they couldn't pay me?

"I just found out myself the other day. Lien doesn't tell me much. Supposably there's no more funding. We're history."

"But." I say. I gaze out at the blur of buildings, feeling at a loss. "I just got home."

"Ravi said you went back home or something."

"Home? Huh?" What's he saying? Nothing makes sense, I seem to have lost my bearings. I clench the balcony rail as my head spins, the cement below my feet feels unsteady. I'm on a listing ship lost at sea. It's hard to breathe; my ribs feel as though they're contracting.

"Back to Massachusetts?" He sniffs, "Funny, I still call it home. Do you?"

"What?" Home? "No," I say, realizing that by "home" I didn't mean returning to my apartment in Silicon Valley. I meant coming *here*. To work. Although I never told Duncan of my now defunct "vacation" plans, I tell him, "I didn't go back East. I was just up at my parents' house." Doing nothing. And now this. *And now what?*

"You went on vacation over where your parents live?" Possibly aware that his verb tense is off, his hand flies to his hair. "Where's that again?"

"Mercury."

This draws a blank look. Although my family had moved to the Bay Area from Massachusetts when I was eighteen, I remember when I, too, knew little of the hot Mercury valley.

Duncan jangles change in his pocket. "They were Flemish,

weren't they?" getting the tense right.

"Finnish," I say. How he could come up with Flanders is beyond me.

"Hmm." I don't think my answer registered. "So where abouts is that?"

"It's between Sweden and Russia." Could this man possibly know where *Flanders* is?

His eyes scan and reflect the cloudless sky. "Mercury?"

Jesus! Why are we talking about this? My brain tries to absorb the news. I'm jobless. I'm stunned. Not the stunned I felt five years back when I got the early morning call. When my mom told me that Dad was dying of cancer. The machinery in my body chunked so noisily that I couldn't hear, couldn't make it out. "You mean he needs an operation?" I asked. He needs chemo, radiation? *What?*

More miserable from these thoughts, I stagger to a wrought iron table. I drop onto a chair, cling to the chilled arms as Duncan wriggles into the opposite seat. Sucking on a new cigarette, he says, "Lien's setting up some kind of resume writing workshop for us. You are honest-to-God the most wicked hard worker I know. I know some places that might be hiring."

"I don't *want* another job." My eyes burn from the smoke, the damn contact lenses. "All this change," I mumble into the holes in the grated table.

Duncan rests his forearms on the table. "I'm really sorry, what can I say, Alina. We're all in the same friggin' boat."

"No, no," I wave my arms as if to banish him, his smoke, his news. "I'm not in your boat! I've never been in your boat and…" I fight tears.

After some silence, he says quietly, "Look, you've been through a lot these past few years. And if there's anything—"

I stand and rush over to the balcony. His tone struck an unbearable chord, the true tenor of unfeigned sympathy.

Clenching the rail, I squeeze my eyes and fight the thickening in my throat. I must have more than strength. I must have *sisu.*

~Minä istun iloissani ja annan surun huilata.~
~I sit here happy and let sorrow catch some breath.~

Meredith's Touch

Meredith holds my head in her lap as I lie on her couch in her calamitously messy apartment. Her hands cradle my head, as she performs some therapy on me called "ray-kee." I have my doubts about this Reiki and her other healing techniques. Mere's an ex-Lit major—we met years ago through a book group—who worked for a while as a masseuse. When her fingers started aching, she got into a form of massage therapy where she didn't actually *touch* people, but floated her hands all over their bodies. She says it provided some sort of healing psychic energy. The clients stopped coming. So she got an M.A. in Social Work and now counsels girls with eating disorders.

I'm glad she's back to touching now, as I am relaxing. With Steffen and Lou off somewhere, I ranted to her for half of an hour. I called and drove here directly after talking to Duncan, flooded with relief to find her home from vacation. Over calming if unsavory yellow tea, I railed about the lay-off, the unfairness, all of us working so hard for so many years for worthless stock options. I whined. And like a mother she's commiserated, consoled. Like a therapist, she listened.

When things get tough, I always turn to Mere for advice. After Mom died I wanted to flee, considered moving back to Massachusetts. She told me it's not a good idea to make any major changes after a traumatic event. "The wisdom is to wait at least a year," she said. Lying here, it occurs to me that I'm *laid off with my mother dead just ten months.* Indignant, I pop up and cry, "This is a blatant violation of the one-year rule!"

With a puzzled expression, she presses me down under her still hands. Motionless and warming. She rests them on my stomach for moments, and then moves to my face—some kind of laying on of the hands. "Let's create a still space for you," she says in her therapist-talk. "I know it's hard, Ali, but try to relax."

I feel my body loosen under her touch, the spinning of my mind slow. Maybe her Reiki is calming me. More likely it's just the presence of my dear friend. I smile up at her, as always, taken with her beauty. She's as lovely and messy as the shedding magnolia in front of her duplex: tall, with a dancer's long neck, glossy black hair, and the kind of thick milk skin that is oddly impervious to the harsh California sun. Her face always looks cool and creamy, even when it swelters. She has the kind of delicate beauty women envy and men often overlook.

She's my best friend, my sole soul confidante, the one who helped me through the deaths of both parents. By nature, I'm private, not a gad-about or a gab-about. Not someone who attracts others, as Meredith so easily does. I can count my friends on one hand: Meredith, Cleo, Ravi and Sri from work, and April back in Massachusetts. Meredith's the cream of them all, the one at the top.

When she positions her hands to cradle my head, something stirs in me that prickles my skull, unsettles my stomach. I liked the ear press better, as it dulled the noise from the nearby freeway. I squirm and sit up, scan the chaotic living room.

She says, "It's worse than usual, I know. I'm on the phone for like ten minutes and Lou destroys the place with finger paints." She waves a lissome arm to the room, which smells like a pre-school classroom. Streaks of red paint are slashed across the white walls, and trails of the color stream across the shag carpet, splattering toys, the thrift store chair, and ending on a tiny tennis shoe that steadily blinks a red alert from its heel. Her bounty of bargain clothes—she favors flowing skirts over ballet-style tops—

overflows from open suitcases near the front door.

The screen door makes me anxious. "Where did they go again?" As much as I'd like to see little Lou, I don't feel like dealing with the easy, teasing ways of my ex-boyfriend. Especially today.

"Probably the park. Steffen came right after you called and I literally banished them." I wriggle off the couch and walk to the door, where the freeway roars, and scan the street for signs of Steffen's truck. Meredith, Lou, and Steffen live twelve minutes from me on a street of worn duplexes and fatigued bungalows. Forties and fifties-era military housing for the nearby air base, it's a low-rent district, generally starved of trees. In the Bay Area, mature, lush greenery relates directly to cash. The apartment's only 600 square-feet, but has two bedrooms and a front yard flanked by a magnolia, half its petals already fallen and curling brown, and a privet gone wild, tall enough for a kid to climb.

I feel I should run before the boys come back. But go where, my studio apartment? Do what? "My feet are cold," I say, despite the heat, always at odds with my internal and external temperatures.

"That's because you don't *breathe*."

"Technically, Meredith…" I decide not to point out that I get by. I take one of the deep breaths she recommends. The thunder from the freeway makes me wonder if deeply inhaling carbon monoxide can be considered salutary. She pats the sofa for me to return. Maybe just a few more minutes with her…I sit beside her. "I'm hoping you didn't tell anyone I lost my job?"

"No, don't worry. Steffen and I have barely talked. He needs time with Lou, and I definitely need a break."

I'm so self-absorbed! "Your trip, Mere. How was it?"

"It was Disneyland, Ali. It was hell. But Lou loved it, of course. I'm broke, but now at least when the other kids at preschool ask him how many times he's been to Disneyland, he won't have to ask what it is." She yawns. "I'm so tired. We got in late, and this morning I get an emergency call from one of my girls. I can't be home for a day!" Girls and young women with bulimia, anorexia rely on her like a lifeline. Not unlike me. "But how was *your* trip? I'm actually surprised you're here. I thought you'd still be back East."

She takes my hand. "You managed to take care of everything, then? Sorry we couldn't talk much, too many relatives down there. Lou was in his element, but I was *so* ready to leave." Meredith, with her ganglia of step- and half-siblings spread throughout California, relations too numerous and complicated to sort out, has family to spare. She continues in a softer voice, "So you got your mom's ashes buried? How was that for you? How are you feeling? I'm surprised you had time to close up the house, though. Did you find a realtor?"

Too many questions. Meredith might be showing her weak side as a shrink. Isn't she supposed to ask open-ended questions such as, "Do you feel like talking?" Used to my recalcitrance, she presses. "Alina, talk to me." *Use your words.* That's what she says to Lou when he's kicking mad. Something buzzes in my purse. We both look at it. "What's that?"

"I don't know, it sounds like my phone," I say. "But it's not the ring." I pull out my phone and flip it open. A phone number foreign to me appears with some text:

April 28, 2007 11 a.m. Regards from...

I say, "I think it's a text message." I slap my forehead, "Geesh, I forgot to tell you, Mere, I have relatives coming—from *Finland*."

"What? You're kidding!" She beams, "I knew those letters would work!" and squeezes me hard. "Ali," she says, holding me at arm's length. "This might be just what the doctor ordered." I click on the message:

Regards from LA! Alina it is soon we will meet. My cousins have not been able to come to US, so it seems that I am only relative coming to see you. We drive up the route 1 and come to your house. Now you knows also these plans. We will see you short time! It was very teasing for Paavo when he hears you live near Stanford. We go to the mool now for shoping. Ps SMS is best way to talk.

As I try to absorb the information, Meredith says with glee, "You've got to have a party!" I stop reading to picture it: Meredith, Steffen, Lou, Cleo and me with some unknown visitors squashed uncomfortably close in my tiny apartment. I clear my throat, return to the message: They're in L.A.! *At a mall? Teasing? Stanford?* And will they see me *in* a short time or *for* a short time? Those vexing prepositions my mom always left out, as in "Come house now, Alina."

"Highway 1 could take days," I say to Meredith.

"More time to plan some fun!" She claps as if I'm Lou and she's trying to build excitement in me for a doctor's visit, one requiring shots. I gnaw at my lip, unable to share Meredith's uninhibited enthusiasm, given my current plight, and feeling more troubled by her questions as I do not know the answers and do not like the unknown. "And now you'll have plenty of time to show them around."

"I suppose."

"Ali, I know you're processing a lot just now but try to enjoy this. You wanted this, remember?" But what I remember is Meredith convincing me to write to these strangers. Once she calms down—you'd think they were visiting *her*—she says, "Let me 'Finn-ish' you up. Get it?"

I smile at my sweet friend, settle back, close my eyes, try to clear my mind of jobs and visitors, and begin to melt again as she cups my hot, tired, eyes. Maybe I am a sensualist, something Steffen always asserted. Dreamy green and red splotches swim under my closed eyelids "My eyes always hurt," I confess.

"It's because you think too much. I think Reiki can help your vision and finally cure your headaches." My mind-blowing cluster headache bouts, so unbearable they call them suicide headaches, which I've suffered from since adolescence. After a few minutes, she moves her hands to the space between my eyebrows. "Right now I'm working on your third eye."

"Just what I need. Another bad eye."

"I'm a beginner. I'm just learning how to clean out your chakras, but—"

"You and your cleaning," I tease, using the words she so often directs at me. I am, after all, the daughter of a mother whose favorite saying was "*Cleanliness is half a meal*."

"Well. Your good humor's back," she says. "See how powerful this stuff is? Now, *shh*, don't talk." Should therapists say things like that? When she moves her hands to cover my ears, I experience a pleasant hum as if I'm in a sensory deprivation chamber—no sights, no sound. Just as I feel I could doze off into a pleasant oblivion, she abruptly slips her hands to cover my mouth and, being a mouth-breather, I gag, "Agh!" I rear up, suck air and opening my eyes I start at the sight of six-foot tall Steffen looming over us, Lou slung over his shoulder.

With a speedy heart—I have a sensitive startle response—I sit straight and sputter, "Jesus, did you *sneak* in here?"

"*Shh*, not so loud!" Meredith whispers.

With his intent but merry blue eyes and a trace of his British mother's speech, Steffen says quietly, "Would you have me slam the door and wake Lou?"

I hold my thumping chest, whisper loudly, "You scared the shit out of me!"

"If the sight of a man is so frightening, I really don't know how you make it through the day," Steffen says. "And speaking of scary, what's with the wig?"

Meredith shoots him a look. "I like her hair. It's edgy. She can pull it off." I'd actually like to be able to whisk it off, swap it with a quick swipe for my old dull hair. "Ali's had a rough day, Steffen. Please just put Lou down in the bedroom?"

He nudges his son's cheek with his long, arched nose, a nose softened by a fine, narrow bridge. His damp, longish hair curves up at the neck in an inviting smile, Lou's baby arm curled around it. I glance away from the graceful arc of that neck; away from the memory of its salty taste and the scratch of stubble on my tongue. That Steffen scent: the smell of sea, salt, sweat.

It's not like me to be so discomfited by him. Our way with each other tends toward light and breezy, easy and teasing. Maybe today Cleo's words reverberate, I've been without a man for so long, I'm excessively libidinous. And today his humor feels off-key, too callous, although I know he's unaware of my calamity at DRIP.

I notice he wears a white painter's jumpsuit. Even Steffen, the frequently jobless artist, has a job. "Looks like you've got work," I say to him, trying not to sound rueful.

"I'm fo-ing," he says. I think this might be a Lou word, like "ba-ba" for "bottle" or "da-da" for "diaper." While I ponder the syllabic choices for what Steffen might be doing, Meredith spells it out, "F-a-u-x-ing. Fauxing walls, you know?" I don't know, but I studied French and it sounds as if Steffen is faking something. (After all, who could believe that he was "in love" with me after just a few months of dating?)

"Sounds like another verb we don't need. Tell me, what's fauxing walls?"

She says, "Making them look like old faded plaster, like an Italian palazzo gone to seed. It's really popular now. You wouldn't believe how much it pays." She adds with a small smile, "Steffen calls it 'ho-ing.'"

When Steffen and I first met, he was doing commercial photography, but this new work seems even further from landscape painting, his dream. I think about this fauxing. There are probably plenty of fake walls to paint in Mercury—Spanish missions, French chateaux, Greek revivals.

"Speaking of money." With his free hand, he pulls from his pocket a fat stack of bills and thrusts it at Meredith.

Lou raises his groggy head, sees me. "Ah-ah-ee?" Aunt Ali? He looks wary.

I reach out. "Hey, Lou." A real smile takes over me. "Can I, would it wake him too much if I held him?"

His father places the beautiful three year-old in my arms. He's inherited Steffen's blond hair, but his translucent green eyes are all Meredith. In general, I study Lou like the Anthropology major I was and he studies me like a scientist, like a child. He appraises me with those clear marble eyes of childhood that tell you nothing. Childhood is an unfamiliar tribe, one I never really belonged to.

"Uh oh," he pulls at my hair. Who knew hair could ruin so much? I never understood that "bad hair day" stuff till now.

"It's just me, Lou. Someone painted my hair orange." He tugs my bangs with a frown. "Maybe you can pull it all out for me."

"No," Steffen says. "Mere's right, you can manage it. Just buy a pair of very large shoes, a big red nose—" Without looking. I know that Meredith cut him off.

I cradle Lou. Still dozy, he struggles to keep his eyes open. His hand drops to my shoulder and his head tips aside, his leaded lids straining up again and again, only to drop lower after each attempt. In the end, his eyes roll back and close, defeated. The weight of those eyelids, thin as paper, light as feathers, heavy as lead—how he struggles to keep them up, aloft.

I suppose everything has a relative weight. Maybe it's why I don't fully feel the weight of the news about my job. I've never had to worry about money. My job paid well, and my parents left me so much: all their savings and a house that's now worth a million.

Now Lou's soft, rhythmic breathing beats with mine. I squeeze his pudgy arm and stroke his full pouty cheek. Roundness. The human animal has an attraction to it. Plump bottoms, breasts, full cheeks. The beautiful curve of a child's forehead.

I had no particular interest in children until my thirtieth birthday, which struck close to Lou's birth. Since that sudden chiming of my biological alarm, the cherubic cheeks and cupid bows of baby mouths everywhere—in supermarkets, on the street—call out a strangely stirring siren song. But regularly witnessing Meredith's earthbound struggles makes me question my ability to plow through the rocky terrain of motherhood. Before Meredith even rolls out of bed at 6 a.m., Lou pounces, pelting her with demands—for toys, TV, cereal. I'd have to take my cue from the airline industry. I'd put on my own air mask first: get coffee, then think about dealing with the child.

I drop my head to his. Hormonally hungry, I clutch him, want to absorb him, pull him into me so that his soft body morphs into mine, filling all the holes. I suck in his breath, fresh as mountain air, drawn from the pure heart of a child. I inhale him like unadulterated oxygen. His soft arm falls to rest on mine. Unexpectedly overwhelmed, a teardrop falls to our commingled arms. Meredith, sitting beside me, strokes my back. "This is good, Ali. Go ahead." But I don't feel like crying, don't even know what I feel.

"Man, I'm sorry, Alina. Really, you look great. As always." Steffen's paint-splattered boots shift.

I jerk my head up. *What?* And why did he have to come ruin my alone-time with Meredith? She shakes her head as I pass Lou into her arms. I stand and walk to the door. "Really, I've stayed too long. I should get going."

"Oh, don't go!" Meredith passes Lou back to his father like a delicate football. From the cradle of Steffen's arms, Lou lifts his head with a small wave. "Die die!" he says. I don't take it personally.

As we walk to my car, Meredith slings her arm around my neck.

I say, "His teasing's beginning to bug me. It's like he's always laughing at me."

"Ali, you have so many blind spots." A sigh escapes her, "At least he's a great dad."

"When he's around."

"You judge him too harshly."

"You *don't* judge him." I say. "He should marry you. Lou should have a regular family."

The phone rings and Meredith dashes inside with a finger up signaling me to wait. At my car, I lean against the warm metal, heated by the unseasonably hot spring day. After a while, I give up on waiting and slide into the car as Steffen lopes across the lawn to the low fence. "Meredith told me what happened. Terrible news, Alina, I'm sorry."

I gaze down the short street to where it ends at a cross street. A triangle of crooked telephone poles connect a mass of crisscrossed wires and cables. "Yeah."

He says gently, "Let me know if there's any way I can, we can help, OK?"

Again today, I find myself close to tears. *Sisu.* That's what my dying mother wanted, not crying or self-pity. The last word she uttered as I held her hand in mine. Before she slipped into a semi-conscious state, she squeezed mine harder than I'd thought possible, through drooping eyes shook her head at the tears rolling in hot streams down my cheeks. Although the only word she'd been able to utter for weeks was "*piru,*" or "devil," her aphasic, determined soul miraculously forced out her final wish for me: "*sisu.*" She wanted me to persevere, hold tenaciously to life, to the Finnish spirit. To never give up.

Meredith hurries out, phone pressed to her chest, sticks her head in my car window. I say, "Thanks Mere. So much. Talk soon?"

"We've got to. About your relatives and, well, because I actually have some news too." She smiles. "Good news." Isn't that the way: bad news always trumps good. Standing to look at Steffen, she adds, "*I think.*" But he's turned to walk back to the house.

~*Ei tule lasta, eikä paskaa.*~
~Not producing baby, nor shit.~

Pregnancy Scares

Meredith's pregnant. That must be it. My thoughts swirl as I drive to my apartment. Meredith pregnant—*again*? I push away the thought that nags: *But it's my turn*!

Three years ago, Meredith announced her pregnancy just months after dating Steffen. The two of us were grabbing fruit smoothies on the run, and it bubbled out. She wore a peasant blouse tucked into a skirt, and I involuntarily looked at her flat stomach. I dropped down on a metal chair.

"But…" I was speechless. I had introduced them, after all, had encouraged their relationship. "It's kind of soon, isn't it?" I almost whispered, as if we were talking about something illicit. I counted the months since I'd introduced them; realized almost a year had passed. The blenders whirred, they shrieked. The smell of oranges cloyed. Meredith leaned forward, making me repeat the question.

"I know." She sat back, patting her stomach as if she were nine months in. "It wasn't planned." She glowed. I felt sick. "I felt really queasy and vomited for a couple of weeks, then—

"Are you sure?"

"I've had a blood test and everything."

"But those don't mean anything!" She queried me with her face. I'd never told Meredith about my close call with Steffen, my own pregnancy test…in fact, it was the beginning of the end for us.

Within days of meeting each other, Steffen and I had rabid sex everywhere—in bed, naturally, but also on chairs, in cars, and once in his apartment's communal laundry room. He tapped into an underground wellspring of passion, unearthed in me a bawdy sexual geyser. I think it was biology. The shade of dove grey that spread over his eyes when he looked at me, along with the bulge of his rising cock, made me wet, made me instantly spread my legs and bury my head in the scratchy hairs of his chest—regardless of where we were. It made me reckless. Parked in the passion-heated car I might raise my head, concerned about passers-by, but Steffen would just plunge his tongue in my mouth and bear down. My head sank back, my pelvis melted and rose to him as my eyes slid back into blissful oblivion, forgetting that I was half-naked in the middle of the day, screwing in a steamed-up Toyota on Camino Real.

I couldn't take the pill because of my yearly bout of torturous headaches. Although my cluster headache spells struck but once a year, the pill could make them more frequent. And death would be preferable to more of that debilitating pain.

When there was no protection on hand, Steffen would pant that it'd be OK, he'd pull out. But the force, the intense suction of our desire, made it excruciating. I'd push him away at the last minute, biting his shoulder, then worry that something leaked in. These incidents, which were not infrequent, caused me to fret non-stop until my monthly bleeding began.

Then one month I missed a period. After two weeks of looking dolefully at dry underwear, I bought a home pregnancy test and literally kissed the urine-dipped test stick when it turned a negative blue. Steffen, certain that six weeks without bleeding meant conception, insisted that I go to Planned Parenthood for more conclusive proof—a blood test.

"Why would I do that?" I said.

"Because you're not bleeding. You still could be pregnant."

"But I'm not." By then I'd had two negative home tests.

"I doubt those are truly accurate," he said. We argued back and forth until finally, to appease him, I called the clinic. After telling them about the home results, I had to plead to get in. The technician glared at me as she poked my arm. Heat flamed my face with her jab—we both knew it was a waste of everyone's time and money. The next day I got my period.

Two mornings later, I sat with Ravi filling out a work spreadsheet when the phone rang. It was the clinic. After confirming my name, the woman on the other end said, "Your blood test came back positive."

"No," My eyes darted to Ravi, sitting close by in my cubicle, then to the computer screen full of rectangles, the cursor like an empty Red Cross symbol. I turned away and said into the mouthpiece, "This is *Alina Eskala*."

"Yes, and you have a positive result from the lab. You're pregnant."

"I can't be."

"Your blood test shows you are." The screen blurred to a bad dream. I dropped the phone onto the receiver, and without saying a word, fled Ravi for the lavatory, stunned. Filled with dread.

Steffen was thrilled. He drove over at lunchtime and thumped the hood of the car with a hollow thud, "I knew it!"

I looked at him glumly. "But I have my *period*, Steffen. It's got to be a mistake."

"Women often bleed when they're pregnant."

I didn't ask how he knew this gynecological tidbit. "I don't. I mean, I'm not spotting. It's a totally normal cycle." His smile faded a shade off brilliant and he put his arms around me. "We'll buy another kit."

We found out two things: I was not pregnant and we wanted different results. Although my body urged me to conjoin with Steffen, my mind did not. It was all too soon. I didn't want to be crazy-reckless, out of control—*pregnant*! At home, I drew a red circle with a slash through it on a pair of his white briefs—an international interdiction sign on the crotch—and mailed them to him. Later I listened to his message on my answering machine. "Only you," he laughed. "Only *you*!"

Nonetheless, I grew cautious, withdrew. And when Dad got sick and died, consumed with grief, wanting to be alone, I rejected Steffen's efforts to console me. What did he know of death? Grieving? Loss. Introducing him to Mere felt like weight lifted. They hit it off, freeing me from his frightening, feverish fervor. Freeing me to mourn alone.

But that day at the juice bar, I looked at pregnant Meredith with mixed emotions and a kind of fever of my own. "Did you go to a clinic? Because I don't think they even *test* the blood. It's like they just assume that if you go to the trouble of a blood test you're pregnant!" I leaned in, "I think they *actually throw away the samples.*"

She squinted at my lunatic, frantic face and took my hand in hers. "Ali, calm down. I know about your pregnancy test. Why didn't you ever tell me? It's what best friends are for."

"It was over so quickly." I looked away from her vivid gaze, recall fixating on the little containers of sprouting green grass behind the glass counter. "And I guess I was ashamed at not being more careful." Soon it was too late to tell her. It's not the kind of thing you tell someone who's actively having sex with the man you were actively having sex with.

Her face clouded. "Is something wrong? I mean." She faltered. "You've never shown any regret about Steffen, and he told me how you guys didn't want to be pregnant and—" I nodded. Exactly right, at least on my part. So why did I feel so wrong? Why didn't I feel her happiness? She looked down and wrapped her fingers around the tall white cup with its cheery bright flowers. "Maybe you're not in touch with your feelings? Ali, have you been listening to your own heart?"

"I'm just…confused. I mean, it's not about Steffen." Or was

it? "It's just that your life will change so much." And mine won't. "Maybe I'll feel left behind."

"Never," she assured me and we sat in silence until she said, "It's hard to believe, isn't it?" Yes, I thought. Nearly impossible. She took a long sip through the straw. The thick pink fluid flowed up and into her mouth. My own drink remained untouched. I'd never questioned my introducing Steffen to Mere, the three of us got along just fine. But my stomach churned…it became clear for the first time that I was ready, that I *longed* for a man and a belly fat with baby.

"Steffen must be delirious," I attempted a smile.

"He'll get used to the idea," she said.

I had to leave. I hugged her, stretching over her shoulder to squeeze out a mute congratulations.

Now Meredith has a family. And I don't.

Ten minutes in my apartment and I want out. Compared to the cluttered thicket of Meredith's bungalow, the rooms feel as bare and sparse as a stand of winter birches. The air is stale, and I'm struck by the starkness, the lack of personality here. It's as if nobody really lives here, a place for a transient. I look at it as if for the first time: a generic, modern, one-bedroom in a generic, modern complex. White walls, beige carpeting, passed-down furniture. A large black and white Ansel Adams photo of Half-Dome the only "décor," aside from my shelf of books and towers of CDs. Pathetic, really.

Starving, I open the refrigerator and quickly close it. Like a hospital, it's gleaming white and unpleasantly lit.

I dial the number from Jukka's text message only to hear a recorded Finnish message, unintelligible to me. No email from him, either. But when I dial my voicemail, a chirpy male with Mom's Finnish accent tells me that they've arrived safely in Los Angeles and will be seeing me "*after some time has passing.*" I text him asking for an ETA, but after staring at my phone for an indeterminable time with no reply, I give up.

I'm starting to hope the drive up Highway 1 takes weeks, long enough for me to find a job. According to Dad, Finns value hard work above all else. Former underlings of the Czars, peasants under Swedish kings and queens, the hardscrabble Finns forged their advanced industrialized country through sheer manpower and grit.

I raise the kitchen window and stare into middle space. The light rail rumbles past, as I wave listless air into the apartment. Maybe I should give up this place, live in my parents' house until I sell it and find a job, as this apartment has never been much more than a rest stop for me, an exorbitantly expensive place to lay my head after work. My father decried the amount on my lease; any mention of California rents and property prices invariably outraged him. Finland has laws preventing profit from the ownership of property, he reminded me. Such a fount of knowledge, it was hard to believe he'd visited the country only once in his seventy-five years.

We flew Finnair to Helsinki when I was eleven, when I endured the long flight over the North Pole squeezed between my snoozing mother and a garrulous Italian hiker. Dad, drink in hand, was immersed in a book across the aisle. The striking Italian informed me that he traveled to Finland "for the women." I looked over at my gently snoring mother with my mouth ajar, hairs sprouting from her nostrils. I snuck a look back at the young man and tried to connect the dots. Did he need his house cleaned?

My memories of the trip are few, but I recall a laughing towhead throwing my plastic sandal into the sea. Could that have been Jukka? We were swimming at their *moekki*, their summer cottage, on the Baltic. Russian guards in tall towers, wooden boxes atop stick legs, stood watch as my bikinied cousins laughed at the unseen soldiers surveying them. The boy tossed my favorite Cinderella slipper, sparkling clear plastic, and off it floated and sank. I trod, slipping on the rocky bottom, groping for it in the dark water without success.

Mom said, "That is good thing. A sign you will come back."

"Losing a flip-flop?" I said with pre-pubescent sarcasm. "That's some ancient Finnish wisdom?"

She just replied, "Leaving anything behind."

Waking up is the worst. Another morning when the escape of sleep is replaced with brutal reality. My stomach sinks as I recall yesterday, my new jobless state. Uneasy at the height of the sun filtering through my bedroom blinds, I lumber out of bed. Saturday.

My head dully aching from lack of caffeine, I gobble a late lunch of sour yogurt and a soft, bruised banana. I crave coffee but did not think to buy fresh milk yesterday. Tea would be easier on my insides, but the weak, tannic taste never satisfies me. Before heading out, I notice a phone text from Jukka:

Hei, Trip is awesom. Paavo likes to get to the north sooner than me. He's the one in the hurry. I'm the yipsy and like take my time. I tell him to chill but watever. He has big visit to make up there. We come to your house if you tell us where this is. Dont be holding youre breth ☺ Moi moi!

Honestly, would some details kill him? Anyway, it doesn't sound like the "gypsy" and this Paavo will be here anytime soon. Slinging my hobo purse over my shoulder, I leave my apartment. I need more than coffee; I need to know what's going on with Meredith. If she is pregnant again, I want to be truly happy for her. And Steffen. If this is what they want.

~Olla hukassa.~
~To be in a wolf (lost in despair).~

Lollipop Girl

The coffee at McDonald's has gone downhill. What was once a decent mellow blend has become "gourmet" in a vain attempt to compete with trendy cafes, which means it's now a darker roast. Not a grind that scrapes my innards like Starbucks and Peet's, but more bitter. Meredith would prefer a cup of herbal tea from one of those places, but I don't feel like interacting with unpredictable counter staff today.

I don't bother to call Mere ahead—even that feels like too much energy. I round the drive-thru to get coffee and a cup of tea for Meredith, along with two miniature apple pies. I squint from the glaring afternoon sun, the hard contact lenses I forgot to remove yesterday grate.

Driving to her house, I sense the streets of the suburban area suddenly too crowded, every square inch packed in, built up, cemented. So citified. Did it change overnight or had I grown used to Mercury: the green between things, cows grazing on hills, clusters of jerking wild turkeys, the fleeting views of deer?

In front of Meredith's bungalow, a waif with indiscriminate facial piercings stands stripping berries off a bush like a child. At my time of life I don't come into much contact with people between the ages of five and twenty. From her actions, the girl could be there to play with Lou. But metal glints in her brow and nose and she wears a long dark coat.

I suspect that she's Meredith's emergency call from yesterday. With her moon face and thin limbs, she looks like a lollipop girl—

one of the sweet young teens she counsels, stick figures topped off by large round heads. My theory about Meredith's clients: that girls with large round faces are more likely to develop bulimia, anorexia. "They're actually trying to shrink their heads, Meredith," I argued once after picking her up from work. "No matter how thin their bodies get, they look in the mirror and see their big heads." Not their wan faces, their poor, decimated bodies. Just round skulls that can't be changed.

"Always thinking," Meredith answered, adding that the idea was ridiculous. Both Meredith and Steffen like to accuse me of having a theory about everything. I have a theory about that. Their analysis of me, their gentle jibes, bond them. Always the patient mother, Meredith explained about perfectionist personalities, family problems with food, the media's obvious obsession with thinness. "Now they're finding it could be genetic." A predisposition, Meredith said, like alcoholism. I said you didn't have to look under a microscope to see that it might be genetic.

I watch the girl toss putrid green berries in the air one by one and catch them in her mouth. They might be poisonous. Maybe the girl's attempting suicide. Jauntily. She shoots the berries out in a stream over the low fence. "They're not home," she says as I approach, eyeing my white bag and cardboard tray of drinks. "She said she'd be here today but oh well. At least *she* has a life." For some reason, I take this personally. "But I'll take some of that," the girl points to the food. I look at my cooling coffee, then at Meredith's closed door and empty driveway. "It's *OK*," says the girl. "I drink coffee, I *eat*."

Reluctantly, I offer Meredith's tea from the grey drink holder, soggy and stained brown from spillage, and set the food tray on the lawn to look for her. "Where are they, do you know?" The girl rifles in my bag of food.

"I bet she's off with her boyfriend." She crams half a pie in her mouth. "God, he is so fucking *hot*," she garbles, crumbs spewing. "Have you seen him?"

Yeah, naked. The girl gulps from the cup. So different from the blond cheerleader types of Mercury and neighboring Blaineville. Even though it's not my home, I say disapprovingly, "Where I live kids say 'freaking.'" And "Gosh" for "God." I've heard them in line at Blockbuster, the Blaineville girls with their designer purses and, I guess from the fancy stitching on their asses, pricey jeans. This girl could practice some of that civility. Or better yet, silence.

"That's so gay. Where's that at?"

"Mercury."

"Oh yeah, ha. Like *Men are from Mars, Women are from Mercury*, right?"

"*Venus*!" I say with more vehemence than expected, searching more desperately for signs of Meredith. This causes the girl to momentarily stop talking, before she asks exactly which planet it is I live on. Ignoring her, I cup my hands to peer in the window and jiggle the doorknob.

"What're you going to do, *break in*?" I turn to watch the girl, who can't seem to keep still. While she devours, she paces the small yard like a wolf. Holding the bag up, she says, "You mind?" and digs for the second pie. Definitely oral. Irritatingly mouthy. "Don't worry, I won't puke it all up," she sticks her forefinger deep into her mouth, revealing a tongue swollen around yet another stud. "I'm cured."

The girl points to my chin, where, having inherited my dad's oily skin, an alarmingly large pimple has erupted overnight. "Nasty. Looks like a herpes sore."

I'm already sick of this girl. Where the hell is Meredith? "It's smallpox," I snap. "I wouldn't come near."

"Oh, I had that in, like, kindergarten." She licks her fingers and wipes amber goo on her dark coat. She opens the tea lid, sniffs, then half closes it, dropping the food litter on the grass. I look at it but do nothing, getting as far away from her as possible in the small yard.

"You're that friend of hers, aren't you?"

"I don't know. Meredith has lots of friends." *Where is she? I need her!*

"But you're quiet, she says that." I stop. *What?* "She mentioned a friend once. You, like, don't deal with things? Talk about your issues? You push things down."

I swing round to face her. *I'm* not the one sticking my finger down my throat. What is Meredith doing talking about me? To *her!* Such an invasion of my privacy. I stutter, "Meredith talks about me?" To *you*?

The girl flinches. "Chill. She just said how I need to talk about my shit too. See, I don't really come from a"—she puts her fingers up in jumpy quotes— "*functional*" family, either."

I'm incredulous. "*You and I* are nothing alike!" I scream. The girl sucks a silver hoop in her lower lip, silent now, Miss Goth Chatty Cathy.

I feel a lightening flash of pain in my temple, like the start of a migraine. This girl suddenly reminds me of a doctor in her coat, like a lab coat drenched in dead black dye. I hate doctors, beginning with the sadistic ophthalmologist I went to in middle school. Making me choose between two indistinguishable rows of letters over and over, scolding me for being inconsistent. If I could tell the difference between blurry and blurry I wouldn't be there! And the green-clad intern with the heart of a mollusk whose words of "condolence" immediately after Dad's death from liver cancer were, "Don't drink." *Don't drink!*

The wind picks up and blows open the girl's coat, exposing her protruding breastbone. Anger flares at everything—at this sick girl who I want to spit berries at, at Duncan and his loser company, at probably-pregnant Meredith for talking about my family and me to this messed-up girl. I jerk my leg back and kick up the fast-food trash, sending paper and tea spraying into the air.

"Don't drink!" I shout as I storm off, leaving her with her empty maw wide open.

~Mikään ei kuivu kyyneltä nopeammin.~
~Nothing dries faster than a tear.~

Drinking (Reindeer Tears)

I down my second vodka-loaded Cape Codder as I wait for Cleo at a bar in Blaineville, near Mercury. A Finnish fireball, vodka and cranberry juice. Better yet would be reindeer tears, a cordial glass filled with clear cold vodka and a few floating, blood-red cranberries. I want my liquor straight tonight.

I barely recall getting here; just that I raced onto the freeway, stomping on the gas pedal. The car wheels wobbled as I sped north, wanting as far away from Silicon Valley, Meredith, and her skinny sidekick as possible. I drove blindly, fueled by hot anger, confusion. Time must have stopped, my car on autopilot, because before I knew it I saw the sign for the Blaineville-Mercury exit. Mad at myself for driving back to the place I escaped yesterday, I sped up and drove past, headed for Tahoe. I drove for hours before thinking it through: I'd need warmer clothing, emergency headache medicine, contact lens fluid—not to mention a reservation on a Saturday—if I were going to spend the night away.

At some point, eyes weary and clenched hands aching, sun setting, I pulled off the freeway and called Cleo. After telling her the news about DRIP, she offered to meet me at this dance club, said there'd be music and men. It would cheer me up. I balked at meeting up here but she said, "Sorry, kiddo. I'm house signing in Folsom tomorrow. Take it or leave it."

I count close to twenty people spread about the large club, waiting for more bodies, louder music. A lone couple moves languorously to a lame top-forty number, nose to nose, as if alone in their home. The alcohol begins taking hold, and my head feels lighter, my body looser, spirits higher. If the music improves, dancing just might be the tonic I need.

Some people dream of flying. I dream of dancing, huge soaring leaps that take me high and far and touch me down lightly only to bounce me back up, bounding weightlessly aloft. Glorious, long extended arcs, a joyful air dance. I sail this way, exuberantly, across the terrain of sleep. When I'm dancing, with a drink or two in me, my inhibitions melt. Perhaps this, too, is genetic, as I've heard that the shy people of Finland flock to the dance halls weekly to entwine each other in the sultry Tango.

Though I doubt that there will be much action on the dance floor in sleepy suburban Blaineville, even on a Saturday night. I order another drink as the music suddenly blasts, attempting to fill the void from the lack of bodies. Cleo arrives and wobbles toward me in four-inch heels. She slings off her jacket to reveal a metallic silver top that hugs her copious breasts. "Hey, kiddo," she pats me on the back, drops her bag onto the table, and hops onto a tall stool near me.

Cleo looks as tired as I feel. She's in pharmaceutical sales now, pushing prescription pills instead of computer chips. She flips off her heels and crosses her legs, exposing a ruby-tipped toe that pokes through a hole in her fishnets. Thrusting her chest in a yawn, she says, "I probably need Flontese."

"Flaunt tease?" I say, "That runs in your veins," but she doesn't appear to hear.

"It's for iron-poor blood. Or low blood pressure, or something." This lack of specificity is not surprising in Cleo, though it is somewhat troubling, given that she sells drugs whose side effects fill pages of magazines in tiny, four-point type. Therapies whose warnings usually include risk of "heart failure." But, as she's said, "There's money in them thar pills."

"So," she says. "Look on the bright side. You have some time off." I don't want to think about the bright side. I ask about her house purchase. "The commute will suck, but I'm actually psyched about moving to Folsom."

"Plenty of men there, at least."

"I prefer the minimum security types," she says. "Oh, shit. I meant to call for a day program out there for Garth." She takes care of her gentle schizophrenic brother, who shuffles from room to room in their place, sedated on medications, a Diet Coke gripped in his hand. It must give the men Cleo takes home pause when they waken, hung-over, and eye the cluster of amber vials near the coffee maker.

"You're sort of like a hooker with a heart of gold."

"You take a pretty dim view of sales."

"Hey, at least you have a job."

"Don't worry, kiddo, plenty of companies are hiring."

"Sure, if you live in Chennai."

"You did some documentation at DRIP. Maybe we have something for you in product literature."

"I wrote technical release notes, that's hardly pharmaceutical product literature." In the revved up world of our start-up, we made decisions over the water cooler and worked on whatever needed doing. I not only tested and found bugs, I helped Ravi design the user interface and assisted the tetchy tech writer with the release notes—high tech's answer to never meeting a deadline—a regrettable necessity because there were never sufficient resources or time to find and fix all the problems before the product shipped. So we gaily shipped our wares to the innocent customer with an enormous *caveat emptor* at the top of the box, a regrettably long list of the slight and not-so-slight snafus one could encounter upon actually using the product. A release note might inform the reader, for instance, that if he or she tried to *install* the software, odds were it would fail and *Technical Support* should be contacted. (This, I always thought, would be more helpful information if we actually had a Technical Support crew.)

It occurs to me that all those pages of medical disclaimers are just release notes for drugs, but I doubt I'd feel comfortable writing them. I say, "It's one thing to tell customers their computer might crash and another to say 'Keep 911 on speed dial.'"

"Yeah, some of the stuff I sell is scary shit." She shakes her head. "Shame about your stock options." I've barely had time to register that loss. Five years of promise gone. "At least you own a house. You should move to your folks' place. No rent." I cut her a look, even though I've had the same idea. "The thing *is* is it makes sense while you're not working. And when you sell it, you'll be rich!" Because of its location in coveted, tree-lined Mercury, which now has enormous *cachet*, the modest home is worth an unseemly sum. When we gathered there after Mom's funeral, Cleo blurted, "An heiress!" cake crumbs spraying, with characteristic indelicacy. But between the house and the inheritance my parents left me—savings from years of frugal and simple living—I suppose the term fits.

"I can't stand that area. I mean, *this* area." I gaze around at the few middle-aged suburbanites gathered here. Mercury, a town filled with aliens.

"You seemed to be enjoying it up here, last I saw." I cringe at the memory of her visit with Greg. "Anyways, you're smart. You'll be scooped up fast enough."

I find I don't want to talk about work. "There's a joke my dad liked. A couple of Finns meet in the woods after a long absence. They go to a sauna and drink for a couple of hours. The one asks his friend how he's been doing. They go on drinking for another hour or two. Then the friend replies, 'Did we come here to babble or to drink?'"

Cleo snorts and heads for the bar. When she returns, she pours from a pitcher of frozen margaritas, giving me a protracted look. "You should go on *Guerilla Makeover*," she says loud enough for the entire bar, now filling, to hear. I sit up and look around.

"Gorilla make-over? You flatter me."

"*Guerilla*, as in they ambush you outside your house. I know, I know, you wouldn't like that part, but you'd be perfect for the show." I've channel-surfed enough to know about all the house-body-life transformations currently popular on TV. A gang of plastic surgeons nab me, scalpels in hand, slice me up, and then rearrange the pieces to tragic effects.

"Perfect for it. Thanks," I say.

"No, it's a compliment. Right now the thing *is* is you're just so, so—*unadorned.* But they do your hair and makeup and clothes and you'd look gorgeous." I scratch at the zit on my chin, which feels like it's burgeoned into a carbuncle, and imagine appearing on a show where everyone I know tells me what's wrong with me, then airs on television so that millions can share in the knowledge. Maybe what's wrong with me is that I'm one of the few people in America who doesn't want a TV crew in my living room.

Cleo goes on to say at random that she was going to have her eggs frozen, but the doctor said she was too old. "So I think I'll have my eyes done," she says.

"LASIK?" I've been reading about it for years, wanting to improve my vision but putting it off due to my inherent misgivings about doctors.

"No," she pulls her eyes out to look Asian. "I'll look like you." Cleo and her needless medical procedures. "Check out those hams," her eyelids flutter then rise to expose her rolled-back irises as if she's in momentary ecstasy, as she points to a man in tight pants dancing with a much taller partner.

"He's a good dancer," I say. Not as stiff in the hips as most men. When it comes to the opposite sex, Cleo's like a teenage boy. She tells me that I'll be the same someday—I won't even notice their faces. In my college years, what I liked most was the foreplay with my gentle-faced boyfriend. And the post-coital cuddling. Years later, with Steffen, it was the urgent, wild, get-your-dick-in-there sex. It was the fucking. It was shocking. I clunk down my weighty margarita glass. "I think Meredith is pregnant."

Cleo's eyes pop, she leans in, "*Again*?"

I nod.

"Wow. Bummer. I mean, weird and all, since they're still not married. And must be weird for you—like that first time when they just start dating and Va-voom! Baby time!"

I frown at my drink. "It was OK with me."

"Liar."

"Shut up." This conversation's dropping to kindergarten-level fast, I'm sorry I even brought up the subject. I pick up the pitcher, heavier now despite holding less liquid, and shakily pour until icy green fluid margarita sloshes over the rim. On top of my woozy state, my internal plumbing is clogged: my eyes drip and my nose is plugged.

I've theorized that Finns, like Native Americans, are allergic to alcohol. Maybe it's the Saami blood. Races without body hair, with eyes that have the epicanthic fold, that flap of skin that extends past the eye toward the bridge of the nose—these people cannot hold their liquor. They get addicted easily, like my dad. Sad thing is, he died of liver cancer after years of sobriety. But me, I get sniffles and sneezes and generally quit early. But not tonight.

I remove my irritating contact lenses, then fish my glasses out of my bag and slip them on. "That's a mistake," Cleo says, tipping her salt-rimmed glass at me.

"Walking into walls is a mistake." I look around at the paunchy crowd. "Picking up a guy here would be a mistake." I go dancing enough to be familiar with mating rituals, and this club has a poor male-to-female ratio.

She stretches her arms. "You'll do great here. You're at least ten years younger than most of the women." I check out the men staked around our table. And at least thirty years younger than most of them, I think. The music volume notches up another level and on comes Elvis—not Costello. Men swing women onto the dance floor.

Cleo sees my grimace. "I know this chain of clubs. They work their way up through the decades," she shouts over *Blue Suede Shoes*. Her lids flutter and roll. "Just wait."

I think I'll pass out before they get to the *Bee Gees*. Couples do the jitterbug on the black and white parquet floor, as if from some 50's movie. That's the problem with this area, I think. It's a time warp. Women stay at home while men work. What they drive proves that they've never heard of global warming; or they believe that it, like evolution, is merely a theory. I voice as much to Cleo.

"You're so European," she tells me. "You want everyone driving around in a Yugo."

I reach for a napkin to honk my nose. "Speaking of Europe—*modern* Europe—those Finnish guys are here. They're in L.A. or somewhere now."

"There you go. Might be some prospects for you. She tries on a lilting Yiddish accent, "Maybe a nice Finnish doctor." I snuffle, grab another napkin from the aluminum holder and scrape my runny nose with it. "Yeah, you know how I *adore* them." Her sarcasm about doctors isn't lost on me—I'm just not fond of the species. From college on, I've felt that too many seem driven by avarice and are unschooled in empathy. Most of my encounters with members of the medical profession have left me cold, if not outright angry.

"You seem to see them often enough." I decide not to argue that I get mind-blowing headaches, have poor eyesight, oily skin…and instead, perhaps spurred by a glimpse of a handsome, clean-shaven man at the bar, envision that somewhat enticing picture of my cousin's friend Paavo. A mustached face frightfully close interrupts my thoughts, makes me dribble my drink. And this damn startle response of mine! I lean away.

"My name is Yanni," he introduces himself. "Not Johnny, not Yanni—Jzshanni," he pronounces. He looks at me expectantly. It seems I'm supposed to repeat his name.

"Je-anni," I say, relying on my French.

He says louder, over the music, "*Jshanni.*" Maybe he's hard of hearing.

Communication has always been hard for me. Feeling the push and frustration of grade school lisp lessons, I spit out, "JSHANNI!" at full volume just as the song ends.

"Close enough," he says with a shrug and a wipe of spittle from his mustache. He pulls a stool close. Cleo seems to have vanished during the speech lesson. He drums gold-ringed fingers and scans the club, "I have a friend," he says. Good, I think. Maybe it's someone who says his name perfectly and he'll leave. "I'll be back." I watch him walk to the bar, where all the men seem to be looking back at me, as if watching a sport on TV.

After Cleo returns, Yanni reappears too, now with drinks and a tall dark gent. This guy's an improvement, as after being introduced as Sam and pushed onto Yanni's stool, he proceeds to silently drink. Across from us, Cleo and Yanni laugh it up. A Rolling Stones number comes on and they dance.

I don't mind this music, though it's my middle and high school 80's-era music I like best—when I found joy early, moving into a dance groove, finding the beat and counter beat. With or without a partner, I whirled and spun in a cocoon of music. I could dance in my room for hours, soaked in sweat, high on endorphins.

I suspect my quiet neighbor might not speak English. I like this about him and smile, keep it simple. "Sam," I slur, nodding. "Sam I am." My head bobs loosely as if we are in active agreement. I read Dr. Seuss to Lou every time I baby sit. Sam smiles warily and looks sideways as he takes a sip. I decide not to ask if he likes green eggs and ham.

Because I'm bored, or more likely drunk, I run through the words of the book. The rhymes I know by heart, I try to set them silently to the beat of the current song...*would you like them in a house? Would you like them with a mouse?* I smile, the happy-go-lucky words, the thought of Lou's soft breath on my neck ...at some point, enjoying myself, I pour us each another glass and say aloud, "Would you eat them in a box? Would you eat them with a fox?" and chortle.

I want to dance so I grab Sam's forearm and pull him onto the dance floor just as the song changes to a laborious slow number. He pulls me close during this unfortunate musical turn, amorous, perhaps, from my recitation of Theodor Geisel verse. He starts to rub my back as we step to a bland song I've never heard. A man sings, a woman sings, they join in a soaring duet and suddenly my partner is nuzzling my neck as if we are the couple united in song. His wiry chest hairs poke my nostrils. I push him back with a swift shove. I reel back to the table, which is empty. No doubt Cleo is on the crowded floor enjoying the forward embraces of Yanni Live!

I finish the pitcher. I lean my head back but the ceiling spins and I feels vulnerable with my throat exposed, afraid of another vampire bite. My stomach gurgles. There's food on the table. Suddenly starving, I bite into a tasteless taquito that squirts grease down my chin.

My phone vibrates on my hip. I squint in the darkness to read Jukka's message:

Hei! I think maybe we get close but not so much. Cal is bigest place it takes long. Now some more guys is with us, some grate duds. Bikers like me. One has give to me his black lether jaket. Reely fly guys. We chill now. Moi moi!

Adjusting my glasses, I re-read this three times. Jesus. Bikers with leather jackets? He's en route to my place with Hell's Angels? I consider volunteering for the Witness Protection Program.

Dropping my head to the table, I rest it on my arms as if in a boring class at school, but instead of smelling dead skin and erasers, I smell beer over disinfectant. The disinfectant reminds me of Mom. I think about the lay-off, my dad, pregnant Meredith, the lollipop girl...each steely, self-pitying thought magnetically attaching itself to the next.

Cleo seems concerned when she returns from the dance floor, alone, perspiration dripping from her hairline. I lift my head, "I do not like green eggs or Sam." I wonder if, at thirty-three, my own eggs are turning green, if I should freeze them before *I'm* too old. I wipe moisture from under my glasses "It's just reindeer tears," I say." Her brows furrow as she strains to hear. "The drinking," I say louder, righting myself, sitting as straight as my sluggish body allows. Then I'm out with it: "I'm really mad at her."

"You know you're not making much sense." Leaning closer to hear over the throbbing base, she needlessly slides the empty margarita pitcher out of my reach. "Did you say you're mad at someone?"

"Meredith." At Cleo's blank face, I yell, "*Meredith*!"

"Oh right. The pregnancy thing." We're both shouting. "But—"

"No! She's been talking about me. Like I'm neurotic or something." Cleo doesn't seem alarmed by this. She asks what the deal is, who Meredith's been talking to.

"To everyone, I guess. Probably Steffen," I sniffle, "The lollipop girls."

"The Lollipop Guild?" Cleo calls over the music. She puts her hands on her hips and sways. "As in," she sings in a high, nitrous-oxide voice, "*We represent the Lollipop Guild…*" When she sees Yanni approaching, she drops the act and leans across the table to me. "She really shouldn't be talking about you to munchkins."

I laugh. She takes Yanni's hand to dance. "That's a bitch about Meredith," she says, squeezing my arm with her other hand. "But it doesn't sound like her. Don't you think you're blowing it a little out of proportion?" They disappear into the crowd. "Caribbean Queen" sucks everyone onto the vortex of the dance floor. It's like the Bermuda Triangle, and I feel an intense need to sail away.

I wait until the song ends to part with Cleo, when the Talking

Heads come on. My first concert, an early introduction to dance ecstasy, was one of their shows that I was illicitly dragged to by my much older babysitter, all the way into Boston. "Burning Down the House" keeps people on the floor, though I don't consider it their best song. Still, I tap my feet to the infectious beat, feel the music surge through me. Unexpectedly, I want to dance, lose myself in the thrumming drums.

As sweaty dancers vacate the floor, I rise and push through the throng. I start moving to the driving bass of "White Wedding." Although somewhat maladroit from drink, I hop and swirl, spread my arms. I've got space to freewheel. Billy Idol snarls about a "nice day"...ha! I fling myself into the song with a ferocity I've never before felt. Skipping and twirling, I spin like a Sufi until I grow warm and toss my sweater to the edge of the floor. Over and over I howl aloud with Billy, "*Start Aga...ain*!" The disco ball splashes dizzying lights on the tilted floor. Faltering, my feet lose their grip. I stop and try to focus on the rolling parquet. My stomach immediately plunges. I lurch for the rail at the edge of the dance floor and bend over. Then everything goes blank.

*

In the morning, my mouth feels dry and corroded, rusted. I sit up, head pounding, blink at the bright light, and realize where I am. Of course, the house in Mercury. I sip stale water from an *Itala* glass at my bedside, feel the corrugated streaks, the vertical rivulets that pour down the glass like rain. Like sorrow solidified. A peoples' melancholy nature imprinted on housewares.

My gut feels hollowed out. When I stand, woozy, I hear wind rushing. I squint out the window at the obnoxious sun. No wind, just my aching head churning with white noise.

I slog into the kitchen, where a white sticky note with a pharmaceutical logo, purple atoms rotating around a nucleus, is posted on the refrigerator:

Drove you here last night. Lots of fun. I crashed on your couch. Catching a ride to my car with your new neighbor (cute!!). Feel better kiddo (you puked A LOT last night)—Cleo

A lot! Fun? What neighbor? I bang my throbbing forehead into the cold surface of the fridge and groan. I back up and peer at her *PS:*

You really should move here. The people are sweet!

Move to Mercury? I rip down the note and crush it. No friggin' way.

~Oma tupa, oma lupa.~
~Your own living room license.~
(One's own cabin, one's own freedom.)

Au Revoir

I'm moving to Mercury.

Ten days after my lay-off, I'm almost settled in. The decision was practical, the move temporary. The lease on my apartment was up in June, and not renewing it frees me from rent payments until I find a job. Besides, I can get a realtor and sell the house more quickly living here, not to mention have more room for the incoming Finns.

I'll miss the diverse liveliness of my area and the library near my apartment, where they know me. Though not a joiner, I saw that a book group was discussing Henry James, an author I started reading after college. I went to the room at the back of the library and Meredith was there, an ex-Lit major—talk about impractical, Anthro looked like a genius career path by contrast—along with a handful of middle-aged women and one chubby pre-pubescent daughter who rolled her eyes theatrically whenever her mother spoke.

My new friend Meredith and I dropped out after two of the evening meetings and walked to the nearby downtown. (I ended up reading *The Portrait of a Lady* and more James to my brain-damaged Mom for hours on end, my mother often nodding off, until *The Golden Bowl* put us both to sleep.) Newly renovated, this Silicon Valley downtown bustled with packed Asian and Indian restaurants, bookstores and cafes, the air dense with MSG and roasted coffee. In contrast, Blaineville, the town closest to

Mercury, is wrapped in a blanket of suburban sleep by nine each night.

In the few days it takes me to move my trifling life from south to north, west to east, I do not call or stop by Meredith's, despite the numerous voicemails from her.

"Ali, why aren't you returning my calls? Would you please tell me what's wrong? Between us? Cleo claims you're mad at me. She started rambling about the Wizard of Oz or something crazy before she lost reception in the tunnel. Typical. Anyway, *I miss you.* I want to understand if I've upset you because I'd never do that intentionally. *I've tried dropping by your apartment but you're never home. Is your family here yet?*" Her plaintive voice cracks a notch. *"Please call."*

I don't. Although my father always told me not to be like him, not to harbor grudges. *Resentment devours nothing but its own core.* But I justify not phoning her: didn't he also say, *Silence is gold, talking is silver? Closeness without conflict only exists in the cemetery?* Besides, the man never forgave the Russians for taking his family's land—back in a country he'd only visited a few times.

I don't know if his wisdom came from the *Kavela*, the epic poem about ancient Finland, said to be a source for *The Lord of the Rings*, but he was fond of such sayings. They were brief and didn't require much extra effort in the speech department. Teaching was not the ideal profession for such a taciturn man. I attended one of his lectures once, squirming in the uppermost row as he mumbled into an overhead projector and scrawled formulas into the dim yellowy light. Mom polishing the lectern or squee-geeing the whiteboard would've been more riveting. Which is why his move from M.I.T. into research at Cal—conveniently after my senior year of high school—was beneficial for all concerned.

For me, though, living at home during my four years of college might've been a mistake. We saved money—and now I suppose I'm rich—but I never knew the close camaraderie of dorm life. And with no specific major, rather an interdisciplinary mix of Anthropology, Sociology, and History, I belonged to no collegial clique. The two girls I knew best left for graduate school back East, and when I joined the hectic workforce, we lost touch.

As for Meredith, I'd rather not deal with her pregnancy just now. Cleo, who pops in and out of my life, seems preoccupied with her own move to Folsom, her job, her men.

I cleared out my office cubicle and stuffed boxes of appliances and garbage bags of clothing into my sedan, moving most of my belongings into the old detached carriage house in Mercury. They'll be out of the way when I "show" the house, ready for my next move.

For the past week or more, I've been quite alone, which is fine. Solitude is in my nature. My parents hailed from the least populated country in Europe, a land of forest and water, not people. Besides, I have Jukka…virtual Jukka.

~Yksi tyhmä kysyy enemmän, kuin kymmenen viisasta ehtii vastata.~
~One stupid person asks more questions than ten wise ones can spare time answering.~

Puzzled

My great-aunt might be dead, but not so Jukka Kovanen. He's not just alive, he's *wired.* I'm bombarded with a regular succession of emails and messages—short on useful information but long on graphics. Unfortunately, due to his failure to actually answer my questions and his imperfect English, his messages often leave me feeling more disturbed than informed.

Despite the Finnish literacy rate, which hovers around 110 percent according to my late father, who possibly factored in their knowledge of English, Swedish, and German, Jukka uses some unorthodox grammar. I wrote yesterday that there are just two bedrooms in the little house, and he texted that "*it don't matter,*" and that "*we is down mit that.*" I chalk it up to Finn-glish and MTV. He alternately refers to Paavo as "he" and "she," a mistake my mother often made.

But I receive plenty of pictures, photos of unknown Finns said to be "relatives" standing in front of lakes holding drinks, or dressed in black around flower- festooned caskets, their expressions the same either way.

I zoom in on these people I do not know and study their generically familiar faces: the small eyes, long upper lips, and sensuous mouths; noses like my father's that angle up at the end in an abrupt ski jump, brunettes and blonds, hazel-eyed and shades of blue. I magnify the digital photos until they blur into a mass of tiny overlapping squares, skin and eyes every hue of the rainbow, ending in one small dot of white light at the center of their pupils.

And jokes, Jukka sends jokes, which alas, are no funnier than most recycled Internet humor. Some are in English and others come to me forwarded in long vowel-laden Finnish, umlauts and all. I understand that many are about Swedes and Russians, Finland's former imperial rulers, but most are about the Finns themselves.

I'm just reading the old saw about spotting the difference between a Finnish introvert and a Finnish extrovert—the introvert looks at his feet when talking to you; the extrovert looks at yours—when my phone buzzes with a new message.

To anser all youre to many questions is taking some time. It takes dicsonary and maybe month or so to write so much. ☺ We arrive at your house soon after the surgery. We come for the summer. We is wishing to sees Josemite, Vegas. Holywood, Frisco." Now is busy driving and very winding road so beter not to drive off into sea! —J

Is he texting while driving the treacherous ocean cliff roads of Route 1? So many questions this text poses! "*Soon after the surgery*?" I wonder what word he has misconstrued; perhaps he's coming after a doctor's visit. And I believe he meant to say that they are coming during the summer, not for its duration. It's unsettling not knowing their exact arrival date and how long they will stay with me—an hour? A day? *Ailing bikers coming for the whole summer*?

I'm relieved to hear that they have U.S. travel plans, schizoid or otherwise, as I am not comfortable with the prospect of entertaining him and his friends for long. Or do they expect me to be their travel guide? Yosemite, fine. Vegas? Definitely not. It's also perplexing that they're driving north when some of those destinations are closer to LA....could it be they are eager to meet me?

My phone buzzes a minute later with:

Paavo says don't worry youselfs. We have fun. You will like Paavo. Ciao!"

*

I shift into super-drive. Cleaning. Organizing. Scrubbing. Washing.

When the house sparkles and smells of Pine-Sol and wild roses cut from a sprawling bush out front, and the spare bedroom is cleared, I face the scraggly back yard. Reluctant to be a Mercury landowner colonially overseeing Hispanic help, I decide to deal with the overgrowth myself. Knowing I have to venture deep into the dusty carriage house, our garage, I throw on a pair of Mom's polyester pants, sizes too big, cinched with one of Dad's ties, and top it with his old yellow-checked work shirt. I find a wide-brimmed hat to spare me from the baking sun, then jump when I catch my reflection in a window—that of a scarecrow, especially with the straw-like red hair sticking out. But then, no one's around, and, on the bright side, I expect no crows will bother me.

The Finns shouldn't arrive for a few days. I texted my address but told Jukka to phone for directions. There are people who live within a ten-mile radius of Mercury who can't find the place, tucked away as it is at the base of Mt. Mercury, accessed by one road.

Wedged in the front door, I find a business card. Local realtors are already stalking me. I've seen the large white truck about town picturing an over-sized, toothy, happy couple holding a cat that sports an American flag about its neck. I'm in Patriot Cat territory. The preponderance of flags speared into car antennae and posted in front of houses here has not escaped me. My parents flew the flag on Memorial Day and other apropos holidays, but for some reason I find the aggressive boasting of patriotism around here chafing.

In keeping with the theme, their business card displays an American flag printed in the upper left corner, and a Christian fish symbol on the far right. What love of country and God has to do with selling real estate is beyond me. I throw the card in the trash—I'd sell the house myself but suspect that my attitude toward the area might prove detrimental to closing a deal. Reminded of the need to sell, I call a random realty company I find online, then start out to the carriage house for the mower.

The dim, musky space is filled with junk, stuff I should clean out: rusted tools and cans of gasoline, yellowing newspapers from Finland and Fitchburg, rags, and stacked boxes of who-knows-what.

I try starting the gas mower, a model only slightly newer than the antiquated rotary mower my father preferred. I tug on the cord. Nothing. I find a row of rusted red and yellow gas cans lining a dirty shelf in the carriage house. A luminous, perfect spider's web connects two of them, illuminated by sunlight pouring through the window above. I grab a can that won't disturb the web and fill the mower until gas streams down the side onto the floor. Wiping up as much as I can with an old blanket, I try not to breathe in the fumes and kick the blanket near the door for trashing. I yank the mower cord repeatedly with no result.

Exasperated and sweating in my parents' clothes, I roll the old manual mower out to the yard. But after shoving a few lengths through the thick, unyielding weeds, the grass clumping on the twirly blades and jamming the wheels, the mower jolts to a stubborn halt. Huffing and hot-faced, I try to clear the blades. Another thwarted push, then frustrated, I lean over the contraption, beaten. What happened to the lawn boy Mom used?

After I pull the mower back to the carriage house, I gaze around. Most of the cardboard boxes are filled with Dad's papers…how much did I ever ask him about his life, his past? He was so private. I scrabble through boxes of books and academic writings mixed in with old sepia photos, rifling through what must be hundreds of photos of people long gone. I find a sepia portrait, tinted in pastels, of my *mummu* and *pappa*, who we lived next to in Massachusetts until we moved out here after high school. My sturdy grandmother, no great beauty, and her husband with backcombed hair, pointy elf ears. A short, handsome man, my grandfather stands solemnly next to his stiff-collared wife, whose bossy ways and large bosom seem to thrust out of the picture. How I loved her! Leaving them for the West Coast was one of the saddest days of my life.

Underneath their portrait, I discover a curious page, an ornate certificate in Cyrillic writing. I can't make out anything except for a year, "19" in type, then what appears to be "33" or "38" in faint, barely legible writing. *A Russian document from the 1930's?*

I sit cramped on the sooty floor, baffled, staring at the ancient, yellowing page, the incomprehensible blockish, backward-looking letters, the twining vines of wreath that surround the unmistakable hammer and sickle. My brain swims to make sense of it. What is this paper? Why did my parents keep a Russian document near photos of their parents? My grandfather loathed Russia.

The scimitar eyes of my grandfather, my *pappa*, would narrow as he accused all Russians. "So many Finns has gone there to help. They never heard from again," and I knew at a young age that he referred to the Communist Revolution, the Finns who ventured to help the Soviets pursue their ambitious egalitarian dream. Then he'd repeat his refrain about Karelia, the paradisiacal stolen land, the motherland of Finland, usually ending with, "They has taken everything." *Mummu*, my grandmother, would cup my hand in hers, her pinky finger a stub, and say, "Not everything. We have not lost everything. Don't listen to him. Your *pappa*'s glass is half the empty one."

I become agitated and giddy from the smell of gas and this mystery—is this a birth, marriage, death certificate? The year is puzzling—but someone born in 1938 would be only 69 years old!

I rifle through more papers, hoping to clear the mystery, when an unfamiliar voice with a familiar lilt calls, "Alina? Alina are you here?" No way!

Since my parents died, no one says my name like that, accenting the first syllable.

"AH-lina?"

~Ilta on aamua viisaampi.~
~The evening is wiser than the morning.~

The Finns

Flipping off my scarecrow hat and hitching up Mom's drooping slacks, I hasten to the house where a young man stands at my front door. There, in the flesh: my second- or third-cousin twice removed, Jukka. There's no mistaking the smiling Viking, his Swedish side evident in his lanky blondness, yet despite his height he somehow looks smaller than that online picture.

Grinning broadly, he shakes my hand with both of his upon my approach, vigorously not letting go, repeating, "*Hyvää päivää, hyvää päivää*!" His teeth are not so white after all, but stained brown with nicotine or coffee or both; I wonder if he doctored his digital photo. He's dressed in the tight leather pants from his picture and appears over-heated, his face flushed the red of his tucked-in Stanford t-shirt. It smells of starch, crisp and new.

"The traffic," he rolls his r's like Mom, "is really something. So. Finally we are meeting, Ah-lina." I feel a grin break through as I greet him and open the front door, inviting him in. He strides inside ahead of me, slips off his high-tech zippered mesh shoes and places them by the door, Japanese style.

"It's nice to have you here, I say," thinking perhaps his eyes have my mother's impish twinkle. "Really, it is nice," My mouth won't stop smiling.

Looking at me, he cocks his head, folds one arm across his waist, and rests the other elbow on it. I yank up my trousers. As if evaluating a painting, Jukka says, "Your hair is not the color I was thinking." It's not what I'd been thinking, either. I push my red bangs aside. My earlier self-description as a brunette is not so accurate at the moment. "You should learn to send the pictures," he says.

"I know how to email pictures," I say. "I just don't have any." No one to take photographs of me. Blushing under his gaze, I mumble something about wearing "work clothes." Jukka looks around with an appraising eye, "Your apartment is very dark." OK, I understand why Finns have to take seminars on how to finesse business with foreigners. I switch on a lamp to brighten the perpetual dusk of the low-ceilinged rooms. "It is better if you paint the valls vhite," he tells me. The walls *are* white, but I don't argue.

This talk of my hair, my house—perhaps instead of a biker gang, an SUV full of gay men is outside waiting to rush in, eager to make over my life, a band of boys who would roll their eyes at my mother's traditional wall weavings and advise me how to keep my oily skin under control. Who'd whoop with derisive laughter at the polyester pants sagging from my waist.

I look around him toward the door. Wonder about Paavo. The Hell's Angels "duds." "You said something about others?"

"Well, yes, there are. There is. I am afraid that Paavo is sleeping now that it is taking so long to get here and the trocks."

By "trucks," I know he means the Explorers and Yukons. "Yes, we have too many large cars here," I say. I feel the need to apologize for global warming. For the war and the Kyoto treaty.

"*Ei*, no, it's not the SUVs. Drocks." He says, "You know, the medicines."

"Oh, *drugs*." Drugs? "Is Paavo the only one?" On drugs?

He sucks air as he says, "*Yo, yo,*" as Mom used to, that Finnish habit of inhaling a sigh. "Yes, yes. It is yust him and me coming. Now it was not supposed to be Paavo today but I'm afraid that something has gone wrong which I need to tell about. But the surgery has gone fine."

As he does not immediately pursue the subject, I peer out at the small white rental parked in front. Through its half-open window, I discern a human form leaned back in the passenger seat. He appears to have a shield of some sort over his eyes, perhaps to keep out the sun, to sleep.

"Do you think we should we leave him out there?"

"Yes, yes, of course." Jukka waves dismissively. "The surgery has gone fine but if that is OK, she's going to be here now as well." If I hadn't been raised by a mother who habitually reversed her "he's" and "she's," I'd think that Paavo had just gotten a sex change operation. But weren't the Swedes experts at that?

I clasp my hands. "Well! Would you like some coffee?"

Jukka shakes his head with a sigh, "I was thinking you were never going to ask that." He leads the way into the kitchen.

*

Coffee: the Finnish ritual. Growing up I drank it only in the morning, but as time passed I joined my parents on weekends with the drink at mid-morning, after lunch, in mid-afternoon, and after dinner. On Wednesdays and Saturdays, we capped the day with coffee after sauna. Now as Jukka and I finish ours, after he's devoured two of my store-bought blueberry muffins, no need to say much in a comfortable Finnish way, I'm startled by a dark-haired man in goggles peering through the kitchen window. Ski goggles in the summer heat. I glance at Jukka, who rises. I follow him to the door.

"It's time you are awake," Jukka says, pulling him inside. The man's clear plastic goggles have a million little holes poked in them. I wonder if he sees a kaleidoscope of a million little me's, like those bugs with the weird, multi-faceted eyes. By way of introduction, Jukka says, "*Here now is Paavo.*"

"Welcome!" I say too loudly, somehow intuiting that his eyewear makes him hard of hearing.

"He's had the LASIK today," Jukka informs me, pointing at

the curious glasses.

Paavo and I shake hands. He's brunette, not as tall as Jukka, with more of a farmer's build, and thick Slavic forearms. His nose has that squared off look as if unfinished, but he has sensuous, full lips. His eyes, well, it's hard to see them through the holy plastic.

"Thank you for letting me come to visit with you," he says. "This is most kind."

"I'm happy to have you here." Again the smile. "Come, have some coffee." With them settled at the table, I fill mugs.

"You found the place all right, it seems. I'm a little surprised." The Ford Taurus doesn't look like it has a GPS.

"Of course. We have maps," Jukka says, not knowing that there are area residents who wouldn't be able to find my house with or without a GPS. "I'm loving this country. It's my first time, but not so for Paavo." He points his cup toward his friend, who, fumbles for the sugar spoon.

"I have never before have the Valium," Paavo says. "Funny I'm the doctor, but myself I never try this medicine."

"You're a *doctor*?" I try to sound neutral, not wanting to divulge my prejudice. Shrugging, he says he works at a health center, what we would call a general practitioner.

"Surely they perform eye surgery in Finland?" I address them both, not sure how 'with it' this drugged Dr. Paavo is.

"Oh, yes, on every part. But he's coming with me because his friend is the best doctor in the world. For the eyes." Jukka makes a V with his fingers and pokes them at his own eyes, talking about Paavo as if he isn't here. Paavo remains silent. "Don't get me wrong, I'm glad he's coming. But Finland has plenty good doctors."

Paavo speaks up in his defense "But these are my *eyes*."

"Did it—" I was going to say, "hurt?" as I know I should get something done about my vision.

Jukka continues, "John is the guy," pronouncing his name as 'Yann.' Here Paavo's traveling thousand miles for this. John says 'leave your eyeglasses here, you're not needing them no more' but Paavo says 'no.'"

Looking down at his plate, Paavo mutters, "They are my only pair over here."

"But you come because he's best doctor in the world and then you don't believe him. That's crazy." Jukka shakes his head and smiles his stained smile.

"You said that something has gone wrong…" I say.

Jukka explains that Paavo was to spend the night down on the Peninsula with his eye surgeon friend, but his wife just miscarried. The men thought it best that Paavo stay here. I express condolences and insist that both are most welcome here, although this Paavo is not living up to my fantasies. I also learn that Jukka's twenty-eight and single, while Paavo is thirty-four, also single, and they both live in Espoo, a suburb of Helsinki. Jukka says the two met "*avantouinti*," or ice swimming. "This is good for many health problems," Jukka assures me, though I have no intention of ever finding out.

"Do you like to swim?" Paavo joins the conversation.

"Yes, yes I love to swim," I say, though generally in warmer waters. "I just don't seem to do it much anymore…" I trail off, dismayed by all of the pleasures I've given up since my mother died—swimming, hiking, bopping around the house to my favorite music. Sex. "Um, I'd like to know how we're related, Jukka."

"Our grandmothers is sisters." That verb is problematic on more than one count. "You will not believe how many of us—Virtonens and I'm sure the Eskalas too—there is in Finland. Virtonen is my mother's family. You come and you will see."

"You answered my letter by email—that was a surprise."

"My *mummi* has given me the letter. You are on the web."

At my astonished face, he says, "You have written some kind of paper and it's from the company you work for, so I'm just typing AEskala at DRP.com and it is working." After a moment I

recall a paper on test case scenarios from some obligatory conference, co-authored with Ravi when I first started at DRIP.
"It is easy," Jukka says.

Paavo says, "It's not magic."

After calling for take-out pizza, I suggest a quick walk along the golf course before it arrives.

"This is killing me," Jukka says, admiring the expanse of green, the ponds of sand. "So beautiful." Me, I've never found tamed nature so great—golf greens, baseball fields—just so much man-made prettiness. I like my outdoor scenery more wild. "And I have brought with me my clubs," he says.

I'm taken aback. "But you didn't know there was a course here?"

"No, but I don't travel without them. There is very nice courses here, one not far I'm thinking. Bubble Peach." Pebble Beach. They came to *golf*?

About the Mercury country club I say, "I think it might be private."

"Yes, yes, so I think. That is why it is killing me," Jukka says as we walk on. An older couple walking their dog passes us, says hello.

"Can you see?" I look back at the phlegmatic Paavo, dragging behind.

"Yes, I'm looking but feel funny being out here with these on. And I'm thinking John said not to use my eyes too much yet. Maybe it's better if I go back to house."

Jukka sighs, "*Yo, yo,* we all go back."

~*Pessimisti ei pety.*~
~A pessimist will not get disappointed.~

No Russians

The setting sun casts the yard in golden light, as we eat pizza and drink beer on the back deck. Mellowed by the alcohol, the pleasant temperature—companionship—I put my feet up on the deck railing. While Jukka and I drink Heineken, Paavo sips his own bottled water, having informed me that the tap water here would most likely upset his stomach. "We have the pure Arctic waters," he said. So what's he think, we're some third-world country?

"Our water is fluorinated and chlorinated," I state. "It's perfectly healthful." They both laugh.

Jukka says, "One thing: I'm really going to miss *Juhannus* in Finland."

"What is that?"

"You must know the mid-summer party, just few weeks away, the bonfire, party all night. We go to our *moekkis* to celebrate."

"Oh, right. The summer solstice thing. I remember being at someone's summer cottage for that holiday. There was a bonfire, we were near the Russian border and..." the Russian certificate! I run to fetch it.

After a quick glance, Jukka tosses it on the table, claiming to know nothing. Although Paavo admits to reading and speaking some Russian, he says, "I am not supposed to be reading."

"Maybe you could try? It's just one page."

"Well John says yes go ahead look round but not do the reading." I purse my lips, joke, "I think the doctor meant don't tackle the *Kalevala*." Assuming he'll be impressed that I know about Finland's national epic, he merely squints. "This writing is very old, not so dark… and this Cyrillic, it's difficult."

"But you know Russian, right?"

"Ya, little bit…but these letters is harder for my eyes." Cyrillic letters are harder on his eyes than the Roman alphabet?

Jukka gives a dismissive wave. "That paper is probably something you should throw way."

I look to them both, "But why would my parents have it? Do you think it's a family document?"

Jukka says, "No. There's no family document from Russia, that I am sure," pronouncing the country name as my mother had with a rolling "r": Roos-i-ya.

With a sagging exhale, I say. "Well, if you can't help me…" I reach out to snatch the paper from Paavo when he says, "Maybe I see some numbers."

"I know, I read that part."

"Maybe this is 1933 or 38, I'm not so sure. But also I'm seeing a month. December. Twenty-four of December. 1933."

I reel back. "That's Dad's birthday! Are you sure?"

"Well, this date here is on your father's birthday perhaps but I cannot say what rest is. This handwriting is very bad, some kind of paper from the small village." But what *willage*?

Jukka shifts back in his seat as if to distance himself from the document. "That is very strange paper for a Finn to have." His arms crossed on chest, he says, "Russians are not so good. We have lost thousands kilometers fine farmland, nice houses, you Americans don't know this history."

I set my beer bottle down. "Yes I do. I studied Finnish history." Part of what I called my "ASH" degree in Anthropology, Sociology and History, a waste in that it amounted to nothing as I ended up working, like so many other liberal arts majors, in high tech. "But the document, what does it mean?" I ask no one in particular. "My father's birthday?"

Jukka points his forefinger finger, thumb up, at the paper as if shooting it, "That must be some kind of mistake."

"Maybe you have the Russian relative," Paavo suggests, placing the paper on the table, sitting back. "You are *Karjalalinen*, after all."

I know that most of Karelia, heart of Finland romantically if not geographically, home of the epic poem of Finland, the *Kalevala*, is Russian now. It was ceded early in World War II. I remember visiting ugly Soviet "Vyborg," and hearing *pappa* tell of how *Viipuri* was once Finland's second largest city, a bustling seaside, cosmopolitan town—hard to imagine in that grey, decaying place. And though the feisty Finns started a conflict to regain the territory, after years of struggle almost half a million defeated Finnish Karelians were forced to leave their land. Those events were over half a century ago, but people like my grandfather, my *pappa*, and then and my dad, never forgot. Never forgave.

"I really doubt we have a relation there, what with my grandfather's attitude. He was so bigoted." I color with shame.

Jukka shakes his head, "*Ei*, no. There is no Russian."

Paavo says, "If this is your father's birthday, then perhaps he is."

"You mean, perhaps he's *Russian*?" I'm confounded. "My dad was born in this country. My grandparents moved here when *Mummu* was pregnant with him. Or just before. Or something like that."

"There is no Russian," repeats Jukka. What's with this incantation of his? What does he mean *there is no Russian*? There are bazillions of them!

Paavo hands it over. "Jukka is funny. He has perhaps your father's and his own father's prejudice. It's not uncommon in the old *Karjalalinen*, but most young people they do not care. Why you haven't taken this to someone at Stanford? They have the experts over there."

"I just found it. And actually, I'm closer to Berkeley. But." I stare at the paper until the blockish letters blur. "I need to find out."

*

"We go to bed early tonight," Jukka says as I produce a bowl of fresh strawberries for dessert, large and ruby-red. After a bite, he says, "These is looking good, *mutta*..." But. Always the "but." Just like Dad, who liked to speak the hybrid "Finn-glish" of his parents and typically viewed the glass as half empty.

"But what?" I swallow the remains of my bland berry.

"But not so much flavor."

"They are OK," Paavo offers, evidently trying to smooth over my cousin's insult to the local produce. But I recalled my first bite of a falsely voluptuous California strawberry, so perfect in color and tempting in size, and my own dismay at its remarkable lack of flavor. All show.

"We had sweeter berries back East," I admit. "Smaller."

"Best berries are from Finland."

"*Oma maa mansikka; muu maa mustikka.*" When I ask Paavo the meaning of his pronouncement, he stands, stretches and yawns, his muscular frame and broad shoulders on display. "Other land blueberry; own land strawberry. Is something like 'Foreign places are nice enough, but home is better.'"

"Best," says Jukka.

Suddenly tired and ready to be alone, I rise, hugging the bowl of fruit, and offer them the two bedrooms. Although I insist I don't mind sleeping on the couch, they readily dismiss the idea and trot off together to the guest room.

Climbing into bed, those words toss in my head. "*Other land blueberry; own land strawberry.*" Yes, home is best. But where is home? Where is *my* home?

~Pienikin tähti loistaa pimeydessä.~
~Even a small star shines in the darkness.~

The Neighbors

I can't sleep. Feeling restless, I drape an afghan over my shoulders and step out into the chilly evening. The overgrown grass chafes my ankles. Secluded by a border of trees, the long backyard slopes down to a small creek. In the solace of the moonless night, the murky, benevolent shadows of pines, eucalyptus, and the craggy oak centerpiece stand sentry. I breathe in the mentholated air. A breeze carries flakes from a row of elms like aimlessly floating moths. One sticks to my cheek.

I walk to the front yard to pick up the accumulated newspapers—the monthly Finnish *Raivaiia* from Fitchburg, which, like the electricity and cable, I never cancelled. Bending down, I hear voices and a low whirring noise approach, then spy a golf cart jumbled full of people pull up and jerk to a stop in front of the house next door, where the new family's moving boxes are still piled on their Tuscan veranda.

"Christ, Taylor, look out," a man shouts.

A boy of about eight or twelve, I have no idea, whines, "Why can't I drive some more?"

"Because it's late," his mother says flatly. A ponytail fluffs from the back of her baseball cap, and she cradles an infant in one arm while gathering a sack with the other.

"Kyle gets to drive his dad's Escalade," the boy insists.

"Maya, wake your sister up," the mom commands someone in back. A girl, I think. I do not see well in the dark, and unincorporated Mercury has no streetlights (no mail delivery either, which seems quaint until you arrive at the historic post office after weeks away to a whale-sized bucket of junk mail). Shooing her brood along, the woman, already slim despite the new bundle, retreats into the house. I catch my breath at my last view of her entering the lighted hallway, the baby's head nuzzled into her neck, its slanted eyes closed, mouth open, its magically tiny fist resting on her back.

She and I are the same size, and probably about the same age. The difference between us being four—maybe five—children.

And a husband. The husband, who stands over six feet tall, lingers by the cart with a bottle of beer. "Hey there," he says, startling me. Unlike his family, he's noticed me, poised as still and quiet as a garden gnome. Some male territorial thing, I figure. He takes a step in my direction, extends his hand and says, "I've met your friend Cleopatra but I'm afraid we haven't met. Marty. How you doing. Hear you're quite the party girl." The stars wink in the darkness.

Great. All he knows of me comes from Cleo. If he's noticed I have male visitors, he's no doubt concluded I'm taking a brief break from an orgy.

I shake his hand. "I'm Alina." I step back.

He points the tip of his bottle at me, and asks, "Cold?"

I look down at my woolen mummy wrap. Like a typical northern Californian, he's oblivious to the thirty-degree drop in temperature brought on by the night and is dressed in a short-sleeved shirt, shorts, and flip-flops.

"Guess so," I say. My northern blood doesn't make me immune to the cold. Quite the contrary: I could tell him that my cold extremities would save me in a blizzard due to the blood surging around my vital organs. I might lose a few fingers or toes, lose a pinky like my *mummu*. At a loss for words, *dull and uninteresting*, I blurt, "My grandmother got frostbite."

Marty's head shoots back. "Is that so?"

I hold up my left hand, wiggle the middle three fingers. "She lost her pinky. Her wedding ring lined up with the nub."

He looks at my fingers. "Well, we're from Maine and it doesn't exactly feel like frostbite weather—"

"No, I know that!" I shoo him off the subject. Clutching the blanket, I toe the ground as we stand there for a few long moments. Why isn't he going in his house? I cannot think of one more idiotic thing to say. The old joke comes to mind about how Finns are good at silence in two languages: Finnish and Swedish. English, too, it seems.

"Maybe you should warm up in that sauna," he offers, pronouncing it the American way, rhyming it with "fauna" instead of saying "sow-na."

"Huh? The sauna? How do you know—"

"Our realtor. He's on the planning board. Your dad had to get a permit to build it, right?"

"Oh. I guess so." Maybe my parents' sauna is still the talk of Mercury. For me, taking one is as natural as taking a shower. I should inform him that it's not unusual for American Finns to have saunas in their basements, garages, backyards. Tell him that homesteaders built saunas first, before their houses.

My eye is drawn to the sliver of light that brightens his front door, left slightly ajar. A gnawing yearning seizes me. I stare with unabashed longing at the doorway, at the recollection of that impossibly tiny fist.

"Babies were born in them." I say aloud.

"What's that?"

A side effect of spending time alone, I've begun talking to myself. I say, "Nothing. I better go in now," I pirouette toward the house, arm raised to wave the newspapers at him as if I have a lot of reading to do. This is a mistake, as one side of the afghan falls in my way, making me trip up the front steps. "Lumsy," my mom always called me, having trouble with the "cl" sound.

He calls out a hearty "Take it easy!" and I feel his eyes follow me, the blanket—what's left hanging—prickling my neck. Once inside, I hear the golf cart cruise down the driveway. This maddening place!

I walk through the house to close windows. In the end bedroom, I hear the mewing of the baby next door and linger. My mother was over forty when I was born, which in the mid-seventies seemed downright elderly. Pragmatic if not prescient, my parents tried to reassure me about my future without them: "You have good job," Mom stated over dessert one night, pronouncing it "yop." I was just out of college. She nodded her head with its practical short hair, her gold helmet of authority, "And you will have a family of your own by then."

My father, worrying an after-dinner toothpick in his mouth, plucked it out and said pointedly that I must have *sisu*, like the spunky, determined Finns who fought to the last man against the formidable Russian army. I groaned inside. His Karelian family had lost their farmland in the Winter War, but would this distant discussion, too, boil down to a sour Russian stew? "Pig-headed, you mean," said my mother, who was more objective about her countrymen, and that was the end of our talk.

I look up at the new neighbors' two-story mansion, which swallows the whole length of their yard. I shut the window and go to bed.

*

I lie under the covers early the next morning with an emerging sense of pleasure. Jukka's my kin and he's here! His speech alone comforts me, so like that of my mother and grandparents, where all is stated without inflection, and all sentences tread downward from the start. Mom used to ask, "Where this is," when she searched for something. And the sounds: in Finnish the "t" pronounced so softly it sounds like a "d," the "k" melded to a "g," and the "p" a buttery "b" sound. My visitors' talk feels familiar, familial.

But something still nags at me, feels off. I stare at my cell phone on the bedside table. All these events not shared with

Meredith? I rise and lift the window blinds. Up and down the street, blankets of creamy white flakes spread over the lawns like snowflakes covering the ground and listing through the air. This sudden change in the landscape—how did I miss seeing it happen? Two mourning doves perch on parallel phone wires, one on top, the other directly below. One dove flies off and the other lingers before following. I call.

Although it's seven on a Saturday morning, I know she'll be up. When she answers my call, words pour out of her. "Ali, could you please tell me what's up? Are you mad at me? Cleo told me you're moving!" Her voice wavers. "I know it makes sense, but now it's like you'll be so far away." And here I thought I was the only one who needed us to be close… She goes on to tell me she ran into the girl, still in her yard, just minutes after I'd left. "She told me that you'd been there looking for me. Said that you got pissed off and left because she ate your McDonald's food. What a head case."

A big head case, what have I been telling you?

"So is it about that, really?"

"I don't know." I think about the miserable day, the lay-off, pesky Steffen, the girl, Meredith's 'good news.' "It wasn't a good day."

"I know. You poor thing." She exhales.

I blurt, "Do you talk to your clients about me?"

"Never."

"But she said…"

Meredith pauses. "Oh gosh, maybe I was talking about needing to open up, I have no idea. I don't always know what I'm doing in case you haven't noticed. Sometimes I think I'm in the wrong line of work. My job is so stressful, the pay's awful, and then these girls call me in the middle of the night like I'm a doctor or their mom and what can I say? Eat. Don't eat. Don't puke. Am I really doing any good? If I'm making my best friend mad at me, I'm really screwing up." *My best friend.*

Men don't realize how girls and woman court each other, how in the beginning, a new friend as simpatico as Meredith feels as exciting as a love affair. Anticipating each new meeting with her early on, I compiled her a mix CD, while she presented me with books, including the complete collection of Henry James, and yellow roses that smelled like peaches. That urge for friendship that's entirely non-sexual, yet can feel more important than wooing a man.

"Friendships for women are survival," I say softly. When a female baboon loses her grooming partner she becomes depressed. After that she searches and searches for a new one, who's possibly more important to her wellbeing than a mate. "A female baboon without her grooming mate might never get over it." I gaze out at the snowy blanket of flowers.

"I'll consider that a compliment. Anyway, I'm really sorry if there's something I did or said to upset you. Sorry that I wasn't there for you, Ali."

I feel any residual resentment dissolve, rise, fly out and away like the mourning doves. My ire seems so distant, so trivial. Why was I so mad? "You don't always need to be there for me." Was it the thought of her being pregnant again? Mere and Cleo are probably right about me: I'm basically clueless about myself.

I fill her in about my move, to her dismay. "Alina, you can't just cut us off, *we're* your family now." By this, she means herself and Lou, and her immoderate circle of friends, many of whom are social workers and psychologists and therefore highly suspect as "family" material for me. Adding Cleo and Steffen makes the mix far too combustible. And maybe a new baby on the way?

I hold the phone tight. "You said you have some good news."

"I'd rather tell you in person. I have a busy week, but…when can I see you?"

I tell her about my visitors, still sleeping, it seems. In response to her delight and her asking if they're cute, I say, "I think they might be gay."

She laughs. "You and your snap judgments. If every guy you thought was gay really was, the world would be *under*-populated, Ali. You're so weird."

"No, no, I know I'm like that. Guilty until proven innocent." Not that I have anything against gay men, it's just I don't want them asking me out on dates, which occurs with statistically improbable frequency. "No, they chose to sleep together and they just seem very domestic, like a couple."

"Looks can be deceiving. Maybe they just wanted you to have your own bed."

"Maybe." I say skeptically. "Anyway, they're OK. The friend just had eye surgery though so he's kind of out of it and wears these plastic glasses. My cousin's nice enough. Seems pretty opinionated."

"A relative of yours *opinionated?* Shocking."

"Yeah, yeah. How soon can you come up?"

She tells me that Lou's sick, running some crazy high fever like 104, assuring me that it's normal enough for a child.

"But they said they're leaving Monday." My shoulders droop, as it hits me that two days is too short, after all this build-up.

"Only the weekend? Shoot."

"They're going down to Stanford Hospital for an appointment Monday…" Since Meredith lives just a few miles from the university, we devise a plan for dinner at her place Monday night, providing Lou improves. She thanks me for calling and says she loves me. "I've got to run, Ali. Sick kid."

I want to ask about her own health, if she's worried about catching his cold because she's pregnant, but instead I say, "Meredith? I'm going to try be less weird."

~*Kaikki on kaunista, kun silmä tykkää.*~
~Everything is beautiful once the eye likes the view.~

Paavo

Newly energized by the call, I fix breakfast Finn-style. I lay breads and butter, cheese and tomatoes on the table, then move to the stove to boil coffee and eggs.

Within minutes, Paavo pads in wearing navy long underwear, a bit too tight—I feel I can see every muscle and rib of his body—and big rubber slippers only slightly smaller than swim flippers. Atop his goggles, his hair bubbles out like a Shitake mushroom.

He mumbles a quiet, "Morning," the way the Finns say it "*Huomenta,*" a statement not a greeting. None of that cheerful American-ess; after all, who knows if the morning will actually be a good one? I reply, and he stands there until I offer him a seat at the table. I pour water in the metal coffee pot, listening to him crack into a piece of hardtack.

He pipes up, "The cock was really growing last night." The coffee lid slips from my fingers, clanging on the stove. "It was feeling to me like that was going on all night," he adds. I rub my eyes. Too much information, as they say. I click the burner on high.

Behind me, I hear Jukka laugh. Barefoot, in a loosely belted yellow robe that reveals his hairless chest, he sits and says with great cheer, "*Hyvää huomenta*, good morning!" I turn to greet him while he says a word, "*kananpoika,*" to Paavo, who seems to dispute this in Finnish.

Paavo says, "*Mutta*, but *cockfight.*"

"But that's not the way. Rooster. That other word..." I keep my back to them but hear Paavo sputter. I turn to see Jukka, not great with English grammar but the possessor of slang, pointing to his crotch. I should've understood. In Finnish the consonants blend, the "p" muted like a "b," the "t" and "d" not so distinguishable. The cock, the rooster, was *crowing*. When I turn around, Jukka pats Paavo's shoulder, "Sometimes my friend here can seem little bit strange." No kidding. Paavo's eyewear appears to fog as he reaches for more bread.

I watch my pots closely, not knowing what to say, not wanting to get back into the subject of how they slept last night —or didn't. With a quick glance back I see Paavo looking at me. "Is there some help we can do for you? I'm not the bad cook."

"Ha!" Crumbs fly from Jukka's mouth. "That ain't the truth. I'm the one who can do the cooking."

"But you're not the one offering." He adds, "And you don't say 'ain't'."

I set down the eggs and coffee, interrupting the domestic quarrel. We eat quietly around the table as the caffeine kicks in, and I have the uneasy feeling of being stared at. Looking up, I see Paavo's goggles close in on me. What I can see of his peering eyes gives me the uneasy feeling of a fish in an aquarium about to be netted by a deep sea diver.

"I am seeing you clearly now," he says excitement entering his voice, "Yes! You are looking good!"

After my shower, I find the house quiet. Dressing quickly, I step onto my front porch to find the neighbor children congregated in front of their house with Paavo, as their dad Marty loads his golf bag in the back of a cart topped with a fringed canvas roof. Jukka slams the trunk of his rental car shut and steps into view wearing a pink polo shirt and khaki shorts, a pair of white golf shoes that look too big capping his feet. A bag of golf clubs stands by his side.

"What's going on?" I towel my damp hair.

"We golf today. Marty," he points to my neighbor, "has lended to me these clothing. I left without the thing—unlike Paavo, of course, so much clothes I think he stays for the winter."

"You're going *golfing*?"

"He's kind enough to invite to the private club," he smiles over at his newfound friend.

"But..." what can I say? He's obviously thrilled and I don't exactly have a plan for the day. "Can Paavo golf?" *Please say yes.* I don't know what to do with strange, bespectacled Paavo.

A tiny girl, maybe five years old, points at his goggles and says, "He's sick."

Marty chuckles. "That's 'lay-sik,' Riley." To me he says, "We're doing eighteen holes but I think we're getting a good start."

Paavo trots toward me. "They gonna be back by Monday for sure." I look at him alarmed. "I was yoking," he says. "Choking," he over-corrects himself.

As I load the dishwasher, I spy Paavo sitting on the rear deck staring at the backyard. He's switched to sunglasses, which is a definite improvement. Although I only glimpse him from the side, I feel the appeal, the instinctive attraction I felt at first seeing his online picture. Since his arrival, I've sensed that he can't see me clearly, and this feels safe, comfortable. He isn't peering into my soul the way Steffen did, his direct stares making my insides feel exposed.

I call out to him, "Would you like to go somewhere?"

"I'm not feeling like doing much." He points to his eyes. "But I like to walk round this yard."

I watch him open the sauna door. *Mom's ashes.* Days have passed and I haven't even thought about them, sitting in there on the top bench, a place that felt respectful. I feel a pang of guilt and rush out to the deck, "Let me know if you guys want to take sauna, will you?"

Shutting the door, Paavo says, "We are not staying long, it won't be necessary. The shower is fine."

I join him as he paces the yard, stopping to look at the various species of trees. Despite his recalcitrant personality, which could be due to his recent surgery, he has a sexy Bono look. I smooth my hair, move closer beside him, sneaking peeks, feeling a surge of heat. It's been so long since I've been with a man. "I know you have that eye appointment on Monday, but you should stay longer."

"Well, it seems we have the changing plans. Jukka is something like a wild gypsy so there is not much set into cement." Then he waves his thick arms in a sweep of the yard and states, "Everything I see is bad!"

"I'm sorry? Maybe your eyes aren't adjusted." Did that LASIK work?

"Yes, yes. Such amazing how good I'm seeing. Every little thing. It's wonderful!" I push up my eyeglasses, suddenly self-conscious. "You would not need those if you go have the surgery." He peers at me, but I cannot decipher the look, just feel its penetration. "Your glasses are too hiding. I see your eyes. *Kaunis.*" Pretty.

I feel a blush rising. "It's just a little scary."

"It's not so bad." And just as I'm warming to this Paavo, this handsome visitor, he scans the yard and repeats, "But here," another arm sweep, "I only see bad things out here."

What? In this jewel of a yard? OK, so the lawn needs mowing, but even Cleo is impressed by the deep green glade, the emerald oasis of trees here. As we walk through the scratchy, ankle-high grass, he points to water draining into a small oak, heavy pine boughs hugging a telephone wire, a shallow-rooted eucalyptus like the leaning tower of Pisa. He stops at the majestic oak, so aged my parents had some of its branches wired, yet so lush and gorgeous it almost makes living here worthwhile.

To my surprise, he shimmies part way up the hefty trunk and

stands in the V of a low branch. "This one maybe it needs to go—it's got the—*kovakuoriainen*." He puts his thumb and forefinger close, "some little bug." Leave it to the Finns to have a word that's longer than the thing itself. "See these leaves someone is eating," but I cannot see anything up there but glossy green leaves. "I'm not sure it's possible to save. It is very old."

"No," I say. Cut down the oak? I grimace at him perched in my tree. "How do you know all this?"

"Well, before medical university, I was working in the forest industry like so many others." Perhaps he notices my crestfallen face. "On whole, it's going to be OK."

"But you just said everything you see is bad."

"Maybe I've said this wrong. I am trained to see the problems." Oh. He sees only the bad. Such an unpleasant trait in a person!

"They won't be my problems for long. I'm selling the property. In fact, a realtor's coming tomorrow."

His forehead wrinkles. "That seems a mistake. Where are you living then?"

"I'll move back down to the Silicon Valley. That's where I work." *Will be working.* "Not far from where you were yesterday."

Paavo says, "It is nicer up here. I've been to the States before—and to John's near Stanford. It really is too much crowded there now. I have not seen the properties like this." He slides down and stands close, again I feel my heart beat quicker, warm and eager, near his firm body. He beams a striking, full-lipped smile, leans close to squeeze my arm. "This is nice yard for children to play for when you have the family."

*

Later, I drive Paavo up the mountain, spring the only time of year it's in fulsome glory and tolerably temperate. Soon from a distance it will turn camouflage, then the color of dry camel fur, forbiddingly hot, living up to the name Mt. Mercury. From the peak, a beautiful vista spreads before us, wide blue sky, the valley, actually a series of rolling hills and valleys, the verdant high ridge to the West, beyond which somewhere, too far, shines the waters of San Francisco Bay.

We stroll along an easy trail, a gurgling creek off to the left, mirrored blue in the sun-drenched meadowland. Vast stretches of low-growing shrubs, called "elfin forest," according to a brown park sign, are shaded by coastal live oak, sycamores, California laurel, and my favorite: the gorgeous gnarly, red-roped madrone. In a thicket, I run my hand along the twisted burgundy wood, soothed by its cool, smooth surface. Tiny blue butterflies dance in the tall grasses, while in a shady glen a small waterfall splashes us with spray.

Paavo points out species of plants and trees, saying Finnish names, asking for the English, telling me their Latin species names: *pinus strobus* for the pines, *quercus robur* for the oak…is he trying to show off?

"Very beautiful here," he says. "If I am living here I'm coming to this mountain all the time."

Seeing the mountain through the eyes of this stranger, I agree. I breathe in the fresh, moist air and say that I should be taking advantage of my current proximity. I marvel at the whole scene—it's not just a hot-as-hell monolith but a wonderland of variations, hidden glens with water, shady secrets. It's hard to see a mountain when you live at its base.

Walking back to the car, I notice women look his way. I sidle closer. I swear he smells like cardamom. "I'm going to start hiking here. You might want to join me? Maybe you'll stay longer, or come back soon?"

"Well you never know with Jukka. But I am thinking we will come back." He faces me for a long moment. "I most definitely want to come back here." I pivot to open the car door so that he won't see me redden. The vibes I feel are definitely species *Finnus Heterosexuous.*

~Ei se tapojansa muuta, joka ei mieltään pahenna.~
~One won't change his habits if he hasn't hurt his feelings.~

Marty

"*I* could live in this crib, I'm telling you." Jukka jumps up the front steps in the late afternoon, jovial, high cheeks sunburned. Inside, with malty breath, he extols the virtues of American golf carts and greens and clubhouse beer, and tells Paavo that he missed a great day.

"I've had quite the nice day with Alina," Paavo says.

"I doubt as much fun as we are having."

Hmph. I march into the kitchen, where I've been cooking, and scour the old farm sink hard, like Mom, who scrubbed away most of the porcelain veneer as if striving to expose its cast iron core. When Jukka enters, he says, "This is smelling good. Marty eats alone tonight, I think."

"Why?" He shrugs. I shrug it off, too, but Jukka continues, "I'm thinking he likes food. We have talked much about that."

Since there's no shortage of pasta and sauce, I say, "I suppose we could invite him over." I squeeze out the steel wool, surprising myself by my offer. Maybe Paavo will see me as outgoing and generous, like Meredith? Without hesitation, Jukka jaunts to the house next door.

"Nice to meet you again, Alina," says Marty. "Or as I sometimes call you, 'Alona.'" He grins at this witticism. "Alina Alona, get it? You know, because you spend so much time on your own."

I blink at him. I had him pegged as something of an ass from our first meeting, but this confirms it. And why is he talking about me? "Come eat," I say abruptly.

Seated at the table, I thrust food at him to keep him from more inane chatter. It works, as he devours the simple salad, three helpings of pasta with Bolognese sauce, and four slices of buttered Italian bread. We're on our second bottle of Pinot Noir when Marty leans back, satisfied. "First decent meal I've had in months. Thank you." He suppresses a burp. Jukka brings up golf and the two talk about their play on various holes, boring me to the point of interruption.

"Can riding around all day in a motorized vehicle and occasionally swinging a club be considered a sport?"

Jukka, who's on his fourth or fifth glass of wine says, "Maybe it is more of a game. But I like. And racing. Finland has many good racecar drivers. This is very big sport in my home."

"Sounds dangerous," I say. Especially given the modest size of most Finnish homes. Only Marty smiles at my silly joke. I frown at him. "Would've been nice if your wife and kids could've come for dinner." I feel like odd woman out.

"Rebecca dropped the three off with our oldest at some kid flick. Not sorry to miss that," he shakes his head. "She's home now resting with the baby." He leans on the back legs of my rickety chair, cradling his stomach. "She does that a lot." At our silence—I've been wondering why I don't see his wife much—he looks up at us, "Breastfeeding, you know. But I'd like you to get to know her," he nods at me. "Would do her good."

Paavo asks how old is the baby and Marty says ten weeks. "I guess you're not 'alone-a'," I say with some sarcasm, which jovial, sated Marty doesn't acknowledge.

Red-face glowing from drink, Jukka belches. "You have too many children. In Finland we have one, maybe two. That is plenty. People don't like you have more than four." I cover my mouth with a napkin, having had the same thought, but knowing Jukka has gone too far.

Marty jerks forward on his chair. "What do you know?"

"Well I'm seeing you don't want to be over there."

Paavo admonishes him in Finnish as the neighbor wipes his mouth and stands. "I'd better get going." He shoves in his chair. "Thanks again for the meal." When he turns, I rush after him to the door.

"Come again!" I call. Feeling contrite, I add, "I'm sorry. My cousin doesn't know what he's saying. His English isn't very good."

"His English is fine," the man mutters as he stomps toward his dark house.

"I'll visit your wife. Tell her!"

Back at the table Paavo talks in stern Finnish. Jukka holds his head in his hands.

"You can't talk that way to people," I say. "He's probably a jerk, but they're my neighbors, I live here."

As I start clearing the table, Paavo says to him, "You are drinking too much." Jukka doesn't reply.

Piling plates, I say, "My father drank. He said all Finns drink too much." And I know the Finnish statistics.

"It's true." Paavo says.

"I think all northern peoples do. All the dark days of winter. But the sad thing was, he quit. A few years before liver cancer got him." My voice wavers.

Jukka sits up, "That's too bad. Well. I guess it does the business to the body and so."

"*Viina on viisasten juoma*!" I snap, surprising myself with Dad's frequent saying. A quiet drunk, my father defended his drinking to my mother with those words: *only someone who can control himself should drink.*

"*Piisaa*! Enough, Jukka! And perhaps then you better watch out," Paavo points at Jukka's scarlet-stained goblet. "It's time I think for you to go to bed." In the Finnish that follows, I hear Paavo say, "*nenänvalkaisu*," and recall that it means something like "nose-whitening"—sobering up.

Jukka scrapes back his chair and slurs, "*Yuota.*" *Night.* I hasten to the sink, slosh water on the dishes. *It does the business.* Of ruining the liver. Of ruining the lives of others. I blink back tears. I'm starting to forget the sound of my father's voice.

Paavo quietly places glasses on the chipped countertop. He puts a hand on my wet, soapy one for a gentle moment. "*Kauniita unia,*" he says, just as Dad used to say. *Pretty dreams.*

*

Groggy from the wine and late night, I wake to find a note on the kitchen table. I rush outside to discover Paavo, wearing sunglasses, jacket draped over his arm sitting on the steps. Rubbing my eyes I say, "*Huomenta.*"

Jukka, in shorts and a thin t-shirt, jogs over from Marty's house. "He's good guy. It's all good. Now we go to Frisco. We leave you to your own business today. You have your own life."

Who says I have a life? My un-caffeinated brain isn't processing this sudden departure. "But." They look at me expectantly. A bleary montage of the obligatory tourist sites: the drive down crooked Lombard Street, snapping pictures and walking windblown across the Golden Gate bridge, slurping greasy noodles in teeming Chinatown, waiting in a long line to hop a cable car, topped off by a stroll through Pier 39 and a stop at the Disney store. Still, I haven't been a tourist in the city for ages, and its natural beauty always awes and enlivens me.

But they're leaving now and getting ready would take me time: coffee, a sweater, windbreaker, my headache medicine... "If you can wait," I say, then recall that a realtor is coming this afternoon. Which feels about as fun as wart removal. But I don't break appointments, and I've stalled long enough on the house. "No. Have a nice time," I say half-heartedly.

Paavo whips off his sunglasses. "I have just called John and he said it's silly I'm keeping these on for so long."

An involuntarily, "Oh!" escapes me. Where Steffen's gaze is

all flash, electric, charging people to stop and stare, Paavo's large hazel eyes are a handsome copper brown, drawing in the radiance of the sunny morning. "Your eyes. You look—so different."

"My mother says they are always changing. Maybe I am always changing." No, I think, you're like me, like Meredith, solid and stable. Not flighty like Steffen.

Jukka says, "If it's OK, we stay one more night before going to John's."

"Of course it's OK! You should stay longer. *Please.*" Only I hear the pleading note. They smile as they slide into their rental car. "Dress warm!" I advise.

Jukka laughs, spreads his short-sleeved arm out the window in the temperate spring air. "*Moi,*" I say, attempting to sound cheery.

"*Moi moi,*" he calls, "*Moi* is hello and now you say, *moi-moi.* Goodbye!" And they speed away.

I slump toward the empty house muttering *moi-moi-moi.* My grandparents and parents always said *oi, oi, oi* when something was wrong. And this being alone feels very, very wrong.

~Ei auta itku markkinoilla.~
~Weeping does not help at the marketplace.~

Moping

The only thing worse than sleeping during the day is watching TV during the day. I plunk on my parents' couch, slurping Cheerios in front of the muted television, and cringe as I watch a blandly handsome couple act out Hollywood's idea of the perfect, intimate moment. The man kneels before his co-star on a mound in a preternaturally bright green field, a baseball field. With one hand he pulls from his pocket and presses toward her a ring, all the while holding onto—and talking to her via—a microphone. There's a close-up of the ecstatic blonde, her joy outmatched only by that of the thousands of complete strangers shown cheering in the stands.

I shudder in the cool house—such a contrast from the heat rising outside—and draw up my knees, wrapping them in Mom's scratchy afghan. I imagine her walking by clutching a dust rag, pausing at the screen only long enough to wave an ammonia-soaked rag at it and say "oi, oi, oi" in accented English. She'd say that Finns would never make a movie like that. They wouldn't even *film* a private moment because that would mean that *someone* was watching. And yet they all drop their clothes at the drop of a birch leaf to sweat cheek to cheek in a sauna.

I've watched a few of these "romantic comedies" in recent weeks—clearly a misguided attempt at entertainment, as the witless dialog, insipid plots, and sadistic slapstick have only served to gall me. Only two were even mildly interesting, both about weddings, one Greek, the other Indian, with their large, boisterous extended families butting into every aspect of the nuptials. Such a daunting profusion of relatives! Like the Sri Lankans I worked with who get together with their "cousins" every weekend. After being a guest at one of these huge all-night gatherings, I discerned that "relative" is only a marginally narrower definition of "human." After a second and third invitation, I began to feel cousin-ish myself.

Reminded of Ravi and Sri, whom I haven't seen since we cleaned out our offices, I click off the TV and go into the kitchen to phone them. Sri's acting as an untraditional house husband, caring for his young children, while Ravi, a decorous single man in his mid-50s, tells me that after years of dating Americans, he's planning a summer trip to India for a bride. I choke up talking to him, already missing our daily contact, and impulsively announce that I'm going to throw a party. Hosting a party has always seemed such risky business, but I insist I'll have one, in June, before he leaves. We'll celebrate the solstice. *Juhannus* for the Finns! A big blowout with all my friends and newfound relatives, a large happy dancing affair—possibly with confetti.

Desperate to get out of the house, I surf the web for a comedy at a local theater. One shows an interesting plot with not-so-promising critical reviews, but, atypically, I decide to ignore the critics and scan the user comments. Repeatedly I read rave reviews that include terms involving a wetting of the pants: "pee-in-your-pants funny!" and "it's LOL and pee-pants fun." After reading three such remarks, I check to see if the movie is G-rated and meant for the fresh out-of-diapers crowd. While I love to be amused and am quick to smile or chuckle—these being my physiological responses to humor, rather than urination—these reports of bladder-control issues during the film make the thought of sitting in a theater amongst pants-soaked viewers, the acrid smell of urine in the enclosed space, eating my popcorn and drinking lemonade, lose all appeal.

Giving up on the flick idea, I pace the lanes of Mercury

before the realtor comes, gathering house flyers, noting the list of luxe features and the multi-million dollar prices. Quaint cottages lay nestled in the woods, some entirely hidden by foliage, others are picturesque backdrops to expansive, well-tended lawns. A few sleek and ugly 70's houses hang on. All are overshadowed by the mansions of the nouveau riche. A huge stone structure stands half finished down a long dirt lane, where short, Mayan-featured workers haul cement in wheelbarrows, dirt-covered and sweating under straw hats and baseball caps. I think of their ancestors, toiling to build grand testaments for the elite.

The original houses in the larger Blaineville area are California ranches in what was once true ranchland. Long, low-slung shoeboxes, their "porches" are plain cement slabs covered by an overhang of roof supported by a four-by-fours. Simple, practical, dark houses to beat the valley heat, no character, no charm. By contrast, the new houses springing up all over the hills have charm oozing out their dormer windows.

The truck with the supra-human-sized photo of the realtor couple with their jingoistic cat passes. Another local realtor lists a 7,000 square-foot house that boasts twenty-foot "coiffured" ceilings, spectacular views of the 10th green, and "Wayne's Coating Throughout."

I look into an open house with a "family room" so large you'd be hard-pressed to find your family in it, and wonder if that's the point. I pass a weathered Mexican snipping a hedge, a tuft of white sprouting from one side of his bangs like a patch of weeds. I nod and smile, as I do to all the workers in Mercury, and the gardener flashes a metallic grin. "I'm one of you!" I want to shout to them all, "I don't live here. I work! My mother cleaned houses!"

True, my father was a math professor and my mom cleaned others' houses only because an inbred genetic detail made her actually *enjoy* it—and we'd all had the advantage of a good dentist—but we didn't belong here. We shared more with the cleaners, haulers, gardeners, and carpenters—the myriad laborers who daily poured, like migrant workers over the border, into Mercury. The irony of paying to live in pastoral peace is that there is always noise. Buzz saws, cement trucks, leaf blowers—everything ceaselessly torn down, rebuilt, and blown about. I know. I lived here to care for Mom in her final weeks.

Church services must be ending, as I'm forced off the road to evade a caravan of cavernous vehicles, a couple of bodies in each. The roads, built in a different era, are too narrow for any two to pass each other. Smaller cars are invariably driven by "the help," unless they are high-end German models.

Out of nowhere, a swift, seasonally-late rain shower breaks through the morning heat, dousing me. The fliers in my hand wilt. I take off my rain-splattered glasses, and the misty lanes blur like an impressionist painting, my astigmatic eyes taking in general ideas, first impressions I stick with, trusting my gut.

A golf cart pulls up next to me, driven by an older, plaid-capped man. He asks if I'd like a lift. I don't need one, but something in his smile and forlorn eyes makes me accept. We introduce ourselves and he chats as he drives, occasionally stopping to pick up trash, stashing it in a black garbage bag behind us. His profile reminds me of Dad, the stooped shoulders, the protruding lower lip. Noticing my brochures, he asks if I'm looking to buy. "Sell," I say, "It's too rich for me here," though I don't mean that I can't afford it. I tell him about my parents' leaving the house to me.

He shakes his head and expresses condolences, says he knew of my parents. "Fine people. Kept to themselves, but I had the pleasure of talking with your father a few times up at the post office. He was going to join the Preservation Committee, help us keep the 'old Mercury.'" *He was*?

Driving slowly as if he craves company—I get the feeling he's a widower—the man points out the small houses that date back to the 1920s and 30s, and shakes his head at all the new construction, the outsized, incongruous add-ons to the old cottages, the brand-new mega-mansions. I agree heartily and hop out the next time we spot a crushed soda can.

Pulling up to my house, he says, "Have you been to the Newcomers Welcome? Might convince you to stay." I smile but say my life is down in the South Bay. I walk up my steps with less confidence in my judgments and an odd melancholy creeping over me. Is it because he reminds me of my father? Because we might be kindred spirits? Or just two lonesome souls. I turn back to ask him in for coffee…but his cart has zipped away.

*

I implore Meredith on the phone. "Is there any way we can get together today? I need to stay for a realtor but can you come? I just can't be on my own."

"On your own? What happened to your guests?"

"They left." I tell her about their trip to the city, then plead again to get together.

"As it turns out, Steffen's not working today." I can't help wondering if he's on board for another child. While Cleo belongs to that camp of women who think it's impossible to see an ex-boyfriend with your girlfriend, I'm not. But when pressed, I once admitted to her that the advent of Lou—their having a baby together—did make me envious.

"I can't wait to see you Ali, and I have a few free hours. Though I'm disappointed your family won't be there."

Family? "Oh, right. But guess what? There's this Russian document, some family document we think, that I found up here."

"Russian? How coincidental! What is it?"

Coincidental? "I don't know, maybe some kind of certificate? I'm going to have to take it to a translator. It's definitely from Russia."

"Do not go there!" she barks and I hold the phone away, "Sorry, I've got to run, Lou's healthy again," fatigue in her voice.

"We have so much to talk about, Ali. And I have—well, *Steffen and I* sort of have—something that might cheer you up."

When we hang up, my head drops into my hands. I seriously doubt that news of her pregnancy will cheer me *one bit.*

~*Siitä puhe mistä puute.*~
~One talks about what one does not have.~

New Life

At last Meredith rushes into the house, carrying a loaf of dark bread that looks suspiciously healthful, not unlike the dense rye *demo* Mom served daily. She plunks the bread on the kitchen table and squeezes me long and hard. In a rush of words she says she was delayed because she had to help Steffen unclog the toilet after Lou's long bout of constipation.

We sit at the table, Meredith across from me in Mom's spot. I place a piece of buttered bread before her and she looks up. "You'd be surprised how much poop can come out of a three year-old. I complain and Steffen just says, 'Tough shit' to be funny." I smile. "You can laugh. When he says something like that, I just want to throttle him. I'm so tired all the time." She munches and says, "Don't ever let your child go three days without *going*."

What child? So many hurdles to jump before I get to jammed toilets: the finding-a-man hurdle, the marriage hurdle, the sex hurdle, pregnancy…by the time I jump them all, I'll be as old as my mother, needing the prune juice as much as my blocked-up kid.

"I'll keep that in mind," I say, pouring iced tea in her glass. "Oh darn, I made black tea," I start to pull it back. She wouldn't want caffeine in her condition.

She grabs the glass. "Caffeinated's OK, Alina. I can use the buzz."

"God, I'm so glad you're here." I dig into her grainy bread, which tastes only slightly moister than the hardtack I grew up on. After a moment, I sit back, folding and rubbing my arms. "I'm excited to hear your news."

"I've been wanting to tell you this ever since my trip to L.A. But with your lay-off that day and all."

Impatient, I say, "So, are you…are you 'with child?'"

Meredith chokes on a mouthful. "Did you just say, 'with child?'"

"I think so." I scrunch my face. "Well?"

"Well, I guess you could say not yet. *Almost.*"

"Not yet?" They're just *trying*? What kind of 'news' is this? Like, I almost have a boyfriend? Or, more apropos to me, 'I *almost* have a date?' Makes me presuppose that telling Meredith about my attraction to Paavo might be a tad premature. I let out a sigh. Her not being pregnant feels like relief.

"You know how Sue adopted twins from Russia?" I know her sister and partner down the coast have a boy and girl, I forget how old. "Well…I want to adopt too!" Her eyes glisten. "From China, or more probably the Ukraine."

My jaw drops in bewilderment. "*Adopt*? But I thought… but you have Lou. I don't understand."

"Ali, you know my uterus is damaged, right? Well, I just had a check-up because I've been getting *broody*, wondering if I could have another baby. Not that I brought it up with Steffen, we're barely scraping by. Anyway, my gynecologist says it's unlikely I'll be able to carry a baby to term now."

"God, Mere. I'm so sorry. How long have you known?"

"For a few months. Long story. Anyway, I've been thinking, and talking with my sister. And seeing her with her adopted twins really changed me. I already have Lou, and now I can help another child."

"But…" Strange feelings stir in me.

"It's just that I want more. More of a family. I want Lou to have a baby brother or sister. You know how I grew up next to my Dad and Sarah, Mom and Paxton in my house with Sue, David, Sunny, …" as she starts with the half- and step-siblings on both sides my eyes glaze over—I consider suggesting she fill out a spreadsheet for me someday—and my mind travels back to her news. With Steffen off on odd jobs all the time, Mere's often on her own. She told me he has so much work in an up-market town near his parents', he's been sleeping more and more at their house.

"Sometimes you're like a single mom," I say. "Won't it be hard with two?" I think of the work Meredith goes through just to get her toddler to nap; that when he's finally down she spends the better part of his sleep unplugging phones and closing windows, tiptoeing around squeaky floorboards so that instead of getting rest, she exhausts herself from the effort of keeping quiet. But in response to my remark she just shrugs and sips her tea. "I know you come from a big family, but foreign adoption? Isn't that expensive?"

"Sue and Germaine are totally into it. They want to pay, can you imagine? Course, they're loaded. But they're so supportive of the idea."

"Think about it all, though." There are *so many* cons to this idea. "Does Steffen want this?"

"Hardly, but I can't live my life waiting for him to decide. It's hard to explain, Ali." Her face softens, her eyes glow dark. Pupils of adult females dilate at pictures of babies; male pupils dilate when they see photos of naked women. I can see by her dewy eyes that this is not so much about Lou—or Steffen.

"If anyone should adopt, I should," I say. Here I am, nearing thirty-four, no man in sight. "But of course I wouldn't." I want to have my own baby. "Adopting from another country...how would you know what you were getting?"

The caffeine brings a rush of roses to Meredith's cheeks, blooms to cast off any concerns. "Just think. Ali. A little *babushka*!"

"I think that would be adopting a grandmother." I'm

thinking Mere would be better off with that—someone who could keep a cocked eye on Lou.

But she says, "Whatever, a little Russian baby. A girl would be great, you should see my niece's curls. She's a little doll."

"Yeah, but if Steffen doesn't want it—"

"Oh, forget him. He's so slow to come around to anything. I'm moving on."

What? Is Meredith giving up on waiting for him to marry her? This is starting to feel like my fault. "It's not me, is it? What happened with him and me."

She drops her bread. "Go on."

"Just. You know, how when I broke up with him it was because he was basically crazy. He drove women away being in such a rush to marry, have kids, all that. So now he's like the complete opposite and you—"

Meredith cuts me off abruptly. "Sometimes I don't know if you're blind or if you deliberately don't see things."

"Huh?"

"I thought you were finally going to say he's still in love with you."

"NO! Jesus." I stand to clear my plate. "What nonsense. Besides, I thought you said you guys had something to cheer me up and this talk about adoption and Steffen is hardly—"

"Oh my God!" she rushes for the door. "I forgot. I brought a surprise for you and she might be thirsty." Mouth agape, I watch Meredith run to her car.

~Neuvottu mies on puoliksi autettu.~
~A man who is given advice is helped half the way.~

Puppy Love

"She was sleeping so I left her with the windows cracked. Now she feels too warm. Someone should report me to Animal Services." Meredith cradles a large puppy: it has pink-rimmed eyes and a mottled coat of white and brown. Except for its floppy ears, it's an ugly dog. But having been raised in a rusting New England mill town, I have an appreciation for things not pretty.

She hands the dog to me, and, because the pup looks so calm and drowsy, I accept. I hold it still, my hand vibrating with the quick breaths from its silky belly. I'm glad for this distraction after Meredith's ludicrous accusation. My face still burns. I bend to scratch its head and the dog awakens with alarming alacrity. As it starts to squirm, its velvety softness dissolves. It opens its jaws and pierces my arm with a mouthful of tiny daggers. "Ow!"

"She's going through a teething stage," Meredith says, pushing a rubber bone into its mouth. I hold the dog at arm's length. I do not like this stage. Naturally, my hygienically-oriented mom never let me have pets—the smells, the fur, the *accidents.*

"Steffen got her impulsively with Lou, you know how he is, but of course we can't have a dog where we are now. And we sort of thought she might be good for you. *Temporarily*, of course." Before I can object, Meredith says we need to take the pup out for a walk. I leave a note for the realtor with my cell phone number, while Meredith fastens a leash on the dog, and we head out.

Late spring in Mercury already feels too hot for outside exertion after noon. The puppy leads, pulling and sniffing her way.

Her perky loop of a tail is high in perpetual waggle like Lou's little spout of a penis, sometimes erect as he runs around naked, his enthusiasm for life on display, irrepressible, a body bursting with generalized excitement.

As we walk, I recount my time spent with Jukka and Paavo and the puzzling Russian document. I tell her, "Doesn't adoption take years? And you know, Russia's pretty corrupt."

But Meredith counters by saying that her sister has an insider working for her and everything is being arranged quickly, outside the regular channels—which actually seems to prove my point. "When you get to Russia, there's this guy called a "roof" to help translate and sort of protect your interests."

Meredith controls the dog as we walk on the lacy shadows of oaks and the spiky feathered fronds of palms, then into patches of bright, harsh sunlight. We pass the country club lot, divided between the cars of golfers—BMWs and Mercedes—and the more modest cars of the workers, today including a maroon Pontiac Bonneville, its sun-bleached paint faded in blotches like Rorschach spots.

I'll never feel comfortable living among the rich. My parents were charmed by the bucolic nature of the place, not caring a whit about the community's perceived *cachet.* In earlier years, when Dad taught at MIT, we didn't live in a gentrified Cambridge neighborhood, he insisted we live in working-class Somerville, known by all as "Slummerville." And when we moved to California after high school, we didn't land in Berkeley's *chi-chi* north side. No, we settled in decidedly down-market Albany. With all my parents' saved money and the value of the Mercury house, it's possible I'm financially set for life.

Meredith and I speed up and slow down at the puppy's will, taking the route along the golf course road. A string of squat white posts, like grave markers, line the grass, separating the golf course from the road. A buzz saw sears the silence.

She inhales deeply. "These yards, these houses. Such a nice

place to raise a kid. Wow," she points to a Mediterranean hacienda with a Spanish mission bell tower, like in *Vertigo.* She stops in front of a variegated-rock house featuring peaks and gables and a large turreted tower. Spaced cypress trees look like pikes guarding the castle, symbols of a fighting culture. Or do I just feel the need to battle it?

"Looks like a medieval fortress," I comment. Complete with moat, as a stone bridge spans the creek in front of it. "If there were enough water, they'd probably put alligators in there."

Meredith rolls her eyes and hands me the puppy's leash. "Take her for a spin." and I jerk forward as the dog tugs me with improbable strength. The next few yards are a struggle of control: any movement—the scuffling of a leaf, the flutter of a bird or squirrel's tail, the swing and click that launches an invisible golf ball—causes an arm socket-wrenching surge in that direction. My right arm quickly aches, and my underarms grow damp. "Strong dog! How old is she?"

"Not sure. But we're going to enroll her in puppy school, of course," Meredith assures me.

I don't think puppy school is going to cut it. "Give me a dog with a post-graduate degree."

As we turn a corner, three blondes approach, straight backed, posture-perfect—so different from the Hispanic women here, their shoulders rounded from cleaning, carrying children, pushing strollers. They stride quickly our way, looking as clipped, shaped, and manicured as the pampered landscaping we pass. One carries the leash of her dog high in front, as though a Louis Vuitton handbag is hooked on her arm. All three wear white tops and sporty black pants with white stripes down the sides. All three. Blond. White stripes. The one jerks on her dog's leash, looping it around her hand, and her wedding diamonds sparkle in the sun. Diamonds are very big here. I see them on all the women, the mothers, in the supermarket, the stroller brigade sipping lattes in front of Starbucks. The women power-walk past quickly, talking, taking little notice of us, despite the puppy's desperate lunges toward them and their pet.

The woman in the middle glances back at us, eyeing Meredith in her gypsy dress, and me in khaki shorts and a thinning olive top, camouflage gear. The maverick evidently, her hair is sawed sharply from short in back to long at the jaw. The ponytails of the other two bounce peppily along.

"Look at this place—everyone trying to be like everyone else—only better."

"Alina, stop generalizing. Rich, poor, Democrat, Republican…with you everything's so black and white!"

"Black! Ha. Do you see any people of color here? Just Hispanics—cleaning, mowing, doing the work." A golf cart buzzes past, pushing us onto the shoulder grass.

Meredith grips my shoulders. Her eyes narrow as we stand face-to-face, the dog tugging, swirling uncontrollably around our feet, binding us together with the leather leash. I look away from her eyes, which bore into mine.

She says sternly, "Stop. Don't. *Grow*." My face flames, it blazes. I look down. S*top, drop, roll*—isn't that what you do in a fire? I look back at her softening face, "I just wish you'd see some of the good here, let yourself be happier," she says. *I see only bad things…*

Reminded of Paavo and our trip to the mountain, I say, "The place *is* kind of growing on me." As I try to step away from her close range, I stumble, our feet bound by the leash. I lose balance and topple. The dog jumps and yelps. Meredith collapses flat on top of me.

The triplets with diamonds walk back our way to find us rolling with laughter on the mossy lawn, the puppy yipping in our ears.

Out of the corner of my eye I see a gold Lexus slowly approach. We lie face to face, bushed from giggling. I grin. "I really love you. But not *this* way." She pinches my cheek.

"Excuse me," a suited young man with grey hair but a pink baby-face, like a boy in a businessman's wig, leans out his car window. "Could you fine young ladies tell me where *Alameda Calido* is?"

My street? Shoot. The realtor. He's early. We quickly unwind the leash and beeline through a short cut to my house.

~Hullu paljon työtä tekee, viisas pääsee vähemmällä.~
~A fool does a lot of work, a wise man gets off easier.~

Reality

The man leans on the Lexus in front of my house fiddling with a calculator until he sees us approach, when he tosses it through the open window of his car and stretches out his hand. He shakes Meredith's hand, then mine, passionately, and introduces himself as Troy Champlaine of Ralph Barker Realty. He pronounces it *real-i-ty*. "You might say that was *kismet*, ladies. Me asking you for directions." When he smiles, dimples show.

"I wasn't expecting you so early," I say to the chipper fellow.

He puts up both hands, "Waiting is not a problem." With a glance at his car, he indicates, "I had work to do." He smells like peppermint and wears a brown suit two sizes too big: his sleeves descend to mid-knuckle, and his pants—or trousers—bunch up at the ankle. Bending down to the dog, who currently gnaws on his loafer, he says, "Do you live here too, lucky guy?" I tug the leash away from his shoe and let the dog pull me toward the house.

While Troy Champlaine grabs papers from his car, Meredith motions backwards and whispers to me, "He was playing with a *Game Boy.*" The dog leads us all inside, then kicks into full gear. Suddenly she strains with the strength of a bull to sniff everything, and I struggle to pull her back. Before I know it, the dog helter-skelter has tugged through the realtor's legs and in an instant I find my arm in the man's crotch.

I jerk my hand off the leash as he says, "Well, I'm happy to see you, too," bending forward to the puppy, now skittering around the corner. "He thought he saw a pussy cat," the realtor says in a cartoon voice. I look around for Meredith. He just said "*pussy cat.*"

Meredith retrieves the hyperactive dog, and as we head to the front door, Troy raises his right arm as if swearing an oath. "Ladies, I want you know I'm a modern gentleman."

Mere mutters to me "an oxymoron," then buries her smile in the dog's fur. "Ouch!" she says, as the puppy nips her chin. I begin to think he's more of a moron when he continues, "I understand today's living arrangements and…*fancies*, and you can expect the utmost diplomacy from me."

Meredith leaves with the canine, grinning and giving me a big smack on the cheek for the realtor's sake, and I ask where the dog will stay. She says perhaps Claire can take her for a while. Claire being Steffen's English mother, Lou's doting grandmother. She and Steffen's father Louis live among beautiful redwoods on the western edge of the Peninsula because he got rich pouring cement over the plum and peach orchards of the Santa Clara Valley back in the aerospace days. Steffen said when they met, his construction worker dad thought Claire very posh, but I know from PBS reruns of *East Enders* that she's no Crown Royal. With that cockney accent, she requires an interpreter.

"A galley kitchen," the realtor says, turning to me expectantly, like a proud pupil. We're doing the "walk-through" he requested, Meredith having departed, thank God, with the crazed canine.

"Sounds nautical," I say. He walks up and down the wooden gangplank of the narrow room, running his hand along the kitchen counter and appraising the fixtures. "Original," he tells me.

"Pardon me?"

He waves around the kitchen, "These are all original to the house. The appliances, the cupboards."

I look at the chipped tile, 1960's mustard yellow, the grout worn away by my mother's excessive scrubbing. "I think this house was actually built at the turn-of-the-century."

"Precisely. *That,*" he points behind me, "looks like a very old dishwasher."

My skepticism about this Troy Champlaine mounting, I ask, "Have you been doing this long?"

"*Ralph Barker*? Ralph Barker Realty, which has been serving the East Bay for over twenty years?" He waits for a response. "You called me, remember?" I remember. But that was only because he wasn't the Wayne's World guy or the couple pictured on the Felines-in-Support of-the-War truck.

"We might need to paint," I suggest, looking around with a seller's eye. Though my father had painted most of the rooms white, the passing years, along with the low ceilings and northern exposure, give them a dull grey cast. Jukka, in his frank Finnish way, is right.

"Maybe. Maybe *not*," Troy says enigmatically. His lips pout as he jots a note on a clipboard stuffed with disheveled papers. We pass through the front room adjacent to the kitchen, then make the length of the hallway, touring the bedrooms at each end, the small bath in the middle. Off the family room in back, I open the double doors to the deck, and we step outside.

"Holy shi-moley. I thought these were all small lots." I explain how this property and the lot next door are large, almost an acre. As the street progresses to its dead end, the lots become shorter, following the creek line. My parents figured that the original dwellers, servants for the vacationing rich, must've tended a pasture or garden, although saplings now sprout in the area near the house.

Troy says, "Tremendous potential!"

"I think the sprinkler system broke, it needs some lawn work."

"This lot could fit two *domiciles*." With a smile, he says, "That would be *houses*. I learn a new word each day. And study Dale

Carnegie." Dale Carnegie? Isn't he from the 19th century or something? "I find it really enriches my..." Troy pauses, evidently stuck for the word of the day. *Vocabulary*? I want to suggest. "Enriches my...*persona*." He shines a smile. Then he walks toward the deck steps and says, "I see three, maybe four houses!"

"What? No! You'd have to cut down so many trees."

He quickly says, "Not that you *would*," with a shake of his head. He looks down at the redwood decking and taps a foot. "This is nice." My father built it. It's where we sat after sauna when I visited, listening to shrill cricket mating calls in the cool air. I look out at the live oak that graces the middle yard, its shadow stretching east, its twisted branches covered with spring green leaves.

"I think that tree is protected," I say. "It's a Heritage oak."

Troy adopts a reverential tone, "Yes. And so it should be." He places the palm of his hand on the clipboard as if it's a bible. "Mercury is a deeply historical place," he intones. Then he perks up and nods at the sauna, "Nifty shed."

Despite my reservations, I start to enjoy the quirkiness of this Troy Champlaine. Bubbly, idiosyncratic, yet sincere—that's how he'd be described if he were a Napa Valley wine. With his stiff suit and dandy ways. "You seem to be something of an anachronism, Troy."

He frowns slightly, then smiles. "I try to be." He jots another note, then tosses the clipboard on a deck chair and jumps down the steps. "This zip code is highly prized," he declares. "These lots are in a great deal of demand."

Suddenly his repeated use of the word "lot" becomes clear; I smell teardown. Like the cleared field at the dead-end of this short street that has a sign in front: "Black Diamond Development." It isn't much of a house and I don't belong here, but demolition had not occurred to me; the thought of destroying my parents' home, where Dad lay on the floor figuring math and listening to Bach and brooding Sibelius, where he cut the lawn with the antiquated rotary mower, sweat beading his low brow.

Where I cared for Mom in her final days, reading from "*The Portrait of a Lady*" as it was originally published, in installments. My mostly mute, brain-damaged mother sat in her wheelchair and nodded me along. She formed crooked smiles or wrinkled her forehead at the right moments; her eyes brightened and, on rare occasion, tears welled. Sometimes the bark of a laugh interrupted my reading. Mom shook her head and said "*Piru,*" "devil," when it became clear that Isabelle would return to her deceitful husband. Often, I would re-read chapters because Mom softly nodded off, slumped in her chair, listening to the lullaby of my voice.

As Troy paces the yard, I fix my gaze on the magnificent oak at its center, now wired to hold its aging branches aloft. Trussed like my mother, who, after her stroke, had braces on her right arm and leg, until finally being relegated to a wheelchair. She'd moved from intensive care to rehab to nursing home. The Philippina staff there talked to her like a child, loud and falsely cheerful, while my comprehending but aphasic mom stared them down. They must've wondered why Americans went to such length and expense to keep alive these hapless aged, perhaps coming from poverty-stricken towns where children died before the age of five. The supported elderly were like the old oaks of Mercury, their heavy aged branches propped with wire, protected, cared for past their time. Doomed luxuries. Maybe I should bury her ashes under its sweeping canopy, feed its roots with the stuff of her strong bones…

I tilt lethargically back in the Adirondack chair, a seat designed for inertia, and glance over at Troy's clipboard. He's written "*dish-washer!!*" "*Wash gym shorts*" and "*anacronism?*" in loopy penmanship. He approaches me patting his brow with an old-fashioned white handkerchief. Suddenly he spreads his arms and sings out in a tenor, "Al*ee*na Es*cala*," pronouncing my name like an Italian opera house, "You are a very lucky girl!" He hops onto the deck, hugging my space, "Am I right?"

"Technically, you'd pronounce it *Ah*-lina *Es*-kala—you stress the first syllables. But nobody does." Nobody left living, anyway.

His buoyancy only slightly deflated, he says, "Oh, pardon my grammar, *Ah*-lina. I'm sure many realtors are interested, but at the end of the day, I hope you'll use us, Ralph Barker Reality for your reality needs. But don't ask for my uncle—call me." He hands me a thick folder and throws out a jaw-dropping asking price. Before I have time to answer he says in a serious tone, "Please, don't get up. Stay here." He drops his arms so that the clipboard rests in front of his crotch and bends his head as if in prayer. "This is a profound decision. *Profound*," he repeats before skipping off to his car.

I look at the glossy folder, the business card clipped on with Ralph Barker's name crossed out and Troy's written in careful pencil. When I go back in the house—minutes, maybe an hour later—I see that he's left a book on the coffee table: *Historic Mercury*. Skimming through the section on Mt. Mercury, I spot a picture of a huge granite boulder that looks like a mini version of Half Dome at Yosemite. Yosemite! In a rush of inspiration, I slam the book shut and get online.

These Finns are not going everywhere without me.

PART 2: LOOKING FOR LOVE

~*Ei elämästä selviä hengissä.*~
~You won't survive life.~

~Piru tanssii missään niin paljon kuin välillä pari.~
~The devil dances nowhere so much as between a couple.~

Yosemite

I lucked us into reservations at Yosemite for a night, perhaps because someone cancelled, or late May nights are not warm enough for most campers. Five days from their arrival, the Finns are still in the Bay Area. After their blustery day in San Francisco, Jukka returned predictably wearing a new sweatshirt, Mickey Mouse, and it was all I could do to refrain from saying *told you so!* Unbeknownst to outsiders, summer in San Francisco all too often chills to the bone.

And then they went back to Stanford to visit Paavo's doctor friend John and wife, and what else exactly I'm not sure, because wide-eyed, enchanted-with-all-things-American Jukka evidently no longer has time for texting. (I text him asking what they are doing, if they're having fun, and he replies with a smiley face. I ask when they'll be back, and he replies with a wink. It's like talking to a mime.)

We all had dinner one night at Meredith's, as her place is proximate to John's, and, unlike me, she possesses the entertaining gene—always eager and ready to spontaneously erupt into a hostess. It was a pleasant evening, with Meredith gliding around feeding us healthful, vegetarian ratatouille, baked garlic whole wheat bread, and a salad with more nutritious, unpalatable greens than I knew existed.

Paavo, pleased with the menu, mentioned how he wished to eat less red meat; Jukka, on the other hand, kept glancing into the kitchen, perhaps hoping to see marinating steaks and potatoes with butter magically appear on the counter. And when Meredith brought up the subject of her new Reiki lessons, Paavo was all ears. "This is very interesting for me as a doctor," he said. "We are not treating our patients well with just the Western medicine, I believe."

Jukka pointed out that he'd just traveled the globe to be treated by a Western doctor, doubting that Reiki could fix Paavo's extreme near-sightedness. I piped up that Meredith had treated me to a session, not revealing that it occurred on the awful day of my lay-off.

"And how did this feel to you?" asked Paavo with interest.

I thought back. "Warm, comforting." I smiled at Meredith. Then I recalled the one pose, where she held my head like a tender baby in her hands, and the uneasy feeling filled me again. "Maybe kind of scary, too."

"Ah," Paavo said knowingly, like some Dr. Freud, just as Meredith appeared with herbal tea and—thank God—a pot of strong coffee.

On leaving, I felt pleased that my best friend liked my Finns and had even found common ground with Paavo—a promising sign for the future. It was then that I suggested they all join us for a two-day trip to Yosemite.

Now we find ourselves at a fine campsite by a bubbling stream: one tent pitched for Meredith, Steffen, and Lou, another for Jukka, Paavo, and me. Cleo bowed out due to the venue, summing up her view of the proposed outing by saying, "Sounds kind of outdoorsy." Although I love this place, it's Meredith who knows its striated granite walls up and down. She calls Yosemite hallowed ground.

On the first day after a late start—Meredith and Steffen took a while to drive to Mercury with Lou and all of their toddler gear—we hike around the valley floor. We wander into a pine grove where shafts of sunlight filter through the trees and view the Cathedral Rocks, behind them two slender columns of granite like church spires.

Come evening, Meredith puts down Lou, who's tired from a day chasing butterflies and climbing small boulders. Like me, Paavo watches through the open tent flap as she places her hands over his eyes, then on his tummy. "Reiki," I murmur, but Paavo says nothing. At first Lou wiggles, but gradually succumbs, grows still. When Meredith squats out of the tent, Paavo, obviously curious, approaches her, and I watch as they go back inside. Kneeling over Lou, she seems to go through the different hand positions, quietly explaining. In the soft glow of evening, they look like a family in there. It's the wrong picture. I search for Steffen, but he's not in sight.

As darkness descends, we gather on canvas chairs around the campfire, built with wood provided by Steffen, chomping into juicy wieners washed down with cold beer and vodka. The sun sets early behind the tall rocks that encircle the valley and the stone walls exude a wintry chill. The stars emerge in the dark-domed sky, the firelight dances on the faces of my friends. In my warm, hooded sweatshirt, I feel cozy and content. The beer loosens my limbs, the gorgeous crisp night makes me wish our time here were longer. I've no desire to return to the hot, suburban Mercury valley.

Meredith holds up her beer bottle, "*Kippis!*" she says somewhat shyly to toast Jukka and Paavo. I'm surprised by her use of Finnish.

Jukka replies with thanks, "*kiitos*," and holds up his plastic cup of vodka, filled to the brim. He's been drinking a prodigious amount, which I find somewhat worrying after the incident with Marty.

Paavo says "To our American hosts," and looks from me to Meredith and Steffen.

Jukka adds, "You must all come to Finland soon. In the

wintertime. We will ski in Lapland."

Meredith hesitates, and then says, "I might actually be coming to your neck of the woods." I stop mid-bite in my sausage. She goes on, "To Russia, anyway."

Jukka cries "Russia!" with his characteristic dismissive wave. "Why are you wanting to go there?"

I ask, "You're really going through with…?"

Meredith says, "It's a bit complicated, but." She and Steffen exchange a swift look, then she faces Jukka. "I'm going to adopt a Russian baby. I'm traveling there this summer. Just decided." Her tone sounds almost defiant.

My jaw drops. Jukka, puzzlement in his voice, asks, "*Adopt?*" Paavo explains to him in Finnish. Jukka shouts, "A Russian!" his face red with heat and drink. "Ha!" Meredith shushes him with a nod at the tent where Lou sleeps. He says still loudly, "Why go to Russia? Besides, you have the boy."

"As I said, it's complicated," she says. Steffen stares at the untouched bottle of beer between his knees. I want to flee to Siberia.

"Complicated, sure," says Jukka. "Have you been to Russia lately?" Paavo seems to rebuke him in low, stern Finnish.

"No, Jukka, I haven't," Meredith says firmly, plainly annoyed with my cousin. "My sister adopted two children from Russia and they're wonderful."

"Yes, they're wonderful!" I agree heartily to shore her up, though I've never even met them. And I have my own doubts about Meredith's decision.

"When has your sister got these children?" Jukka tones it down a notch.

"I guess it was five, six years ago."

"I'm not thinking it is so easy anymore. And many of these children have the…" To Paavo he talks in Finnish.

Paavo says, "Let's not talk about such things."

But Jukka continues, "The mothers drink when they

are…knocked up." He rolls his arm out in front of his stomach. We groan. Jukka and his slang. Jukka and his mouth. "You gonna see that *everything* in Russia is complicated. You want a child you yust go in there with your man and do what needs to be done." He leans toward Meredith and Steffen and waves them toward the tent as if willing them to go off and screw.

"Jukka!" Paavo and I say in unison, "That's enough!" In the brief silence that follows, I hear the stream rushing, firewood snapping. Jukka downs the last of his vodka, shakes his head and mutters, "Complicated. You don't know nothing." I watch Meredith's usually steady complexion turn crimson in the firelight. Her mind's made up, so I say, "Well, I support her. Lots of people here help children from abroad."

"Thanks, Ali." Mere tosses her beer into the fire, causing a sizzle of smoke, and then marches off to the tent. My eyes sting as I search Steffen's face for what to do. Paavo says something again to Jukka, who rises, then trips and stumbles down to the creek.

I say to Steffen, "I'm so sorry. Jukka gets this way when he drinks," as if I've known him all my life. "He can be a bit of an ass, but…maybe he's right?" I don't say *just go in there and do what needs to be done.* Meredith's recent assertion that Steffen is still in love with me suddenly makes me self-conscious. Looking down, I say, "I think she just needs you to commit or—" when I raise my head, I see he's headed for his family tent.

Paavo, who sits quietly on a tree stump, watches Steffen retreat. He says, "Now I'm thinking this trip is some big mistake." And I'm starting to agree.

~Kaksi ei yhtä asiaa aattele.~
~Two do not think the same thoughts together.~

Native Princess

Besides the birds, the only one chirping the next morning is Lou. Hangovers abound, the air bites, and a paltry stream of white smoke filters toward the grey morning sky—a reminder that we foolishly did not fully put out the fire.

Jukka leaves at dawn for the trek up Half Dome. Meredith and Steffen take Lou on the mellower, shorter hike to mirror lake, which I advise Paavo against. As spectacular as the views there are, the "lake" is little more than flooded grassland in spring. I've witnessed hot and weary tourists staring about confused at mid-summer, dismayed to find the destination a grassy meadow. Besides, I like the idea of having Paavo to myself today.

After the hikers depart, I savor the tranquility and sip my morning coffee. Paavo is showering, and I've got a warm and mellow brew in my cup, clear, brisk air to breathe, and the start of a sunny May day. I don't feel alone at all as I gaze up and around; the rock faces have literal faces if you stare long enough. Yesterday I'd watched Steffen viewing the painterly rocks with his artist's eye. "You should get back to painting landscapes," I said to him, breaking him out of his reverie. He just sighed and said something about money, starving artists and families to support.

When Paavo returns, he asks, "What was that waterfall we drive by yesterday?"

"Near the entrance?" I tell him it's called Bridal Veil Fall. "Let us go there, " he says, so off we walk, taking in most of the valley floor first, growing flush as the sun rises higher, heating the cliff-enclosed meadows and dappled forest.

As we climb the path leading up to the falls, I brush my hand along the cool iron railing. Paavo wipes his brow. "It becomes warm here already," he says. I tell him he can cool off ahead. We hear the rumble of the rushing water, encounter an oncoming international family of tourists laughing as they walk back, dampened by the spray. I'm glad now for the late rains, happy we've arrived early enough in the season to experience so much water.

Standing near the base of the falls, side-by-side, alone at the moment, we gaze at the gauzy plumes of water that descend, widen out, and spread to a thunderous drop. Under the sonorous falls, mist on my face, I feel blissful. Paavo, from my vantage point, seems to feel the same. "Why are they calling it Bridal Veil?" he asks.

On shaky ground, I mention the legends I recall. I say perhaps it appears like the bridal veil of an Indian princess who fell into the water and died. "I think some chief saw her spirit there or something and followed her in."

"Not the smart fellow," he chuckles.

I say I've also heard that inhaling the heavy mist here at the bottom helps your chances of getting married. "Maybe I should breathe deeply here."

He turns from the flume to me. "You are liking the fairy tales, I see." And since he smiles at me like a prince, I blurt, "I really want to go to Finland." It comes out abruptly, like a swift spray from the cascade. "I'm thinking of spreading my mother's ashes there." I can't leave them in the sauna forever.

He reaches his hands out to mine. "Come with us. You will like it very much." My feet slip—such a sudden, startling proposal—but Paavo catches me. "So many relatives there will be for you." My heart pounds like the water. Our feelings are mutual!

He puts his hands on my shoulders. "Close your eyes," he instructs me. Oh my God, is he really going to kiss me? My heart thuds, I shut my lids, tilt my face up slightly to his, feeling the spray wash over it. Then I feel my shoulders quickly being swiveled, and a cold splash from the falls hits me like ice. A gush of water drenches me. Argh! Brrr…*huh*?! I rear back, head soaking.

Paavo laughs. Taken aback, I shake off the water. But he smiles broadly, his face full of merriment. I try to smile. Still laughing, he puts his own head under, shaking it around like a dog. "Feels good, ya?" He straightens out of the cascade, swipes water from his face with both hands. "Like the lake after sauna."

I give into a smile. I guess…yes. I laugh. "It actually does feel good." I duck my head into the spray for another cold douse and he does the same. We play lightheartedly together, dunking and splashing. If I squint hard enough through the vapor, I think I can see a future with this Paavo…

*

Before we leave, alone in the late afternoon, I enter a grove, an ancient wooded cathedral. This is where I want to marry, in the first primal church, sunlight filtering through the towering pines and sequoias like light through stained glass. The heavens shining in. For some of us, the ultimate spiritual experience.

I daydream of a forest wedding, like the people of Mari-El, current relatives of the Finns in the Caucasus who still practice pagan ceremonies, worship nature, and perform weddings in sacred groves.

I did my senior thesis on the early Finns. My father's family hails from Karelia, the eastern-most part of Finland, regarded as a treasure-chest of poetry and the paradisiacal primal home of the Finnish people. I'm not as interested in the Nordic mix of current Finland; my anthropological interests lie to the East. I imagine my roots lie under the Ural Mountains to the Altai's, extend through the primeval, virgin forests of the Volga region, span over the granite of the Caucasus, and stretch far across the vast frozen plains of Siberia all the way to the Mongolian Steppe.

Dreamy, I lie back on a bed of pine needles with a sweet blade of grass in my mouth, staring skyward through the towering trees. A swath of vertical feathered clouds shaped like an Indian headdress springs out of the blue sky. Am I too old to wear bridal flowers in my hair? I turn my head to the meadow wildflowers: lupine, Alpine buttercup, purple asters. Meredith will bless us with some spiritual *feng-sui*, Mom and Dad will sing with the wind in the pines. We'll dance like pagans after the wedding ceremony…I'll name my little girl Mariel.

I awaken to Lou pounding on my chest. The shadow of a tall figure with a camera disappears. Steffen?

Lou cries, "Die die!" I sit up languorously in the fading light. Right. I smile and hug his plump body. "Time to go bye-bye."

*

Their departures come to me as unexpectedly as their arrival. Back from camping, over my home-cooked American breakfast of bacon and eggs, I ask, "Where are you off to now?"

"We go to Vegas to gamble way the money." Jukka laughs.

Paavo says, "I'm thinking his plans take us in circles. But I'm looking now forward to really *seeing* everything. I'm not caring much where we go."

Jukka nudges him, "You're coming here to see the women, I think." I bite my lip.

Paavo smiles, "Maybe this time I'm going to see them better." I'm not sure I like that future tense. "We have not the exact plan. Jukka has just quit his job so he has all the time in world." I've learned that Jukka's a graphic designer, an unemployed techie like me. "But I'm only taking a sabbatical," Paavo says, pronouncing it "SUP-pat-a-gal." They tell me they plan to travel around the West more before flying to New York, and then home. "I must return to Finland early in July," Paavo says, and I feel a surge of sadness.

"You *have to* come back to my house!" Their faces imply that this came out rather urgently. I insist they return for *Juhannus*—

that I'll throw a party for Midsummer, the longest day of the year, the summer solstice, a few weeks away. I say urgently, "We'll build a bonfire and it will be just like home for you."

In front by the car, instead of shaking their hands, I hug my cousin hard. Turning to Paavo, I squeeze his solid torso, warm and comforting. As we hug, I wonder if he feels what possibilities lie ahead for us.

They hop in their rental, eager for an early start to their travels, but I call, "Wait!" I dart inside, then come out and toss Jukka my extra house key. "In case you need a place to stay while you travel around out West. This can be your…your *home base*."

~Älä laita kaikkia munia samaan koriin.~
~Don't put all your eggs in one basket.~

Blind Date

Juicy, juicy, juicy. Sometimes nature, screaming, can be unseemly. After Paavo and Jukka leave, I wake up one morning feeling moist and desirous. In the middle of the month, I ooze estrogen. I feel like a Queen Bee with an overflow of Royal jelly, rich with ripe, ravenous eggs. Or egg, I suppose. And tonight I have a date!

I don't want to get out of the sheets. I squeeze my hand between my legs and groan. Outside my window the sun bursts on a tall row of scarlet flowers, making them stridently bright, jarring, inappropriate. Like the loud Hawaiian flowers Steffen sent to the hospital years ago, each a red heart with a yellow stamen curving out—Anthurium. One of my dad's nurses, snapping off her latex gloves, called them "penis flowers," and I blushed, even though by then my father lay in a coma.

Not willing to put all of my eggs in Paavo's roaming basket, I've cruised online dating ads per Cleo's advice. "Men like competition," she said when I told her of feeling some attraction to Paavo. Yesterday, my groin hot and courage strong, I called a promising guy—and he eagerly agreed to meet me after work. Since he's a Silicon Valley engineer, I suggested a convenient Mexican restaurant where Steffen and I used go for happy hour. Steffen's dad was somehow connected with the owner, but they had a falling-out and we stopped going there.

I call Cleo for advice about my clown hair, which has faded to pumpkin orange with poorly matching brown roots. She claims to be an expert with store-bought color, and although it's Friday, she zestily offers to come "fix it." I chew my lip in silence. "Come on!" she says. "Hair is the first thing guys notice. After tits. And ass."

"That would make it third. So maybe I should focus on a good bra."

"Hair says *everything* about you," she declares.

"So my hair says *Bozo*."

"Exactly. You need to change it before your date. First impressions."

After more cajoling, I assent—with reservations. "Nothing red, right?" I instruct her: "Don't buy any color that has the words "sunset," "fire," "chestnut," "rusty," "strawberry," "burnt sienna..."

"I get it—"

"...burnished, molten..."

"Molten?" she stopped me.

"You know, nothing with "hot lava" on the label."

"You're so weird."

"Obviously. You've seen my hair, right?"

Upon inspection, Cleo rebukes me for not using color enhancement products. "What'd you do? Use that brown soap of your mother's to wash it with?" Briefly I recall Fels-Naptha, its old-fashioned lye soap smell, which Mom used for washing laundry and even scrubbed on me when I was covered in mosquito bites. The name itself carries its distinctive smell and a surge of memories.

Cleo pins a towel around my neck, then smiles at me in the bathroom mirror and rubs her hands together. "Let's get going!"

*

Must everything be about hair? And why does it always turn out so dreadfully wrong? I need to avoid mirrors altogether. Cleo picks up the damp, caved-in box of hair cream. "It said, '10N, *Dark Brown*.'"

We stare at the dead-black strands framing my pallid face. My complexion has adopted a greenish tinge. Briefly, I consider shaving my head. The total effect, including my dramatic, dark-rimmed eyes, also courtesy of Cleo, is regrettable. "He'll think we're going to Rocky Horror," I moan.

After she leaves, I rub the black eyeliner without success, concluding that Cleo used permanent marker, then spend my remaining half hour choosing what to wear. The straight black skirt I try on looks too form-fitting, and the jeans feel hot. I unclip from a hanger a flouncy skirt I wore to a Cajun dance with Meredith. I twirl and love the sound of the soft fabric swishing, the fluttery feel of the cloth flirting against my bare legs. With a red knit top, an old birthday gift from Cleo, I feel satisfied. The skirt requires sandals, so I slip into a strappy pair. The only viable solution for my hair is to pull it back and wear a very thick headband. As I recall, the restaurant was darkish.

On the way out I grab a sweater because inside or out, sooner or later, I'll be cold. I'd like to take socks too, but fashion-wise that might be like slapping on a fur hat with flaps. If only the world could stay inside my comfort zone, that agreeable range between 74.5 and 76.5 degrees Fahrenheit! Excited anticipation overriding my temperature concerns, I swing my patent-leather purse and dance out to the car.

~Ihmetapauksiin voi toivoa mutta ala luota niihin.~
~Hope for miracles, but don't rely on one happening.~

Casa Loca

The property that once housed "Casa Loca" looks decrepit; the sign now reads "Hog Rider." A parked motorcycle tilts by the front door, which is propped open. I peer in. The long dim room is empty. Really empty. The wood bar still runs lengthwise from the front halfway to the back, but aside from that, it's completely changed. The cheery red booths, wall piñatas and plants have vanished; only one table and the barstools remain.

A bartender reads a paper behind the bar, behind which hangs no mirror reflecting bottles of liquor but lurid posters showing women on motorcycles. One displays a gal wearing only leather chaps, captioned, "Good Girl Gone Biker." Another shows dueling biker chicks brandishing whips.

Stalled in the doorway, I rub my eyes, almost laugh. How could I pick such a ridiculous place to meet a new man? After considering calling him, I decide to enter and wait for my date out of the sun. Consider where we might go from here.

The boxy bartender raises her brows, appraising me as I step in. It's early in the evening, but maybe any customers at all are a surprise. At least the temperature is cool, the darkness soothing from the glare outside. The sun still heats at seven p.m. but in here it could be midnight. When I ask when the old restaurant closed, the bartender shrugs. "Did you see a guy?" I ask.

"Oddly enough, yeah. He looked in and checked out. Fast." She snorts. "What'll you have?" After hesitating—maybe it wasn't my date, or he'll return—I order a cup of coffee with some skepticism, then retreat to the table in back, the only seating aside from barstools. I sit facing the door.

Near me, a plastic Tiffany-style lamp hangs over an empty slab, the ghostly footprint of a pool table. The jukebox sits out from the wall, unplugged; only the thick reek of beer feels permanent, a thing that will linger long after the building is dust.

The bartender saunters back splashing an un-lidded Styrofoam cup. She's squat and square in her un-waisted denim overalls. Except for the hair that bristles vertically upward from the round of her crown, she is bald, and I can't help but feel somewhat superior in the hair department, a rare sensation of late. She hands me a cup filled with brown sludge that instantly offends my nostrils and roils my stomach. I never drink coffee that's older than ten minutes. Serving this muck is reason enough to demolish the bar.

Setting the cup at arm's length, I ask, "What'd the guy look like?"

"Like a nerd."

"Did he? I'm a nerd!" I say with enthusiasm.

"Own it, girl," she turns away.

I clasp my hands, hoping that he'll return. Meeting a software engineer sounds nice, a man like my work colleagues—kind, stable, logical. Unlike artists, Steffen being case-in-point, who are too impulsive and unpredictable, unsuited to my temperament. I push out of mind Meredith's awkward and totally inaccurate assertion. Why would she think Steffen still loves me after all the years they've been together? After Lou?

"Cute?" I call to the bartender.

"You're asking the wrong person, doll." Right.

After waiting for twenty minutes, during which I order and drink a tall screwdriver that tastes more of harsh vodka than sweet orange and watch the bartender play with her cell phone—a monotonous chirping noise emanates from it—I slump and give up. I call Cleo to tell her that either the guy left or stood me up.

"Stood you up? In all my years of Internet dating, that has never happened to me."

"Thanks for soothing my ego." My phone beeps, warning me of low battery.

"I was wondering if you'd come. Have a drink." Beep. I look around with Cleo's eyes. She likes to go where the action is. This place is the opposite of action. Unless a wrecking ball drops soon. But I could meet her somewhere, I'm all dressed up with nowhere to– *beep*. "How about we meet at—" My phone dies.

A dark-skinned woman wearing a business suit, wooly hair cropped close around her skull, walks in, kisses the bartender quickly on the cheek, then sits on a barstool across from her. From the side, her head and neck form the fuzzy silhouette of a shapely question mark. Her briefcase thuds as it hits the floor, sounding full of bricks. Her high-heels clatter down after it.

The two converse inaudibly, glance at me, then evidently start to text or play games on their respective cell phones. I drink more, regarding them, quiet in their contentment together, not unlike my parents' gentle compatibility—though I never saw them playing Half Life on their cell phones.

I walk over. "Could I borrow a phone?" The bartender saves her game and hands me her flip phone. I take a step away to talk.

When Cleo says, "Hey!" I jump back from the sheer volume, hold the phone away from my ear and tell her where I am.

"Sounds like a dive," she says.

"It is," the black woman says, drawling out 'eez,' not looking up from her phone.

That's the problem with Cleo, her voice. Its earsplitting decibel level never varies. I take another step away and hear her bray, "Sounds dead there." The women at the bar sniff.

"We could meet somewhere else." I whisper, "I think this might be a lesbian bar."

"We're not really even open," the bartender says.

Huh? She served me drinks. And what is this, a four-way

conversation?

Cleo cracks up, "A dyke bar and you're wondering why the guy stood you up?" She's driving, she says, and getting too near home to go to Silicon Valley.

"We could meet closer. Go back to that dance club in Blaineville," a false note of gaiety in my voice.

"I used to live over that way," the bartender's friend says, looking up. "In Mercury." I'm dumbstruck, and I guess she notices. "Oh yeah, there are blacks over there. Well, we were the only ones in Mercury, but we had a black club at Blaineville High. All five of us. Until Michael and Natasha Brown left after sophomore year…"

"I'll call you back," I murmur to Cleo.

"…then there was only three of us. 1200 white kids and Jake and me and Shayla. Then her little sister came along in senior year, when we renamed it the African-American club. What was her name? I can picture those ugly shoes she always wore. Every damn day. Shit, there was girls there wore a different pair every single day. Three hundred sixty-five different pairs of shoes!"

Sounds like a rigid school year, but I don't quibble. In fact, I wouldn't put it past those over-achieving parents to add weekends and holidays to the academic schedule. The woman's throaty voice runs on, melodic and soporific. I sway on my feet and look past her through the tinted window to gauge the time, the sun lowering behind the neon Budweiser sign. This singsong could go on for a while. For me the world is not so much divided between gay and straight, white and black, as much as talkers and listeners. Very few, it seems, manage to strike a good balance between the two.

"…but I learned. That's how I put up with this chick," the black woman aims her phone at the bartender like a remote control. I'm thinking the bartender should click *her* off. The talker dodges the swipe of a dirty bar towel. "It's not that bad, really. But I couldn't wait to get the hell outta there."

"Yeah, I can relate," I say, handing the phone back. "I *so* do not fit in there."

The black woman snorts outright. "*You*?"

"Touché," I mumble, stung. I return the phone, then walk back to retrieve my purse to get the hell outta here. I'm not straddling the worlds of the horse set and homies, gay and straight. What right do I have to feel like an outsider?

As I drop a twenty on the table, a tall man in a worker's suit, his face dark and indistinguishable with the setting sun at his back, appears at the door. Is it my date? My heart quickens at the appealing outline of his physique. I can't see with the backlighting, and he looks taller than described, but then he opens his mouth. "I'm here to pick up the contract." I instinctively stoop, heart pounding, wanting to duck under the table. No way!

~*Joukossa tyhmyys tiivistyy.*~
~In a group stupidity condenses.~

Judge Ruby

I watch from a squat in the recesses as the bartender hands Steffen a thick manila envelope, which he proceeds to open. *Damn.* Of all the lesbian biker joints in all the towns in all the world he walks into mine. Maybe if he's busy with paperwork at the bar I can sneak out behind him. In the air of shifting attention, I clutch my bag and try to drift out. I don't get far. The bartender says, "Take it easy, babe!"

Steffen swivels. Drops the papers on the bar. "*Alina*? Is that you?"

God. "Steffen? Gosh, what a surprise."

He squints, takes in the new Goth hair, the skirt, the me. "What are you doing here?" The bartender and talker watch, obviously perked up with this development

"Oh, just having ...*coffee*," I know how absurd that sounds—how could anyone mistake the Hog Rider for a café?—but my brain's intent on splitting, fast. I am not going to discuss my humiliating non-date with him. "Just leaving, actually. Nice seeing you," I say airily, and, with a swing of my handbag, begin striding past him to the door.

"You two know each other?" the bartender asks.

"Yeah, we're friends." Steffen says, eyes still on me.

OK, this is awkward. I turn to them. Obviously I cannot leave without the usual pleasantries. "What the hell's up with that?" I point at the papers, knowing a good offense is better than a defense.

"Dad bought this property as a side project. I'm simply picking up some papers for him. But I should be asking what the hell is up with you. And is that another new wig?" The two women exchange looks, think this might get good.

"I thought your dad and the owner were on the outs." *This is the last place you should be.*

He shrugs. "Business is business. Dad's a developer. They let bygones be."

"I thought they hated each other. Seems like an awfully short grudge."

"An utter shame, I know," he smirks at me, then takes a visual sweep of the dark, decaying barroom. "Coffee must be good here, yeh?"

Ha ha. Such a comic. I fold my purse in my crossed arms and face him head on. "Truth be told, I was meeting a date."

His eyebrows raise and his chin tucks, as a thinly suppressed grin grows. "And he, or excuse me, she is … where?"

"I really don't know."

"He bailed," the bartender interjects. I grimace.

"Oh, so it was a guy. I suppose that's reassuring."

"Hmph," comes from one of the women.

"And do you two regularly meet here?" He looks around, as if to say 'At a run-down lesbian bar?'

"It used to be a Mexican place, you know that. The last time I was here was with you." Now I see the women fully tuned to our conversation, making no bones about tending to their own affairs whatsoever, the cell phone games long forgotten. Shouldn't you check to see if you've lost all your lives? I want to ask them.

"Anyone I know?" Steffen leans, his elbows propped on the bar behind him, apparently enjoying the topic.

An honest man would rather sell his land than tell a lie. I just wasn't raised to dissemble. "Just some guy online," I say off-handedly, knowing this is a mistake.

This brings forth a remark from the audience, "OH," the

black woman murmurs a laugh. "Little match-dot-com girl," she chuckles. Yeah, that's me, a little match girl out in the dark, trying to get into the light bright world of couple-dom but miserably failing in some dead bar and running into my ex while I'm at it.

He says, "I can't picture you with a stranger."

"I dated *you*." I never did get to know him.

"Oh, so you two ...I see," says the bartender's friend. "Now ain't that something? You two connecting here like this, you'd almost say it's fate..." I don't hear the rest of it. My face flames at the two women with their wide white eyes and Steffen with his questions. The subject needs to be changed, fast.

"So you grew up in Mercury?" I address the talker.

"That's right, sure enough. Not exactly the hood. But that's not what—"

I interrupt. "That must have been hard for you being bla-African-American." I press my lips at the blunder.

She sits up straight-backed, "Did you just say *Blafrican-American*?"

"Mmm... I meant—"

"Ooooo! That's rich." Her face contorts and then she lets loose a huge guffaw. The bartender spews her Bud-Lite, they double over, repeating the word through deep, husky, belly laughs. I can't help but smile. When Steffen grins too, they stop.

"So now you got your date for the night," says the bartender's friend, suddenly ready to shoo us off.

"He is most definitely *not* my date. He's got Meredith and a kid." I turn to him and my opinion comes out for all to hear. "Meredith deserves someone who can commit. That's what this crazy adoption idea's about, you know, Steffen. It's because you're not a hundred percent *with* her. Maybe she's forcing your hand."

The women now look at me with astonishment. And blessed silence. Steffen's tan deepens. "You know, sometimes I think you just foisted her on me. So you wouldn't feel guilty dumping me."

"I introduced you, Steffen. I didn't make you impregnate

her."

"Uh oh. OH girl, you best be running the other way," the friend points an unusually long forefinger to the door as she shakes her head.

"That—" he stops. "You can't really say it's a mistake when you have a beautiful kid like Lou."

"That's right," pipes up the bartender, as if she knows Lou.

"Meredith was supposed to be on birth control," Steffen says.

The friend says, "Like you know anything about raising a kid! You let that girl get away with murder and here she is in the fourth grade already talking 'bout steppin' out—"

"Look, Steffen, I should go."

"That's right, you go on now, girl. And don't look back."

The bartender says, "I wouldn't say it's necessarily his fault if she was supposed to be on birth control. Come on, Ruby, who hasn't had it happen?"

The friend, evidently named Ruby, turns to her, arms crossed. "Like I said, it's OK you went ahead and had your baby girl but that don't make you a good mother." When the bartender mutters, "It don't make me a bad mother, either," Ruby snaps, "Doesn't!" This interchange over slang reminds me of Paavo and Jukka, and I wish I were off traveling with them now. She repeats that I should get on my way, shooting Steffen a reproving look.

"Steffen's a great dad," I say.

He says, "Thanks."

"Give him a chance then," the bartender shrugs. "Your other dude's not coming back, that's for sure."

"What other dude?" I say, having already forgotten my blind date.

The black woman draws herself up regally on her stool and says with authority, like a judge at the bench, "Now let me get the facts straight. Who's this bitch Meredith?"

"NO!" I say it so loudly I drown out Steffen.

Ruby mutters an aside to her cohort, "White chicks got some

issue with that word." To us, she says, "Chill. I'm a bitch, she's a bitch," she jabs her friend, then points at me, "you're a bitch."

"Is he a bitch?" I cock my head to Steffen.

"He the biggest bitch o' all!"

I make a small circle of our group. "So we all bitches."

"*We're* all bitches. You're not black, girlfriend. Fact, since you're from Mercury you are *exact opposite* of it. Polar bear, white fox opposite, if you catch my drift. My *snow* drift." A husky chuckle at her own wit ensues. I explain that I just have a habit of mimicking the way people around me talk…then think how I've been leaving out my articles with the Finns. "Let's get in car," I'll say to them… but Ruby cuts off my thoughts. "What about *Meredith*?"

"Oh yeah. She's my best friend."

Her eyes widen, then narrow. "*Was* your best friend, sweet-cheeks. Get the tense right. But sounds like she's out of the picture, so what's stopping you from getting with this fine man here?" she says, slipping in and out of allegiances as quickly as she does slang.

"She's not out of the picture at all. They're still together." Obviously these women have a listening issue.

"Holy shit." This from the bartender. The judge calls out, "Get me a pencil. I got to be writing this all down," her demeanor so imperial and commanding we don't question it. After the bartender produces a stubby one from behind her ear, "Paper? Could I pul-eez get some paper?"

"Could I please get a drink?" Drinks are poured as I plunk on a barstool. "It gets worse. Meredith wants a child from Russia or China, like her sister."

Steffen says, "Her sister's from Pismo Beach."

"Deanna here and I were going to adopt from over there." The two smile at each other. "Russia, the Ukraine."

"Same thing," says the bartender.

I say, "No, actually, they're separate—"

The judge stops the cross talk with a loud, "We're not here to discuss our situation!" I didn't know we came to discuss mine.

"And you," she points that long sword of a finger at Steffen. "What do you have to say for yourself? How do you feel about this Chinese baby?"

"I don't think it would be good for Lou."

Parents, I think. Is it what's good for their kids or what's good for them? Ballet would be good for her, start lessons at age three; Harvard good for him, Advanced Placement Tests at five. It makes me grateful that my parents were so laissez-faire; despite my grades and test scores, my dad recommended only public universities. "You don't need to go to school with all those rich kids," he said.

"Lou." She writes on the bartender's pad. Then she faces Steffen. "Do you love her?"

"Of course he does!" I chime in.

"I'm axing *him*."

"Who, Meredith?" Steffen says dumbly. "Of course I feel affection for the mother of my child."

"*Affection*, hmmm." She nods her head at me. "What about her?"

"I've got to go." I jump up, sway off balance. The floor wavers. I grip the bar to steady myself.

Judge Ruby rubs her eyes. "This situation," she swirls the pencil around in a rapid whirlpool, "is what you'd call highly unorthodox."

"It's different," I admit, trying to gather my wits and car keys from the depths of my bag.

"From where I'm sitting, it's beyond that, honey. Let me think."

We all do as she says, we wait for the verdict while she thinks. With a dramatic sigh, she sets down the pencil stub, crushes her paper napkin notes and faces us: "There's just one too many."

After a pause in which we digest this enigmatic morsel of

wisdom, I jingle my keys and announce, "I've got to run… meet up with Cleo." Though this might not be technically true, as I think I hung up on her.

Ruby un-crumples the napkin and lowers her head to peer at the writing, and as I stumble through the door I hear her call out, "Do we know Cleo??"

~Ei halu halaamalla lähde.~
~Hugs won't remove the desire.~

Pusu (The Kiss)

Getting away from this place appears to be impossible, as while my tires start to crunch on the gravel parking lot, Steffen hops in the passenger seat, splashing a lidded cup of offal—the bar's coffee.

I jerk to a halt. "What are you doing? Where's your truck?" He points across the lot.

"The bartender thought you might need this. So do I." He hands me the white cup, settles in next to me. "Thought maybe we could talk for a bit while you sober up."

I tilt my head back and the car ceiling moves. I cut the engine. But this offense to the coffee bean and my olfactory sense isn't going to help. I buzz down all the windows and toss out the rancid liquid, then squash the cup and stare at my lap covered with little white bits of clingy, malodorous Styrofoam. "It's embarrassing about the guy."

I feel him appraise me with his overly-keen artist's eye. If only I knew what he was thinking half the time. He says, "Would you like to discuss your hair issues?" which actually makes me laugh.

"I'm surprised it took you this long to tease me about it."

"As if I could get a word in edgewise. But I'm sure your blind date would've been pleased."

I sniff, finger my slick black hair, "Yeah, no doubt." A warm blush rises as I feel the heat of his gaze, tug at my low-cut top, too hot and clingy. Leave it to Cleo to give me polyester, something that doesn't breathe. Either my sweat or our proximity to the Bay moisten the air with a slight sea scent. Or him. The last rays of sun hit Steffen's face sideways. With his green shirt, his blue eyes appear truer than ever. The alcohol and his nearness make me light headed. We stare ahead at the bar. I smile, thinking of the loopy duo inside.

Steffen interrupts my thoughts. "That Ruby was having us on, eh?" His use of his mother's English slang makes me smile more. I still have affection for his parents, although I rarely see either Claire or Lou Sr. anymore. For some reason, our brief relationship included regular visits to both our parents' homes: Sunday dinners at mine, random calls at his.

"We always did have fun here," I say. Perhaps it's why I picked the place to begin with. "That circus in there was better than some stilted blind date, anyway." I turn to him, see his perpetual damp-haired look, from sweat, from showering; whatever the cause, it makes me think of how drenched and stuck together our bodies were after making love. Unbidden memories wash over me—of Steffen walking in my door and pressing me up against the wall with fierce passion, his tongue thrust in my mouth, my urgent mouth wanting to suck the whole of him in. I feel the juices from the morning flow. This car is too snug and full of salt air and ocean. I'm starting to drown.

"We've been rather stilted with each other of late," he says. I don't reply. It's my fault. It's his fault.

As we sit in silence, I try to get a grip, remember why we aren't together, how our relationship, once so free and fun, took a turn for the serious following the false pregnancy test. The hot sex was replaced by the cold fear of pregnancy and my increased withdrawal from the pressure of his passion. He said he loved me—after just four months of dating. He said he wanted to marry me. *After just four months*! I told him that he didn't even know me.

And then my dad got sick, died within weeks, and everything was too much for me. I withdrew from Steffen and his efforts to console me. My sex drive vanished. I blocked him out. All I could focus on was my mother and my grief; I buried myself in work as never before. Maybe guilt eventually made me steer him toward Meredith. I'd come up short, and Meredith was the answer. But, as I breathe his scent here in the close car, the passion we shared comes back with a vividness that reaches through time.

"Steffen, I never told you. I'm sorry."

"Sorry?"

"For the way I broke it off with you. For being callous." What do I want to say? "You know, there's a big difference between twenty-eight and thirty-three…at least for me. I didn't know what I wanted then. And I was afraid."

"No doubt I pushed you."

"Maybe. Who knows? You know they say 'timing is everything.'" I pause. "But it's all good, as it turns out, right? I mean, you couldn't do better than Mere."

Presently, he says, "At the moment, it seems Meredith and I are a bit estranged."

"I know you stay with your parents sometimes, but still. You'll work it out."

"It's different now. We've been arguing about the adoption idea. And now she's talking about running off to some alternative medical conference in Big Sur." To me this sounds innocuous enough, it's her passion. She's a natural healer. Besides, what mother doesn't need time away? "She said 'we might be gone for a few days,' and I don't even know who 'we' are."

"When did all this come up?" I, too, feel left in the dark.

"Just mentioned it today, actually." I think I see fear, loneliness in his face, I reach out to touch his shoulder.

"Don't worry about some conference with her co-workers." I sense he feels he's losing her—how ironic—when she's been waiting so patiently all these years.

"We're both so unsure these days," he says. I wait, listening. It's been ages since he and I have talked, really talked. "It's like I kept thinking that at some point it would all cosmically come together, that we'd be in the same place at the same time. That I'd feel certain, know for sure."

"I don't think you ever know for sure, Steffen." He averts his gaze from the front to the side window, away from me. "Get this," I tell him how Cleo once contacted a guy online who wrote that he literally thought he'd hear bells ring when he met the one perfect woman. For their first date, she slipped her cat's belled collar in her purse. "'Just in case he's hot,' she said. Then she goes, 'Hopefully Fluffy won't eat any birds while I'm out.'"

Steffen smiles wanly. "Maybe you're right. I'm over-thinking the whole thing." He leans forward, elbows on thighs, runs his hands through his hair. "But here it is. I'm feeling like quite the fuck-up."

"Oh, God, I know how you feel."

"And this new family she's got in mind." For the first time I see how Meredith and Lou and another child feel threatening to him, how he feels left out. I lean and impetuously give him a reassuring hug. An inept, inebriated hug. He smells like beer. He twists his torso to squeeze back, and I let him, knowing it's wrong, somehow, for us to hug here in our condition. But I can't help it, I stay in the warm comfort of his arms for moments, unable to move out of his familiar enveloping embrace… Then he turns his head and kisses me gently, feather-like, at the corner of my mouth. The sweet spot that teases, begs for more. My lips find his. We kiss.

~*Kyllä siinä melua syntyy, kun kaksi hullua yhteen tulee.*~
~There will surely be some noise when two madmen come together.~

Darda and the Iron Curtain

"You kissed *Steffen*?" We're talking on the phone but I can picture the dark silver fillings in the back of Cleo's dropped jaw, pewter pebbles set in her lower molars. Like me, Cleo does not own a perfect California smile.

"He kissed *me*. And it was totally unexpected. I didn't want it at all." Now that I have it off my chest, I'm not sure I want to talk about it. My left temple throbs.

"Ohhh, this is good," Cleo says. "Listen, I want to hear all of it but I'm about to go in." She's at a dermatologist for some anti-wrinkle procedure. "What're you doing later?" she asks. I tell her about my hair appointment.

"You're getting your hair done? *Again*?" She's right, it's possible I need a twelve-step group. *I admit I am powerless over my roots, my hair has become unmanageable...* Of course, she's conveniently forgotten that her botch-up is the reason I look like Morticia. She says, "Never mind. Where? I have time, I can come." This is double allure for Cleo—beauty parlor and gossip.

"It's near me. Kind of out of the way for you, I think," I say, picturing the small basement salon whose arrow-shaped sign, "Down Hair," and "We take walk-downs" caught my eye. I contend to Cleo, "Don't you have to work?"

She makes me tell her where the salon is, then says, "I make my own schedule. Besides, my new dermatologist's not that far from there. You might've heard of her in Blaineville—she's famous. She's, like, fifty or something and she looks twenty-five. And it's not because of plastic surgery. The thing *is* is she doesn't smile."

"Is she Finnish?" I wonder if my somber face is why they still card me at dance clubs. It comes naturally to me, but how strange to deliberately not smile. I wonder if the doctor is a mother. Young women freezing their faces with Botox. Primate young learn from those smiles, those crinkly eyes. What do babies see these days? What soft stomach and plump arms caress them when all these new moms work themselves into hard-bodies within weeks of giving birth?

I hear Cleo say, "Yes, I'm here for the *Parfait Plus*." Then into the phone she asks with the full force of her monumental voice, "Why were you two even *together*?"

"See you soon!" I trill and hang up. *Maybe*. I just pray I'll be in and out of the hairdresser's before she gets there. The full tell-all would be much easier on the phone.

I walk down the stairs and open the door to the small, dim salon. A bell tinkles overhead to announce my arrival, but no one is here. Only a large framed black-and-white picture of a model's head titled back, lips pouting, with voluminously distressed curly hair. The room has just two stations, one against each wall, worn vinyl chairs a vintage shade of burgundy. It's basic, functional. It could be a barbershop with a twirling red, white and blue pole out front, except for two bubble dryers in back, like empty-headed aliens from outer space.

It's what I want, not a slick, disco-throbbing, product-plastered, chatter-infused place. I wait under the poster until a tall woman who appears to be in her late fifties, clips forward with stiff arms from behind a curtain in back. She's pale, with jet-black hair tightly knotted in a chignon. If her hair were down, I imagine she'd look like an aging Natasha from Bullwinkle.

She eyes me with suspicion. "I have an appointment," I say

into the harsh odor of cigarette smoke. "For color." I made it this morning, from the looks of it with this very woman. Either the hairdresser is forgetful or I'm forgettable.

"Well, color takes a while," the woman says, dubiously looking down at a spiral notebook. I scan the empty room and wonder why that could possibly matter. The hairdresser's voice is husky, with a heavy Eastern European accent. I watch her page through the appointment book with long squared-off nails. Pink with white tips, a French manicure. A small mole dots her chin, a few straight hairs stick out like cactus thorns. I have a smattering of moles, "beauty marks," like all the Finns I knew growing up, and wonder if they'll start sprouting as I age.

Once I'm seated, the hairdresser stands behind me and fingers through my hair with the nails. Déjà vu. The license wedged in the corner says Darda Lantos. A Hungarian name. Darda regards my image without remark. She scrutinizes my strands from top to end, still silent. She keeps her cards close to her chest, this one. Obviously too much time spent under Communist rule. Her eyebrows are plucked to a suspicious arch, which manages to make her face appear permanently distrustful. Rivulets form over her top lip, minuscule, winding tributaries that pour into the rim of her hard mouth.

"I was thinking of returning to my roots, as it were." She doesn't smile. "My own light brown color, maybe? With highlights." Again I feel the need to mollify a hairdresser, again uncomfortable with being at the mercy of a stranger.

She looks skeptical. "This dark color is good."

"But it's not what I want." Do I have to come out and say that her Transylvanian look is just not for me? I hesitate, take a breath and state, "Listen, I want it like this." I describe my old hair, its natural color, the way it streaked with gold during the summer. I don't look at her until I finish my speech, and when I do, she stomps off. And I'm not entirely sure that she's going to return.

When she does, she works in silence, first guiding me back to the sink to remove Cleo's color. "You are lucky this is not permanent dye," she says only, as she roughly scrubs and rinses, scrubs and rinses. I shiver from the cool water.

Back at the chair, she starts painting cold paste on my hair. We haven't said a word in minutes, the place is quiet as a tomb. As an ice-breaker, I finally say, "You're Hungarian, aren't you?" Darda nods at my reflected face.

"You know they're related to the Finns. Distantly. Linguistically." Finns, Estonians, and Hungarians – somewhere there was an ancient connection in the Carpathian Basin…I remember Dad telling me that only one sentence could be understood by the three peoples, but I cannot recall it. Something about fish and water.

Since Darda doesn't pick up the conversation, I try a version of my dad's joke: "The Finnish and Hungarian tribes were migrating from the Steppe when they came to a signpost—'To Civilization.' The ones who could read went south to central Europe, and the Finns went the other way." Instead of smiling, Darda nods as if this is true. This makes me want to inform her that Finns tell the joke the other way around.

Irked, I say, "Anyway, the Finns did pretty well by staying free of Soviet rule." Darda tugs a piece of hair and clips it tight to my skull with a long metal pincer. "They were lucky."

"Lucky? That's crazy. That long border, the Winter War. You've heard of '*Finlandization*?' They were smart!" First fighting, then years of guarded cooperation to stay free. It took finesse. I feel like my father.

Color rises in Darda's dark face. As she slaps on more frigid goop, it occurs to me that this discussion might not be good for my hair. To soften things, I say, "I kind of feel like that where I live now. In Mercury. Like I need to live there, around my new neighbors, but not become one of them."

"I'm taking a short break," she announces, shoving me under a dryer and heading toward the curtained back. Great. My hair's in process and she's probably taking off for lunch.

I shuffle through a pile of dog-eared magazines searching for one that doesn't feature outrageous hair on its cover, and settle on a bland women's rag. Flipping through, I find an article about a study proving that women can actually sniff out the pheromones of intended mates. Researchers rubbed smelly men's sweatshirts on chairs and then had women come in to choose a seat…it turns out that they gravitated to chairs that matched some pre-chosen male they'd seen in a picture. I wonder if I've been drawn to Paavo's scent, suspect that Steffen's insistent pheromones are the cause of my current predicament with him.

I shut the magazine when Cleo bounces in wearing a shiny black skirt and leopard-skin top. The skin around her mouth is bumpy and red. Glancing at the small shack of a salon, she asks, "What is it with you and these hole in the walls?"

I feel like Meredith when I correct her: "Holes in the wall."

"Yeah, and you're like a little mouse ferreting them all out."

"You do sales in that get-up?" I say, poking my head out of the heat.

"I have a jacket but hey, it works." She sits in the seat of the empty hair dryer. "Anyways, speaking of sluts, what about you. Why were you alone with Steffen? *Kissing him.*"

"Shh," I say, cocking my head to the grey curtain at the rear of the salon. The *Iron Curtain,* I think, where Darda went to either smoke or listen in. "I think I pissed her off."

"Who? Your stylist?" She glances around. "Or should I say barber? How could you piss her off? Are you crazy?"

"She's probably totally messing up my hair."

"You know, it's like you're pissed at everyone these days. You've got to chill, girl." She's talking like the boys she's dating. "So what'd you do?"

"We were talking about the war."

"Politics? Get over it, already. Bush won. *Twice.*"

"The *Cold* War."

Cleo rolls her eyes. "Didn't that end, like, *months* ago?"

"Very funny." I'd laugh but I'm worried about my hair turning some dreaded color—this time irrevocably. I tell Cleo in a theatrical whisper, "He came into the restaurant—it's some old bar now—where I called you from. Where I was meeting that online date!"

"And then he kissed you. *Of course.*" She smirks. I press my palms down on the air to keep her voice down, as if Meredith, not the hairdresser is within hearing range. As if Darda knows Steffen and Meredith and me, the whole newly messy triangle. I stick my head back under the dryer.

After a few minutes Darda returns smelling of strong tobacco. With a business-like nod at Cleo, she leads me for another rinse. Head back in the sink, I breathe out and close my eyes, wishing Cleo away. What could have been pleasurable, having my hair massaged by quiet hands is now just barely tolerable. I shiver from the arctic spray, suspect Darda can't pay her hot water bill.

When we return to the chair, Cleo, who's pulled a chair over from the waiting area, clears her throat to speak. Before she asks a prying question in front of Darda, I try to explain the episode without getting into details. "Steffen was doing some deal for his dad. Renovating that bar, or something. So I ran into him and we ended up having this weird conversation with the bartender and talking about Meredith's adoption..."

"That does not explain the ki—"

I'm fast. "The kid? No, there's no kid yet. Just a puppy. The one Meredith tried to give me the other day. Steffen picked it out with Lou at the pound." I need to keep talking, to keep Cleo from belting something out. "I asked him why he picked such a homely dog and you know what he said? He said, 'I like the unusual.'"

Darda's thick brows wrinkle as she strokes white cream on strands, folding them into squares of tin foil. Cleo shoots me an annoyed look and presses the area around her mouth with her palms. "OK, so Steffen got a puppy from the pound. *Fascinating.*"

"Yes, and I ended up talking to him…Steffen, not the puppy." I run on and on, don't even know what I'm jabbering about, just trying to keep Cleo from opening her bee-stung lips in front of Darda.

Cleo doesn't ask about the adoption, it's the necking she's interested in, and she's both annoyed and squirming. I refuse to talk about this humiliating episode in front of anyone. I look at my reflection in the mirror, under the spotlight, and then over at Cleo, sitting to my left, ready for the ride. The ride, the smell of ammonia is already making me sick. My darting eyes land on a paperback of *War and Peace* with a bookmark near the front. I say to Darda, "Are you reading that?" I don't recall the plot, just that all the good characters were described as ruddy cheeked, full-faced, dark-haired Russians. I look at my own pale visage in the mirror; I'm a bad character.

She answers that she's in a reading group. Must be a speed-reading group, that's no Oprah book. When I ask, "How often do you meet?" Cleo sits back and rolls her eyes with an exasperated flutter.

"Once each week. We read only one chapter." There must be over two hundred chapters in that book; obviously they're in it for the long run. Her people learned patience, I suppose.

She finishes up, tells me to sit for a while. Flaps of aluminum drape down each side of my face. I'm sure they contain some purplish hair dye—like Chi Chi's—and I'll go out with brash "sun-kissed" hair.

Darda straightens into order the hair products and combs on her shelf, not leaving, and I think maybe we can wait silently like this until Cleo has to go. If our roles were reversed, or our chairs, if Cleo sat front and center in the glare of the mirror and the overhead halogen bulb, she'd be talking full volume about the night, sparing no shameful detail, drawing Darda intimately into the conversation like an old friend. She and I are definitely from different gene pools…I think how Cleo would revel in a public marriage proposal, a strange crowd oohing and aahing and clapping. No Finn in her right mind would want to be on display at such an intimate moment!

The bell rings over the door and a man steps down, stooping through the doorway into the salon. Darda goes to seat him in the opposite chair. He and I can see each other reflected in our mirrors. He's nearly bald, it doesn't look like a long job.

"Tell me quick," Cleo says, leaning in. "About the kiss." I look at my miserable face in the mirror. The slick black smock chokes my neck. I can't deal with any of this, the hair, the questions, the screw-ups.

"I went out to my car," I whisper, "and he jumped in. I was sort of tipsy."

"I bet."

"Then, this is the really bad part, he sort of kissed me near the mouth." I look over to where Darda flirts with the bald man. She's pointing to pictures that line the mirror and saying things that make him smile into her chest. Everybody flirts. Females and males want attention, want mates. Finlandization—it's not easy living around a super-power, a super force, like Steffen.

Cleo's poised forward, pressing for details. I say only that a simple hug turned into a kiss that shouldn't have happened. I don't say how the pure suction of our desire led to a long, deep kiss, our tongues tangled and looping, searching, sucking, as if we were trying to find something—possibly air. As if we were trying to breathe.

I conclude by saying that Steffen and I parted ways (leaving out the slight medical mishap that occurred as I pulled away) and tell her how awful I feel. Not content with this surface version of events, she says, "OK, but you're going to have to tell me the juicy bits later." Then she asks, "You're not going to tell Meredith, are you?" She's relentless. I look for Darda, who's possibly off for another smoke. Shouldn't there be a timer? Isn't it time to get up and clear away this mess?

To distract Cleo, I say, "I had this really weird realtor come by. He was talking like Tweety Bird or something." I lower my voice even more, "He said, 'I tought I saw a *pussy* cat.'"

"You have a cat now?"

"No, he was talking about the dog."

"You hired a blind realtor?" I shoot her a look. "Sorry, you hired a *visually impaired realtor*?" I'm not in the mood for her sense of humor. "You don't have a dog, either."

"Haven't you been listening to me? Meredith brought a puppy over."

Cleo says, "Of course I wasn't listening to you. Were *you* listening to you? God." She considers the issue. "Did he say 'puddy cat' or 'pussy cat?'"

I glance over my shoulder to where Darda's back trimming the bottom rim of the man's hair. I whisper, "He said '*pussy.*' And the problem was, my hand was *between his legs*."

Cleo barks, "You're juggling his balls and you wonder why he's talking pussy! Alina, you are too funny." Her silver fillings glint as she laughs. Since this is said as if through a bullhorn, the chair opposite swivels and Darda and the man look straight at my foil-framed red face shining in the mirror. Cleo is such a mistake. But she's bursting with jollity and, seeing Darda and man exchange looks, I can't fight her anymore.

Aloud, I say to Cleo, "I *so* need a man."

Cleo stops laughing to press her injected face back into place and says, "No shit." She stands and peers into the mirror, "Do I look lumpy?"

Darda walks over, possibly trying to rid her basement of the both of us. She snappily rinses, shampoos, and, back at the mirror, blows my hair hot, pulling strands out with a round brush. It's hard to see without my glasses, and at this point I just want out of here.

Cleo cannot leave until it's finished, she says. After my hair's dry, Darda spritzes on alcohol-scented spray, fluffs it just so, and for the first time smiles. She hands me a mirror and says, "Outside. You will see it better."

We take the mirror up to the street. I look at my hair in the sun and am blinded. *Whoa.*

Who knew? I just might be beautiful. My hair is the color it once was, light brown or honey blond woven through with streaks of pale gold. I shake it and it swings, catching light. Shining gossamer threads reflect the sun. Fingering it, I look like a happy model in a shampoo commercial. This is the color my hair would turn after a few weeks on the Cape, camping, jumping and riding the bracing waves at one of the beaches during the day, rinsing off as the sun lowered onto the silky green waters of the campsite pond.

Back inside, I croak, "Thank you" to the proud Hungarian, who takes the mirror and my check, and turns back to her flirtation.

"Oh my God," Cleo says as we collect our purses and leave, "Steffen should see you now. You look so *hot*!" Outside, she says in the quietest voice she can muster, now that we're alone in the parking lot and it couldn't possibly matter, "I've got to get back to work. Details about the necking later."

"It was *one* kiss! There are no details."

"I'm not one to judge. But you…"

"What?"

"You've got to stay away from Steffen, kiddo. That's just messed up."

"I know, I know." I suddenly want to tell Cleo more, open up about how he really makes me feel when we're alone together. Back when I met Steffen, his insta-love might've beggared belief, but by the time I could observe him without the weight of his outsized love, learned how generous, decent, and kind he was…he was unavailable. I grab her arm. "But. But what if he was The One?"

"The *One*?" Cleo shrugs. "What're you going to do about it?" I think of Meredith, my best friend, struggling as a virtual single mom while Steffen figures out his life, and of sweet Lou, an only child, who needs both his parents.

I exhale, dropping her sleeve. After a pause, I set my jaw. "Find another *One*."

*

When I return home, another business card is stuck in my door from the patriotic cat couple pictured on that roaming realtor truck. The same card with the flag and the Christian symbol of a fish in the corner. I puzzle over the empty fish outlined in blue ink until it finally comes to me: *The living fish swims in water*! The one sentence intelligible by Hungarians, Estonians, and Finns alike. I pocket the card and quickly dismiss the thought of calling Darda.

~Rohkea rokan syö, kaino ei saa kaaliakaan.~
~A brave man eats the soup, a shy one won't even get cabbage.~

Nature Hike (Save the Tick!)

Thank God for spandex-wrapped Ryan! And thank God Meredith has been working hard all week, preparing for time off at that Eastern healing seminar. I'm still consumed with guilt about kissing Steffen.

I've scanned the Employment section, checked out housing prices, and read in the local paper about guided hikes on Mt. Mercury. Hikes to learn about the flora and fauna. Open to everyone, not just geared for the kind of desperate single I've become. If I'm going to find love in this Mecca for the Married, I better work at it. These past many years, while I've been working and my family dying, my fertility's been plummeting…my almost thirty-four year-old eggs might be rotting. What if all I have left to offer a prospective mate are green eggs and spam?

I arrived at Mt. Mercury in the crisp early June air with some anticipation—a little thrill that came when I thought of my trip here with Paavo—hoping the mountain would hold more pleasant surprises for me. I need to be out and about and steering clear of my ex-boyfriend.

Over the last few days my eager realtor Troy has trotted in here and there, once with a plumber, another time a paint estimator. Little actual work has transpired, making me suspect that despite his enthusiasm, we're getting nowhere. "Miss Eskala," he used his serious tone to assure me that he, Troy Champlaine, seller of zero houses, is a true realtor, "it pains me to say this, but it's best if you're not around when I show the house." I thought of saying it might be best if *he's* not around, but didn't.

When I spotted the hiking group milling about at the advertised trailhead at seven this morning, the air chilly, the sky overcast, I realized that my jeans, thick sweater, and sneakers were all wrong. The dozen or so men and women here, mostly middle-aged, wore khaki shorts, light vests, tall socks over ropey calves, hiking boots and wide brimmed canvas hats. I wore a bandana around my neck for the cold, brought no hat. But mainly the hiking boots alarmed me—were we going on terrain that basic sneakers couldn't handle? Moreover, it wasn't exactly a hopping singles scene here, at least not for my demographic.

"We're waiting for Dave," a man obscured by huge wrap-around sunglasses and a low-slung hat informed me. "He's the guide. Great guy." After introducing himself as Jake he turned to walk over to his grey-haired wife. On his back was a wide-eyed baby in a huge framed backpack.

In theory, I always wanted to be a young mother. But by the time I actually wanted to be a parent—now—I am destined to be not so young. I used to look at the aging hippie couples in Berkeley, the Birkenstock-clad dad with his wiry grey hair awry and the mom with her crow's feet magnified through eyeglasses and think, not me, never me. It's not fair to the kids.

"Are they your grandparents? Is that your grandpa?" I was asked often enough. Especially in heartless middle school. My dad, waiting for me, would be slunk low in the Volvo wearing his brimmed fisherman's cap, sound asleep in the Cineplex lot when the movie got out. At 9:15! No, I never planned to revisit such humiliation on my own children.

But my adolescent angst has given over to harsh reality, and now when I see them, those not-so-chipper couples with strollers, lugging diaper bags and jerking up with stiff knees from pushing bottles and toys at a wailing baby, I tend to, well, *root* for them. Moreover, I now appreciate my own parents, always one on the sofa when I came in late during my teen years. Sure, they were snoring and dead to the world as I snuck upstairs, but they were there.

Dave appeared to be late, so I wandered around, checking out the brown shingled rest rooms, the signs near the lot: one warning of fire hazard, not uncommon in our dry summers, and an odd sign that said "Save the Tick!" showing a picture of an exceptionally large spidery bug.

"Are ticks an endangered species?" I asked, aloud to myself. Jake, near me again, chuckled. I heard a whirring as a contingent of neon-clad, helmeted, bicyclists buzzed past, all in loud shirts covered in writing which I find perpetually puzzling—advertisements for Italian soda?—and chatting genially, no doubt, because they hadn't yet started up the steep incline.

"Read the fine print," Jake advised. It said that ticks are a thriving insect and should one decide to attach itself to me, I should remove it with tweezers, then take a moistened tissue and place it in a plastic bag. I should *save* it, yuck. Someone at the park service has a sense of humor, evidently. "You should wear a hat," Jake said.

No hat, no baggie, no damp Kleenex…throwing fashion to the mountain air—no one here remotely my age or dateable—I untied my red neck bandana and threw it flat on top of my hair, securing it around my forehead with my headband. I sensed a Yasser Arafat look, but it beat the prospect of Lyme disease. And it's not as if I was with a bunch of fashionistas here. Then I sat on a boulder to wait, morosely growing warm as the sun burned off the overcast.

Sweating, I seriously thought of ditching, when a cyclist pulled up, sunglasses and space helmet, thighs straining to bust out of his spandex shorts, skidding to a halt in a flurry of dust. The waiting hikers gathered round him as he shook his hair out of his helmet, a crown of black curls glossy in the sun.

So this is our trail guide. Young and slim-hipped and bursting out of his nylon shorts! I wander in for a closer look. He exchanges his helmet for a backwards baseball cap, smiles a dimpled smile. "Hey," he greets the group. "Dave's sick so I'm, like, filling in. I'm Ryan. So, well, yeah." As he bends to pull hiking boots from a high-tech backpack, I cannot take my eyes off his thighs, feeling like one of those men who talk to you while staring the whole time at your breasts. Those thighs could certainly hold him up during a good romp in bed. "I'll just roll with my bike shorts on today," he says to no one in particular.

"Wassup?" he startles me, now erect and addressing me directly as I avidly peer at him. I look at his face to make sure my gaze doesn't wander south. His eyes appear directed at my head, which I've gotten used to due to my rainbow of hair colors, until I realize it's covered in a hiker hijab. Pulling it off and shaking out my hair, I say, "I didn't bring a hat. The ticks."

After a pregnant moment when I feel the heat of a blush rising, he says, "You should, like, worry more about your feet. Pull your socks up over your jeans." He says if I don't wander off the trail I'll be fine.

"Sure," I say, "Sounds fun." Which it does not, the way these people are dressed, water bottles and tweezers—I bet some of them already have fat plucked ticks inside their baggies—all of them fit and ready. With the escalating heat and the arrival of Ryan, I'm already feeling toasty, though we haven't moved an inch.

After the pleasure of briefly meeting our young and fetching guide, I trek behind him as we start the hike, checking out his padded bike shorts, refraining from patting his bottom as I would Lou in his puffy pull-up. But I become quickly winded as the trail steepens, falling behind, plodding at the back of the line of older but much more athletic hikers. With the advent of a lengthy vertical ascent, I curse myself for everything, the wrong clothing, my lack of exercise. The kiss with Steffen. My head throbs from the heat, I fear a spell of headaches coming on. No, that cannot happen! I cannot suffer weeks of debilitating headaches now, just as I'm coming to life.

Jake extols non-stop about the fauna: rare mountain lions, some coyotes, snakes, hares. The flora, he says, include oak canopies over other evergreen trees, California bay laurel, manzanita, and nutmeg. I try to recall some of this for Paavo, for when he returns at mid-summer.

Jake warns of poison oak—which is where I mentally stop listening and start watching the trail as we walk. Without my realizing it, Ryan's dropped back to where I act as caboose of the train, and when he abruptly stops, I bump into him. There's an electric shock that passes between us, possibly from his spandex.

Charged by a sexual surge, I blurt, "Do you want to go out?" After this outburst, I minimize it, "For coffee or something?"

"Awesome. I'll give you my number when we get down. We're almost at the top."

Blessed top of trail, if not top of mountain. I heave down in the shade by a rippling creek, and Ryan offers me water from his bottle. A jet far above draws a pair of white lines against the blue sky. Lower down, red-winged hawks swoop and circle, watching the weaker inhabitants of the world below. A vista of hills covered with sunny meadows, savannah grassland, and chaparral spreads below, alternating with shady green glens of oak. "Pretty here, but I'm not sure I can relate to the people," I say to Ryan.

He gurgles his water. "Seriously. Some tweaked dudes here." A duet of birds trill to each other, the one calling "too-too-too-too" while the other caws back. Ryan looks about, possibly searching for them. I wish he'd take off his sunglasses. "Nature calls," he says, stirring. I nod, feeling his warm arm brush against mine as he rises. "Gotta take a leak." He hesitates toward me as if he wants to ask me something—to join him?—and then traipses off into the bushes. When he returns, head tilted back, he inserts eye drops. Nice, long-lashed, nut-brown eyes, if a bit red-rimmed.

"Must be hard having allergies around here," I say, lamely.

"For sure," he laughs, a sunny sea change in his mood. He pulls me up and gathers everyone for the descent. Back an hour later in the parking lot, I say, "So...can I get that number?" After a baffled shadow appears, then clears from his face, he takes a pen out of his nylon pack, holds my hand steady and writes it on my wrist, tickling my skin with his ballpoint. I giggle. This is just what the doctor ordered.

~*Raja se on raittiudellakin.*~
~Even abstinence has its limit.~

Date Night

Ryan swooshes up on a skateboard, leaning, curving, carving a C until he stops and steps back to kick the board up with a flip into his arm. Oh Lord. How old is he? I'm waiting in my car in front of the address he gave me, a generic apartment complex in Blaineville. When I get out and approach, he shows no sign of recognition.

"Ryan," I call.

"Dude," he smiles at my approach, and I get the distinct impression he's trying to recall who I am. "Hey," his face lights and he grabs my hand with his surprisingly soft fingers, then pulls me to a numbered door on the first floor. His friend's apartment, he says. Inside, a small gathering sits watching some MTV reality show and drinking beer. Three boys and one girl, none of them close to thirty. A long-necked red vase sits on a low, glass coffee table.

I'm briefly introduced to the congregation, but no one pays much attention. The only light emanates from the blue flicker of the dim TV show, which the others watch with rapt attention. Ryan pulls me and I sink with him into a slouchy couch. He slings an easy arm around my shoulders. Despite my misgivings, I angle a degree toward his warm body, blaming biology. I haven't been intimate with a man since Steffen, and that was well over three years ago…how is a lonesome female of reproductive age to tolerate it? An intense yearning for closeness, the contact of flesh, a physical connection with someone fills me.

But casual sex is more Cleo's department; I've never even had a one-night stand. For the time-being, I accept a can of beer from a tattooed arm, its indiscernible designs colored dull green and pink, and realize that the vase in front of me is a bong. A boy on the floor lights a joint. I stiffen. OK, time to go. I've got to tell them I'm in my mid-thirties, a Silicon Valley test engineer, I don't do drugs, tattoos, or call people "dude!" Unsure of how to make a graceful exit so soon, I stay as sickly sweet smoke fills the air. And maybe I stay for the distraction, to be near a man who will keep me from doing horrible things like kissing my best friend's boyfriend.

I guzzle my beer. I'll finish it and then say I'm not feeling well, which is starting to be true because this dismal place with the plaid couches, wood-paneled walls and lack of natural light depresses me—I'd like to suggest they paint the "valls vite." This room wouldn't have bothered me before, but I've viewed too many 'open houses' in Mercury, wandered through too many high-ceilinged Tuscan villas with opulent interiors—maybe it's altered my aesthetic.

On the television, blandly pretty boys and girls lounge around a living room confronting each other about bathroom time as if such banality in front of cameras is not only natural but *interesting*, while the real-life, non-verbal company here seems even more boring—if that could be possible—than their television counterparts.

The girl says, "This show's so sick." Which is how I feel. I don't like TV, especially while it's still light outside. I want to run out the door to view the last rays of the day's sun. But mainly, despite the warm comfort of his thigh against mine, I want to run because I don't know Ryan. "I can't stay long," I tell him, and in reply he caresses my neck and plants a soft kiss on my cheek. Oh God.

The joint is being passed around. I swallow more beer and my body relaxes, but my brain buzzes. The pot-smoked room starts to fog my synapses, my heart speeds, I feel claustrophobic. I fear I'm getting a contact high from the thick incense smell filling the small space. Having tried pot in high school with disastrous effects, I grow fidgety.

The language issue looms in my brain, my trouble understanding the simplest conversation when stoned—how a simple sentence took on so very many shades, so many gradations to be sorted through before answering, as to render me speechless. As ambient smoke fills my nostrils, I grow light-headed, puffed-up and fuzzy, like a desiccated dandelion head. One breath and my mind would be scattered.

"My roommate's sister might of like went to school with that chick," announces the girl, evidently the chatty one in the group. She points at the TV. Her large kohl-rimmed eyes and spiky pink hair remind me of Japanese anime. She has Pokémon hair. I know about this because someone bequeathed Lou a Pokémon card collection, which now fascinates him, and since neither of us knows what to do with the cards, we use them to play a silly version of Old Maid.

My mind wanders to Lou, who I miss. How does he come up with "pee-nee" for "smoothie," those healthful fruit concoctions Meredith feeds him when he's not eating orange macaroni from a box? And why can he say "ba ba" for "bottle" but when saying *bye-bye*, he calls "die die?" Now almost three years old, Lou can't keep pace linguistically with his duplex neighbor, a reedy girl several months younger who seems capable of reciting Shakespeare. Lou struggles as he rattles off something unintelligible to us, searching our faces, repeating it with an adamant stomp of his foot, *willing* us to comprehend.

Like my mother's frustrated attempts to talk after her stroke. Aphasic, her speech and reading wiring tangled, she could understand but not reply. I heard her actually *having* the stroke. We were talking on the phone, she in Mercury, me an hour away in my apartment, when her speech changed mid-sentence. It was as if she started speaking in tongues. A tangle of mangled words poured out, syllables misplaced from word to word. Sounds like letters tossed from a Scrabble sack, tumbling out at random, all wrong.

After months of hospitalization and rehab, my mom's ability to voice her wishes and thoughts in Finnish, in English, in Finglish was gone. In the end she said only "*Piru*!" Devil. *Piru* for "yes" and *piru* for "no." *Piru* for devil and for damn it all to hell. My head falls back against the wall, I squeeze my eyes shut. *Don't think about that.*

Ryan coughs sweet smoke into my face, "Having fun?" Is he being sarcastic? During a commercial for sex—or is it beer?—I come back mentally to the room, swivel my head and see Ryan's leaf tattoo next to my face. He'd told me it was poison oak. I jerk forward, check out Pokémon Pink, then the boys, one shaped like an inflated beer can, the other stringy, all strangers. Glazed eyes on the bizarre TV show, where the combatants have squeezed into the bathroom to shout about toilet paper. I start to hoist up from the sunken sofa. "Ryan, I don't really think I can take this seriously."

He shakes his head. "*Seriously*," he coughs. What the hell does that mean? He passes the joint.

"I think I'm getting a headache," I say, feeling my temple tingle as I rise.

"Weed's good for that." I grimace. So I've heard, but this isn't exactly medical marijuana being passed around. Anyway, with what I've probably absorbed by osmosis, the possibility of a rebound headache worries me. The girl laughs and says, "This show's so sick."

Ryan jumps up and grabs my hand. Without a word to the others, he pulls me just outside the apartment door and kisses me hard on the mouth, the sickly sweet taste of pot mixed with the sour malt of beer on his tongue. I hate it. I love it. The feel of his fleshy tongue looping around mine, long and lingering. I pull back to catch my breath. "Sick," I murmur before grasping his neck in a death grip and glomming onto his lips for more.

Now this is a drug. His hands slide up and down my hips, then up my torso to my breasts. I groan. His pelvis presses mine and, growing moist, I long to wrap my legs around his ass. The intense pleasure I feel when his hands slink under my shirt fire me with pure, uncontrollable lust. My body hasn't forgotten. "Like riding a bike," I mumble into his ear.

"You rode your bike?" he asks, then locks lips with me before I can answer. After another long, devouring kiss, I pull back.

"Dude," I say, "Let's book."

By the time we reach my car, I begin to doubt my actions. But he's so hot. Cleo's right, I just need sex, like a thirsty man in a desert, a life-saving glass of water. Just a quick dip after this very long and arid spell. It's OK, I tell myself. As long as we're safe.

"Let's go to your house," Ryan says.

I think of my neighbors, the kids on the street. Marty and his "party girl" remark, the snug lane with its tight houses, everyone aware of each other's comings and goings. "Can we go to yours?"

"My parents are home."

Right. After chucking his skateboard into the backseat of my car, he starts tugging on my shirt. "Wait," I say, knowing that if we start kissing here, I'll jump on his lap. And I have to get home—for protection—for a bed to savor this.

We ride through the quiet Blaineville streets, already closing up for the night, then through the back lanes of Mercury, his hand stroking my thigh, his tongue nibbling my ear. I tingle everywhere, all ravenous female. I just know if we don't use a condom I'll end up pregnant. "Don't—stop," I joke, but I mean it. "We'll be there in a minute." I literally cannot wait to rip off his clothes, to strip out of mine. I drive faster than normal, pull quickly into my driveway.

"Is someone here?" he asks, bending to look through the

windshield at the lighted house.

I kiss him, murmuring, "I always leave a light on." We leap out and run up the steps. I fiddle with my key but the door opens easily and we fall into the room in an embrace. Dropping to the floor, we tug at each other's clothing. He pulls out a condom and, primed, I think we might do it here in the entryway…when Ryan suddenly stops. I pull down his zipper, cup his bulging crotch.

He presses down on my hand, whispers, "Is your boyfriend here?"

"What? I don't have a—"

He raises his head, pressing his finger on my lips. "*Shh.*" And then I hear them—the male voices laughing from the direction of the deck.

Only then does it dawn on my hormone-flushed, substance-addled brain what a terrible mistake I've made…

~Itku pitkästä ilosta.~
~Weeping will follow a long delight.~

Three Wise Guys

Three naked men lounge on my deck. After jumping up, straightening and smoothing myself, I took a deep breath. Slowly, I trod toward the laughter to see them, Ryan trailing.

I freeze in the double doorway that leads out back as a burst of cool air hits. Not only are Jukka and Paavo there, towels draped over their laps, beers in hand—Marty, the neighbor, drinks with them. Flanked by the smooth-skinned Finns, Marty's chest appears festooned with yak hair. A bottle of empty vodka sits on the table before them, and drained beer bottles line the railing of the redwood deck.

Paavo rises, his towel slips so I see the V of his pelvis before he recovers it. "We have come back little bit early, Alina." His speech is fuzzy, his face a mixture of shame and alarm. Looking at Ryan he says, "I did not think it was going to be much the good idea."

My scalp burns, as if someone struck a match across the part in my hair. In three seconds I've gone from hot and horny to freaked-out. My brain's paralyzed, my tongue frozen. Three naked men plus Ryan, a regular embarrassment of riches. Well, an embarrassment certainly. "Jukka here has something in his mind about taking a real wood-smoke sauna. He's needing this like some drug so we come back from Portland." But Portland is full of drugs! They should've stayed.

"I thought you'd be away for longer."

"Your phone is going to message right way," Jukka says.

Damn. I couldn't find my charger and have felt strangely free without my phone for the past few days, not even logging onto email, realizing that I don't miss being perpetually hunched over a laptop under the unnatural glare of fluorescents, rather enjoying my days free to roam about the sunny neighborhood, feed the horse, breathe fresh air, and wonder what the hell Troy's doing. Jukka slurs, "We are family so I'm thinking it's not the problem we come. Since you are not home we take sauna like you always want. You have given the key to your house. Home run!"

Home run—*not.* Looks like no one's scoring tonight. "Oh yeah. Home base," I say, ha ha.

Beet-red Marty laughs uncomfortably and tucks his towel more tightly around his soft middle. "Your cousins here introduced me to the *sow-na.*"

"You have changed your hair," Paavo says. Smiling, I smooth it back, flushing at the sight of him here, bare-chested, so similar to his initial online picture, the one that made me catch my breath. "There are the stripes in it."

"Highlights? Yeah." Are they that noticeable? Fake-looking? "I guess you can tell…" I finger some strands.

"They are quite realistic, I think," Paavo tells me. *Right*, that's the look I'm aiming for. Not pretty, not beautiful. *Real.* Never turn to a Finn for a false compliment.

Ryan rocks on his heels. "Thought you looked different." I scrunch my face at him. Nothing's changed in the hair department since I met *him.*

"And who is this young guy?" asks Jukka, evidently enjoying himself immensely, making no move to cover up more than the square of his groin or do anything that might require physical coordination.

I sneak a peak at Paavo, then turn to unconcerned Ryan, dopey smile on his face, hands in pockets and—his fly open! "He's…just Ryan." I check my jeans, tug on my t-shirt again, try to communicate to Ryan with wide eyes that his crotch is unzippered.

Marty stretches his arm to Ryan, half-rising while clutching onto his towel, "How you doing?" and I mumble introductions, "My neighbor Marty, and this is my cousin Jukka. Over there, his friend Paavo."

With slurred enunciation Jukka says, "Well surely"—which comes out 'surly'—"Paavo is your friend now too, Alina." While Paavo rises to shake Ryan's hand, Jukka chuckles and says, "*Hevoset karkaa*," with a thick roll of the "r," causing Paavo to grin. I demand to know what he said, and he tells me it's an expression for a man's unzipped fly: "the horses gonna run away." Ryan grins gamely, hands glued in his pockets.

"Oh, for God's sake," I pitch forward and yank the damn zipper up with excessive zeal, as Ryan instinctively trips backward. Clearing more distance from me, he says, "That's some tweaked language. You guys Hawaiian?"

"They're Finns!" I say in exasperation, despite that remark being the most astute he's ever uttered…all the vowels, the limited consonants, so much use of L, K, and M. Melodious tongues, both. I flash on my grandmother's name, *Mielikki*, a Finnish myth name that sounds Polynesian.

Paavo coughs and says, "We're here a bit early for *Juhannus*, I am afraid, and now surprising you and your boyfriend. Come have the drinks. We will clean up bit." I don't want to drink with them and I don't want Paavo to think Ryan's my boyfriend. Nor have I even thought about *Juhannus* and the freaking mid-summer party.

"He's not my... uh, it isn't mid-summer yet is it?" Christ, we're barely into June.

"That would be the weekend next," Jukka pipes in.

"No, no. Really? The weekend after next weekend?" So soon!

"Weekend around 21st is always going to be the party," Paavo says. "But if you have not—"

"Is your man here coming?" Jukka asks.

Ryan breaks into a goofy smile and swivels in his Converses.

"*Coming.* Not yet." Argh.

I say, "No, I haven't invited...anyone." I turn to stutter something to Ryan about the bash. The one I haven't planned, the one no one's been invited to. The one I, at this moment, very much do not want him at.

"Awesome. Sick," he takes a beer from a six-pack on the deck, leans against the deck rail near Marty's chair. *Great, make yourself at home. Forget me.* I didn't have big plans for Ryan—except for tonight—which have turned out to be blasted to hell.

I slump into the Adirondack chair. "You'll come too, Marty?"

He says something about getting a sitter and not missing it for the world, clinks beer bottles with Paavo, then Ryan. "Cheers, my friends."

I'm suddenly feeling left out of the male bonding party. Sighing, I say, "I guess I should invite some women." When I ask, "Will your wife come?" Marty says, "Definitely."

Paavo says, "Meredith is coming?" I look at him quizzically.

"Of course she is." But I haven't planned a thing. I feel a twinge in my temple. "And Cleo. I've just been a little busy..."

Jukka says, "Sauna is still hot, Alina. Goot for you guys now." The chill night air makes me miss taking sauna, and I actually understand Jukka's desire for a true one, so much more invigorating—and brutal—than the tepid, wood-paneled types found at American hotels and health clubs.

Steffen used to want to make love to me in there, and I said, trust me, you don't. A true Finnish sauna is by turns a searing steam bath and diabolically hot dry box. But after suffering through the dimensions of heat and sweat, you come out transformed, feeling invigorated, elated even—maybe just the relief you'd feel after you stop banging your head against a wall. I shiver, long for a purifying sauna, think of how I don't bother with such pleasures anymore.

Then it hits me. The sauna! My mother's ashes, the pine box...were they on the top bench? I run down the steps, open the door, am struck full on by a furnace blast of heat. Nothing there. "Did you see a box?" I shout at them. The drunken losers. Why did I ever give them that key? I'm shaking, I think I'm going to cry. Paavo reaches me, takes my hand. I shake it away "I said, *did you see a pine box*?" slowly and loudly like a teacher to a student with an attention disorder.

"Alina, Alina," he pulls me away and says quietly, "I have put that box in your bedroom. Don't worry." Naked from the waist up, he draws close. "I'm sorry. Really, I am sorry."

I shut the sauna door and look down. "It's so stupid." I shake my head. "It's crazy. *I'm* crazy. For some reason it's hard for me to deal with Mom's…" I fight to keep my voice steady.

"No. It's not so crazy." Paavo reaches to pat me on the back but still shaking my head, I rush toward the house, note in a blur Ryan talking to Jukka, oblivious, no Marty in sight. I hurry to the bedroom where the cube of ashes sits upon my mother's dresser. Grasping the solid sides of the smooth pine cube, my lips quiver and I squeeze my eyes, trying hard to follow my mother's stoic lead.

From behind, Paavo gently touches my shoulder. Choking up, I mumble toward the box, "My mother said she wanted me to have *sisu*." I sniffle, snot dripping from my nose, "On her death bed," which comes out clogged, "on ha da ba," like something Lou might say.

Paavo says to me in the mirror, "And you think *sisu* is not to cry?"

"She never shed a tear after my dad died."

"Maybe this is for you. How is it you are knowing what she does when she is alone?"

I turn to face him, melting as he wraps his strong arms around me, my head fitting perfectly into the nook of his neck. Feeling I could rest in the comfort of his embrace forever. Feeling this is so much more right than being with Ryan.

~Jos ei viina, terva ja sauna auta, niin tauti on kuolemaksi.~
~If tar, liquor and sauna does not help, the disease is fatal.~

Suicide Headaches

I awaken with a metal spike thrust in my head. My suicide headaches have arrived in full force. Napa, which Paavo proposed last night, is impossible for me now.

Excruciating pain radiates across my temple and down the left side of my face. Involuntary tears pour from my left eye, my clogged left nostril drips. An ice pick stabs directly on a nerve that runs from the top of my skull, through my eye, down my cheek. Pound-pound-pound. I press on the pulse of it, on a vein at my temple, bearing down hard in a hopeless attempt to make it stop. A turnpike of burning, throbbing pain shoots up my neck to bore into the entire left hemisphere of my head.

In the pre-dawn light of the bathroom, my free hand scrabbles through the bathroom cabinets for my medicines. The drug spray I inhale turns the metal spike into a faintly softer wooden dagger. I find the remaining Imitrex pill from last year's pack and two liquid-gel Motrin, grab a Coke from the refrigerator and wash them down. I try to breathe through the pain. For two hours I lie in bed and suffer in the dark until, on its own schedule, the pulsing ache subsides. The house is quiet. I cannot worry about anything, least of all Paavo and Jukka, still asleep. Or any daytrip with them.

Suicide headaches. That's what they call them. The searing one-sided pain that comes daily for weeks on end—cluster headaches. A form of migraine that typically strikes men, my theory for the dramatic nickname. I have no idea if they're worse than migraines, a more female affliction, which come with an attendant stomach upset that sounds like misery on top of misery. I know only that they are unbearable, and I suppose it's true that I've wished myself dead more than once during an attack.

My headache spells usually occur in a bell shaped curve of frequency, where I feel a tingle here and there for days and then one day awaken with the real thing, an axe in my head. Only to look forward to increasing frequency and intensity for days, weeks, until the "cluster" diminishes and passes, gone for six months or a year, the pain forgotten, I suppose, like labor pain.

Now my spells are completely unpredictable. When I was younger, my spells occurred in autumn when school started, and during spring after finals, waking me each day at the exact same hour before dawn. More recently, they strike randomly—like lightening. Like electrical bolts shot straight into my left temple at any hour, during any season. And since my mom died I haven't had one, which worries me, for already this spell feels different, has crashed down on me strong and hard, unexpected. I fear a more protracted, diabolical cycle.

I've been on every drug imaginable, some of which were almost worse than the pain. Years ago, when I was twenty, a headache specialist made me fill out a ten-page form. Balding, rheumy eyed, with an accusing hawk-beak of a nose, he told me, "Cluster headaches usually affect *men*. You have all the symptoms but you don't fit the diagnosis." He pointed at a fat book. "Middle-aged men, hard-drinkers with leonine features." I was flummoxed, not to mention in need of a dictionary. *Leonine features*? And was he implying that I was a hard drinker or a closet male? He squinted at my forms. "Cluster sufferers don't lie in bed when they're in pain. They thrash about, bang their heads against the wall."

"If I banged my head against the wall would you believe me?"

"Are you having an attack?"

"I wouldn't be sitting here if I had a headache." Jesus, I wanted to say, isn't it possible women—or some individuals—with cluster react differently than those documented men? Maybe I've had bad luck, but my doctors generally have been arrogant and dismissive.

When my pain abates mid-morning from time and medicine, I explain the disease to Paavo and Jukka over cereal, tell them I need to see a doctor today, which could be a drawn-out affair, as I have no appointment. Despite Paavo's creased brow and protestations, I refuse to hear of them hanging around—particularly when a headache onslaught makes me want only one thing: to be alone.

And when I am alone, when they're off to some Bay Area attraction, I go to an urgent care office and leave with prescriptions for Imitrex, pain pills, and life-saving oxygen, the quickest, safest remedy—providing I'm home when a headache attacks. The Finns promised to save the wine-tasting trip to Napa for me, despite my telling them it could be several weeks before I can touch alcohol.

*

After my two-hour bout with the demon headache the next morning, I do the usual: make the most of my pain-free day. I busy myself with the house and insist that Troy have it painted before the summer solstice holiday, *Juhannus*. When I return from the paint store, a thick fan of every conceivable color in hand, Paavo and Jukka sit hunched over their laptop on the deck steps.

They greet me and return to the screen, while I take in the verdure of the flourishing spring trees, the backyard bowered, luxuriant. I inhale deeply, smell sweet jasmine as I glance over Paavo's shoulder at the computer screen. They're reading an online article about cluster headaches. An ache pierces my heart...this is how it feels to be cared for. Perhaps emotionally unstable from the morning's meds, I feel like crying. I feel love.

Paavo pivots toward me, "I have never heard of this luster headache," he says, omitting the "c" as Mom used to. "Is this better if we leave you alone now?"

I gulp, compose myself. "Leave? You just got back here. No! No, please don't go."

Jukka holds up the back of his hands, "There is old Karelian medicine for such problems I'm thinking but hard to find these doctors now. Well, they are not really the doctors. They are old men with some kind of magical hands." He talks to Paavo in Finnish.

Paavo inhales, "*Yo*, some old kind of healing. But anyways, I'm going to check into this problem. Perhaps this Reiki Meredith has shown me is helping."

"Meredith? Reiki? When was this?" I ask, suddenly confused. They explain that yesterday Paavo visited John's wife, while Jukka rented a motorcycle to cruise the green western hills. When John's wife had to leave, Paavo phoned Meredith. I ask him how he got her number, and he reminds me that I gave it to him.

"She is inviting us all to dinner but it is just me."

"Alone? You could have invited me down."

"We have tried to call you many times. Your phone is off, I think." Of course, lights off, phone off, I crashed early and prayed I'd make it through the night without a headache. Jukka grabs my thick stack of paint color swatches, fans them out. "What is this?"

I sigh from the diversion of topic, tell him I couldn't decide on room colors, the choices overwhelmed. He chuckles, "With all these you gonna have some kinda gypsy circus tent." Following a quick scan of the strips, he points to a pale yellow rectangle. "This one. It's going to be good." Skeptical about "Soft Moonlight" but knowing he's a graphic artist and wanting to get off the paint topic, I say I'll think about it. But Jukka, primed with coffee, is not to be deterred from yakking, it seems. "You are like Paavo, cannot make up the mind. He's that way with everything. We order from the menu and takes him hour or so, then he changes it. Like his girls, Kirsi leaves him because he's so slow and thinks Suvi is best, then course he wants other one back. Really crazy." With that and a remark about "taking the leak," he leaves us.

"Is that true?" I sit next to Paavo on the hard step. He turns a puzzled face from the computer. "Um. So Mere showed you Reiki? Was Steffen there?"

"No, he's not. And it's all right because I am very interested in this. For long time now I'm wanting to learn more kind treatment and she is good teaching."

I press my temple, swearing I can feel blood vessels expanding in the hot sun. "But Lou must've interrupted."

"He's sleeping at night," says Paavo, in his matter-of-fact way. I tug on the sweaty underarms of my top, envision them alone in the evening, alternately caressing each other's head—on the sofa, her bed? I recall her soothing hands the day I was fired…so tender, sensual. My friend's phone numbers, my house key—why the hell do I have to be so friendly?

But my thoughts stall as Paavo covers my hand with his, sturdy and reassuring. "It seems to me you are strong girl living with this problem." *Strong*. The word touches me. Flattered, I smile, grateful for this doctor who's actually *sympathetic*—and handsome, with his dark hair tousled, longer now, sexily covering one eye. Anyway, he and Jukka were home last night, their car here when I awoke. "Are you walking fast and hitting up your head on the wall?"

"No, and I don't have a penis, either," I kid. "I'm sorry. It's just that mostly men get these headaches, as you've probably read." He nods. "So when some specialist tells me that just because I don't react according to *the book*, I don't have cluster, it makes me crazy! Maybe I don't bang my head against the wall—I just want quiet and darkness. I have this theory that men and women probably react to severe pain differently, you know? No one's thought of that? Experts, ha!" From Paavo's silence, I realize that I spit those last words, am possibly foaming at the mouth.

"I'm sorry about that," he says. "Our medicine has failed many people. This is why I like to learn the Eastern ways. And Meredith knows much."

Meredith again. "Do you like Meredith?" I ask, facing him head-on, close enough to kiss his lavish lips.

"Oh yes, very much," comes the rapid answer.

I squirm on the step. "No. I mean, do you *like* like her?" *Say no!*

"What is this, like-like?" He shrugs. "She has teach me quite some good Reiki. This I like very much. No, *I like this* very much. Meredith is helping me to speak better English."

Sounds like a busy night, healing *cum* language lessons. I could teach him English! "I didn't know you wanted to be corrected. It can be rude. Besides, you speak fine English," I state.

"No. It's good she corrects."

"*You*. Me. I can help you too. You say, "She corrects *me*."

He shakes his head. "Now I'm confused. That is not how she is doing it."

"*Does* it."

"Does what?"

I fan myself with my deck of color strips. "It's not how she *does* it!" And does what, I'd like to know! OK, so maybe she does it better than me. Or I? Or everyone. Perfect Meredith! Who's on first here?

Paavo mentions my stress, thinks this is part of my head problem. "Meredith is helping you."

"No! She's not." I bark, slamming the fan on the deck. The clip breaks and scores of samples scatter, sliding down the steps. Leaving the mess, I stand to go inside. "Once you learn that Reiki, you really should lay your hands on me, Paavo."

~*Parempi karvas totuus kuin makea valhe.*~
~Better a bitter truth than a sweet lie.~

The Confession

I wish I could fall into a deep, oblivious sleep, like Lou. The day is bright and clear as we cruise down the freeway. When my morning headache subsided, I drove down to Meredith's, arriving at naptime. So now I'm back on the road, riding shotgun, readying for The Talk as Mere drives Lou in her regular attempt at lulling him to sleep. "Shh," she says, as I clear my throat, so I fidget, not knowing how to address the subject of my kissing her boyfriend. And wondering how things got to be so complicated…

What was it about Steffen? Although my body urged me to conjoin with him, my mind did not. An impetuous artist was not for this reticent Finn. When we dated, his immediate intimacy was frightening.

After the pregnancy scare our easy affair became more difficult. I began noticing all the things about him that bothered me—aside from his impulsivity. First, he stared at me. A lot. After sex, instead of doing the normal thing—falling conveniently asleep—he propped himself on his elbow and peered. He traced his finger along the scimitar-shaped scar on my left cheek, caused by a teenage fall onto a sprinkler head. The permanently raw nerves prickled. He examined me from different angles, making me feel like the subject of a portrait, or a still life.

He said odd things, made irritating pronouncements. "You're a sensualist," he said, one rainy winter Sunday as water pounded on the roof and streamed down the windows of the room he was renting. We'd made slow love to the steady drip of water pinging into an empty paint can in the corner.

Naked, I blushed and tucked the worn blue quilt up under my armpits. "Just because I enjoy sex."

"Quite a bit. And swimming, and dancing." He paused. "Maybe 'primitive' is more the word. You're a primitive."

"Ever the flatterer."

We lay in bed, listening to the downpour quiet to a patter. Steffen told me that he found my background "exotic." I replied that Worcester was not exactly the mysterious East. Then I allowed that there was a German anthropologist back in the 1700's who divided all the world's peoples into five races, based primarily on skin color. The Finns didn't fit into any of them, so this anthropologist lumped them with the Asian Mongols.

My senior thesis research taught me that the blond hair and blue eyes must have come from the conquering Swedes, as the Finno-Ugrics originated centuries before near the Ural Mountains and Volga River. I told Steffen that even though most Finns are genetically more European now, originally they held more connections to Asia than Europe, that their language is entirely distinct from the all the Indo-European tongues; their origins possibly from the steppes of Mongolia.

I tried to recall the unusual tribes: the Khantys and Mansis from Western Siberia, and the small island of Finno-Ugrics in the middle of Russia called the Idel-Ural …Mari-El and Udmurtia still trying to maintain their strange language and pagan ways, the only places in Europe where nature-worship is an authentic, organized religion. I grew animated teaching Steffen as if I were Dad: "Did you know that the Mari, Komi, and Udmurts still practice shamanism?"

Head propped on one elbow and eyes at half-mast, he said, "I love it when you talk sexy." I pushed a pillow at him. "You should teach," he said.

"Yeah, I can tell you're captivated." But I thought on. Along with the reindeer people in the north, the Arctic Lapps, the

Saamis, Finland seemed a strange melting pot that had frozen hundreds of years ago. It was, perhaps, what set the Finns apart—their belonging to no classification. I remember saying, "I think Finns are just an odd, unnoticed meeting of East and West."

"Genghis Khan meets Alfred Nobel," he said, cradling my face as if searching for a resemblance. But maybe he had something there—the peaceable Finns with their stubborn ability to fight. Was that me? Outside, the rain stopped, all was still. He rolled on top of me and we made love. Then he wound me tight to him, wrapping our bodies in the sheets like mummies. Despite our short time together he whispered in my ear, "Can't you see that I love you?"

I looked up through the high window. Dark clouds raced by. He held me tighter. "You're cold, Alina." I shivered as a chill passed through me like an errant Arctic wind. It must have been a premonition. Not long after, my father was diagnosed with cancer.

I know one thing: you can't be too happy. That's life out of balance. But it was a good day, overall. When I look back.

I nearly jump in my seat to see Meredith's gaze fixed intently upon me. "He's almost out," she whispers.

"Shouldn't you keep your eyes on the road?" I flush as if she were boring into my brain, spying on that intimate image of Steffen and me.

"You looked dreamy, there." She smiles. I try to smile back. Before commencing, I turn in my seat to check on Lou, watch his head tip toward the window, his eyes droop, and then pop open. He repeats these valiant attempts to stay alert at least three times. But in a moment, he's out, the steady speed, humming tires, and soft music from the tape player being weapons in his mom's arsenal too great to battle.

With a glance in the rearview mirror, Meredith chimes her refrain, "A sleeping baby is a beautiful thing!" Victorious, she punches out the lullaby tape. "I am *so* sick of Brahms."

I sigh. That kiss has been weighing me and everything around me down, even the air feels too heavy to maneuver through. I observe Meredith before starting my slow and calm admission. Her profile is elegant, a long neck with hair casually gathered at the nape. But her chin, on the meek side, makes her seem so vulnerable just now. My heart races. My head pounds. It will pound and hurt until I tell her.

Staring straight ahead, I inhale deeply to start my spiel. I've planned how to say it, beginning with the whole story of my no-show blind date, when Meredith says, "What would you think if I stole Paavo away for a few days to a Reiki conference?"

"What would you think if I kissed your boyfriend?" My hand flies to my mouth. Oh my God!

The car slows dramatically as our faces meet in mutual shock. When she returns her attention to the road, I expel a non-stop monolog. Cars rush past. "Steffen ran into me in a restaurant the other night. Well, if you can call it a restaurant. It was really more like a run-down bar. A lesbian biker thing I guess was going out of business and who knew? I was going to meet this guy from love4ever.com like Cleo suggested but I guess for some reason he didn't show so there I was, the place was empty except for these two women—"

"He said you met up." Long pause. "What's this about kissing?" Her voice cracks.

"One! One…ki…iss." I hold my breath as time suspends. She looks at me expectantly. We've slowed to a creep, cars charge past, horns blaring. "Maybe we should stop?" Like, stop talking about this? Why did I have to spurt it out that way? What was that about Paavo? She drives to the shoulder, kills the motor. "Go on."

Drawing another huge breath, afraid of a real headache coming on, needing air, I roll down the window to hang my head out. Oleanders line the freeway in full bloom, fresh and breezy, showing off their brief day in the sun. "Steffen and I ended up hugging in a friendly way." This is impossibly hard. "Then there was this short kiss, like, on the mouth. That's it!" I pull my head inside to see her face. "But I know it's awful! I'm so sorry, Mere, you have no idea. It feels so incredibly bad and ruinous and I just need to tell you that I have no feelings for him and wish…"

Momentarily I run out of words, don't know how she's taking it. "I was drinking and he got in the car—I *so* wish the whole thing never happened." I wait, head bowed, in silence. Car tires hum on the freeway, the floor of the car is littered with fast food papers and small, disposable toys: a snail wearing a hat and tie, a fuzzy goofy-smile dog that looks like the Cowardly Lion. Quietly, I say, "So. Guess he didn't mention that part."

Meredith's never been mad at me in any real way and I cannot stand her silence, the whirring of passing traffic, each speeding vehicle tugging at the small sedan. My thoughts race: she's too quiet, horribly angry. She hates me and we're growing distant and apart and I'm losing the only true family I have…

At last she speaks, her voice gravelly. "He didn't have to. There was something in his tone—we were talking on the phone—and somehow I knew what I've known all along."

"What? You know nothing! There's nothing going on, Mere, I swear." Hand clutching her arm, I say, "Honestly, I've been so horny I'd jump a frog, I was really looking forward to that blind date coming—I mean *coming*!—because I haven't had sex in like decades and then somehow I was in proximity to a male. Unfortunately it was Steffen." I look at her frozen profile and think it begins to melt.

Eyes glistening, she says," Don't worry, Ali. Steffen and I are in counseling. Who knows."

Huh? Not me, I guess. I swivel to see Lou's head cocked, asleep in innocence, exhale all the air I've been holding in. Darling Lou. A fleeting memory of my parents arguing, perhaps over my father's drinking, and my mother threatening to leave him while I, an only child—how old?—shuddered in panic all night at the prospect of being left adrift.

I tell Meredith I don't know what's going on with her ever since I moved, and she says the same. "So...counseling. It'll get better, right?"

"I hope so. For Lou's sake, if nothing else."

"Yeah," I sigh, feeling drained. The strain of talking over the roaring traffic wears on me. I roll the window back up with some effort. "Please don't read anything into that night. I think Steffen was feeling lonely. He's worried about losing you."

She sniffs. "Funny way to show it." We sit in miserable silence for a bit before she says, "Our relationship has always been a bit complicated by you."

"It wouldn't exist without me!"

"Don't you think I know that? But don't deny it isn't complex."

"It doesn't have to be."

"Ali, you can be in denial all you want but—"

"Denial about what?" I return to look at the oleanders, which by August will look withered and scraggly.

"Your feelings. I don't know. Steffen's feelings, certainly." She's reading way too much into this. I was just *in heat* that night. She thinks he's still in love with me? *It's because he hasn't made the final commitment to her.* "I guess I can't really blame *you*," she says.

"Yes you can! I was as much at fault as anyone. I mean, how could I possibly let that happen? It's so terrible. You're my best friend!" Now *I* want to cry, to hug her, re-bond and put it all behind us. I cannot lose her. "I'm so incredibly sorry, Meredith. Can you ever forgive me?"

"Don't be so hard on yourself." I gaze with love into the green pool of her eyes, the amber around the pupils like a pond's soft, sandy bottom. Then, as if something stirred up the sand, they cloud, turn opaque. I reach out and we embrace, and I squeeze her tighter than ever before. As if this physical act will wring out all the emotional anguish. After a moment she pulls away, her lips straight. "You need to start listening to your heart. And I have to start thinking with my head. The heart, mind, body connection," she says. "We can both learn from it." Straightening her back, her complexion clear, she clicks on the ignition. "Let's not talk about it." Such a new and refreshing line from Meredith!

As we head homeward, I switch to a better topic. "Mere, you know I'm dating—or trying to—but guess what? I'm really interested in someone. It's a bit premature, but you need to know this. As my best friend." *And, because he might be getting the wrong signals from you.* "I think you'll be glad to know I've got a crush on, on Paavo." The car slows and swerves to the right as she turns to me. "*Paavo*?" She says this so loudly that within seconds Lou is wailing.

*

"You sounded surprised when I told you about Paavo." Back at her apartment, Lou wide awake and munching animal crackers, she throws lingerie and toiletries in a quilted bag, head down, while I hang around, feeling helpless, still guilty. Sitting on the bed, I watch as she grabs things from the dresser squashed in the corner of the room, its top a crowded mish-mash of dangly earrings, uncovered jars of face cream, and bottles of "essential" oils, which I've thus far managed to survive without.

"Ali, I just …I had no idea, really. Weird. It surprised me. You never said anything. But it kind of explains your outburst."

"We've both been busy."

"Obviously you haven't spent much time with him and you need that. Of course he *cannot* come with me! I just thought that since Cynthia bailed, he might like to go. But you have to get to know each other while he's here, right? You're a lucky girl," she says, slouching onto her futon, black lace bra in hand. "But he's luckier." Unaccustomed to much personal praise, it not being the Finnish way, first from Paavo and now Meredith, I smile in gratitude.

She talks quickly of her trip just two days away. She says that Steffen has a lucrative house-painting job in Marin County over the weekend, and, since his parents are off on a cruise, she's hired a sitter. I tell her that I'm glad she's getting a break, she needs it. We're getting comfortably back on track when the phone rings. Wanting to part on a normal note—and because I miss her—I stick around for a bit, feeling how I long for her regular company, wishing I could bop over to her bungalow without notice to tickle Lou, sit at her table and drink tea. I wander off to give her some privacy, tripping on a ballet flat as I enter the living room.

In my focus on her, I haven't registered the exceptional disarray of her apartment. I recall the order that reigned when Meredith first moved in, when everything from shoes to toiletries to kitchen utensils was sorted and contained. Lou's toys were relegated to neat wicker bins: cardboard storybooks separated from bumpy plastic blocks, wood puzzle pieces kept away from crates of stuffed animals. Meredith sidled up to me and theatrically whispered the secret to her domestic success—"*Baskets!*"—as if to Dustin Hoffman in *The Graduate*. Now a given bucket is as likely to contain shoes, a spatula, *and* toys, mixed in with a stale Pop Tart and last month's electric bill. How many times have I seen Meredith dump out these bins of iniquity in a mad hunt for her car keys?

When she enters the room now, her bent posture hides her face. "Let me help you straighten up," I chuck an unidentifiable plastic toy, or piece thereof, into an empty blue basket. But in answer she kicks at a suitcase, half-full at the foot of the rocking chair.

"*Shit.* I guess my plan just wasn't meant to be."

~Kolme yötä koiralle kodin tekee.~
~It is home to a dog after he has been there three nights.~

La Vida Mercury

Dogs and children, it turns out, are the key to popularity in Mercury. Pulling into the driveway, the neighbor kids run out as if they've been watching all Spring from behind curtains, awaiting this very instant, when something out of the ordinary, something actually fun, might occur in our lackluster neighborhood. Upon my arrival with Lou and the dog, a swarm of little people appears. A charming, noisy, frightening swarm that appears to want to stay once they hear that I have both Lou and a dog for the next three days.

When Mere told me her sitter came down with the flu, my remorse swelled—guilt about Steffen, regret that I dictated she not invite Paavo to the seminar, and now this: no one to take care of her son. This is the woman who, after two years without a vacation from new motherhood, flew from Waikiki, where she'd been whisked by her sisters, back to my side when my mom had the stroke. Left paradise to comfort me in the cold waiting room at the ICU. Because I called her choking back tears, because she knew I had no one else to call.

Taking Lou for the weekend felt like some sort of atonement for the ill-fated kiss. When I offered, we argued; I insisted that I'm free and unemployed, Jukka and Paavo can help, and so on until my obstinacy prevailed—she agreed to go to her conference while I cared for Lou. As we talked, I scooped him up to touch noses. How I've missed living near him! "Auntie Ali wants to live closer," I said.

Then I heard yelping from his closed bedroom. I asked warily about the puppy, and Meredith quickly said she thought something could be arranged. But I saw the doubt on her face. Lou looked up at me with his marble eyes and pleaded "peas peas." While I considered this new quandary, Meredith assured me that the dog, now trained, knows commands: *heel, stay, sit.* She showed me arm motions, which I watched closely, in hopes the overactive pup would do all of these things—preferably continuously—if I took her.

And so I consented, causing Lou to skip to open the bedroom door. Mere mentioned something about "how fast they grow," when a new, unrecognizable dog, half the size of a cow, spotted me and immediately lunged.

*

A dog and a new kid, both of them much alike—scanty language skills and a love of balls—appear to be all the neighbor kids want, along with my yard to play in. Within minutes, they're all over at my place, carrying tennis balls for the dog to chase, and at first it seems that I don't have to do much except watch.

Inside, I find Paavo packing a duffle bag. "You're not leaving again, I hope!"

"Just for few days," he says, handing me a paper.

I gawk. "You're going with Meredith?"

"She is going? I don't know this. She has told me about learning Reiki congress some time ago. I have registered to it online just this morning." *I* register that he is now going to the same conference as Meredith.

"You'll probably be in the beginner classes," I think aloud. Unlike Mere, who knows Reiki. I sit on the edge of his bed.

He finishes packing, and I hand him back the paper. "Yes, I suppose so." I walk over to point outside the window, where Lou and the small neighbor girl chase after the dog. A broad smile brightens Paavo's features, transforming his often-serious face. "This looks good," he says.

Boldly, I say, "You look good."

"Now yard is being used right. I'm happy for you," he shakes my shoulders, then picks up his duffle. "You are the good friend to take her child."

I trudge after him. "What about Jukka?" I ask. "Does he like children?"

After Jukka speeds away on a rented Harley, headed out to "chill" for the weekend, I find consolation only in thoughts of next Saturday's bash.

Marty's three middle children race, run, and play tag non-stop, dodging in and out of the elms and oaks, trailed by Lou. They've discovered the gap in the old chicken-wire fence at the far end of the yard, out by the dry creek bed. There's a Taylor, Madison, and Riley, so naturally I cannot keep them straight, the boy versus girls. I learn the boy is 11 years old, the middle girl 7, and the youngest girl 5. The skinny oldest girl, a teen or pre-teen, along with mom and baby remain out of sight, and I wonder if it's OK with the mother… Unlike my parents, I figure these modern moms all fear kidnappings and predators lurking in bushes.

I ask #11, the boy, if their mom knows they're all here. Number 7 runs to me, "I'll take you over." Next door, she charges in, leaving the door ajar, and calls "MOM!" while I wait at the bottom of the porch stairs. "The neighbor wants to talk to youuuu!" Such an ear-splitting voice from such a tiny girl. I glance at the house across the street, where I'm sure two kids live. They can be seen rushing out to a honking silver van, perpetually wearing sports gear, toting duffle bags. From the front window I've watched the mom tear that silver bullet out of her driveway at breakneck speed—some day she's sure to crash right into my front parlor.

After a minute, Marty's wife appears without the baby, descends the porch steps to meet me. Her happy, frizzy strawberry-blond hair and loose, yellow SpongeBob top are at odds with her subdued manner. She introduces herself as Rebecca, I notice that, like Mere on sleep-deprived days, her eyes are shadowed. "It's awfully nice of you to have the kids over."

I tell her my name, then say, "So you don't mind them playing in my yard?"

Fingering curls from her forehead, she sighs, "No. It's great. We don't have a yard, haven't you noticed?" Her head tilts toward the back of the long house. "I don't know what Marty thought I was going to do with the kids all summer. He *wasn't* thinking—except about the golf course. But you. Looks like a park over there. You could charge admission."

I feel instantly guilty for having a yard and no kids. "It should be 'free passage,'" I say, like in Finland. Or is it "everyman's right?" Among other things, Dad told me Finns cherish the tradition of allowing anyone to pass over any property whenever they like—enjoyment of the land is for all, equally. Jukka had made a comment about all the fences in California, all the land trapped in, something I also found strange when we first moved from Massachusetts. "Also, I'm having a party, a mid-summer solstice fling, next Saturday," I say, in case her husband hasn't mentioned it.

A wafer-thin girl with a yearning face, wearing abundant eye makeup, which tells me she's in middle school or beyond, comes outside holding the baby. Comparing her to Meredith's clients, I immediately suspect she has an eating problem, is another poor lollipop girl. With a small wave she introduces herself as Maya, and when she reaches the bottom step, I extend my arms to cradle the infant but stop, reminded of Lou. Talk about crummy care taking! "Shoot. I've got to go back, I'm babysitting." But I sense some neediness from this Rebecca, despite her husband and house full of kids. She needs Meredith, not me. Or Cleo, with her boxes of sample medications. Or just some fresh air. "Would you like to come with me?"

The mom shakes her head but Maya hands the baby to her

mother. "I'll go check on the rug rats."

"I could help you out a little for a couple of days. It's a waste, my yard," I tell Rebecca.

"Marty buys this big house and the kids have to play at the neighbors'." She's on a rant, "We move constantly. I wish we never left Maine." Rebecca tells me about all her family there: parents and grandparents and even great-grandparents. I gulp. I don't want to do the math on that. Sisters and brothers, aunts, uncles and too many cousins to count. I want to say that's too bad, I'm sorry you had to leave them. And I am, but the ache in me won't let the words out.

"I'm so pissed at him. And the baby doesn't sleep… I'm just so tired all the time. He wanted this baby but really it's just too much!"

I'd pegged the guy as a jerk, but honestly, five children for a woman who looks my age—it's obviously an injustice. "Terrible," I say, opening the soft blanket to caress the puffy hand, stroke the infant's dove-soft skin. I press the blanket back in place. No time to get all dewy-eyed and drool on the baby. "Sorry, got to run. Next Saturday, come!" I call brightly, wanting her to have something to look forward to. Besides, a friend in the neighborhood wouldn't hurt me.

Back at the yard, Maya says, "You *so* will *not* want them here for long. Just send them back whenever." But it turns out the children have decided, evidently some clandestine vote was taken. They are there at my house, in my yard for the duration. Like a species I cannot rid myself of. A species that eats a lot, like rodents.

But I'm grateful for them. Their infiltration is a welcome intrusion; the children not only divert the dog but they help me handle Lou, who asks incessant questions. Just as my body, at 30, started asking "*when*?" Lou, at age three, has started asking "*why*?" Why for everything: "why?" being his answer to "try to go potty," "drink your milk," and "I've got to take this pill." I have to swallow this pill because my head hurts! And all these "whys" are making it hurt worse.

When I'm alone with Lou, I do the "uh huh" thing after too much chatter, which makes him chatter more, keenly aware of inattention. How do mothers do it? It drives me crazy! "It takes a village," they say. It takes an insane asylum.

Walking with the kids and the dog—given the literary name "Cosette" by Meredith but shortened to "Coco" by Lou—in Mercury, I am a magnet. Strangers smile at me through tinted car windows. Golfers wave. People stop us to ask questions. Young and old have voted me Miss Popularity. Dog walkers, in particular, love me. While Coco yelps and jumps and entangles me, I learn about the best dog parks and obedience schools (that one comes up a lot). They part with a friendly wave, a "See you around."

The fifteen year-old, Maya, helps out sometimes, never eats. She drinks water, eats miniscule bits of fruit. I push coffee breads her way, make protein smoothies, but nothing works. Sweet as she is, her presence makes me penitent, rueful that I'd been so flippant about her problem. I should never have mentally called her—or Meredith's girls—"lollipop girls."

Exhausted by mid-afternoon, I stick the kids in front of the TV, change the channel to PBS because Meredith approves. I get flack from the older kids, who switch to Nickelodeon or Cartoon Network while I sink into an armchair, Coco sleeping beside me. The start of the late Friday lull, I hear the last noises from the ubiquitous renovation that echoes through the otherwise quiet community. I doze off to the beep-beep-beep of a backhoe reversing, the drill of a jackhammer, the last nock-nock-nock of a hammer…

*

The next day, Lou and I take the oldest boy Taylor to his baseball game, the regimen strict and tidy as his shiny uniform, his new titanium bat. A couple of beat-up Japanese cars are parked in the lot, owned, no doubt, by the black umpires from miles away.

Sometimes when I pass one of the myriad sporting events this area prides itself on—soccer, swimming, whatever—all the tinted-window SUVs are black, looking like a Presidential security unit guards the perimeter of the event. Today the SUVs—Escalades, Yukons, Suburbans—lined up are white, appearing like a row of ambulances. Yes, I think these children should be saved. Saved from their neurotic over-reaching parents, from the endless scheduled events, the tutors, teams, parties and play dates planned down to the minute. From the constant shuttling about.

Lou and I stay for this game. While I read on the top rung of the stands, he plays in the dirt in front of the bleachers with a couple of small kids. They've gravitated together like molecules, morphing automatically. Was I ever like that?

The moms and dads shout wildly. "Good eye!"… "Nice cut,"… "Way to go!" They scream, "Go Devon!" stomping their feet, shaking my book. "Nice play, York!" I find myself wondering if Manchester is next at bat… or perchance Stratford-on-Avon.

The ruckus—and the niggling notion that no one is calling Taylor's name—causes me to stop reading and watch. I see him come up to bat and actually hit the ball on his third swing. He runs to first base, safe, so I yell a meek "yea!" He's been bemoaning his lack of scoring a run, so when he runs to second base, I'm sitting forward, rooting for him.

What's the score?' I ask and someone says "1 to 0, them." Not sure who *them* is, who's side I'm sitting on, who these strangely engrossed parents are, I ask, "The ones in blue?" A woman frowns. "The *Giants*." Oh, "them" is not Taylor's team. I know little about baseball, although as a child I watched the occasional Red Sox game with my dad. (TV-wise, he preferred fuzzy black and white re-runs of "Bullwinkle," where he took childish delight in the bumbling Russian spy Boris and his slinky sidekick Natasha.)

So Taylor's on the losing team with a chance to score. On the next play, another hit, he slogs to third, and I watch him almost get tagged. I hop up and shout, "*You can run faster than that*!" A bunch of blond heads with oversized bug-eyed sunglasses pivot my way. "I've seen him," I say defensively to the Google-eyed crowd. Sitting, I mumble, "Good eye." Whatever that means.

As we wait for the next pitch I'm talking under my breath, *pretend your sister's chasing you, get the lead out*! When he runs for home on the next hit, I jump up. He scores and when I yell, "You did it! You did it!" he looks my way with a smile that suddenly makes me want to weep. His mom should be here.

What I didn't know was that the tie score causes the game to run longer…I plunk on the cheesy hollow metal bench and truly want to weep.

When we return home from the game, Cleo, evidently responding to my phoned plea for adult company, is parked in front. Yes! A grown-up to talk to instead of just Troy, who's dropped by with painters and an electrician, easy-going types who typically talk more than work. I should hire Steffen to paint or fix things but that's obviously out of the question.

As Taylor's sisters, no doubt lurking at their window until our arrival, race toward my house, Cleo steps out of her Corvette wearing heels, shorts, and a denim halter-top.

"Wow. Young crowd," she says.

I wipe my brow. "I'm exhausted."

Inside, she nods around the packed family room where they've automatically settled in: Lou lying on the floor with Coco nestled into his neck, the others sitting Indian-style before the unduly loud TV. "What's with this?" Bags of microwave popcorn and foiled juice packets litter the coffee table, pillows lie on the floor, crumbs and dust bunnies proliferate.

I say, "Funny, huh? Instant family."

"Looks like an invasion." She pauses, "Of your privacy." She contemplates the domestic disorder. "This is *so* not you."

"I'm just taking care of Lou for a bit and it's actually easier with the neighbor kids." Being an only child, I never knew how much kids occupy each other. It makes me better understand Meredith's desire to adopt, not to mention her housekeeping woes.

"That's what I was wondering. Why're *you* taking care of Lou?"

As we enter the kitchen, I dump some kid drinks and Cheetos on the table, too tired to play hostess by preparing coffee. I explain that Meredith didn't have a sitter. "Even the grandparents are off somewhere."

She eyeballs my place. "So where are those cute guys?" I'm evasive, saying that the Finns are traveling for the weekend. No way am I telling her that Paavo and Meredith happen to be at the same conference.

Switching gears, she asks if I've told Meredith about the kiss with Steffen. "*Shh*," I say, peeking into the family room at Lou, who's blissfully drugged by a cartoon his mom doesn't let him watch. I mumble that Mere and I are "good" and jump to a subject I know will distract her: my interest in Paavo. I recount the whole night with Ryan, the coming home to naked men, the intimate consolation of Paavo's hug. After she stopped chortling, she got serious, "The thing *is* is he could've just been trying to cheer you up. You know, like a friend." Had I detected the same note of skepticism in Meredith when she asked at one point, after our car ride, "You don't suppose Paavo's just a flirt, do you?" But nothing in his interactions with me has suggested that. He's been nothing but sincere…

Stuffing more Cheetos in my mouth, I stop and exhale at Cleo, orange dust flying out my nose. "No. I'm pretty sure—pretty much definitely sure our connection goes beyond mere friendship."

"Yeah, well, it wouldn't be the first time you were a little "off" in the romance department. Remember when we worked at Sam-Son and you were convinced that Polish contractor was crazy about you?"

Not something I choose to think about. "Sort of. Anyway, that was a long time ago. I was like twenty." An exaggeration. "So?"

"So you had this enormous crush on the guy but you didn't tell any of us—what was his name? Igneous? Sedimentary?" She chuckles.

"*Ignacy.*"

"Whatever. Anyone could've told you he asked practically every woman there to marry him."

"So he needed papers. He was nice."

"My point exactly." She lets a pause hang. "Trust me, kiddo. Even if he is interested, that kid Ryan sounds better than this Paavo. I mean you're going to fall in love with a guy from some country no one's ever heard of and wear mukluks and ride around on reindeer all day?"

This is what I get for opening up to her. "I was looking for real support here."

"OK, OK. The thing *is* is that long-distance just doesn't work. He lives there, you live here. Won't work. *I know*. Stick with *the locals*."

The locals, humph. I suck the life out of a foil packet of sugar water. "Dating any Folsom inmates yet?"

She ignores me. "Besides, I thought you had a rule against dating doctors."

"He's different. Caring. Interested in all those alternative healing things, like Mere."

She raises her brows. "Like Meredith? Just hope she doesn't steal another guy from you."

With a glance around the corner at the drowsing Lou and the TV-comatose kids, I counter, "Meredith never stole anyone." I push the junk food away.

She throws up her hands in retreat, "I know, I know, you introduced her to Steffen. But did you really expect Lou to come along so quickly? I mean, what if you changed your mind?"

Jaw tight, I say, "I never change my mind."

*

Lou and I spend our last day alone, leaving Coco in the neighbors' care. Driving to a park, I crest a hill and see in the distance a long layer of morning fog threading through the western hills like a fluffy boa.

We picnic near a duck pond, where a bird with a tuft that surrounds its face in a cloud of fluff, a white Albert Einstein hairdo, paddles close to us. Plain females swim past, trailed by ducklings, while the colorful males preen, their iridescent blue-green heads reflecting light. They draw attention the way blond, blue-eyed Steffen does, as if he were on display. Can't say I'm sorry to be done with *that.* Too many aspects of him made me uncomfortable. Paavo, now, is much more my style, attractive in his understated way. And I feel calm and at ease in his presence.

As I feel now, watching the swans glide by. When I'm away from the more obsessive adults, this area grows on me: the fat bellied geese flying north, red-tailed hawks circling overhead, cows grazing with their young sidled up. After the pond and ice cream, we walk to the post office to collect the mail, startling a deer and its baby. They stand as still as statuary, their large rabbit-like ears held high in alert, the mother positioned in front her young. I shush Lou and pull him along. Their eyes remain fixed on us as we pass, they twitch not a muscle, and when I turn my head to look back, I catch them swiftly leaping over a hedge.

That night, bushed from three days of running around, the constant demands for drink and food, from picking up the detritus of fun, I snuggle into bed beside Lou, kiss his angelic cheek, and fall fast asleep to the signature sleigh bells of chirping crickets. Then Lou leaves, and Christmas is over.

~Rakkaudesta se hevonenkin potkii.~
~Even a horse will kick out of love.~

Pheromones

During the week before my party, I feverishly shuffle Jukka and Paavo to various Bay Area spots—the city, the mountains, beaches—while taking ever more medication as my headache spell becomes worse. But they're still manageable, even though the oxygen tanks haven't arrived, which is nothing new, as each year I'm required to make several phone calls to get them actually delivered. And I'd rather not drag a tank down onto the sand, anyway.

Paavo and I have limited time alone, due to the lively, garrulous Jukka, but I begin to enjoy my cousin's company—especially at the beach, where he acts as frisky as Coco, dashing in and out of the freezing waves. It could be my meds, but in general he acts more enthusiastic and adorably silly than the taciturn Paavo during our ventures. And he seems to be drinking less.

One day, jumping the frigid waves with Jukka and the dog, I pause to catch my breath and watch Paavo. He sits pensively on the rocks above us, arms about his knees, cutting a fine, contemplative figure. A quiet Finn surveying the landscape, lost in thought. I'm reminded of my professorial father. Although bothered that Paavo won't join us, I admire his stance, his quiet intellectualism. When Jukka chases Coco down the beach, I scale the rocks to Paavo. Panting, I ask what's on his mind.

He lowers his sun-kissed face toward his bent knees. "My own thoughts," he says.

I sit beside him. "Can I ask?" I press, wanting to know him

better, learn what philosophical or artistic ideas the sea and surf provoke in this introspective man.

"To be honestly, I was thinking it has been long time since I have been with the woman."

Whoa, maybe not so highbrow after all…the next question that pops to mind is, *Can I help?* But as I consider asking just *how long since you've 'been with'* one, we're interrupted by Jukka, who trumpets up to us that he's hungry. To my dismay, Paavo readily jumps up in agreement and we prepare to leave.

When Jukka tells me he's dropping Paavo off at Stanford for a final eye check Thursday, I plan to stay home and clean. The party's two days away. But then Jukka says he wishes he could rent a motorcycle for a long day, whooping, "Harley hogs rock!" I gladly offer to pick up Paavo, envisioning an evening alone with him. Now, on the drive to the South Bay, breezing against the late afternoon traffic, I grow giddy with the idea.

As I pass the exit for Casa Loca, my mood briefly dampens as I rehash my last encounter with Steffen. He came to Mercury to pick up Lou—our first meeting since the kiss. Lou was wild and clingy upon Steffen's arrival, leaving me to busy myself packing his immoderate amount of gear—you'd think Meredith wasn't planning on returning! Then the girls next door extracted the reluctant child from his father's arms to play with him one last time.

"Uh, is your nose all right?" I asked, handing over Lou's backpack, though I could see it looked fine—long and narrow, the showpiece of his handsome face.

He flipped the backpack into his truck. "At some point it ran out of blood."

"Sorry about that, I—" He put up his hand to stop me. There'd been a mishap that unlucky night when I realized I was kissing my best friend's man with particular gusto. In a swift but ungraceful motion, I pushed him away and jerked my elbow into his proboscis. All I recall is blood leaking through his hand, a look of pain and anger, and the car door abruptly slamming.

We talked at cross-purposes as I tried to clear the air. Eyes fixed on the kids in the next yard, he said, distantly, "We really appreciate your helping out with Lou." *Steffen, I would never do that again.* "And taking the dog, to boot. Many thanks." *I'm really sorry.* He reached for his pocket. "Let us give you some money." *Can we just forget it and move on?*

Then the kids rushed over. Little Riley, struggling to grip the wriggling dog, nearly her size, pleaded with me. "Why does Lou have to go?"

"His mommy and daddy are back."

She pouted, "Why do they have to take Coco?"

"Because." My answer made me melancholy, already feeling the lack of their vitality. "But she can come back anytime. In fact..." I spontaneously grabbed the dog from her. "I think this is a perfect yard for her," I turned to Steffen. "For now. That is, if it's still OK?" Adding to my argument, I said, "Meredith did bring Coco here to give to me." I clung to the wriggling pup like a life preserver. Steffen's blue eyes bored into me. "*What*?" I asked. "You're doing that thing, that artist stare, like I'm a still-life you're dissecting."

"Would you please tell me why every time I see you your hair's a different color?"

Argh. Three meetings with him of late and three hair colors: first red, then black, now I'm, what, blond-ish. "Oh, you know. Mercurial me!" Meant as a light joke, as I used to call Steffen "mercurial." Lively and unpredictable, I never liked the sound of the word, too much volatility, potential for combustibility. "I live in Mercury, get it?"

He continued his contemplation of me. "I think you are changing." I'm not sure what he meant, if good or bad. Not sure I wanted to know.

"Can Coco stay? Can she can she can she?" the young Greek

chorus chimed.

"I suppose. For now," Steffen said. He nuzzled Lou to assuage him and I assured him he'd see Coco more up here than at his grandparents'. Saying this helped me accept Lou's departure, which now seemed irrationally cheerless, given my fatigue.

After I squeezed Lou and he was tucked inside, I whispered to Steffen, "I told Meredith all about it."

"Of course you did." For some reason I wanted to hug Steffen, his affect was so *not* him, so subdued, his mouth too downcast.

"On a happier note, and I know this is weird coming from me, I'm throwing a party on the summer solstice. This Saturday. All-night bonfire, rite of summer, pagan thing. For the Finns. It'll be fun. You're coming with Meredith, right?"

The engine cranked on. "I'm sure she's planning on it. It seems she's been 'utterly transformed' by this conference. Wants to compare notes with your cousin Paavo."

"He's not my cous—"

"She's quite taken with your Paavo."

Huh? Quite taken? The truck rolled away. Could Cleo be right? Is '*my*' Paavo becoming '*her*' Paavo?

*

The eye doctor's receptionist, a middle-aged Indian wearing an unfortunate yellow smock sprinkled with cartoonish birds, butterflies, and flowers, a roll of fat around her neck like a tan scarf, says Paavo's with the doctor. I sit, thinking how much prettier she'd be in a rich, jewel-toned sari; wonder if there's money in creating fashionable medical smocks, if that's not an oxymoron.

I glance around the vacant waiting room. A dozen empty, plum-colored chairs with curved oak arms line the room in a U-shape. A few intermittent low tables hold rumpled golf and tennis magazines. The only unusual sight is a jar full of abandoned eyeglasses on the front counter, left by patients who—I suppose—now see perfectly. Sitting down, I push my own glasses up my nose. Perhaps I'll book an appointment. I check my face in a pocket mirror, then wait, fingers twisting. I want to remember how Paavo and I felt together. This talk of Meredith and him has thrown me off.

Growing peevish as the time approaches 5:30, I begin to suspect the two friends are back there chugging beers. As if reading my mind, the receptionist says, "He should be right out, dear." At this hour we'll be mired in traffic, but that could be good. I might suggest we stop for dinner.

A white-coated, lanky man with a receding hairline lopes into the room. He looks at me, puzzled, then breaks into a smile and extends his hand, introducing himself as John. "You must be here for Paavo. He and I go way back. I actually met him while studying in Finland." After saying that he met his wife there, he pauses, appraising me. "Is it Mary? Paavo mentioned a young lady near here."

"Alina," I say. "And not so near, really, I'm in the Northeast Bay." I fling my arm out. "Way out. Near Blaineville."

"Oh, I've got a buddy out there. Cool old town."

"You think?" I suppose what's left of the old western downtown has its charm.

"But I could've sworn Paavo said you lived not far from here."

"I moved."

"Oh, so that's it." Wow, Paavo's been talking about me! Now that's a sign. "Well, he has an eye for the pretty girls," he smiles. Leaving me uneasy from the plural, he hands a folder to the receptionist, then departs with a "nice to meet you." Before I can mull over "pretty *girls*," Paavo appears. I jump up, first noticing his eyes: clear and bright, beaming like beacons, and I'm a moth.

"It is nice for you to come to me, Alina. Sorry about so long. John is my friend for quite some time and we have had to chit and chat." He holds out his arm for us to exit. When I ask, he says his eyes are fine, 20/20. To me, his smiling eyes look kissable.

The receptionist dims the lights and presses us through the door, but Paavo halts. "I'm forgetting something." He digs in his pockets, then looks about with knit brows. The woman, holding her purse, shifts her heft, her neck fat jiggling.

Paavo walks over to probe the crease of a chair. Puzzled, I tell him, "That's where *I sat.* What're you looking for?" He kneels to peer beneath it, and then rises, holding his eyeglasses aloft. "These." He proceeds to drop them in the jar. "This time I leave them here."

"It's a sign you'll return! My mother told me if you leave something behind, you'll come back."

"Come back? My eyes is fixed now."

"But you'll come back to the States." I grin. Then my mind flits to the magazine article I read; the study where women actually *smell* men they're attracted to, unconsciously detecting their pheromones by sitting in chairs with their scents. I sat in Paavo's seat for a reason! Suddenly emboldened, I add, "Maybe you'll come to see me." I exclaim, "So many signs!" The two turn to my frenetic face as if to a madwoman. And though the exasperated receptionist shakes her head, I hug her, press my cheek to her sweet, fleshy neck.

*

That night I dream of Dad. Perhaps because I thought I saw him the other day while walking to the post office, his head typically bent in thought, a fisherman's cap shading his eyes. My heart suddenly quickened and I sped up. But he turned, and I saw the face of a stranger. I hastened home, unseeing, with my un-mailed letters.

At the beginning of the dream, we're in the hospital. Dad is very sick. But as the dream progresses, we realize that his skin is no longer orange, the whites of his eyes, previously the color of soft butter, become clear again and sparkle as they did when he teased my mom. By the end of the dream we realize that of course he's in the wrong place, he's going to live, we have to get him out of the hospital.

This same scenario often plays out with my dream Mom: at first she's stricken, half-paralyzed and silent. Then words trickle out, then sentences, and at last we're talking and laughing as in the old days. She's no longer trapped in her broken body. I'm gadding about with her like the other women my age here, those I see at cafes and in stores, browsing housewares or clothing, having lunch.

This morning my dream ends as it often does. I tell Dad, "I miss you," the words clotting in the back of my throat, not coming out clear enough for him to hear. We reach out to one another, we strain, yearning to hug. And just as we come achingly close, I wake up.

Head afire, I snort sprays, swallow pills, and rest. When the head pain subsides, tired, I stay under the covers. Staring at the ceiling, I contemplate my dreams, why I never get to the point of actually embracing my parents. Maybe it's too much for the psyche. Like how I never die in my dreams, the feeling is too powerful, too overwhelming; I wake before the impact of a sky fall, or before a killer throttles me. And I never get to hold and be held by my dead parents. My dreams cannot bear such emotional weight.

I grog dolefully into the kitchen to find Jukka and Paavo at the laptop with the Russian certificate. Paavo surprises me with some information. "I cannot say the year exactly right. It is 1933 or 1938, this print is very vague. But what I see is that you have some official paper—looks like country village, not a big city. And this person has the name…"

"You are not going to be believing this!" Jukka interjects with excessive enthusiasm and a mischievous grin. When I question Paavo, glancing down at the perplexing letters, he says, "Alina Eskala."

"Yes? So tell me, already!" I shake his arm. These guys truly are "teasing."

"That is the name in this paper. *Your* name."

~Puhuen asiat selkenevät.~
~Through talking things will be solved.~
~Puhumatta paras.~
~Best not to talk.~

Caffeine Spa

Meredith, Cleo and I lie in the backyard slathered in coffee grounds. Evidently, they are good for more than just brewing. Sealed in plastic wrap, we lie like mummies on large beach towels, Cleo in the middle, our faces to the afternoon sun. Tickly, oily coffee grounds coat our thighs, bellies, and for some reason, Cleo's face and chest. We wear only our underwear, although Meredith and I have covered our breasts with modest hand towels.

Preparations for tomorrow night's bash are complete: everyone's been invited, the food cooked, the keg of beer arranged—a bit much given the guest list, but Jukka couldn't resist the bargain—the house aired and clean. Jukka and Paavo cleared an area for the bonfire this morning, then took off for the city and a tour of Alcatraz, tickets purchased weeks before their arrival.

Before agreeing to Cleo's silly beauty treatment, I read the "recipe" she cut from a women's magazine:

One-half cup warm used grounds with one T olive oil.
(We quadrupled the recipe.)
Stand on newspaper and apply to cellulite areas.
(Much of it fell onto the paper.)
Wrap areas in plastic wrap and lay in sun.
("Areas" meaning our bodies.)
After, remove wrap, brush off excess coffee mixture. Shower. (No kidding!)

When we began, I wrinkled my nose, "If this is for cellulite, how come you're putting it on your face?"

Cleo said, "Just in case. Might firm everything, never know." She wiped flecks from under her nose and sneezed. When I told her I don't have cellulite, she pointed me to a mirror, where I twisted in the bathroom's uncongenial fluorescent light to see dimples just below my panty line.

"Mirrors are over-rated," I muttered and went along with it, game because I'm zooey from fatigue and daily headache medicines, and grateful for the help and company of my friends. And projecting that I might take sauna with Paavo some day.

As we bake in the sun, glazed and itchy, a strange hot wind blows; last night I heard it, went to the window as it waltzed in, swaying and swishing the treetops. A desert wind from the East, channeling up the Central Valley, careening West, a gale that doesn't cool but rushes in warm. Like offshoots of the Santa Ana winds, though I know those Southern gusts blow later in the year. They make the skin on my arms crawl, put me off kilter. The breeze stirs things up, dried eucalyptus leaves crackle and rattle, skitter across the deck. Some small tree branches fell during the night. Our towels lie atop a thick blanket of fallen pine needles, soft as a bed. The persistent blowing calls like a siren, stirring up dormant emotions, seeming to call to me, "What's next?"

These odd thoughts, the general feeling I have of being "off," are propagated, I know, from the accumulation of Imitrex injections, painkillers, stomach acid relievers, by now all creating a sort of fugue state that will last until my headaches dwindle in frequency and then, as randomly as they began, will stop for a year. These are the desperate days, when my mind floats outside my body, when I lose control of my thoughts and limbs; drinking glasses slip from my hands and shatter on the floor, my feet trip over small warps in the floorboards and I stare at them in wonder. I'm altogether disembodied and disconnected, and I hate it.

I had hoped to get away without the oxygen tanks until after the party—where to put them?—but I've had to call for delivery. They should arrive early tomorrow, and I'll stash them out of sight until after the festivities, away from visitors and their inquiring eyes.

Cleo brought champagne and she and Meredith grow giggly. I cannot drink a drop of alcohol until my cluster headache spell passes, but my morning meds have me feeling light-headed enough.

"Ali, I haven't really had time to thank you for last weekend. Lou loved being with you."

"He really missed you," I answer, eyes shut to the sun.

"But you were wonderful. I guess Auntie Ali won't make such a bad mom after all?"

"Who knows. I'm beginning to think I should go to Russia with you to adopt if I'm ever going to have kids."

"Oh, no. Sounds like you've got a prospect," she says.

I rise to get more champagne for them. As I pad to the deck for the chilled bottle, I'm itching—literally now as I swipe grounds off my calves—to tell her everything about Paavo: how we almost kissed at Bridal Veil falls, his mentioning Finland, his concerns for my health, and now the certificate revelation. And of course the recent pheromone phenomenon. But Cleo's presence prevents me. I don't want to reprise the Darda incident, where everything gets blown out of proportion and turned into a clown show. I need to be alone with Meredith, one-on-one.

I refill their plastic flutes, placing them carefully on patches of barren ground, once again bothered by the state of the yard—recently mowed by Taylor only to have it windblown and messy again. I'm eager to institute Troy's plan to carpet the yard with fresh sod. "That's next," he said. "It's the last step before we 'Wow Mercury with our stunning property!'" Now that the house looks better, the rooms painted a warm golden color, I feel differently, am viewing the place in a new light, thinking of possible improvements, its overall potential.

Sitting on my towel, I say, "Paavo is very open to your Eastern healing, Mere. He wants to learn it to help me." I emphasize the "me," for some reason. I clear my throat. "Did you, uh, run into him at the Reiki conference?"

"Oh, yeah," she says casually. "We were all one big family there. I mean, everyone got to know everyone." I swipe coffee grounds from my knees. Family? What does that mean? Close in a fraternal way? She continues, "Steffen used to scoff at Reiki, but I think Paavo is quite spiritual."

Cleo blurts, "He's quite *hot* from what I hear." She jabs my arm. A grin lights Meredith's face.

"I think this plastic wrap is melting," I say, the clinging cellophane claws at my skin. "This has got to be the goofiest thing I've ever done." A hawk circles overhead, showing glimpses of flashing red. The moon is a thin communion wafer in the cloudless sky.

Cleo says, "It's best if you do this treatment twice a week." Meredith and I snort. As if! Grounds fall from Cleo's arms into her glass, as the two sit up to drink.

"Back to men," Meredith says, obviously getting tipsy, as that is Cleo's line, "What made you think Jukka and Paavo were gay when you met them? You seem to have changed your mind."

"Yeah, guess I jumped to that conclusion a bit too fast."

"Not the first time," says Cleo, and they both guffaw. I'm not sure I like it when they're an ensemble.

Meredith leans forward to see me around Cleo. "So, how's it going, Ali? Tell us about Paavo. Are you in that crazy, fluttery love phase?" She sighs. "God, that is definitely the best time." She drinks. "Goes downhill from there." Cleo chimes "Amen."

Feeling prickly from the coarse grounds, I say, "Well, we're taking it slowly. That's the good thing, see? I think that's how real love works. Like you're friends first, then comes the love part. Not the other way around."

"You're saying you don't want to jump his bones?" Cleo says.

"But you're feeling that intense spark, right?…mmmm."

Spark? "No. Yes. I mean, I think it's more like…" What? Like a few flickers? A couple of damp sticks rubbed together that hasn't quite lit? "Paavo's been a great comfort to me. It's been nice."

"Nice!" They both laugh. I lie down and, after slurping more champagne, they follow suit.

Meredith sighs to the sun. "I guess we all project."

"I'm *not* projecting. It's real."

"Ali, I was thinking more of me. And Steffen." She props herself on her elbows. "So how do you feel? All bubbly around him?" Meredith persists. I wish I could drown myself in some of that bubbly they're guzzling.

"All horny around him?" Cleo insists.

"I'm definitely attracted—of course!" Geesh. The wind blows, coffee grounds irritate my face, I itch my nose. How do I feel? "I guess I think he's the one…the one who'll work out for me. Maybe the one I'm meant to be with." I feel a bit silly saying that.

"You should definitely be *doing it* by now, kiddo. You haven't partied since, like, 1999."

"I've already made that mistake." I glance at Meredith. "Much as I'd like to be with him, I think it's best to know him first. He's really been affectionate and…admiring." I feel as though I'm trying to prove something. "He called me 'strong.'"

Cleo laughs. "What, he wants someone to do the heavy lifting?" I poke her hard.

"Timing is everything," Meredith sighs. "I've figured out that who you end up with is 99 percent timing."

I wonder if it *is* all timing and if so, what does that mean? That Mr. Right is just a biologically-arranged marriage? And is that any more successful than a parentally-arranged one? "If my parents were alive, they'd approve of Paavo."

"I thought they approved of Steffen." What a mixer, as

Steffen used to say. Cleo's certainly stirring things up!

"Shut up," Meredith says, while I say, "Why bring him up?" This beauty treatment's turning ugly.

She ignores us. "Uh, duh. Because he's like, the last *real-world* relationship you had?"

"For your information, Paavo and I have something real. We've had all sorts of close encounters that tell me he's right."

"*Close encounters*?" I know Cleo's goading tone.

I squirm, tired of this prosecution, try to think through the fog of chemicals in my brain. "OK, for your information, I had this amazing experience." I tell them of the study that shows women can sense when they're attracted to a mate, how I detected Paavo's pheromones at the eye doctor's.

Cleo says, "Oh, close encounters of the *weird* kind." She smirks at Meredith, who loyally keeps a straight face.

"Seriously. In that whole room, I sat where *he* sat. I smelled his chair."

"You sniffed his seat? His *bottom*! Meredith's mutt must be rubbing off on you."

I have an urge to splash champagne onto Cleo's coffee-covered face, but Meredith reaches her arm across Cleo's nude body to feel for my hand. She squeezes it tight. "I so want you to be happy, Ali. You deserve it." She hiccups.

Cleo says, "Could you guys get your hands off my tits?" We let go our clasp with a shriek. But eager to escape the subject of Paavo to focus on her, I fixate on Cleo's enormous fake breasts, which don't flop to the sides like ours, but stick up, solid and firm. A bit brazen from my meds, I say, "I wonder what they feel like."

Meredith slurs, "What *what* feel like?"

With my forefinger, I poke the side of Cleo's rubbery, firm breast. "Those. Cleo's boobs."

Meredith, very modest in the chest department, presses her hand towel to her breast. "Yeah, I'd like to know too." She drinks more. Cleo says, "Go ahead. Feel them."

Meredith and I look at each other, grin. I poke again, feel the firm flesh spring. Meredith prods the other side. "They're like rubber balls," she says.

I say, "Like over-filled water balloons."

Cleo smiles too. "Go ahead. Really feel them." Meredith tickles Cleo under the armpit and I jab her in the ribs. She squeals and before you know it we're rolling on top of her, breast on breast on breast, hers solid and unyielding, ours pliant, soft skin on flesh, rolling and laughing, plastic wrap unraveling, bitter coffee grounds dropping into our wild, giggling mouths. From inside the house, Coco barks at the commotion. Wrestling and toppling, spilling champagne, Cleo retaliates by ripping off our Saran Wrap.

"Mud wrestling! Awesome!" a male voice stuns us. Shocked, we stop, reach for our towels. Ten yards away, Troy stands near the corner of the house.

"Jesus, Troy!" I grasp my towel tight as Meredith twists her torso away from him. "I thought you weren't working today."

"Figured I'd bring Joe here to inspect for termites…" his voice trails off as I spot a grizzled head pop around the corner next to Troy. Grizzly Adams quickly disappears from view. Troy's a statue, however, as Cleo glances up at him then falls back on her towel, bare breasts to the open air.

"Not a good time," I call to him. He doesn't answer, but stares openly, transfixed. "*Troy*!" I exclaim. I turn to Cleo, unselfconsciously exposed, her great mounds covered as if in volcanic ash, topped by the little fires of her nipples, erect and greeting the wind…

~Maasta se pienikin ponnistaa.~
~Even the smallest will take off the ground.~

Juhannus

Throwing a party has always seemed such a foolhardy thing to do. But it's happening, and despite the daily cluster pain which now, at its peak, randomly strikes as often as three times a day, and despite my fears that all will be a bust, my excitement grows.

"*Juhannusyö* is the magic night," says Jukka, the morning of the party, as he and Paavo lay twigs and stack logs, surround the fire pit with large stones. He tells me that after staying up during the nightless night with drink and family and friends, "Young women can put flowers under the pillow to see the man in their dreams."

"You mean the man *of* their dreams?" I ask.

"What is this difference? You are going to see him while you're sleeping."

"But we're staying *up* all night…" I say, when Paavo interjects from his squat, twigs in hand, "This is some old nonsense."

Jukka says, "You must put seven flowers. Then you see who's gonna be your husband. But I'm not so sure most women get the dream man," he snorts. "Or look into some kind of a well or lake and you may see this man's….picture there."

"Reflection," Paavo corrects him, having difficulty with the word. Call me superstitious or a romantic, but I glance around the arid, windblown yard for any sign of wildflowers. "Will store-bought flowers do?"

I look away from their inquisitive eyes. "I mean, theoretically. I like myths. Can they be any old flower?" Paavo shrugs, evidently not putting much store in this Finnish fairy tale, while Jukka adds,

"I have heard my *mummi* say that go to run naked in some rye field or such and also you might see your so-to-be. This is night for—" he asks something of Paavo in Finnish.

Paavo pauses, frowns. "Fruityness," he says.

Jukka laughs. "You are fruity." He points at his crotch—déjà vu for me—"It's the time when the woman are getting..."

"Laid?" It just popped out.

"Fertility," says Paavo. "This is the word."

I'm not sure I know of any local rye fields, nor do I plan to cavort nude tonight, but fruity I am, and my 'so-to-be' might just be standing before me, now with his strong back turned, muscles straining through his t-shirt, balancing a tepee of long thick logs. "*Ruista ranteessa*," Dad would say of him. A strong man, one with rye in his wrist.

He wipes a sweat-beaded brow and, hands on hips, shakes his head at the logs. "Enough now of such stories. *Juhannus* is to celebrate the long light of summer. The sun is staying up round the clock in Finland. This fire shows that," he pauses for a word, "*symbol* of light and sun from olden times, that's all." Right. *There's no magic.* And yet I have a strong feeling that tonight something memorable will occur.

Turning to me, Paavo says, "You are the funny girl. Finland is very advanced society but you like to learn these strange old things." He's got me right. All my life I've heard of Finland's remarkable feats: from a country of peasants to a high-tech society of "firsts." First European country in women's suffrage, foremost in education and literacy, only country to repay war debts—Dad's list plays on in my head. But these facts interest me less than the mixed origins, the old myths, the *sisu* that lies at the heart of the Finnish character.

Frowning again, he says something to Jukka in Finnish. They look down at the shallow pit in which the logs lay grounded, situated in the clearing off the deck. The large space where the kids played ball, the area my parents surmised was used for a pasture or garden at one point—a few saplings here and there, but the best spot for the fire pit because the farther yard is too full of huge old trees. The long reaching branches of the heritage oak are far enough off. Paavo eyes the nearby carriage house. "We usually are going to celebrate at our *moekkis*. Fire should be on or near to water."

"But it's gonna be OK if we keep this fire small," says Jukka.

Paavo inhales a sigh, then suddenly seems startled by my appearance. "Alina, you have worked too hard with cleaning and the cooking. You are tired. Go now to rest. I don't know how you do with these headaches." He shakes his head. "You are like strong Finnish woman." Focusing on the latter comment, I beam.

Leaving them to perfect the fire pit, I return inside to research this flower thing. I need all the mojo I can get to woo Paavo tonight, and preparations for the party are complete. The house is scrubbed, vacuumed, spotless; my mother Lempi would be proud. The smell of summer roses infuses the air, thick sausages sit ready to roast, bottles of vodka chill in the freezer. Although the party will be relatively small, Jukka insisted on ordering a half-keg of beer, wanting "not to be running out."

I lay the table: tiny Swedish meatballs, cheeses—including Havarti, of course—rye and sourdough breads, tomatoes, cucumbers, cold cuts, a creamy potato salad with plenty of dill. I sniff my braided loaves of *pulla,* the homey scent of sweet egg-bread. I've even prepared a creamy *kalalautanen* casserole of potatoes and salmon, my father's favorite, and Karelian pasties, adding extra butter to the yummy meat and rice pies. I squinted at the yellowed pages of Mom's old cookbook for *lehtujas,* a crepe filled with local blackberry jam, instead of the hard-to-find lingonberry.

Everyone who's coming has offered to bring drinks or an appetizer—which means we'll basically have enough food for the compulsory Finnish army. I'm looking forward to the party here in my home, to the chance, on this mid-summer night, to reveal my feelings to Paavo. Now this myth about the enchantment of the night has my stomach fluttering, though I can't rule out the possibility of acid reflux.

When I Google Finnish *Juhannus*, Wikipedia says that originally it was the summer solstice festivity called *Ukon juhla*, the bonfire of *Ukko*, god of sky, thunder, crops and all things natural, the equivalent of Zeus. After the celebrations were Christianized, the holiday became *Juhannus,* after John the Baptist. I read about the bonfires, the *kokko*, usually burned at lakesides or the sea—ha, no luck there!—and that one can plant two birch saplings, *koivu*, to flank the front door for welcoming visitors. I don't have time for tree planting, but I can search for the flowers for my true love.

I find the only clumps of flowers left in my parents' yard, yellow globe lilies hiding amongst the tall weeds under the pines. My mother called them fairy lanterns, drooping, egg-shaped, and deep yellow, some already shriveled. I find a few fresh clusters and count seven, then nine to be sure, and run into the house to place them carefully under my pillow.

While the Finns go out for the beer, I shower, choose a diaphanous spring-green blouse to wear with my best-fitting jeans. The top with my suntan and lightened hair all bring out the blue in my grey eyes; but clear lines of fatigue surround them. With headache season at its apex—or nadir—I haven't slept well in days.

Exhausted but full of nervous energy, I lie down, pick up Troy's book, *Historical Mercury,* and leaf through a montage of black-and-white photos depicting a time when an electric train brought chilled San Franciscans into the hot heart of Mercury. Ladies in long dresses and gents in hats sit on horse-drawn buggies, others ride in cars with tall skinny tires and headlights like bulging eyes; horses race around a track, white dirt flying, and cocky gamblers play cards with cigars angled sideways from their mouths. A picture of a swimming hole with boys and girls on a dock catches my interest. I see that a ranch's cattle trough was deepened and widened to create a small lake. My eyes droop as I draw some conclusion, a happy revelation about the place, but before I can nail it down, I drift to sleep to the lowing of cows returning home from the hills.

I awaken to an insistent knock with a fresh realization about the house. Sitting up, I rub the grit from my eyes and adjust them to the early evening light.

~*Seura tekee kaltaisekseen.*~
~The company makes one alike.~

Tanks

Ryan has parked his bicycle by the front steps. I sigh. I bet the guy can't recall his mother's birthday but he remembered this? That forced invitation on our grievous date?

"Hey," I tighten my ponytail, let him enter. Cute but annoying young Ryan in his plaid shorts and Hurley t-shirt, red-rimmed eyes, dark curls springing out from under a blue knit cap. It seems Jukka and Paavo are still off on their keg run, and it makes me wonder if they're siphoning some of it beforehand. Before I can offer him a drink, Ryan draws me to the parlor window. "Dude! There's a nursing home truck here."

I draw aside the sheer curtains. Oh God. *Great timing.* "That's not a nursing home truck. It's Aria Healthcare. It's here for *me*," I say, which makes his eyes grow large, his pot-dilated pupils ready to explode.

"For you?" he looks at me as if I'm 89, like I just stepped one foot into the grave.

"I get *headaches*," I say defensively, turning to the knock at the front door. A young Filipino with a clipboard stands at my door saying he has my delivery. Of course this has to happen now, as my party begins, in front of *Ryan.* I tell the man to bring it in, wishing Ryan would vaporize.

"Don't you want something to drink?" I point him toward the kitchen, but he just stands there, mouth open, evidently in awe. I tap my foot until the delivery guy comes with a dolly holding a large metal box the size of a coffee table.

"Here's your concentrator." This mistake has been made before.

"I need *tanks*, not a concentrator," I say.

"I've got the tanks too." He turns to get them. Ryan stares, transfixed by the ungainly medical cube.

"Don't! Take this out. Please," I say to the retreating guy in coveralls. "I'm having a party—I have nowhere to put this thing!" I take a breath to calm down. "See, I don't need a steady flow of oxygen—it doesn't even go high enough."

"High enough?" Ryan says, eyebrows raised.

"Yeh yeh," the deliveryman says, but then, "I've got to leave it." He waves flimsy pink and yellow papers, "It's on the order."

"No! The order's wrong! Like I said, I'm having a party and I can't have this here." Parked in the front parlor. "People are coming! This is where I want people to dance. *This is the dance room.*" I hold my hand to my newly throbbing head. "This makes me look like some old invalid." Out of the corner of my eye, Ryan smirks as if to say, "If the orthopedic shoe fits…"

"Yeh yeh. Tell your doctor and we can come on Monday to take it away. I'll go get the tanks." As he walks toward the truck, I tug on my hair, huff, and feel my face grow hot. I call after him, "Do I look like I can't breathe?" mad at the intolerable situation, finding it hard to breath.

In come a dozen E-tanks, two-foot tall metal cylinders painted green on top. Twelve is a lot, but with the severity of this spell, I might just need them. I can't look at Ryan. Last year Meredith took me to Tahoe during a spell of headaches, and I lugged two tanks with me. At hearing this, Cleo laughed, "You brought *oxygen* to the mountains?" I retorted that there is actually *less air* up there, but she was right. It looks ridiculous. What 33-year-old needs air tanks?

Evidently Ryan cannot comprehend this new development, the multiple tanks lined up against the wall like mini-missiles, the huge concentrator in the front room. He rubs his eyes as if he's trying to wake from a pipe dream, which of course he is—the guy's so stoned. His eyes redder than before, he says, "This is pretty trippy. You, like, do that shit?" he points at the tanks. "What's it feel like?"

"*Air*? It feels like *air*." *You breathe, don't you?* I'm losing all patience and affection for this kid.

"So, like, is this for the party? You sniff it?"

"It's not nitrous oxide, Ryan." And I'm not in middle school.

"It's pretty heavy duty, dude," he says to me as I sign off on the papers. He walks off to the kitchen, where I see him open the fridge and grab a bottle of beer.

I look up at the Asian deliveryman. "He called me 'dude,' didn't he?"

"Yeh yeh."

I shout to Ryan, "You should drink coffee!" Then, feeling inordinately pissed at him, I mutter under my breath, "*Before you drive home. Oh yeah, you don't drive. Well bike on home before it gets dark. Don't want you getting hit by a truck. A nursing home truck.* I stop muttering to thrust the clipboard at the Aria man. "He called it a nursing home truck."

"Well we do deliver to a lot of nursing hom—"

"Yeh yeh" I say as I propel him out the door. Marching over to Ryan, feeling the beginning of a tingle in my temple, I say outright, "If you want to smoke pot, forget it. Not here." I proceed to spill the contents of my medications on the kitchen table and take a bite of out an Imitrex pill. I'm aware of his ogle. Pointing at the array of colored pills spread before us, I say, "These are for my headaches. And my stomach."

"Why'd you bite that pill? What is it?"

"It blows up my blood vessels or something and I bit it because insurance gives me nine per month. Guess how many I need?" I fume. "Thirty! *Minimum*."

"Those others looks like Vicodin, dude." I challenge him with my stare. Hands up, he says, "It's just. Don't look like a *drug-free* zone to me. You could O.D. on that shit."

I reply with a childish, "Shut up," which sends him slinking off in the direction of the backyard.

Now to get rid of all these tanks. After stashing two of them in Mom's bedroom in case I get a headache tonight, I carry the rest of the cylinders two by two out to the old carriage house, place them just inside the door, then throw the old blanket on top. Not that any party-goers should wander here, but just to be safe. I prefer to keep my infirmity private. I push the last tanks in when I hear Cleo blurt, "Alina, where are you? Garth, come on out of the car."

I close the garage doors quickly and run around to the front of the house.

Cleo's short black dress scoops to show a splotchy pink, sunburned bosom. Following her in the door is her brother Garth. She throws a sweater onto the concentrator, which sits solidly in the front room parlor. "What's that?"

"A concentrator."

Her face furrows in concentration. "And that would be for…?"

"Oxygen. I don't need it, though. It doesn't work for my headaches. It's for people who can't breathe."

"You invited dead people to this party?' I kick her ankle. Her brother stares at a stack of cards in his hands.

"Hey, Garth," I say to Cleo's brother, who has schizophrenia and generally avoids social occasions. I'm glad he felt comfortable enough to come. Enlisting his help to move the cube to the edge of the sofa, I address Cleo, "Why don't you go find Ryan and see if you can pester him into leaving."

"Oooh, I haven't met your cutie," she totters off, high heels ticking. Garth waits while I find a square of floral fabric, not a tablecloth exactly, more like a scrap from some dress Mom never made. "Kind of a weird boxy coffee table, but at least we can still dance here," I say. He nods, shuffles what look to be baseball cards, and I lead him to the fridge for a Diet Coke, as Jukka and Paavo return with the keg.

~Oma koti kullan kallis.~
~Own home is worth gold.~

Juhannus Juhla (Midsummer Party)

"To our *kaunis* American friend in this beautiful place!" Paavo raises his cup of beer to the bonfire. The heat burns my cheeks as a chorus calls, "To Alina!" An embarrassment of voices. The low sun filters through the magnificent oak that reminds me of my mother, now in full summer leaf, alive—a live oak—spreading its protective canopy over the yard.

With everyone gathered in the dusk around the roaring bonfire—Jukka and Paavo certainly know how to create a flamer—I'm finally relaxing. Surrounded by these people, the leaping flames, the nostalgic smell of wood smoke, and the natural beauty all remind me of camping with my family. The wind still blows, hotter than ever near the fire, rippling through my hair, making me feel free, and happy. This gathering of friends is what I need, what I want.

I count each person—everyone made it except Sri, who bowed out due to family obligations, and the sports-nut parents across the street who talked of early bedtimes due to swim meets. There's Ravi with his ravishing date Valeria, Meredith and Steffen, Jukka throwing twigs onto the fire, Marty and Rebecca with their oldest daughter Maya, Cleo and Garth, Troy, and, alas, still hanging around, Ryan.

Paavo walks around the fire with shadows dancing on his face. Then here he is with his arm around me, the two of us facing the fire. "Thank you very much for this *Juhannus Juhla*, Alina." Flames rise in my face, I smile, but my heart remains at ease. This hug, like the previous embrace we shared, feels more comforting than sexual. A peaceful feeling fills me. Perhaps this is my parents' love, more like a calm lake than the raging fire before us.

"*Hyvä tuuli*," I point at the flames, *good fire*, I say to him, proud of my new effort to learn Finnish.

Paavo says, "'*Tuli*' is the word for fire. You have said, '*tuuli*,'" he stretches the u to make the double vowel sound. "That is the word for wind, *mutta*, but—" again the frown. "I'm thinking we have both *tuli* and *tuuli* now, which is not the good mix." I follow his glance to the nearby trees, the dehydrated lawn. "Anyway, this is *kokko,* bonfire," he corrects me.

"Don't worry so much," Jukka says, listening in. He gulps his drink. "We are staying with the *kokko* all night long."

Briskly shaking each of their hands, Troy says to Jukka and Paavo, "It's a pleasure to meet with Miss Eskala's French relations again." I don't bother correcting him, he's met them a few times in passing and can't seem to fathom "Finnish" and "Finland." Besides, I need to be gentle with him, after the news I just delivered.

We hold *makkara,* sausages, on long sticks near the flames. The meat crackles and sizzles, crunching into the succulent pork is sweet. Unlike my guests, I cannot partake of the vodka being passed nor cups of beer, but I feel merry all the same.

With a glance at Troy, who wears a game face, I clear my throat to make my announcement. Even this small group intimidates me, but I forge ahead. "I'd like to tell everyone my news." All faces turn my way. "I'm staying." I sneak a look at Paavo, knowing he'll approve. "I'm keeping the house." Cheers erupt all around. Troy weakly claps me on the back—I'd told him first, paying him too generously for his time spent "working" on the place. To his credit, he quickly adapted and regained a positive demeanor. "I assume you'll be meeting some very *well-off* people in this neighborhood," he said, and I allowed that I'd refer him as often as possible.

Rebecca trots over to squeeze my hand. Her complexion, too, glows pink in the light, and her hair, smoothed into golden ringlets, frames her rosy face. "Yea!" She performs a dainty jump. "You have no idea how happy this makes me. I *so* need a friend like you here."

Her effusiveness is contagious, and I spontaneously hug her. "Me, too!" How great to have someone from back East, my own age, living right next door.

Feeling a twinge of girlfriend guilt, I round the fire to where Meredith stands beside Steffen. "Wow. This is a shocker," he says.

"It's not shocking at all," I say.

"Thought you hated it here."

"I'm changing. You should try it."

Meredith raises her cup to me, "To your new home!" She didn't take the news well when I drew her aside earlier, but I assured her of visits, playing in the yard with Lou, even suggesting she and Steffen move up here some day.

Holding no glass to meet her toast, I grab a nearby cup of Sprite. Which turns out to be someone's vodka. Damn! Even a drop of alcohol can send my head's blood vessels into painful spasms. From my pocket I pull an Imitrex pill and bite half, then do the same with a painkiller, washing them down with soda from the cooler. I try not to worry, but my head begins a slight throb. It occurs to me that here, near the fire, I'm breathing in the opposite of oxygen. I jog to the house, quickly crank up the music, check the food, and retreat to the bedroom to suck from a tank in hopes of aborting an attack. Luckily, I catch it soon enough: within minutes, the ache is gone.

When I emerge, my headache arrested, I see that people have filtered in…my head foggy and vision blurry from the meds and ill-fitting contact lenses, the scene is hazy and golden. The walls glow warm yellow with the paint color Jukka wisely chose, and the rooms are romantically lit by scores of votive and assorted candles brought by Meredith. People talk and mingle, laughter rises.

Intoxicated by it all, I dive into the family room of my new home. A night of light, magic, and possibly love awaits…

*

Paavo's a huge hit. He sits on the sofa surrounded, I notice, by women. Rebecca, Ravi's Valeria, and young Maya sit around Paavo smiling and laughing. Nearby, Meredith gamely chats with Marty, who I'll avoid after meeting his poor, beleaguered wife.

Jukka, followed by Ryan, who's pursued by Cleo, periodically enters to try to shoo us all outside to the fire—"no mosquitoes!" he advertises—but no one listens. Cleo, after following them in and out, soon tires of the exercise and flops in a chair to flip off her heels. Troy's gaze rockets her way when she's in his view. He eyes her like a duckling who's been imprinted, or a suckling, the sight of her bare breasts evidently having left a delectably indelible impression. He stands at the kitchen food spread, his face drooping as Cleo joins Paavo's sphere. I check on Garth, who's ensconced in Mom's bedroom—*my* bedroom—watching the small TV. The tanks sit near the bed, but he's cross-legged on the floor, sorting his deck of cards. "Doing OK?" I ask, handing him a soda. He nods.

Back in the family room, I feel hampered by the feminine blockade around Paavo. Unable to get close to him at the moment, I grab Ravi by the sleeve. I ask about his Hispanic date, the latte-skinned Valeria sitting so close to Paavo, whose thick, fringed eyelashes drop seductively down like shades during siesta. Freaking boudoir lashes. Is Paavo reacting to her allure?

"She's my last fling," Ravi puts a hand on his middle aged stomach, a mound under his button-down shirt.

"Before what?" I say.

"Before I go home to marry."

"Home to, like, *India*?" He drinks, smiling eyes over his cup. "Wow, Ravi, I totally forgot…I think you mentioned that." I squeeze his arm. "Congrats. Tell me about her! Who's the lucky girl, as they say?"

"I'll soon find out," he smiles. "My parents have lined up a few prospects."

"Gosh," I say, surprised that Ravi is succumbing to an arranged marriage after all these years. Ravi with an Indian woman, imagine that, "I hope you like one of them." I loop his elbow and guide him toward Paavo as we talk. Maybe I need one of my own kind too.

He circles his plastic beer cup around, "Congratulations on the house. It's nice to see your place here, to put it in my mind. When you were working from up here, when your mother was ill, I tried to picture you during our phone meetings. Now I see," he nods toward the back deck and yard, where the fire illuminates the figures of Jukka and Ryan.

I stared at this yard for hours during Mom's final weeks. I worked from here, dialing into DRIP meetings from the family room while Mom, now mute, dozed in her wheelchair or slept in the hospital bed in her room. The house was silent as falling snow.

I'd sit at my computer facing the winter yard, the deciduous trees bare, and listen—phone on mute—to an international orchestra, variations on the theme of English. The meetings were, for the most part, a polyglot Babylon of voices, an incomprehensible delight to the ear. I spaced out to the mellifluous voices from foreign lands. The undulating melodies of the recent Indian immigrants, who spoke beautifully but too fast: stressing the wrong syllables, rendering their speech unintelligible to the casual listener. I'd hear the sharp chops from the Singapore manufacturing rep, who terrified everyone, though the woman was the size of a bamboo shoot. On one team there was even the thick rolling accent of a Russian contractor. Listening to them all through my phone headset, I felt like a member of the U.N. I smile recalling the tetchy tech writer, a nocturnal novelist who, judging from the "technical" manuals she wrote, had great difficulty distancing herself from the fictional arts.

Ravi interrupts my memories. "So now I suppose you'll start

looking for a job?" He mentions that Sri's struggling as a contract tester, working round the clock. I hear women laugh at some remark from Paavo. I need to scoop him out of that circle of estrogen. *Why did I invite so many women?* "That doesn't sound so great." I say distractedly.

"So tell me, are you not looking for work?" I turn my face to him. "*Work*?" I gulp my soda. "Honestly, I haven't been thinking about it much at all. I've had these other priorities." I scan the room before setting my sight on Paavo. Ravi bobs his head as I go on, "I've been busy but also thinking. Maybe time I put my liberal arts education to better use, get out of high tech?" After all, I'd just fallen into it after college like so many other liberal arts majors. I tell him that after some travel—to bury Mom's ashes, possibly go to Finland—I might even apply to graduate school. "I'm so fortunate to own this house, to have money... I mean, how lucky am I?"

"Yes, your parents were very good to you, you should take advantage. I think this new thinking is fantastic, Alina. And you seem so relaxed." Yeah, I can barely keep my equilibrium with the scores of chemicals coursing through my veins. He squeezes my free hand in his warm, velvet clasp and smiles conspiratorially. "Now go, mingle."

As I sashay about pouring beer and filling plates with food, I grow lax of limb, feeling floaty and lithe as a little sailboat skimming familiar waters—although occasionally I list to the portside. The accumulated medications render me even more maladroit than usual. A tingle hits my forehead when I bite into a piece of Havarti. "So that is last night I go out with Jukka in Vegas," Paavo says to appreciative laughter as I pass. What are these stories? I don't recall him being particularly witty… Carrying a full plate of meatballs, I sidle into his grouping, which Meredith has joined. The floor lists, I can feel the plate tilting. I right myself and stand in front of Valeria. Her eyelashes pop up. They can't be real, so long and thick. You could hang laundry to dry on them. I resist the urge to tug on one. Leaning gracelessly forward to present her the food, I lose balance and a row of Swedish meatballs pours into her Spanish lap.

A minor hubbub ensues. Valeria shrieks, standing to brush her dress. Meredith grabs the tray from me and takes my elbow. Ravi rushes for napkins. Mere asks if I'm OK, and I insist that I'm fine. "Go enjoy yourself," I say. Her frown lines tell me she's doing the maternal worry thing. "Seriously. I'm just slightly over-medicated." She sets the tray on the kitchen table as I gently push her off.

"*Stay*," she says, as if I'm Coco. "You need to eat."

"Woof," I answer, giggling. She frowns again, so I start to load crisp bread with ham and Swiss.

As she leaves, Steffen ambles in with an empty glass. "That was quite a maneuver. Graceful as ever, I see." I ignore his grating insouciance. He doesn't know about my current headache spell and I don't want to talk about them. "Seems popular with the women, doesn't he?" he tilts his head Paavo's way.

Fixing on him, I say, "You sound jealous. Don't like the competition?

"And to what—or whom—would you be referring?"

"You know, being the rooster in the room, all eyes on you." As he snorts, I know he puts no store in my remark, his redeeming virtue being his unawareness of his effect on women.

"I might say the same of you," he says.

I crunch into my hardtack. "Oh right. That's me. With Mere and Miss Mexico, I'm the great beauty here. Ha ha." Crumbs fly out my mouth.

He stares at me. "You really don't see yourself."

Mouth full of birch bark, I garble, "Who does?" Besides, right now I'm wondering if Paavo over there sees me, even knows I exist. Jarred by Steffen's elbow as he pours himself vodka, I recall one thing: Steffen always made me feel like the only woman in the room. Nonetheless hopeful about Paavo, I say, "Don't worry. Mere isn't going after Paavo and he's not interested in her."

He makes a choking sound, puts down his drink. "You sound quite sure of yourself."

"He's…" I pause. "He's just being friendly and outgoing, I think." I try to come up with a secret smile but it's hard, as the guy has barely looked my way. "I'm going to ask him to dance." With that I make my way to the front room and crank up the stereo

Steffen follows me. "Dance with me first. We both like this music."

"You're trying to make Meredith jealous. Maybe not such a good idea after that—night."

"She's over it. Are you?" He is so trying to annoy me.

"Duh! Fine, let's dance," I challenge. Maybe Paavo will notice.

Cleo's music mixes, music I've grown to love, play her favorite dance music: Talking Heads, English Beat, B52s. She grew up with her older brother Garth's music, and I often think she plays it to remind her of better times; days before the onset of his illness. Steffen and I start moving to "Burning Down the House." A song I know will bring in dancers. I dim the lights. I want everyone drunk and happy—especially Paavo.

"Come!" I shout to the crowd in the other room. *Let's make this a bacchanalia.* I pop a pain pill to stop the throbbing that starts, down it with Coke. Cleo breezes in with Troy at her heels. I ask about her brother.

"I think he's watching TV in your room. He's good, kiddo."

Ryan enters with Valeria—perfect! But where's Paavo? Lithe young Maya joins reluctantly, clearly not wanting to dance with "old" people but soon bouncing along on the outskirts of the group. After the song, I leave the dance room only to find Paavo there on his ass, looking as serious as Meredith. From her hand motions I can tell their talking about that damn Reiki—but then, it might be the only way I'm ever going to get his hands on me.

"Come on, you guys! Where's Jukka?" Out the window I see him squatting before the fire, Coco sitting at his feet, a flask of vodka in his hand. Marty and Rebecca argue in the kitchen. "Music, you guys…everyone's dancing." They turn to look at me. "Maya's out there," I coax.

"I'm no dancer," Marty tells me.

"No one cares," I say, pulling his wife away.

"He's too self-conscious" she says. Back in the parlor, Cleo dances a retro monkey frug atop the concentrator, waving her arms up and down like a go-go dancer out of an old 60s movie. Troy stares up at her, shuffling his feet, spellbound.

"Lost my partner, per usual," Steffen shouts.

Now I notice that Meredith has joined in, followed by Jukka and Coco, who runs about the crowd in a frenzy. So many tromping feet! The room grows hot and dizzy. I twirl to the next song and seek Paavo—the B52s are on and we're all at the *Love Shack*. Spinning, I stub my toe on the concentrator, lose balance, and fall—grasp Cleo's legs, who in turn catapults from her perch into the group like a rock star launching into a mosh pit. I rise up and Cleo, bolstered by Troy, shouts, "There goes our 'lumsy' hostess" to general amusement.

Light-bodied and lax-minded, I smile, completely ignoring the large medical appliance, now fully exposed to the jostling group. Who cares!

"The dog is hurting!" Jukka shouts to the tightly packed crowd. Concerned about Coco, I search for her. He points as everyone gyrates and bumps each other. "Is some kind of sheep dog in him."

Oh, the dog is "*herding*." Relieved, I laugh with him at the compact group we've become, scrunched ever closer by the circling pup. That's exactly how my mom would say it, the *t* and *d* so close in sound. "I'm so glad you're here!" I yell into his ear. "It's good to have family." His arm sweeps the group, "Yes, you have got all these people."

"Yeah. These friends are like family. But you *are*." I squeeze his arm. Then I see Paavo enter the room. I grab his hand. "Take me to the River" comes on, a slower number. Feeling gauzy from the pills—a little worried about a rebound headache—I lock eyes and sing about him dropping me "in the water…" *Take a hint, baptize me!* He dances with a straight Finnish face, jerking rather awkwardly, focusing on his feet. Not quite what I'd hoped for. But then no one's perfect. Steffen and Meredith dance nearby, looking everywhere but at each other.

I tug on Paavo's moist t-shirt. "I bet you're great at the tango."

"What?" he shouts.

I lean in close again, smell his yeasty, earthy breath. "The tango. Finns all love to tango!"

"Well, yes I suppose there are quite a few. Lots of the older fellows. But not me, you see I've got the two same feet."

"Two left feet?" I laugh. How witty! My head is soft mush.

"Yo, that's what I mean. I have the two left feet. Not the good dancer like you." I grin, he likes my dancing! I twirl to show off, then clutch his arm to balance myself.

"But I'm not so bad at the polka," he says.

"Yes! We'll polka together sometime." If only I had a Lawrence Welk album! The song "Roam" comes on and just as the party hits the perfect fever pitch, my dancing endorphins flowing, my inhibitions melted in the mass sweat, I move in and smack Paavo with a full-on mouth kiss. His fleshy lips, moist and beery, begin to respond. He kisses me! No tongue, but all I can do is think in amazement, 'Paavo is actually kissing me!' When we stumble apart, I have to hold myself back from whooping and high-fiving him. I call over the thumping bass, "That's for everything!"

My head swims from the kiss, the music, the drugs, the contact high of dance and friends. I spin into oblivion, enjoying the abandon. When we all dance to the "Bizarre Love Triangle," the party reaches its pinnacle: I couldn't be more intoxicated.

Marty maneuvers my way to thank me for helping out with the kids, saying they have to leave.

"You should get her out more. It's too much for her," I yell into his ear, my meds making me bold. "The moving, the baby," recalling how Rebecca implied, that day on her steps, before I left for a shrill but ultimately minor skirmish among the kids, that she'd had doubts about having another child. "She said *you* wanted it." He winces. "I mean, wasn't four enough?" the confidence in my tone dwindling. From his stricken face, I can tell he feels slapped.

He turns to jostle through the dense crowd, and I start after him. He turns to me. "Maybe you're right. Maybe I was being selfish."

"No, no." My head hurts with regret. "I didn't mean to—"

"I guess I just wanted one of my own," he says. I open my mouth, nothing comes out, then he's gone.

Dizzy and confused—one of his own? He has five! I try to focus on dancing, but the music's too loud, the people too close, sweaty, hot, a crowded sauna with no relief in sight, no bucket of cool water to drench and clear my head. I find Paavo—no one has a partner at this point, it's the kind of loose dancing I'd wanted—and I try to get festive when "Psycho Killer" comes on, and pain like a knife blade slices into my left temple. Needing to act fast before the headache cripples me, I finger my forehead and manage to utter, "I need some air," to no one in particular before rushing out.

~Joka toiselle kuoppaa kaivaa, se itse siihen lankeaa.~
~Who digs a hole for another, falls in it himself.~

Invisible Pain

I teeter into my bedroom sanctuary for some oxygen, only to find Garth and now Maya there watching TV, lights on. Pulsing pain fractures my skull.

I force out a garbled, agonizing, "Hi," and switch off the overhead light, then fall onto the bed. I crank on the oxygen tank, shove the plastic cannula in my nostrils, slipping the strap behind my head. I lie back. Through the tears that pour from my left eye, I see them glance at me, both from the floor where they watch a baseball game. A sharp sword slices through the nerves of the entire left side of my pulsing head. It burns in torture.

I pop a full Imitrex pill and a whole painkiller, knowing it's too much medicine. But I *need to get back to my party*! With rigid fingers I bear down on my left temple, try to stop the pulsing vein that throbs with swift, agonizing regularity, a jackhammer on my nerve. I pull the rough wool blanket up to my chin.

"You OK?" Maya asks.

Tears stream down my cheek. Garth looks over. "Half of you is broken," he says. I know he sees my flushed face, one eye barely open, half a face contorted. I squeeze my eyes to shut out the flickering TV images. The ancients used to remove segments of skull to relieve headaches…at times like this, I conjure up all manner of violent remedies.

I breathe and breathe, the steady flow of air and the dulcet voices of baseball announcers the only sounds I hear. At this end of the house, I can't hear much of my party. I turn up the oxygen dial. *Please, please either kill me or get this over with.* Lately I've been thinking how apt 'suicide headaches' are. When they attach for weeks, this biting, cruel, hidden pain, I become desperate. I have a sudden, wrenching longing for Mom, who used to place a warm moist flannel cloth over my eyes, stay and hold my hand in silence, in the dark, for hours. I feel so terribly weary.

But the oxygen is a miracle and I caught this one fairly early, the burning pain abates. In minutes the headache has released its all-powerful vice. My blood vessels expand like air balloons, relief comes in waves. On a scale of one to ten, my suffering is no longer 99. It's more like an eight, which for me is tolerable, especially knowing it will soon be gone. Though still hurting, I'm able to open my eyes.

I need to get back out there, back to Paavo. My plan's not working out, we've spent no time alone tonight. To clear my foggy head, I ask, "Can I have a sip?" and rise to accept Maya's proffered can of Diet Coke, but the room spins as I take it, the plastic cannula hose tugs, and I fall back onto the bed, slopping soda. OK, so I need to wait a bit longer…

Sipping the metallic drink, I dwell on my thwarted attempts to be with Paavo. I turn to check the flowers under my pillow, finding them wilted and squashed. "At least he's sleeping here," I say looking at the sorry blooms. My companions turn from the TV to me. It seems I said that aloud.

"I was just thinking about Paavo," I say. They wait, Maya suppresses a sly smile. "No! Not *here*." I drop the pillow. "I mean Paavo and Jukka are back staying with me—"

"Whatever," Maya waves it off. The caffeine isn't clearing through the fog of my brain. He kissed me, though. I take another sip and offer it back. Maya hops up, her skeletal frame airy, and reaches for the soda. I notice raised bumpy scars on her wrist, red and raw, still new. I gasp, she turns away quickly. Red lines running crossways on her inner wrist. Slash marks. The wrong way to kill yourself. My God, what has this girl been going through? I'd suspected she had an eating disorder…but.

I want to cry, to hug her. I know Garth has scars as well running the entire length of both forearms. He no longer wears short sleeves. Such suffering! While the world flows on like air from my oxygen tank. All of us with our invisible pain.

"How are you feeling?" Garth asks me without looking.

"Better. Thanks." I'm grateful for these two at the moment, who don't feel like they belong at the party. Garth with his mental demons controlled by scores of medications, called "crazy" by all but those who know him, Maya with her eating problems, daily—perhaps hourly—fighting her battle with food but walking through the world without anyone knowing. Suffering so badly she's tried to kill herself? And me, with this debilitating disease that no one can understand or cure. We three are kin. They don't question my oxygen tanks, my resting here while the party music plays.

When I reopen my eyes, someone has let Coco in the room. On the floor they pull a sock around for her to chase. She chases, circling madly, getting nowhere. "I think I spoke out of turn with your dad," I tell Maya drowsily as the pain decreases.

"You did what? Like with Marty?"

"You call him Marty?" The other kids call him "Dad"… they shower him with affection—so loudly—upon his comings and goings, tackling him on his front lawn when he returns from work.

"He's our step-dad." Maya sits back and stares at the television, where a long-faced pitcher spits. The sports announcers' mellifluous voices converse with each other as if millions were not listening. Their talk is casual, informal, almost intimate. They laugh and joke. How can anyone *do* that?

I try to make sense of it. *Our step-dad. One of my own…*"So the baby?"

"She's his." Then Taylor, Madison, and Riley and Maya all belong to Rebecca? *Before the baby?* Busy gal!

But my God. How can I get everything so wrong? How could I call a girl like Maya a "lollipop girl?" The headache's abated but I feel like shit. "I need to go apologize. I'm your neighbor now." Even Ryan. His only fault is being young… I try to stand but quickly topple, dizzy, back to the bed. "I'm so off-base," I say. "What's wrong with me!"

"You're sick?" Maya says.

"I'm awful."

Garth says, "You're not awful."

"You're kind," I say. "Both of you." Too kind.

And so I stay, for a while, with these sweet, non-judgmental people. Garth shuffling his cards, Maya sitting up with her regal head erect, her thin limbs tucked under her. "Maya means "queen" in Finnish," I say, though it's spelled differently. *Maija.*

"Weird," she says. "How do you know?"

"I played lots of cards with my grandparents." As I mentally go through the words for diamonds, hearts, clubs, and spades, the numbers one through ten, she brings Coco over and places him by my side. I cling to the dog's muscular body, stroke her sleek fur, nuzzle her. "Some day you'll find your "*kuningas,*" your king, I tell her. A shy smile sneaks onto her face. My eyes drowse to the deep, lulling, patter of the baseball announcers.

Meredith pops her head in and says she needs to go. Disoriented and dry-mouthed, I sit up. "Go? The party just started." I rub grit from my eyes. "I was just about to come out."

"Actually, it's midnight, Ali." No music plays through the open door. Garth and Maya are gone, the air is still. Christ, did I miss my own party?

"Did you have a bad one? I came in a couple of hours ago and held your hand but you didn't wake up. So I figured you needed the sleep. You've done so much."

"No! Is everyone gone?"

"Well, Paavo and Jukka and that Ryan kid are in the sauna."

"In the sauna." *Great.*

"The neighbors went home to bed, I think. I'm not sure where Cleo or your realtor are. Ravi and his dish left…who else was there?"

"*Steffen?*"

"Oh yeah, he's hanging out. Decided not to take a sauna with the boys. I think he's afraid of it. Me, I'm beat. Sleep sounds great—the life of a single mom."

"Garth and Maya were here."

"Yeah, Garth crashed in the other bedroom and Maya left with her parents a long time ago." A long time ago. My life. I'm missing it. Recalling the evening's events, I find it hard to drag my bones out of bed. I feel so tired. So tired of being me.

*

After convincing Meredith to stay for just a bit longer, I brew a pot of coffee. Famished after my sleep, I gobble a taste of every appetizer and casserole on the table and begin to come back to life. I want to bring this party back to life!

Steffen hangs out with his hands in his pockets, brows furrowed. I spot Cleo and Troy out by the fire, call out the screen window, "Coffee?"

Troy slurs, "Gotta keep this baby going. Jukka's orders. The fire stays alighted." I hear Cleo say she needs more beer, whereupon Troy trots off to pour from the keg. The three men emerge from the sauna and Jukka, with a white towel tucked at his waist, announces from the deck, "In Finland now we swim in lake or sea."

I lower my coffee cup, my head a pleasant buzz from the caffeine, glad that some fraction of my party remains. I walk to the sliding doors to tell him that—in case he hasn't noticed—we're not on the coast. But before I say anything, I flash on the book Troy gave me, *Historical Mercury*, and the picture of kids swimming in a lake.

I say, "You can do that! There's a lake right here in Mercury.

We can walk to it and swim!" This is such a totally *brilliant* idea! Genius! A romantic midnight swim with Paavo, skinny-dipping in the moonlight. Steffen stares at me open-jawed. "What?" I challenge.

"It's just kind of spontaneous, isn't it? For you. And your headaches…"

"I'm fine! I missed my own party! I'm not going to let it end. Besides," I call to Jukka, "we're supposed to stay up all night, right?"

"Yo, that's the way I'm liking it. And sauna with not swimming on *Juhannus* is not feeling right."

~*Laita lapsi asialle, tee itse perässä.*~
~Send a child to do your errands, do it yourself afterwards.~

Take Me to the Lake

Before leaving, Paavo says something about the bonfire, which we've gathered around once again. The flames leap high, lighting my friends' faces, reigniting my optimism. This night is not a bust after all. We'll have a fun-filled midnight lark!

"We must put out fire or I will stay," he states.

"No!" Everyone looks at me. I tone it down. "I mean, don't *you* stay, you just took sauna." I'm thinking Steffen's a good candidate for fire-tending.

Troy says, "Allow me to remain. This property must be property, ah, prop-er-ly attended." He murmurs, "Even if it's no longer for sale," piercing me with a brief pang of guilt. Oddly, Cleo offers to stay too. It's not like her to decline an adventure, particularly one involving both the opposite sex and potential nudity, but I'm glad it frees Paavo. He cautions them to let the fire die down as I tow his arm.

And so Paavo, Jukka, Steffen, Ryan, Meredith and I trip off—without towels we all realize too late—into the unlit streets of Mercury, quiet and empty, in search of water. When we reach the road that rises to the mountain, I spot the path that I think leads to the lake. All of us either tipsy or drugged, we stumble through prickly brush.

An eerie, otherworldly sound rips through the night. High calls, yips and howls join in a wailing chorus that sounds as if it comes not from the mountain but from the Netherworld. "What is this noise?" Jukka asks, and I tell him I think it's the sound of coyotes. "I'm not liking that," he says, but we push on.

Steffen calls to me, "Alina. Do you know where you're going?"

"Yes!" I maintain, though I'm seeing very poorly, and only walking on hope. It should be back here, where a few cottages lie. I veer right. We pass one old house, dark and uninviting.

"I smell the water," says Jukka. "This way." He leads us off to the left through thickets and trees and within seconds there it is: the lake. Though it's a small pond in actuality. Thrush and reeds grow in the water around its edges, topped by lily pads that glow ghostly white in the moonlight, making the unfettered swimming area unimpressive. A couple of broken docks descend into the water, and an overturned boat and rusted fishing box decay nearby. Only one vacant house is in sight, despite the "No Trespassing" signs that Steffen illuminated with the flashlight he'd grabbed from his truck.

"Well, this is not very much the lake," Jukka pronounces.

"It's good 'nough." Paavo says, and I look at his dark outline with appreciation. The men start stripping, and Meredith and I walk away to undress behind a clump of bushes. I don't know whether to leave my bra and panties on so I look over. They are naked and Jukka stands at the water's edge. I quickly strip and call, "First one in!" dashing past him into the water, feeling the muck suck and slow my feet until I'm deep enough to make a shallow dive. The men follow, passing me with laughter and loud splashing. Meredith giggles and joins, looking like a lovely water nymph, as her svelte body arcs in a shallow dive.

Alone near the shore for a minute, I lose sight of the others. Recalling the Finnish myth about seeing my true love's reflection on Midsummer Night, I stare into the murky water. It wavers, deflects the half-moon light, but I think a pale visage is possibly discernable…I bend closer to the surface, squinting. "You look for something?" I straighten too quickly at the sound of Paavo's voice, fall back with a splash. I sputter, "Oh, just the reflection of…" Feeling silly, I mumble, "My true love."

"Then he's gonna be some kind of fish, I think," Paavo laughs. I smile, but as he darts away in a speedy freestyle, I can't help but feel pleased that *he* was the one there, next to me. The one I would've seen if not for the ambiguity. Paddling out, I hear him call from a distance, "Mar-ee-dee, Ah-lee-na!" and I hear, "Marry me, Alina," but Meredith calls back "Over here!" and I realize he's called our names. We swim farther out together. When we reach him, Paavo says, "Now this is refreshing," taking obvious pleasure in the water. Realizing I need to speed up the action with him, I float on my back, conscious of my buoyant breasts, a possible view of my pubic hair.

I briefly get lost in the weightless pleasure of floating. I look up at the stars then close my eyes and let the water caress me. The slightly fishy smell of lake water conjures memories of the silken pond on Cape Cod, the campsite pond where my family swam each evening after a day bracing the ocean surf. Washing away all the sticky salt and grating sand, the sun setting, the water warm and soft, cleansing and purifying. The best days of my life. I float suspended as my parents come to mind, and I feel cradled—safe and loved.

I see a fresh, new beginning in the sparkling stars—when I emerge from this lake, refreshed, made new, I'll be the better person. I dunk under, feeling grace and cleanliness wash over me, peace fill me.

My thoughts return to Paavo. I open my eyes, tread water, squint to see he's gone. A tug at my leg and I'm pulled under, shocked and breathless. Before rising, I discern through the murk the undulating dark hair. We raise our heads simultaneously gasping and he laughs, then I laugh. At last he's playing with me, flirting! I splash water at him and he ducks under again. I long to touch him, feel his wet skin brush mine, I want to wrap my legs and arms around him and kiss him until I can't breathe. He darts toward the others so I race after, dive under to playfully grab his leg in the murky water. Finding the firm curve of his strong calf, I caress it upward, feeling the fine filaments of his leg hair on his firm thigh, then brush over the curve of his buttocks, until, hand on his hip bone, I surface to stare directly into Steffen's face.

"Yow!" I gasp. "Geesh! Sorry, I thought you were—"

"Stop!" Steffen cries, turning in the water.

I shake water from my ears. "God, Steffen!" I never knew him to deflect a woman's touch.

"Quiet!" he commands.

Paavo, nearby, says, "Have you heard that?" and then I hear the blasts through the night, like gunshots, followed by the boom of a canon—all from somewhere not far off. Within seconds, Steffen's out and dressing on the shore.

"Fireworks on *Juhannus*!" laughs Jukka with a splash, a disembodied voice in the dark. A small orange glow appears above the treetops. "That color is like sometimes the fox fire in Lapland. *Revontulet*."

"That is no Northern Lights," I hear Paavo say, as he joins Steffen on shore. Another explosion. Red fire in the sky. Ominously close. Perilously, perhaps, near my house? Slowly I swim in.

Suddenly lucid, I stand dripping wet in the shallows of the cold black water. Hit by the breeze, I shiver. A chill runs through my core. Every fibrous hair on my body rises. No one speaks. I emerge from the water robotically, sludge through the mud, reeds clinging to my arms like a Swamp Thing. Sirens pierce the still doom. My heart booms. I look to the lit sky. My stomach bottoms out. Then I do what every creature from the dark lagoon does. I run to the bushes and puke.

~Aamun torkku, illan virkku, se tapa talon hävittää.~

~Asleep in the morning, awake all evening; this is the way to lose a house.~

Tuli

Sirens careen through the chill night air as we race home. The roar of fire, men shouting, pressured water whooshing, wood crackling and thundering down. My ears full of water, I feel submerged as we wade, my feet too heavy, as if still sticking on the guano-bottomed pond, slowly in time through the obstructed narrow lane, past the few parked cars, strobe-lit fire trucks, onlookers, their faces strange to me in the flickering lights. Robes, flip-flops, I see one pink hair curler. And then, I swallow the charred stench of a million burnt cigarettes, feel the blast of heat like a furnace, and see it: my life in flames.

My eyes burn, my throat singes. Flames and sparks fly, wood crashes, water hisses, men bark. Smoke billows from the back yard. Firefighters in yellow raincoats pull hoses. My stomach churns at the sight of the carriage house, already reduced to a burnt shell. Noxious smoke clogs my nostrils as I try to breathe. I try to not pass out. Orange flames leap from the windows of my bedroom. My brain clicks on: I start a sprint to the house, jolted by a thick rubber yellow arm. Pushed back. Cordoned off.

"Garth! Cleo and Troy! My *dog*." I shout to the helmeted man. At my side, Meredith says, "They're all here," she strokes my back. "And Steffen's looking for Coco." She says something to the man. Someone covers me with a heavy blanket. But I shiver. I hold tight to the blanket, the blaze blasts heat, burns my eyeballs and scalp, but I cannot stop shivering. My teeth clack and chatter.

I shake and shake. Meredith encircles me in her arms. In front of my blazing house, in this furnace of heat, blanketed and sheltered in Meredith's embrace, I shiver with icy frostiness. Cold emanates from me. I sense my friends around me but I will turn anyone who touches me to ice. I am not warm. I will never be warm again.

I was wrong. I see Troy squatting nearby, arms covering his head, rocking forward and back. He moans, "Uncle Ray's gonna kill me." What the hell? Furious, blood suddenly boiling, I lurch toward him; I'm ready to throttle him before this uncle has access, the incompetent little twerp. But Cleo intervenes, her face black with melted mascara and smoke. I turn away. "Alina," she pleads. "We stayed out there. We *did*." I cannot look at her. The roof of my mother's bedroom crumbles before me. I jump toward the house, stopped again by strong arms. "My purse," I say. Mom's stuff, her mahogany dresser with the Russian certificate. My *everything*.

"You can't go near," I'm told. The photo albums in the front parlor can be saved. I push at the man. He holds his ground. My God. I crumple to the ground. My mother's remains. A lightening bolt of pain pierces my temple.

Cleo stoops, I feel a surge of fury. I want to slap her. Bristling with anger, I hear her say, "We stayed by the fire and then. The thing *is* is we went to sit on the deck in a chair—"

I shout, "*A* chair?"

She whimpers.

I shout, "Then what?" Seething with sudden rage, I screech, "Unbelievable! *You screwed while my house burned!*"

She grabs my arm, I wrench it away. She snuffles, "I'm so sorry!" She moans like a sick cow. My head throbs. I stumble away from her. *I need to get in the house.*

Circling emergency lights pulsate yellow and red. A sharp pain shoots through my temple. I see the pale, frightened faces of the children next door, the baby crying in Rebecca's arms. Oh God.

My neighbor's house. It's bad enough how I've misjudged Marty, now I'm going to gut his home? Firemen shout at us to evacuate the street. The hot wind blows the flames higher. One man herds us farther back. I overhear people asking questions, someone says, "the sauna." An invisible axe chops into my skull. My hand flies to the pain at my eye. I need my meds. I jolt forward. Am pushed back. My purse. My glasses, I can't see. I need my credit card. The Russian certificate. Photos, so few of them…Mom's ashes in the spare bedroom! Ashes to ashes. "I have to go inside." I can still save things!

"This is your house?" I nod. An enormous, helmeted fireman bends to me. "We're getting it under control. Don't worry." *Huh*? Nothing is under control! In the tumult, he calls over my head to someone. A demonic headache of staggering proportion strikes. "I need air," I manage, gripping my temple, head bent, tears streaming.

Another firefighter pulls at me gently, "Let's get you away from the fumes. Were you in the house?" I shake my head. "I'll take you to the ambulance." His eyes search. "It'll be here any minute. Must've had to call the backup. You all right?"

I nod. I can't speak, as a shard of fire charges through my temple. My head pounds with piercing intensity, exacerbated by the pulsing lights, the smoke-filled air. I try to say, "Oxygen." He leans close to hear me above the roar of burning, shouts, pressurized water, the dark chaos. I look toward Mom's smoking bedroom with my oxygen, the shell of the carriage house where I stored the rest. Those popping noises...

The firefighter says, "Come sit in the police car until the ambulance arrives." I shake him off, go to Meredith, now in Steffen's arms. No dog. *Where's Coco?* The Finns talk with them, cast worried looks at me. Another fireman tromps over to ask questions: am I the owner, did I have combustibles in the garage, the house, can he sit me down to get some information?

"*Headache*," I implore Meredith with my face, hand over its left half, now pulsating in agony. She says something to the fireman, takes my hand. "They'll have oxygen here, Alina. Let's go." But she doesn't realize it's too late. Minutes have passed—now nothing short of morphine will save me. I need to get to the Emergency Room.

Steffen, Paavo, and Jukka surround me. I grab the Finns. "Dive me." Puzzled faces all around. *Sisu.* My mouth can barely open. Scarcely audible, I plead. "Stay, Mere. You, Steff. *Pease.*" Stay here and be in charge. Meredith assures me, tells Jukka and Paavo quickly where to go, and Paavo guides me down the street toward their car, just as the blaring ambulance pulls up, two young men in front.

"Now here is the help," Paavo says, arm hugging my shoulders. I shake my head and push them onward. The EMTs won't know what to do. They'll offer me an aspirin. No one knows about cluster headaches, less than one percent of the world afflicted, a pathetic, silent minority. And no ambulance is going to take me to the hospital for a "mere headache" while a fire rages.

Paavo looks at me doubtfully but something in the set of my posture keeps Jukka moving. They charter me through the throng of parting neighbors and more, passing a crowd of slippers, bare feet, and hairy male calves. Without looking up, I see crossed arms and cross looks. I, the interloper, have endangered them all. I turn to look at my house: firemen douse the darting flames with hoses. Smoke pours up in noxious billowing clouds. The charred bedroom is visible through the broken, burned walls. I see my mother's lovely mahogany dresser…

Walking as if in a nightmare, I hear a thunderous crack. Through the haze of smoke, behind the skeletal bedroom, half of the great heritage oak splits off and falls, as if in slow motion, orange sparks flying against the black night. The tremor rises up my legs as it crashes to the ground. Instinctively, I turn to run toward it. Paavo and Jukka tug me back as, both eyes tearing now, I strain out a pained, guttural, primordial cry, "*Mom*!"

~Hukkuva tarttuu oljenkorteenkin.~

~One who is drowning will even try to catch hold of a hay straw.~

The E.R.

The fluorescent lights assault. A buxom woman slides a window halfway open and asks for my insurance card. Her loose shirt flowered in bold, jarring reds, blinding greens. I rub my unrelenting, grinding head. The disinfectant in the air burns my one open nostril. I cannot talk through the pain. "Ack. Ow." I answer.

The small waiting room is packed on this Saturday night: a mother holding a toddler, an old man and woman, a couple of teens, one cradling his arm, and a lone woman. For the first time, I feel what a wreck I am: my unkempt hair damp and clingy, my clothing covered with soot, my sandals abandoned at the lake.

Jukka is parking the car. The woman asks Paavo for the insurance card. I shake my head no. "My pur. Fie!" I spit out. My purse burned in the fire, my license, insurance card, credit cards—all history. The torment of steady head pangs grows. I moan.

Agitated, Paavo puts a hand on the small of my back and says, "Her papers has burned up in the fire. She needs the doctor."

"Are you her husband?"

"What is that mattering!" Paavo speaks in angry Finnish to Jukka, who, breathless, joins us at the reception window. The woman raises her brows and holds back the clipboard paperwork. "Aghhhhhhh!" I wail. I sense all movement in the waiting room suspend.

She says more loudly, as if we are all deaf, "If you can show some identification and proof of insurance we can proceed with the paperwork." Her high voice screams in my skull. "Is your wife insured, sir?" Jukka snorts derisively.

Paavo says, "Yes, yes of course. She has terrible headache. She needs a doctor *nyt*! Now!" The receptionist scowls, shuts the half-window, and turns to talk to a young woman seated behind her. Jukka storms toward the doors that lead to the inner sanctum, where doctors are, where patients are treated. "These is locked," he says. "I'm not believing it."

Red-faced, Paavo pivots to slam his hand on the window ledge. "This is not happening in Finland!"

She opens the window a crack. "No sir, that's correct." She glances back at her wide-eyed cohort. "We are in the *United States of America*."

"Of course I know this!" Paavo shouts. She slips the clipboard through the opening. "Please fill out the form and she'll be seen as soon as possible." Paavo scans the crowded room, pushes the clipboard back at her. Finnish invective pours out of him. "She has the luster!"

"Is that her insurer, sir?"

"No! This is very terrible headache. You don't know."

"SIR! I don't care if she's got a headache. There are people ahead of you." I peer sideways through my one eye at a child sniffling near her mother, the old man leaning with both hands on a cane. Are they dying inside like me?

"Ack! Eeeee!" I scream with each searing wave of pain. It's intolerable! These are *suicide headaches*! Just shoot me. Or give me a gun. I move to the wall at the end of the rooted blue chairs and bang my head into it. Ow! Minor relief. "*Mama*!" the child wrings her arms around her mother's neck. I strike it again, harder. It's true. It helps. I smash my left side *thud thud thud*, to ease the torment, hear myself cry "*Piru, piru, piru*!" with each blow. Because a devil is stabbing a pitchfork inside my head. Piercing nerves. People stare. I'm a spectacle. I don't care. I'm insane with pain.

Harder—*thump*! I'm mad, English Steffen mad, crazy, American mad, angry as hell. *Thump*!

While I pound my head, Paavo yells in Finnish. I hear voices, scurrying. Jukka or someone tugs at my arm. I yank away. I'm going to keep thrashing my head until I pass out or die…

Warm hands pull me away into an open medical area, blindingly, diabolically bright. I cover my eyes, stumble as I'm led onto a bed. I hear the screech of metal on metal, a curtain pulled. "Evidently, they're foreigners, Dr. Mukherjee," a man says. The overhead light is switched off. I'm laid on a bed, my arm is swabbed, a needle poked. It's nothing. Stick a needle in my eye. Stick a drill bit in it.

Then, within minutes—or seconds?—I feel it. A river of cool jello courses through my veins. The vice that grips my head loosens. One arm flops down, the other grows heavy on my eyes. I become slack and drowsy. My head lolls to the side. The soothing dark room cocoons me. *Relief.*

Jukka texts furiously on his phone. "Mere?" I ask softly, and he sucks air with a "*yo*" without looking up. Love pours through my veins. Oh, the extreme pleasure of *no more pain*. The drug spikes my mood to near-euphoria. I grow dreamy, gaze at my cousin, with the blond-blue of Mom's half-Swedish side. How he's been on my side…

Then Paavo, on one knee by the bed, takes my hand like a prince about to propose. He's so beautiful. I'm struck by his resemblance to my dad, the sculpted cheekbones that seem to push his eyes into a high slant, the blunt but straight nose, the full mouth. The rich, dark hair that falls over his concerned gaze. My knight. How chivalrously he just fought for me. Finally, we're together. I smile, hazily besotted, try to squeeze his hand. But mine's gone limp and I'm drifting. I'm drifting, Paavo, falling into a deep, deep sleep. And I never want to wake up.

~Se mikä on ollutta, on mennyttä.~
~What has been is gone.~

Flying Into the Future

A flight attendant floats a napkin my way and I look up only to find her attention already fixed on the row behind me. In the rarified hyper-air of the plane, I hear everything: the crackle of cards being shuffled, noses blown, the snap and click of soda cans opening, the crunch of ice. Voices near but muffled, the constant din of the jet engines and air pressure making sound both subdued and too loud.

The head-phoned woman next to me suddenly sighs, her eyes glued to the movie playing above us. An on-screen audience appears ecstatic after witnessing a young couple's marriage proposal. The credits roll shortly thereafter, and she slips off her earphones. I strike up a friendly conversation. "Why do Hollywood films *always* do that? It's like they think the occasion is more "romantic" if there's a crowd ogling it, you know?"

She's probably my age, but she turns a baffled face to me. "What? I didn't think you were even watching it."

"Those scenes make me squeamish. I mean, what could be a more private moment?" Gesticulating at the screen, I rant, "Besides, the *movie* audience is the audience. *We're* the audience! No wonder foreigners think we're dimwits. They see all these dumb romances and noisy, obnoxious movies with those hackneyed screams and noisy soundtracks that just try to cover the fact that there's no script…films so bad they never even make it to the theaters!" Realizing that I just started babbling, I stick out my hand with a bright smile, "Hi. I'm Alina."

"I really liked it." She flips open the in-flight magazine. Right.

I mumble something about some good soundtracks, then lay my head back and listen to a man wax about finance—the fall of real estate values since last year—the bountiful summer of '06—the stock market, commodities and *futures*, whatever they are. I kick my seat back, hoping to disturb his monologue, careful not to disturb the box of ashes cradled in my lap. The only future I know about—or rather don't—is mine. How fitting that I'm bound for a country whose language has no future tense.

I went to a fortuneteller once. On my thirtieth birthday, late October. I was walking through a Hispanic neighborhood, where more than one house displayed a painted, bejeweled hand sign in front. Most palm-readers, I'm certain, are charlatans, but I keep the possibility open. Perhaps because I possess my mother's superstitious nature.

I walked up the steps to a modest house and knocked on the door of the prophesier. Inside, I heard voices that stopped with my knocking. Male voices. A plump woman greeted me and drew me into a front room, which, like Meredith's apartment, appeared to be the main living area. No one inside, all quiet. Long dark hair fell forward over her ears, ending at her waist, though she must've been fifty. She wore glittery slippers, but they, and her flowing hair were her only concessions to the "gypsy" look, as her shirt was a pin-stripe button-down, tucked neatly into the elastic band of a pair of generous khaki slacks. To me, it was a good sign: true talent not needing all the hokey trappings.

Then I saw the beaded curtains, behind which I knew my future lay. There better not be a crystal ball or I'm out of here, I thought. After welcoming me, she asked me to wait for "*uno momento*." A skewed cross adorned one wall of the living room, and a string of colorful paper-lace squares spanned the space above the plasma TV for the upcoming Days of the Dead. The sacred over the profane. A small bowl of sugar skulls lay on a doily at the door-side table. I fingered the skulls, their sugary coating gritty and sticky. My father had died the year before.

When we settled at a table behind the beaded curtain, she took my hands and looked at me with grave eyes. She shook her head back a bit and, despite the dim lighting, I noticed an earpiece of some sort. Holy shit, how bogus! I saw where this was headed: she was going to delve into my family a bit, then channel my dead dad or something. I didn't exactly enter a *Believer* but for forty bucks I was hoping to find someone who had some pretense of clairvoyance.

Looking down at our joined hands, she said, "You will be loved by two men. Maybe more." The non-specific-nature of the prediction didn't impress me. She had an air of distraction, as if communing with the other world. A good act if she'd been a little more careful with her props. Then she flipped my right hand over, splayed my fingers, and stared intently at my palm. "You have an unfinished history."

I stifled a laugh. "That would be because…I'm *alive*?"

Her eyes narrowed. "Some unfinished business with someone who loves you." I began pondering this, only to be interrupted by her spiel. "You will have two—no—*three* children." Statistically she was on target. Me, I was still waiting for my "dad" to float in on a white sheet.

With a furrowed face, she drew a ticklish line, starting lightly at my wrist. "Your life line…" she continued to press harder fingering down my palm. Her face drooped, and her brows drew together, "a long line… *drive*?" She dropped my hand to the oilcloth then looked up at me, agitated. "*Chucho Christo*!"

"What?!" She had my attention. Some car accident in store for me? I'm not a great driver, too easily distracted by a good song on the radio or the random static that constantly buzzes through my head.

"No, no," she hastily assured. "You will be fine. Just wait one minute." She got up too quickly and a tiny electronic device fell out of her pants pocket. She slipped it back in and hurried out of the room. I heard the muffled sounds of a crowd, and I followed her out.

On the television, an announcer was shouting, as they do when a sporting event gets exciting and they act like kids on too much sugar. Baseball players were hugging and jumping in a dugout. She'd been listening to the frigging World Series! Spotting me, she clicked off the TV.

After I grabbed my purse, we bumped into each other at the chintzy beaded curtain. The plastic clacked. Her expression was one of surprise. "We are not done," she said.

I walked over to switch on the TV, checking the stats in the upper left corner. I placed one palm on the warm flat screen and the other hand over my eyes. "I predict, I predict…" I said, then I looked her straight-on. "That the Yankees will win by two." Her hands were at her mouth, her brown eyes anxious, by my bizarre behavior or my prophecy, I still don't know. "Shouldn't you know the outcome of this game, anyway?" On the way out, I popped a sugar skull into my mouth. The screen door flapped behind me. I think I left during the bottom of the 8th.

Quick footsteps followed me. "*Lo siento.* I'm sorry," she said. "You are missing someone, I think. A parent?" Now all the days of the dead seemed reflected in her sad, dark eyes. Lip trembling, I turned away. "But your love, he waits. He will not come to you. You must go to him," she said. "Be bold."

At the time I thought she was a kook, but recalling this on my flight East, I wonder at the veracity of her words. I *was* still grieving the death of my dad. And her talk of being loved by two men…obviously, Steffen was the first to think he was in love. And now? Is it possible that Paavo is the other?

It seems I'm bound to find out…

*

The month after the fire passed strangely like a dark whirlwind. After a few days staying with Meredith, I moved back to Mercury, where the sauna became my house. For days after the fire, I'd wander out in the morning, and just stare around me at the devastation—the scorched yard, the half-burnt house, the carriage house little more than a pile of ash. I felt lost, empty. Dazed. I didn't know what to do, how to take a step forward, where to go…looking up I'd see the flash of red-tailed hawks circling—or were they turkey vultures? Whatever, I felt like road kill.

Meredith and—I have to say—Steffen, pulled me through. Scarcely a week after the fire, Paavo and Jukka guiltily left on their pre-booked flights for New York, then home, Paavo's sabbatical over, Jukka's vacation done. My farewell with Paavo was muted by my fractured condition and the presence of others. But when he held me at arms length and looked clearly into my eyes: I saw affection and sorrow… "You will be fine. You have *sisu*," he said with conviction. And when we embraced, long and close, it felt like our most intimate moment ever. As he left, he called "*Nakemiin!*" and I knew it was the right word: I'd see him later.

Meanwhile, Steffen got his contractor dad Louis on the job, starting plans to rebuild the burnt portion of the house. While Louis Sr.'s cleanup crew starting arriving early each morning, Meredith pulled me out of my womb to salvage and clean what was left from the remaining half of the house: the spare bedroom, bath, and parlor stood. Destroyed was my mother's bedroom, the kitchen, and family room. In spite of her insistence that I stay with her, I made the sauna my bedroom (grateful that Dad built the top bench wider than normal), my kitchen, and bath using a heavy-duty extension cord with multiple outlets. I plugged in a lamp for reading, the coffee maker, a microwave oven; all powered by the generator used by Louis' crew (I also used their porta-potty). At the Mercury post office, I tacked a "Missing" poster on the bulletin board and wandered about in search of my lost dog.

Before she returned to work, Meredith brought thick clean blankets to pad the top bench, along with a comforter and pillow. I hung an old cloth—something woven by my mother or her mother, a simple cream cotton square with thin red stripes—over the sauna window.

With only a daytime generator for electricity, I couldn't heat the sauna to thoroughly cleanse my body—how intensely I longed for that purifying ritual!—so I hung a shower curtain against the benches. Each afternoon, I showered quickly under cold spray, washing away dust and sweat, making sure the water didn't spatter my sleeping bag or appliances. Or the book on grief by Elisabeth Kubler-Ross, given by Meredith, never opened.

Even the neighbors amazed me. Fortunately, the damage was restricted to my own property. My insurance paid for cleaning expenses incurred by the neighbors from smoke infiltration. Rebecca or one of the kids would bring me muffins in the morning, sweet with tart blueberries, the juice falling onto my white down comforter. Some days I didn't want to leave my cozy hut. The cacophony forced me out: the rumbling of the generator, the growl and crunch of a backhoe, a head-quaking drill of jackhammer, shouts of men at work, and ranchera music. So I'd up and do what had to be done in the house, finally sorting through my folks' things, boxing what little salvageable items remained that were not burnt or water-logged. I made numb trips to Goodwill. Throwing away things became easy—nothing mattered.

As I slogged through the days, everyone was too nice. Rebecca regularly dropped by looking sunny, suggesting we take a walk, go to lunch, check out the country club. Even the psycho soccer mom across the street cooked for me. The woman whose loquacity swells when discussing her sons' athletic endeavors—the kids play more sports than the Olympics, and, alas, I faded somewhere around Lacrosse. One night she brought lasagna dripping with hot mozzarella, then treated me on successive weeks to homemade meatloaf, roast chicken with rosemary, savory fried and fatty pork chops, all accompanied by garlic mashed potatoes. Garlic aside, the food reminded me of my mother's cooking. I marveled at and was grateful for her industry and beneficence. She, with the ubiquitous baseball cap and ponytail, the maniacal sports chauffeuring, the invisible husband, all the wrong bumper stickers. Who knew?

One weekend afternoon I heard Meredith talking softly with someone in the spared bedroom—I jerked to a halt in the doorjamb. Cleo? *Quiet?* I'd never seen her without makeup, let alone with that timorous and contrite look. I backed out of the room. She was, I suspected, the one responsible for the completely useless gifts I'd find outside the sauna in the early morning hours: bath salts from the English Channel (soaking in such an industrial waterway made me think of bathing in Boston Harbor), bunches of cellophane-wrapped, grocery-store flowers that wilted within hours in the summer heat, an Avon makeup kit. Peace offerings I threw in the trash.

Two and a half weeks post-blaze, my headaches started abating. Gone for another ten months or so. But my brain still felt fuzzy, and I dragged through my tasks unconsciously, thinking only of escape. Despite the incense I burned, I fell asleep each night inhaling char. Then, one miraculous eve, a golf cart pulled up and a preppy couple delivered Coco to me—I hugged their alligator-emblazoned chests for possibly too long. I cradled my dog close, her soft fur became my warmest blanket, her company the only I craved.

During that month after the fire, Troy buzzed in and out, sometimes knocking tentatively on the sauna door to offer help. I refused. Meredith, looking haggard, drove herself up after work some days just to check on me. Ravi and Sri called to offer help, but I accepted only short visits. My old friend April phoned from my hometown and offered to come out. No, I told her. Because I was readying to leave.

Steffen proved to be the most tireless. I'd lie in the sauna, exhausted despite doing little, and hear him crashing through walls and ordering workmen around. His father, Louis, who'd spent his life in construction, convinced me to rebuild, or at least remodel. Although Mom's bedroom, the kitchen, and family room were unsalvageable, the other rooms stood intact—just permeated with the odor of smoke.

As I waited for my passport, we drew up modest plans for the rebuild. I stood in the rubble of the remaining rooms with the architect, Louis, and Steffen, as they yelled about a new loft, "joists," and "haunch piers"—a foreign language that sounded vaguely nautical—over the annihilating growl of the generator. It jarred my whole body. I couldn't hear. Instead of pointing out that if we stepped a few feet *outside*, away from the deafening rumble, we might actually be capable of communication, I watched their mouths, their expressions, tried to understand what was going on...but the noise roaring through my head, the whirling thoughts that failed to gel—the general jumble of my life—left me inert. I just nodded. It didn't matter. I left it all in their hands. In a brief lull of the machine, Steffen said, "You want it exactly the same, don't you, Alina?"

"No." I suddenly decided. "Change it. Make it better." Walking away, I glanced back to say, "Just don't make it big." Then, thinking of the neighbors, I caused consternation all around by saying, "And the yard? No fences."

Before I left, I got LASIK. Life felt strange, distorted, my brain immobile. I needed at least to *see*. I could've ordered new glasses and contacts but there's a freedom in feeling you have nothing to lose, in not caring or fretting. Prior to his departure, Paavo fit me in with John. And afterward, when the goggles came off, I saw the violet sheen under Meredith's eyes, each stubborn hair of stubble on Steffen's chin, darker than his blond hair, the mottled mauve on Coco's black nose. And on the few occasions he visited, I felt as though I could see to the bottom of Lou's endlessly clear eyes. Everything became brilliant.

I gave Louis power-of-attorney with access to all my funds,

Steffen a hefty salary from those funds to benefit Mere and Lou as well. Coco went to the neighbors, giving the dog free reign to my scathed yard. For my chef across the street, I purchased a gift certificate to a local sporting goods store, though I sensed I was only abetting her obsession. *Live and let live*, as Dad often said, after he stopped drinking, one of his AA, twelve-step mantras.

Before packing it, I logged on to my laptop. Piled up were scads of messages from Finns, relatives of all stripes, some in English more masterful than mine, others in pure Finnish, far too many to respond to. I wrote to Jukka and Paavo about my plans, signing off with "*Nakemiin*:" for I had no home, a Russo-Finnish mystery to solve, relations to run to, and…Paavo.

Unable to say goodbye to anyone, most especially my Mere, my Lou, and even Steffen, I merely hinted at leaving soon. Meredith deflected the enormity of this by saying she was still planning on going to St. Petersburg—that we'd be together then—and I wanted to believe her.

I left Mercury feeling wistful. These "rich" were good to me. And, perhaps, good *for* me. And one person I had to see. Before my taxi arrived in the dark of the morning, I checked to see if his light was on. Living so close, I know when Marty starts up his car each morning for his long commute, so I knocked at his door. He came out with a coffee cup and we sat on the steps in the fresh hours, our first personal encounter since the fire.

I'd apologized through Rebecca and the kids, but had yet to face him. Sitting side-by-side, I said, "I can't leave without apologizing to you, Marty." I sighed and scanned the sleeping street, my bags at the curb. "See, I made all these assumptions about this place, these people. You know, the country club, golf carts—it's just not me. Then I got to know it—and you—a little and, my God, you're like some saint step-dad. I was awful. Anyway, I'm sorry I said what I did." I turned to face him. "I really admire you."

He shook my hand, asked when I'd be back. Accepting the

business card he offered, I shrugged, and as the taxi crawled down the narrow lane, I waved goodbye to him with my one-way ticket.

PART 3: FINDING HOME

~Ei kannata mennä merta edemmäs kalaan.~

~One should not go farther than the sea to fish.~

~Kenen leipää syöt, sen lauluja laulat.~
~Whose bread you eat, his songs you'll sing.~

Suomi

I am loved. From the moment I arrive in Finland, I am greeted by hands thick and gnarled with age, others soft and vigorous. The full-leaf aspens and pines reach out their branches to welcome me. Ferns wave hello. Waters lap me in. I am welcomed by the land itself, the soft, spongy ground, the "bog land" for which my new home is named, *Suomi.*

Jukka meets me at the airport with his younger sister, Taimi, a plump college student with a buttery tan, and his parents, a robust chatty couple in their 50's who run a charter sailing company. Taimi holds a tiny infant, whom I admire only briefly, pushing down feelings and memories. When we're alone at the baggage carrousel, I ask Jukka about her. He'd never mentioned being an uncle. He shakes his head. "You can see this baby is new."

"Yeah, but they take time to percolate!"

"Well it is mistake Taimi has child so young and the father is not with her." He says that she lives with their parents, who, along with government-subsidized daycare, help her out.

Back at their small house, a dozen people await my arrival. They are all related to Mom, Kovanens of some ilk, young and old, shy and curious. The house is bright and sparely acquitted with modern furniture. Everything is minimalist except the food. A taupe linen cloth covers a large table spread with natural cuisine from the lakes, fields and forests: salmon, Arctic char, and crayfish; dried reindeer, blueberries and lingonberries. New potatoes smothered in butter, spring peas and onions. Wild chanterelles in sauce. In the kitchen, a huge coffee urn sits on the counter next to an array of cookies, breads and pastries. I hold my stomach, regretting the odd-hour meals I'd eaten out of boredom on Lufthansa and Finnair.

Jukka's parents, fluent in English, promptly put me at ease, fill my plate, introduce me one by one. Although I'm too tired to recall any names, the gathering feels very familiar, like those in Massachusetts with my *mummu* and *pappa*, so many Finns and Finnish-Americans, the quiet and the garrulous.

I speak what little Finnish I know to the older folks and try to draw the English out of the younger ones. "They ain't going to talk in English," Jukka tells me after I unsuccessfully try to draw a young, white-haired metal-head into conversation. "They are understanding you and can say everything but they are afraid to make mistakes. I was like that one time but now it don't matter." Obviously. I smile at him, glad to be close to his familiar face again, hear his loony version of English after our four plus weeks apart.

This is a family gathering, so I don't expect to see Paavo, but I am dying to hear news of him. Jukka and I take our desserts to a loveseat. Exhausted from the long flight, I down more coffee. "Are you still doing that swimming now that it's summer? With Paavo?"

"Oh ya. Many days we wake up early for that. It's healthy habit." He takes a bite out of a berry pastry and slowly finishes chewing. "He's not coming yet. I don't know why." His shoulders rise in a shrug as he glances at the door.

"Coming yet? *Where?*"

"Here. To greet with you."

"You mean you invited him here today? Now? *Nyt?*"

He stares at me strangely. "Yes, of course. You want to see him too, I think?"

I draw a breath. "Yes, but—"

"And maybe we take sauna later."

My coffee cup clangs on the saucer. A sauna with Paavo and Jukka? I'm not sure I'm ready to sauna co-ed! These Finns with their nudity…I envision a scene from my youthful trip here, where, to my preadolescent horror, someone's mother walked past her sons through the house wearing waist-high underwear and fastening her bra, pushing the bottom of one fleshy breast into her cup. Evidently, the comfort of nudity outside the sauna was squelched in my family after one generation in New England.

My vanity gets the best of me. I hop up, grab my backpack, and ask to use the bathroom. Jukka points me downstairs. An oval mirror hangs over the sink. My face is haggard, dark circles dull my eyes, my hair is stringy with oil. The lurking acne mound threatens to burst out of its regular home beneath the skin of my chin.

I rinse my face in icy water, dry it with the thin cotton hand towel, then pull from my leather backpack a brush and some acne concealer. I fix my skin, pull my hair back into a ponytail, and dab on lip-gloss. I try on a tired smile. I didn't want to reconnect with Paavo in such a large grouping, looking like this. I'd imagined something more private, intimate, with me looking rested and radiant. If such a thing were possible anymore.

Looking down, I see a coffee stain advertising my right breast, encircling the entire nipple area. Ugh! Never should I wear white. Then I notice another large coffee stain on my inner thigh, shockingly close to the crotch of my pale jeans. When did I spill all this? On a plane? Here? No matter, I need to change my clothing so that I'm not a walking advertisement for sex.

I run upstairs, backpack held in front of me and mumble that I need something from the car. I scamper outside to Jukka's Fiat, which I know will be unlocked—no one worries about theft here. Leaning into the back, I fumble through my luggage for a long shirt. Unfortunately, my wardrobe was highly limited in packing, as most of my clothes burned in the fire. I find a night shirt long enough to cover my crotch…then through the rear window, I see him, three feet from me, locking his red Volvo! He cuts a striking figure, trim but broad shouldered, a deep summer tan, his dark hair longer. I bend lower, burying my head in my suitcase.

Crunching graveled steps pass me, then stop. "*Moi, hei.* Hello. Is this Alina?"

I swivel up too quickly, knocking my head as I stand out of the car. I see now that he holds a bouquet of violet flowers in one hand—*for me?*—as he spreads his full lips in a winsome smile. I'd forgotten how handsome he is.

Flustered, I shout, "Paavo!" as I draw him in fast for a hug. Which causes him to pull back and finger his ear. "Oh sorry," I step back. "Sometimes I talk too loudly when I'm near someone's ear." I rub my head where it banged on the car.

With a smile he says, "You are still moving too fast. This is what makes for clumsy."

Despite practicing for this reunion, I forget what to say. "Anyway, look at you!" I exclaim in an avuncular tone, as if sizing up a boy who's sprouted two inches since I last saw him. He glances down at his feet, then up questioningly. I say, "You look…" *Sexy* is the word that comes to mind, as his hair is damp, his face flushed, and I notice that his loose cotton pants cling to his brawny thighs.

"I look? What you have said."

"Oh. Just perfect!" I gush, which causes him to avert his eyes.

"Well, I doubt this. But I have just come from the swim, which I need because now I'm working very hard." He pushes that thick, moist hair from his face, saying something about being tired, while I sense his male-ness, and suddenly picture him in that skimpy Euro bathing suit, then nude, a vague blurry memory of the night we swam, his wet, hairless chest glistening under the half moonlight. Warmth grows in my groin as I imagine wrapping my legs around him…if he pressed me up against the car… It must be the middle of the month for me. All this inner talk of saunas, nudity—I'm overly worked up.

"You must be feeling this way, too," he says.

"*Huh?*" My surprised face meets his expressionless expression.

"Tired. After such long trip."

"Oh, tired! Whoo! Right." I look down at my clothing, "Afraid I'm a mess after those flights." As his eyes follow mine, I think how disheveled and unappealing I must look. "I was just going to change my shirt—"

"You really are the Finn." He takes my hand, shuts Jukka's car door. I can't help but grin with pride. He says, "Too much in your head," *What does he mean by that?*

We start up the long walk to the front steps. To move the focus from me, I say, "You said you're working a lot?"

"Yo, I have taken such long time off and now I'm very busy. But I like."

"Yes! There's really nothing like hard work, is there? I miss it," I say, thinking I've barely had time to. But I know exactly what he means; we are like-minded people.

"Well, you have had too much troubles." With his rolled "r," the word pours out like "ruples."

"You were so helpful...I've wanted to thank you. And Jukka, of course." A gentleman, he allows me up the narrow stairs first.

"*Ai*, no. That's not the truth. We have not stayed long enough. And from what I see, Steffen is the one."

"The one?" I pause on the steps. This Finnish business of stopping mid-sentence.

"He's working all the time for you. He's quite some man. Now I've been thinking about him and Meredith and their child."

"He's been good, it's true. But now I'm here and…" *This is our time*! I don't want to talk about Steffen, or even Meredith for that matter.

"Come in house now." He opens the door. "We'll talk about this email from Meredith."

What?

*

"I doubt that you have seen this," he hands me his phone. "This message has come today. For you and me and Jukka." After greetings all around, a presentation of Paavo's flowers to Jukka's mother, and food and drink provided, Paavo, Jukka and I sit around a sleek low table.

Wondering why my most un-techie friend has sent email, and to the three of us, I begin to pore over it. After reading a few lines, I nearly shout, "She's following me here to Finland! Already!" I love her!

Paavo says, "Well, this is bout the baby business in Russia too. She is thinking maybe it's OK to visit to us first because this baby is at St. Petersburg."

"Seriously?" I can't believe it's actually happening—and so soon. How was it arranged so quickly? Did Steffen finally agree? My heart beats too fast. This is all too fast. So much change—I just left!

I read on and see he's right. Meredith's sister has been busy activating the adoption plans, and it's possible she'll fly into Helsinki first, before summer's end. "But no guarantees," she writes. She writes using "I" instead of "we." What about Steffen? Lou? Perhaps Steffen will stay home with their son, as surely Russia is no place for him. Am I becoming biased like Jukka? My mind whirls as I digest the news, my hand gripping the phone.

Jukka says with a sniff. "No guarantees is for sure. You better tell your friend to save the money and stay home with family."

~Maassa maan tavalla.~
~In a land by its customs.~

Getting Busy

They have plans for me. I have little time to ponder Meredith's situation, for the Finns take over. It's immediately decided that I should stay with Jukka at his apartment in Espoo, a former bedroom community for Helsinki but now a city that boasts the largest population outside the capital. A place conveniently close to Paavo's, I think with anticipation.

Jukka's to be my chauffeur, facilitator, and translator, his family allowing him this form of activity because he is not employed. The parents have created a list of myriad summer events, an ambitious schedule, and I recall how much Finns pack into the long temperate days of their short summer.

Still jet-lagged, I listen bleary-eyed over breakfast on Day One to Jukka and his sister Taimi propose an itinerary. In addition to the usual activities of swimming, sailing, mushroom and berry-picking at family *moekkis*, their summer cottages, they discuss much choral and instrumental music, including the huge opera festival in Savoliina, so large it lasts from July till August. And by contrast, lots of heavy metal, which surprises me but perhaps shouldn't, it fitting the Finnish character, young people here drawn to its wintry dark, raw power. Taimi, who does not appear Goth-ish, tells me that I missed *Tuska*, the largest heavy-metal concert of the year. She wishes I could've gone to the three-day fest, held just a couple of weeks ago. "*Viileä*," very cool, she says, and I silently hope her baby was not subjected to that screeching event. Being more of an alt-rock girl, I'm not too regretful about missing it. I ask if "*Tuska*" refers to a town in Finland. They laugh. Jukka says, "'Tuska' is word for 'pain.' It is when you have the headache, some sort of misery."

"Well I didn't come for that!" I joke, and he agrees that my agony is best left behind. Then there are goofy events only Finns would think of, such as boot throwing, mosquito catching, and an air guitar contest, as well as wife carrying (the winner earns his wife's weight in beer) and a cell phone throwing event—perhaps a manifestation of their conflicting views of the tool they rely on so heavily for everything from buying to banking.

I deliberately mix events. "I'll go to the wife throwing."

Jukka smirks, "That we are not permitted. But maybe some men would like it. Anyways, the Finnish women are the strong ones—they throw the men round."

Although I love music and wacky contests, I'm not interested in going to large gatherings of strangers. I tell them I'm happy to visit my relatives. I've arrived in my new home with specific plans but no knowledge of how long I'll be here. By the time I arrive, it's mid-July, and the full Finnish summer of play is underway. This makes my goal of meeting my family members much easier, as many are taking four or more of weeks of vacation. Besides meeting more of my mother's family, I want to learn about my father's side, meet the Eskalas, and find out about the Russian certificate. My other plans—one awkward to discuss, the other too private—I keep to myself. For now.

While Paavo immerses himself in work—he's a physician at a health center—Jukka whisks me off to visit relations. Old ones. Lots. I meet with Kovanens and the like, my mother's side, without seeing Paavo at all for several days. But it's July, the days are long, the Finns make the most of these few lengthy days, and we are busy for twelve hours straight. The energetic Finns rise before I do, and go to bed long after I drop off to sleep. My cohorts young and old party into the twilit night, into the sun that never sets. I wonder if eons of hibernating like Arctic bears during the sun-starved winter months has made them actually need less sleep during the few but long summer months, allowing them this prolonged burst of energy.

As I'm drawn into the houses and apartments of my mother's many distant relatives, offered coffee and cakes, meals, and saunas, I come to believe I might just be related to the full five million inhabitants. And this is just my mother's side!

We see *mummus*, lots of them. Straight-haired, straight mannered people. We visit farm homes and city condominiums and vacation *moekkis*. Jukka escorts me around Eastern Finland from Helsinki to Turku to Vaasa. These older Finnish women suck air with a high soprano sigh, in unison, "*yo, yo, yo,*" when Jukka translates tales of my family—my grandparents and parents. Mom visited twice with my father and me, once after I was born, and another time when I was twelve or thirteen. But she packed in visits on her own as the years passed, perhaps longing for her homeland. And a few of these grey-haired folk have visited us through the years, though I recall little of them. When we talk of her, they smile or shake their heads in sympathy, and suck more air. More than once I hear the ultimate compliment about my mother: "very clean," they say. Which, said in English, often comes out "very lean"—not so accurate as the years advanced and the *pulla* piled around her middle.

The elderly speak to me in fast Finnish, with some miscomprehension that I am fluent—perhaps because I can say *hyvää päivää*, hello, and *kiitos,* thank you, and a few handy phrases. Or perhaps because I am my mother's daughter and look like a Finn. They grab my hands and search my face as they speak, and I nod and smile, respond *yo* or *kyllä*, yes. Sometimes I venture, "*se on hyvä!"—that's good!*—though I could be hearing about a death, for all I know. Their small eyes twinkle at me and tear up when, via Jukka, I talk of my parents. And invariably when I depart their homes.

At one house, a woman fingers the gold cross that dangles over her ample, aging bosom and says my parents "are with God now," reminding me of a lady who occasionally attended Mom's coffee klatches, spouting religious aphorisms while the others talked politics and gossip. Lutherans in name only, my mother's Finnish friends had little religiosity, believed firmly in separation of church and state, and even more resolutely in keeping God out of a nice coffee hour.

Everywhere I see my father and mother, in the forward slant of an old fisherman, the way his mouth noodles his toothpick as we boat out to someone's *moekki*, in the round red cheeks of the caffeinated women, filling me with cup upon cup of *kahvi*...to a fault they are a generous, warm, sentimental people, and I feel grateful to be here.

They all ask why I came, how long will I stay. The answer is complex. I tell them I'm searching for an aunt, perhaps, a close relative on my father's side. These women are not Eskalas nor related, so they cannot help. I also tell them that without a house or job I'm free. Perhaps too free, I think. Rootless, but searching, hoping for roots to take hold here in this swampy land.

~Ollan hiljaa, saadaan kaloja.~
~Let's be quiet, we'll get some fish.~

Moekkis

Lingonberries, gooseberries, and Arctic cloudberries. Mushroom and blueberry picking. Leisurely, we comb the woods for all manner of berries and mushrooms, summer's national pastime. One doesn't go to Finland so much for the urban life, I feel, but for this: the wandering through kilometers of open forest and lake-land.

After a cursory tour of Helsinki with Jukka's family, we've traveled all over southern Finland visiting waterside cottages, *moekkis*, the second homes owned by most Finns. We've sailed and slept overnight moored at islands, slumbering in the cozy beds closeted in the hold, cradled by calm waters. We've roasted meat on common grills, leaving them clean for the next passers-by.

Until now I've been contented picking fruit in the temperate, pine-scented air, absorbing the calming quiet of the forest. But today I'm anxious to spend the day in a noisy, English-speaking crowd, the night dancing in a noisier club. I'm eager to ditch the fruit and fish for a decent pizza. Enough nature, already!

After a few hectic, peripatetic weeks, Jukka's whole family and I spend a rainy day at a *moekki* owned by his mother's sister and her husband. Situated on the Gulf of Bothnia near Turku, it's typically snug and rustically decorated, warmed with wall weavings and rugs. But due to the weather, we stay indoors for hours on end.

The couple, it seems, are remodeling their condo in Helsinki, and don't tire of describing every detail to Jukka's family in Finnish. Jukka cannot translate it all or grows tired of trying. The only word I recognize in the fast talk between the hosts and guests is "house."

As we sit around the table after an early supper, I listen to the patter of rain and conversation, my mind wandering to Dad's attempts to teach me the fifteen cases for "*talo*," *house.* If I said I'm tired of this house, I think the word changes to *talon*. If it were my house, I think I would say *talossa*? One sentence Dad taught me comes to me in full, so during a brief pause in the discussion, I say, "*On vaikeaa elää talotta*." The conversation halts. Everyone stares as if the coffee pot just talked. After repeating myself, I'm forced to ask, "Did I say it wrong?"

"That depends," says Jukka. "You have said—"

"*It's difficult to live without a house*!" I spout. And suddenly I need to get out of *this house! Talostani*? *Argh*. I bolt outside.

Sitting alone on the seaside dock, legs dangling over the water, I shiver, drawing my sweater tight from the waning drizzle. I watch the clouds clear and try to fix on what's wrong…*is it* my lack of a house? Home? The fact that Finland isn't my home yet and learning Finnish is impossible? I think of my lack of progress with my agenda: meeting my dad's side, connecting with Paavo…but if I'm to stay here, I suppose there's no great hurry. Uneasy, I jiggle my feet above the murky sea.

Jukka comes out with two bottles and swings his legs over the dock beside me. He hands me a beer and, after some time says, "I think you want to say, '*koti-ikävä*.' '*Koti*' is 'home.' Or 'base.'"

"But my dad said that '*talo*' is—"

"Yes, yes. Also you can use 'house.' But I think you are wishing for the home. Or missing your home, ya?

"No," I immediately deny it. "I mean, I've only been here…how long?"

"Fourteen and one-half days. But I am not counting."

I chuck him on the arm for being amusing. And because I have nothing to say—I've been here such a short time! Why does it feel so long?

Jukka says it's funny that he still calls his parents' house "*home*." I nod. For years after moving to California my version of "home" meant Massachusetts. Perhaps my birthplace is my true home…my friend April still lives there and at least they speak some semblance of English. Thoughts of California only disturb me.

"You are growing tired of so much visiting, I know this," Jukka pronounces.

"It's what I came for, I mean you're only doing what I asked." I feel contrite, embarrassed by my outburst in the house. "*You* must be sick of it, Jukka. Speaking English and taking me everywhere."

"It's OK. My parents is mad of me without job. So I keep you busy visiting round and they can keep working." Their sailing business does not give them the customary summer weeks off.

"I'm glad I'm providing you with an excuse to be a bum."

He gives out a small laugh. "I like that. You can be funny girl. Letting me be the ass. That's what my sister calls me anyways."

"No. I don't mean ass! I mean your not having to work…it's letting you be lazy."

He laughs more. "Oh, ja. *Laiskuri*. Lazy worm. Well Taimi is calling me that, too."

Gratified by Jukka's company, I sling my arm over his back. "Well, I like you, lazy worm." Maybe this is what it's like to have a brother. In the twilight, we stare toward Sweden, the dark trees of the Åland archipelago visible against the silver sky, the leaden water lapping below our feet. "They've asked me to stay on longer," I say, speaking of the hosts here. "In the sauna your aunt invited me. If you need a break…it really is beautiful here."

"Yo, this is best sailing in Finland. But they talk off your ears. And I know you. You like be left alone. They gonna be with you seven by 24 and you need some time down," he says. Jukka insists I remain at his apartment, and I don't argue.

"OK, your place will remain my *koti,* my *home base.*" Besides, I need proximity to Paavo.

As if reading my mind, he narrows his eyes. "You have not seen much of Paavo."

I pause and attempt a blithe tone. "It would be good to see him more."

"*Yo*, I thought so."

When we finish our beers, I feel the need to remind him about the certificate. "The one from my father's side. I don't know any Eskalas, and I'm dying to meet—or learn about—this *Alina*. I mean, she could still be alive. If that year was 1938, she'd only be sixty-nine. Do you think we can search for her?"

He takes my empty bottle. "*Yo, yo.* I have not forgotten that paper." He frowns as always when contemplating the Russian implications of the other half of my family. "That we gonna take care of."

A burst of laughter peels through the night air. Inside, the lamp-lit *moekki* grows more boisterous. Standing, I see Taimi rocking her infant and listening to the group around the table. The picture reminds me of Meredith breastfeeding Lou in his early days. The yellow kerosene lamp floods the family in golden light. "What are they laughing about?"

Jukka listens as we walk toward the lively *moekki,* then says dismissively, "This is some silly story they talk bout every year." When I press to know more, he yawns and says, "It's hard to tell in English. It don't—doesn't—matter." I smile at his correction. But when he says, "Anyways, it's old family story, nothing you know," I feel my smile vaporize and a strange lurch in my heart.

~*Oma apu paras apu.*~
~Own help is the best help.~

Morning Swim

"We go to swim now." Jukka shakes me awake. I squint up at him from my futon, at the grey day showing through the thin curtain. What's up with the sudden, mid-week dawn aquatics?

"No thanks," I say, snuggling under the covers. We've been back from the *moekki* for a couple of days but last night I was up late. After many tries, I got hold of Meredith. It was 3 a.m. here, the low night sun filtered through the window, and though our talk was brief, it was wonderful to hear her voice. I relish going over the plans today in the comfort of my bed.

He shrugs his shoulders. "OK. But you miss Paavo," he says, shutting the bedroom door.

Huh? "*Paavo*?" I scamper up and after him to the kitchen, where he quietly prepares coffee. "You're—we're—going swimming with Paavo today?"

Jukka, evidently not in a chatty mood, simply says, "Yo."

"But…why? I mean, why today?"

"He's busy doctor and this is some way you can see him. Unless you get sick and make appointment at clinic. But even so, I think maybe they give you different doctor."

Digesting this with some *pulla*, I grin. "*Kiitos*, Jukka. It'll be great to see him." He sets the usual rye crisp and herring onto the table…I haven't even thought to help. "I mean, just to see someone I *know*." I distance myself from the fish by pulling milk from the fridge.

"Well, that is hard to say how well you know him."

"Better than most of the *mummus* I've been meeting," I tease. I sip my creamy coffee. "And besides, I have news for you both!"

After a short hike down to the beach on the Gulf of Finland, we undress on the rocky shore. I shiver, hobbling over the biting pebbles to the water—so different from the sandy beaches back home. Nothing like the coarse sand of the Cape, nor the soft sand of Southern California, a delight to the toes, like shuffling through tawny flour. And the surf here laps gently, unlike the crashing waves at Nauset Beach, where Dad and I would play in the rough swell until I turned blue.

Finland's sea and landscape are mild, like its people. No smashing surf, no soaring mountains, except perhaps the treeless peaks and deep ravines of Saami Lapland. The land is modestly flat, undramatic; lakes and sea alike wave calmly. This land of endless forest and water could only have shaped a quiet people. When Jukka points to Paavo swimming in the distance, I peck my way into the shallows, and with a cold shudder dive in. I swim fast but cannot reach him. Calling out, I sputter and wave, but he completes a few vigorous laps, then swiftly heads toward shore fifty feet from us. I clamber out, wrapping myself in a thick towel to go greet him. Invigorated by the cold water, I reach him before Jukka.

"*Moi*, Alina," he says, drying himself briskly. I'd never noticed what a classic swimmer's body he has: strapping broad shoulders and muscular arms, narrow hips and spectacular thighs. "It's good to see you. Jukka said you might come today." I answer with "*Hei*" and watch him dry. He wears the very swimsuit he wore in that first picture, saved on my computer and oft lingered over…blue and tight, low enough to imagine the private parts beneath. Though a quick glance now shows that the chilly day does not show them to advantage.

Before I can tell him the news, he asks about my house. I summarize that I regularly talk to Steffen and his dad, that when it's finished I'll sell it. At this he looks up, brows raised. I don't want to go into my poor financial planning, how the house was under-insured for its value and required me to take out a loan. How I have nothing to go back to…

Once Jukka joins us, I say, "Guess what? I got a hold of Meredith last night!" Both men take the news calmly. "Mere's not very high-tech. I can't Skype with her and forget email—she hates computers. We only talked for, like, two minutes because she was worried about the cell phone charges at her end. But guess what? The adoption is definitely happening!" Paavo tilts his head, while Jukka flings his back. I continue, "But she's—I guess, I should say *they're*—not coming to Finland. It got too expensive. So they're flying directly to St. Petersburg. And whenever that happens, I'm going over to help and see the baby!"

Paavo says, "So this actually comes round. Her boyfriend has agreed. Who takes care of the little one?"

"Lou? Steffen's parents, I guess," although I don't recall her giving me the details or how she got Steffen to cave in on the adoption. I remember asking, but she either didn't hear me or was in too big a rush to get off the phone. Jukka maintains silence. I ignore him, though it does all seem surreal. "Anyway, her name is Natalya, and I'm going to see her first!"

Paavo says, "I cannot believe Russians will give away this child so quickly."

"We all need to think positively!" I chirp.

"Yes, Americans are very…*sinisilmäinen.* Blue-eyed," he answers.

I know he means "starry-eyed." Mom used that expression for me more than once. But as we all walk off the beach I feel my "blue-eyed" optimism about spending more time with Paavo waning. I need to act. When we reach Paavo's car, I announce, "This is kind of out of the *blue*, but I haven't gone dancing here yet."

Jukka lights up and mentions a nightclub, adding, "I thought you just wanted the boring things."

Ignoring that remark, I ask, "Anyone up for a polka night?"

"Poker night?" says Jukka. "All of sudden you want to disco and gample."

"*Gamble*," I correct him.

He says, "That's good. Any time we can play poker."

I'm not sure if he's deliberately misunderstanding. "*Polka. Polkka.* You know, the traditional dance."

Jukka finds my choices odd. "Old peoples know. You gonna ask that *pappa* over there," he nods toward a pot-bellied man struggling with a bathing cap. "He's gonna take you for sure."

"I will take her," Paavo says. "I will find *polkka*. This Saturday I am free." And although this is stated rather matter-of-factly and feels nothing like being asked out on a date, I can't help but do a little two-step in my bare feet.

~Tyhmä kaiken tietämänsä kertoo.~
~A fool tells everything he knows.~

Girl Talk

I'm starved for girl talk. Real conversation, where feelings are explored and secrets revealed. Although she's a few years younger, I feel that Jukka's sister Taimi and I could be good friends. We're cousins of some sort, like sisters. Providing, of course, I stay, find a job, and realize my dream of love... She'd be my Meredith. And her baby daughter Aino could be my little Lou—although I know in my heart that I could never replace either of them.

On the Friday before my dance date with Paavo, Taimi and I take the tram from Espoo to Helsinki. She has no classes, and her mother agreed to babysit. We're headed for the Cathedral, as I've already toured much of the city with her parents: the modern, musical pipes of the Sibelius monument, the harbor *tori*—an outdoor market where I bought a multi-colored scarf for Meredith and a carved reindeer for Lou—and the old *Suomenlinna* Fortress, built across six islands.

Riding the uncrowded late morning train, I mention that I could see myself moving to Finland. Two fine lines appear between Taimi's brows, as she tells me with certainty that the idea is crazy. After all, I live in California. Just say the name and you can feel the sunshine, smell the ocean, right? "The weather here is not always so warm like this." I tuck my arms around my middle, as the day has barely reached—what is the Celsius temperature? Well, it feels like 60 degrees Fahrenheit today, at most, hardly "warm" (and obviously there's the issue of learning the decimal system). "And you would be missing your family." She lowers her gaze, fixating on the clean tram floor. "Or, your friends."

"*One* friend. I wouldn't include the one who burned down my house." Even as I say it, the old rancor against Cleo feels feeble. I recall with an inner smile her gutsy walk, her quippy, frank talk. No lack of girl talk with sassy Cleopatra Crumm! I insist, "I feel a connection with the people here, the land." I look out at the boring landscape of office buildings, not dissimilar to Silicon Valley. "I actually feel quite Finnish."

"And what would you do?" Obviously she means work, for even she works part-time, despite being a student and mother.

"I could work in high-tech," I suck in a sigh. "Or who knows? Get married and raise kids?" She looks at me askance.

"You gonna marry some Finn guy? They got sexier men in *Germany*!" She laughs. "Anyway, I'm not sure you gonna find work. You don't speak so much Finnish." Of course her assumption is that I'd continue to work after having children, as the great majority of women do here. After they and their husbands have taken their generous paid family leave, they take advantage of the extensive network of daycare. How refreshingly different from cushy Mercury, where women parade around in tennis skirts all day, parrying their kids from one event to another.

At a long stop several people board the train. An attractive man in a suit sits across from us. His gaze flickers briefly on mine then moves downward—another rider excessively interested in the clean floor of the tram. If it doesn't work out with Paavo, *could I even meet a man here?* "Tell me, Taimi, how does one go about dating here? I mean, no one ever makes eye contact!"

"It's not so polite in Finland to stare for strangers."

"Then how do you flirt?"

She emits a high-pitched giggle. "You can meet the guy when he's really drunk. Then if he is thinking he likes you, maybe in a few years he gets up the courage to send you SMS." Ha ha.

We ride the smooth train in silence. After another stop, I ask quietly, "Do you know Jukka's friend Paavo? The one he swims with? You know, he came to the States with him."

"Yes, yes, I know who you talk about." She chews on her pink lip. "I don't really know him. Not so well." She continues, "At first I like the way Paavo looks. My brother has told me he's too old for me, I should be with my baby's father."

"Oh, I agree. With the part about being with Aino's daddy." Funny, how her situation parallels Meredith's in a way.

"But I get to learn Paavo little bit and I'm not so interested. He's so dull!"

I sit straight. "Oh, I don't think so at all! He's just the quiet, serious type. He doesn't talk unless he has something true to say...what do you Finns say? *Ei suuret sanat suuta halkaise*?" She corrects my pronunciation, then says, "Yes, I suppose actions say more than talking. But hard to know someone so quiet."

"Well I know he's kind...and good. And he *is* handsome," I add. Taimi gives a non-committal nod. And *available*, I think, but she wouldn't understand how a mid-30s woman feels when she has no children, no prospects. And how can I explain to her that he's just my *type*? Something one feels instinctively.

She stands to get off. "Well Henrik—that is my baby's father—doesn't have job but he's fun and looks much better than Paavo. I think you are...*pihkassa*. I don't know how to say." She rubs her fingers together. "It means in the sticky stuff from the tree."

Hmm. "Sap? Resin?"

"I'm not sure those words. But in Finnish we say '*pihkassa*' when you are liking someone very much. I think English is 'crush' for him." I suppose the Finnish word applies to me as I persistently stick to my dream of Paavo. Like sap.

"I think Paavo might be—I think he is—*pihkassa* for me, too." That came out more like a question.

Her back shrugs as I follow her toward the city center and Senate Square. "I don't know about that. I don't see Paavo and Jukka doesn't say. But I can ask."

"No! I mean, I'll find out. We're going dancing tomorrow night and..." We get caught up in the city lunchtime crowd and have to walk single file. Like Jukka, she gives a dismissive wave. "Paavo is gonna be *kuin tervan jontia.*" She laughs. "That means something 'like drinking tar.' Kind of slow and hard. You don't have a boyfriend at home?"

"Nope," I say. "No one."

We grab *kahvis* and meat pasties to take to Helsinki Cathedral, walk past the statue of Czar Alexander II to the majestic green-domed church, which is perched high atop several wide and spacious steps. I like this sunny spot near the university with its view of the Russian-style Senate Square. "I remember being here with my parents. These yellow buildings really are like St. Petersburg."

"Yo, and the church was meant to look like St. Isaac's Cathedral there." I observe the graceful white columns, the large green dome flanked by the two smaller ones visible in my line of sight. Scattered about the steps sit students and sun-seekers. We join them to eat our lunch, watch pedestrians cross the square below; it's a relatively homogeneous crowd compared to most capitals—I could be in Blaineville or Mercury.

"Looks like everyone here is using their cell phone," I observe to Taimi. Easy communication for a shy people, I suppose. I've just gotten adept at thumbing SMSs. "At home, texting seems like more a teenage thing. And you guys do way more with your phones...you use them like credit cards."

Taimi shrugs. "You can blame this on Nokia, I suppose." Abruptly changing topics, she says, "Jukka has told me that you have given away your boyfriend to your girlfriend." What's Jukka doing talking about old history?

"That's not exactly right. But yes, after I broke up with Steffen, I introduced him to my friend Meredith. It worked out great." My stomach rumbles from my third or fourth cup of coffee today. I've no doubt this country will give me an ulcer.

"And you still are her friend?" I tell her of course we're still friends, it was my decision. Steffen wasn't for me. Then I start talking about Meredith and Lou, happy to be off the subject of Steffen, but I can tell she's not listening closely.

"That's a strange thing here in Finland. To give away boyfriend and stay the friends with everyone. We don't do that so much, I think."

I sigh. " Well, it's actually kind of strange back home too."

"I could never do that," she shakes her pale, silky hair emphatically. "Afterwards, didn't you have—what is the word—some rejects?"

I laugh. "Yeah, plenty." My mind runs to Ryan and some of the dead-end dates I've had over the past years.

"No. *Regrets*. That is word." A pair of lovers wearing Converses, with messenger bags slung across their bodies, stop their climb up the steps to kiss and nuzzle.

"Regrets? About Steffen? *No*." I stare at the lovers, who stand nose to nose. "Not so much, anyway."

"Really that is hard to believe." The sting of jealousy hits suddenly, out of nowhere, the feeling I had when Meredith told me of her pregnancy.

"To be honest, I did get a bit jealous about Lou. Her getting pregnant, I admit." I feel a flush rising. Taimi might be the first person I've admitted this to.

"And they are married now?

"No." I think of the adoption. Maybe they are? They might as well be.

"Perhaps you can still have him," she says.

"Oh no! I would never do that to her. To Lou." I squirm on the hard granite steps. "Besides, my relationship with Steffen has been over for a long time." I say how her situation is similar to Meredith's, that Steffen hasn't married her yet, doesn't have a steady job. Except for now, as he's rebuilding my house.

Or *was* building it, I muse. He'll be stopping that with the new baby; his dad and crew will finish up. "I bet they'll get married soon." Steffen will love the new baby, of that I'm certain. I stare at the young couple, open in their affection, seemingly rare in Helsinki.

I look down at my worn sneakers. I've barely had time to register all of the ramifications of this adoption, I'm so busy from waking till well after midnight, when I collapse. Suddenly I feel very tired, and agitated at the same time. Why? Meredith is getting her dream fulfilled, while I'm still mired in uncertainty.

Taimi says, "I still want to be with Henrik, I suppose." She points to her gut. "Inside my heart. I think we are *hengenheimolainen*. This means something like spirit connection. I thought we were meant to be together. And Jukka's right: it's good to be with Aino's father, even if he's not working. He is something like a loser, my parents say. Living off the government when he could have job. He's not really studying so much, after all. My parents say we are going to be paying for all the lazy people in Finland, and immigrants from Russia and Eastern Europe. Soon all the lazy people in the E.U." She sucks her lip. "But that is old people talking. I don't worry so much." What would my father think? I grew up with the stereotype that Finns only worked, worked, worked! I try to think about Finland's social-democratic state but my thoughts are derailed when she says, "Finland also has plenty lazy guys like Steffen don't want to take care of their kids."

I fire back, "Steffen's a great dad! And a hard worker. And very generous, he gives Mere almost everything he makes. He's an incredible artist but we don't support the arts like you do here…he's no loser." *And did I mention he's funny and freaking gorgeous?* I lean my elbows on my bent knees, head heavy in my hands. Eyes closed, I think of Steffen and the qualities that drew me to him. It wasn't only sex, after all. I allow myself to remember his smile and how much we laughed together. His attention, though daunting, was new and surprising. I was flattered, for the first time, by total admiration. Before my anxiety about how quickly and deeply he claimed to fall in love with me, before our pregnancy scare and the stress of Dad's illness, we had hours of…how would I express it? Delight, that's the word, sheer delight. I raise my head and open my eyes. The lovers are gone.

Taimi says, "I think you are in love with him still." A flush fuels my face, I feel heat to my ear tips.

"No way." I stand and walk across the steps to get distance and stretch, to forget this talk…my gut aches. I feel like crying. I've been over Steffen for so long…is it just that I want what Meredith has: a partner and children? I don't know, I can't think. I only know that I've had enough girl talk. Didn't we come here to enjoy female company and talk about—*what*? My muddled brain just knows I want to move on. "Let's go," I walk back to pull Taimi up.

We take a blurry tour of the dark church, then walk along the windy harbor before heading back to the train. Because it's rush hour, we're forced to sit apart, which is fine with me. Although I miss talking with my girlfriends, I'm not sure I know Taimi well enough for her to replace Meredith. Or April, whom I visited briefly in Massachusetts before flying on to Finland…

*

When I called April to tell her about the fire, she wanted to fly out. But I declined the offer, promising to come later in the summer to finally deal with Mom's ashes. With only two days there, I explained to April en route from Logan that I had a plan for my mother's remains—a plan that did not involve the Cemetery Commissar Edna Smythe-Burr.

"Who?"

"Never mind," I said. "Let's go visit the dead."

She drove me over miles of country road until we turned onto the narrow dirt path that led to the rusted iron arch. The entrance to the cemetery. Inside, we sat to take in the beauty, the huge maples, the utter solitude and tranquility. In the middle of this bustling state, a mere hour from Boston yet so far away, the dead truly rested in peace.

I had doubts as we trudged through the headstones, many tilted with age, until I spotted my father's marker, the space near it for mom. Together we swept the pine needles off his grave, left thorny but fragrant wild roses. "Edna claims Greendale is a '*Yankee* Cemetery,'" I snorted to April. *As if!*

"So no Red Sox here, eh?" April, the perennial Red Sox worshiper, joked. "So old-school. My grandma used to talk about Finns…like they were Commies with all their co-ops." We grinned at each other, easy friends despite all the years apart. April, with her spray of friendly freckles, looked like Raggedy Ann grown up and now wearing her pigtails in one long braid down her back. If only I could hold her in my arms like a doll, take her with me. "But your parents were great. Your mom serving us that sweet coffee with *boola*…and your dad, always teaching. Remember how he tried to teach us kids Finnish?"

I choked a smile. Another thing I'd forgotten. I was forgetting his voice, the exact way he'd roll over on the rug like a Russian bear to read papers on his back. Tears involuntarily sprang to my eyes and I wanted thank her, so dear to me because she knew my family. She knelt to rearrange the flowers. "It is gorgeous here. So old."

I dropped beside her and put my arm around her waist. Unsteadily, I said, "But it's lonely, way out here. And it's not my home anymore, April."

"Seems like it could be now," she inflected with a question. I shook my head, just didn't know. Had a gut feeling that what I was going to do—with her help—was right. I had to stick with my plan: Finland-bound I would remain.

After making arrangements with the Kalevala Funeral Parlor, who would deal with April, we wandered the hilly old town I know so well, walking down the street I grew up on next to my *mummu* and *pappa*. "Finn Hill," they called it. I quickly looked at the two houses, before we raced downtown, past the closed woolen mill, a Dickensian brick fortress straight out of the Industrial Age. The route to April's house took us past Town Hall, where I had an inspiration. *Edna.* I used to quake at the sound of her voice, but now that matters were taken care of, I was ready to confront her. (Though my heartbeat quickened as I pulled on the heavy glass door.)

The office, with its open seating plan, held half a dozen desks with only two desultory workers. I spotted Edna Smythe-Burr up front immediately. I didn't recall her hair being so gaudy a red, but the pasty, jowly face and thick, pampered hands were unmistakable. I was surprised that she seemed short behind her desk, for in my mind the doughy woman had bloated—as if inflated by yeast and hot office air—into a massive menace. Squat or not, her implacable presence unsettled me. Reminded me of past injustices in the form of mocking insults: "Finns and Yankees," "Spacey Californians"…"One for the books!" I'd been grieving for Christ's sake!

I drew a deep breath. "Ms. Smythe-Burr? I'm Alina Eskala."

Only at this did she strain to look up. "Who?"

"The *Californian* you've talked to. You met my mom and me when we buried Dad at Greendale. We've talked on the phone." *A lot.* "I've traveled here with my mother's ashes."

She surveyed April and me in a blank way until some spark of intelligence appeared in her lackluster eyes. Without moving any part of her bulk other than a neck muscle, she directed her voice behind her, "Hey, Harold. Get a load. This is that gal who couldn't manage to get her motha's box out here for ages." *So I've been the talk of the whole Town Hall?* A thin man lifted his eyes from his computer screen to half-glance at me over half-glasses. "It's about time you got your poor mother buried," Edna sniffed.

"Yeah, her ashes are with me." I stared her down. "But I'm not burying them here." Edna's jaw dropped. "She doesn't belong at Greendale," I declared.

"But she's got that plot next to your father—"

"Dad's leaving."

She dropped her pencil. She shifted in her seat. While a neck muscle twitched and her mouth opened wider, she seemed unable to toss a pithy comment back to Harold about this development.

I secretly squeezed April's hand under the tall reception desk that blocked the public from the civil—and uncivil—servants, and gave my friend a small smile. We turned to leave.

Edna found her voice. "Well I never! This has gotta be the wicked nuttiest—"

April piped up. "You want a Yankee or two in Greendale? I hear there's a whole team of 'em down in New York!" At that we pushed ourselves giggling out the glass door.

My new friend Taimi and I reach Jukka's apartment to find him reclining in front of a TV car race. Without taking his eyes off the screen, he tells me a notice arrived for me. "You have some kind package to pick up at airport." So April did it! She worked with the funeral home to exhume Dad's ashes and have a courier service deliver them here. Now Mom and Dad will be together. With me.

In leaving, Taimi grins impishly. "That's going to be hot night tomorrow with Paavo, for sure." Her brother laughs. I march to my bedroom and sprawl on the bed. What a day. *Puhumatta paras.* Best not to talk.

~Kuu on nuorten miesten aurinko.~
~The moon is the sun of young men.~

Polkka

I want to polka, be swept away, as I was by my dad at some Finnish wedding. I was a child, and he lifted and spun me with abandon. Later, I recall seeing my parents dance together—my dad clunky at first, Mom self-conscious after all the years, until smiles broke out on their whirling pink faces, and my mother's head fell back with laughter. I watched from beginning to end as if it was a foreign movie with hard-to-read subtitles.

I've been determined to enjoy a true Finnish *polkka*, have longed for Paavo to make my feet soar, but my step drags when he picks me up the next evening. At the door, disheartened, I exclaim, "You cut your hair!" His clipped hair now exposes a widow's peak that points to his sharper features, and he wears a neat, button-down shirt.

"Yes, feels good to be back to old self." But I'm not sure I like the look of "old self." Where's that sexy head of thick hair, hair you could stroke your fingers through, clutch at the nape? "Now we go to dance," he states.

I forget the hair once we're on the dance floor. We're in a large restaurant, tables around the periphery. A three-man band plays a lively tune at the far end. On the dance floor, my feet can't keep up with Paavo's, his so energetically adroit. I take one step for each of his two. "I don't know what my feet are doing," I gasp, as he circles me about.

"Don't think," he says, so I hang on as he leads

authoritatively, each hop and twirl a leap of faith. We spin faster and faster. As we circle, tables holding dishes of food pass by, women and men sitting against the wall swirl, the accordion player and fiddler flash past. When the music speeds up, I fly, feet in the air, hanging onto his neck. I throw my head back in abandon.

Paavo stomps and jumps and spins, I laugh and whirl wildly. He turns me about the room with hopping steps until I'm breathless. Ecstatic. Flesh in flight, a celebration of life. Flushed, delirious, Paavo spins me into orbit, lifts me out of this world.

When the dance ends, red-faced and panting, we sit and order massive glasses of dark beer. I gulp the cold, tart brew, then lean back, intoxicated with joy. "I'm in love," I gush. Paavo says, "Dancing can do this. This one is more like *humppa.* Fast polka. I'm thinking you like it better."

"It's great—polka on steroids!" Although he doesn't smile, I think how considerate of him to find music for my taste. He might just know me better than I thought. "Where'd you learn to dance like that?"

"I took some lessons. My girlfriend before liked such things." His girlfriend *before*? *Before me?* Would that make me is girlfriend *now*?

Not wishing to explore his past loves, I say, "Speaking of lessons, I'm thinking of studying here. So that I can work. Obviously, I'd need to start with Finnish!"

He seems to consider the idea. "Maybe you can be student here for while, but to work in Finland you must be needed."

"I might not have to work right away…you know, my parents left me quite a bit of money. And the house. And since education here is free…"

"Yes, but if you want to work and you are not from E.U., they want you have job that is…*harvinainen.* I don't know how to say."

"I get it. You have to be needed in the labor force."

"Yes." Reality sobers my mood. He adds, "But studying

Finnish would do you some good, for sure." OK, now I feel insulted. I turn to face him and see a wide smile—oh, he's kidding with me. We're having fun! "But you can learn Finnish from Jukka. I have other ideas for you." His sly smile surprises me; maybe he has some experience at this dating game. "Anyways, it's good we have tonight because tomorrow I visit up with family."

Although I'm dying to know about his "ideas" for me and how much of "tonight" we have together, I finally get the voice to ask about his family.

He shrugs, "There's not so much to tell. I have the brother and sister. He is married, so I suppose I have two sisters now. They are expecting a child, and tomorrow I go there for Sunday dinner." He tells me they live near his parents in Lappeenranta. So his family is close. How wonderful! How I would love to be someone's daughter, *tytär,* again.

"I'd like to visit that city."

"It's easier you meet my sister, Sirja. She's in Helsinki and I can arrange." Great! Maybe it's too early to meet his parents, anyway.

Head leaning against the wall, smile pasted on my face, I take his hand. "I would *love* to meet her."

After we finish our beer, he pulls me up to dance again. Skipping about the room, faces hot and close, our sweat mingles. When the song ends, Paavo picks me up and spins me. My feet soar. My mouth hurts from smiling as I land. Panting, he plants a juicy kiss on each of my cheeks and, during the lull in music, says, "Next we go to my apartment. You have been wanting something for some time now, and tonight is good night for it, I think. You are open."

Whoa! Open? This night just keeps getting better and better…

~Vian ei tarvitse olla suuri, jos se on päässä.~
~The flaw doesn't need to be big, if it is in the head.~

Seksi?

"*I* think it's good if we do it on the rug," Paavo says.

Drenched from the dance, heart aflutter, I followed Paavo into his apartment, primed for romance. After mumbling something I couldn't hear about his "key," he unlocked the door and took me aback when within moments of entering he announced this, adding, "You have asked for this but I have not given it. Now is the time." Right now? *On the floor?* I clear my throat. Obviously he's not as dense as he'd seemed; I've been sending messages to the guy for months. Not in vain, obviously! But his matter-of-fact approach puts me off. I want to talk a bit first, have things flow naturally…"Uh, I'm not really ready—"

"If you want, you can lay down on sofa here instead."

"I'll *sit* down for now." I watch in wonder as he pulls his light cotton sweater off to reveal a clinging, damp t-shirt.

"I think it goes better laying down," he says. The speed with which he wants to get to it alarms me into stalling.

I glance around the small room. "Jukka said you live with someone. A roommate? And could I have something to drink first? Maybe some coffee?" I arrived tipsy from the beer, giddy from the dance—and he might need to sober up, tone it down a notch.

"Well, I suppose I can make *kahvi*." Walking off he says, "It's good I have my apartment alone tonight. I have wanted to try this for some time now."

I jerk forward on the couch. *Try* this? Oh lord, he's a *virgin*!

My thoughts scurry. When was the last time I slept with a virgin? Never? If he wanted to get right down to it, why aren't we going into his bedroom? Maybe he sleeps on the couch, the condo appears typically small…

I stand abruptly, not wanting to wait for sex on the sofa. I don't even want to think about it at the moment. Around me, the living room walls are covered with more *ryijys,* wall hangings, than usual. To take my mind off the Virgin Paavo, I pace the room, half taking them in, wondering if he'll bring coffee with a side plate of condoms.

Paavo's talking, cup in hand, as he approaches, "—ee is good for the body but also for the head." I didn't catch the word…what's the word for "sex" in Finnish? How awkward! Would it have killed my parents to teach me some sexual vocabulary? Sex…sexy…seksi! That's it, *seksi.*

"I still like it better if we do it on the floor," he states. I half-spurt my coffee. I mean, I'm getting used to the forthright ways of the Finnish people, but *this*! Although the floor rug he motions to appears thick enough, I'm not prepared to just strip and lie down, if that's what he has in mind. "Speaking of rugs," I say, wishing to talk before I de-flower him—the man's obviously clueless about getting a woman in the mood—"these wall *ryijys* are wonderful, Paavo. Did you know they used to serve as *bed* covers?" *Like maybe there's a bed we can go to for some foreplay?*

After correcting my pronunciation with "*Reu-i-yeus,*" he says, "Yes, of course I'm aware of that history. As you can see for yourself, I am collecting them."

"Let me have a look!" Anything to protract this. His *ryijys*, standard in Finnish homes just as they were in mine growing up, are conspicuous here in their number and variety. I walk to one that reminds me of a geometric Navajo rug. I sense him behind me as I circuit the room trying to focus on the animal imagery of one rug, the intricate oriental pattern on another… I bring up the history I'd read for my thesis, how they've found *ryijys* from the sixth-century, how they reflect the Finnish culture and style so well—simple, practical, beautiful. For some reason I recall that the Nordic people—perhaps because of these *ryijys?*—thought that Finns had magical powers. I tell him that the ancient Nordic word for "magic" was "*finngerd*," meaning "a Finn's work."

"Well, that I have not heard and I do not believe much in that."

"In what?"

"Magic. I am a doctor. Anyways, now we should get started. It gets late." He shows me his palms. "You will feel much better once I am touching you."

God, is it that obvious I need it? I mean, can doctors tell when you're not getting enough? Are my nipples popping out or something? This is becoming way too clinical. More like a doctor-patient relationship than a sexual experience. I get the impression he's going to produce one of those cheesy gowns with strings that tie in the front. Or back!

I reach for my sweater to leave, huffing, "Well *I* believe in magic—at least some wooing—and let me tell you, there's not much going on here!"

He tugs gently on my arm, kneels on the rug and pleads, "Please, Alina. I really think this is good. I thought you wanted."

I think of telling him he needs it more than I do, if he's truly a virgin. But it's true I crave the touch of a man…and it must be mid-month because seeing his fine, eager face in the glowing light, in the warm room, I start to unwind. Beginning to relent, I take his hand and sit down beside him.

I pat the carpet, joke, "What's this, *virgin wool*?" He doesn't get it so I tell him that it's dumb humor, you'd have to be American, British…whatever. "So we're really going to *do it*?" I ask, too embarrassed to say "*seksi*."

"*Kyllä*," he nods, *yes*, and smiles, his luscious mouth sensuous and inviting. I move my face close to his when he grabs my shoulders and says, "OK now. We do this Meredith's way."

I jerk back, slap his hand off my shoulder and stand. What? Virgin, ha! "Meredith's way? Tell me, Paavo, what is '*Meredith's way*?' And when did you two do it?"

He holds his hand, wounded, appearing innocent and confused. "Just few times at her place. Why such rudeness?" Rising, he declares, "I cannot do this with you arguing. You should be peaceful and quiet."

I get in his face. "Well guess what? I will not *do this* at all! This is Not How I Have Sex-si. Especially with someone who's done it 'yust few times' with my best friend!"

He gapes at me, then says, "What is this crazy talk? This is not for sex-ing! *Sukupuoli*. Do you not want me to give you the Reiki treatment?"

I reel back. My hands fly to my hot face. *Reiki*? *Huh*? After moments of burning, confused silence, I croak, "When did this turn into a healing session?"

*

Finally calmed and lying down, I begin to feel comfortable, anticipating a pleasant experience. I recall Meredith's soothing touch, her 'laying on of the hands,' the day I lost my job. He places his hands on my eyes, relieving the strain that still lingers there, despite my LASIK. Strain from the pressure of holding back tears, Meredith would say. He caresses my neck by palming its sides, and my body slackens. Despite my outrage seconds ago, I can see how this intimacy could be arousing, could lead to groping and kissing and… God, it's been so long! I wonder how he feels—

"You must try to not think," Paavo says, startling me. This man is psychic! I try to relax, to stop my spinning thoughts and feel the warmth of his large and capable hands. In a low tone, he says, "And now I just hold you." He holds my whole head in the comforting cradle of his hands. "Let the weight down," he tells me. I know he wants me to let go, rest my head, which proves difficult. I try to unwind. "No, you need to let me be support and you are not." I recall this pose with Meredith. I didn't like it, something messy. Something missing. A thing I didn't want to think about.

I try to comply, to enjoy the sensation. "You are not putting down your weight. Make your head heavy into my hands." Why is this so hard for me? I will my neck to drop, pretending that he's a pillow and I'm falling into it. He's my resting place, I'm coming home to Paavo. So l let gravity do its work, dissolving the heavy thoughts that fill my head, everything that makes me reluctant to let go, until I fully melt into his hands…and when I do for a few minutes, when I truly let my head drop like lead so that he fully bears the load, unexpected tears spring to my eyes. Ever more tears flood, until I'm outright crying. My head cradled in his warm hands, the strain of holding it up gone.

I'm back at some primal time before memory, my head supported so. I try to make sense of the wetness dripping down my cheeks into the cup of Paavo's hands. I suppose my parents held my bobbing head as an infant, when I was too young to remember…and yet now I remember everything. A hot rain of tears cascades silently down my cheeks. Embarrassed, I wipe at them.

"It's OK," Paavo says in a soft voice. As he holds me tenderly, I want to talk. Tear-soaked and sniffling, occasionally wiping my nose on my sleeve, sometimes choking on my words, I lie in Paavo's embrace and tell him…

~*Kauniita unia ja enkelia kuvia.*~
~Sleep well and dream of angels.~

God Calling

It was a weekend when God called. Arms loaded with musty books from the library across the street from my apartment, I rushed in to the second ring of the phone. The air was dead when I picked up, as if someone were on the line but not talking. "Hello?" I repeated until my voice sounded hollow and the dial tone buzzed. The call reminded me that I hadn't phoned my mother that week.

I dropped my books and called her. She said she was going to dinner in Berkeley with Impi Vaho, their neighbor when Dad worked at Cal. The air crackled. She was wrapping a blueberry *kaakku*—Finglish for "cake"—in tin foil. I heard the crinkle of aluminum as she talked. But suddenly her words dribbled out all wrong in an incomprehensible language—not English, not Finnish, not Finglish. A brain misfiring.

I panicked. My mother had high blood pressure, and instinctively I knew. "I think you're having a stroke, Mom! Hang up and dial 911!" But my mother, dazed by the crossed wires of her speech or whatever else was scrambling inside her, said nothing. Of course I was asking the impossible. "Mom, I'm going to call an ambulance. You've got to hang up, do you understand?" My voice broke, "*Mom*?"

The paramedics called me back from my parents' house saying that my mother, suddenly lucid and able to communicate, speaking perfectly her broken English, would not go with them. Had I imagined it? Could someone have a stroke one minute and then be normal the next?

But I hadn't dreamed it! I told them that she must go to the hospital. On my cell phone, I argued back and forth with her and the medics as I plummeted crazily northward, my worn tires wobbling at the speed, the forty miles to Mercury taking a lifetime. Taking a life away.

"We can't make her go if she doesn't want to," the calm young voice said. "She seems fine." He sounded bored.

"Put her back on," I commanded. I don't remember what I said to my mother, whether I raised the specter of my recently-deceased father and cried about being an orphan. Some plea, some arrow of guilt pierced through, and made my mother Lempi acquiesce.

But feeling that a silly fuss was being made by her *tytär* in the South Bay, she agreed only to travel to the nearby medical center. I urged the medics to take her to a *real* hospital, to an ugly facility in the city with all the machines and all the experts, but Lempi, stubborn Finn, got her way.

Maybe my mother was shaking her head as she climbed effortlessly, supported at the elbows by two young men, through the rear doors of the ambulance. Maybe she said, "*Oh, piru!" devil!,* on the ride through the bucolic Mercury valley, past the lazy cows grazing on the ranchland, to the neat office buildings of the regional medical center.

The day after her stroke, a female doctor at Oakland General, whom I saw only once, said, "Good work. You saved your mother's life." But I had not. My mother's true life disappeared, was snatched away in a day, though at the time I didn't know it. "It's a miracle you were on the phone when it happened."

I've had time to think about that oddly timed call from no one—as if from a God I was not raised to believe in—that set in motion a series of events perhaps better left undone. Because Mom did not get the right drugs in time. By the time she was transferred to Oakland, the CAT scan was inconclusive. They didn't want to make the damage worse, or risk killing her. So they said.

I "saved" her to a life that took everything from her but the use of her right arm. And the cruel ability to understand what was being said without being able to reply. She would've been better off dead than waking the next morning brought down to nothing. One day walking, talking, and dusting. The next—

Months of rehab followed. Lempi worked like a determined Finn and I had hope that her *sisu* would pull her through. Therapists led her, right foot dragging, up and down the slick hallway. They rotated and cocked her right arm back and forth. She got braces to prop her damaged limbs. Then a wheelchair.

At first they spoon-fed soft food to her like a baby. But my mother learned to use her left hand to pull a shaky spoon to her mouth and sip through a straw without choking. I would sneak a dab at her lips to clear something orange (vegetable?) or brown (meat?) that might linger there, unfelt, indefinitely.

Through it all Lempi watched me watching her, her head cocked sideways to use her good eye and ear, her small eyes birdlike. Sometimes she smiled at me, a half smile, one side of her mouth tugged down.

She worked with speech therapists. Initially after the stroke, my mother spoke a bit; some words dropped out, little nuggets of golden hope. But as the weeks passed, talking became harder, the words fewer, the speech lessons more frustrating. She could not read, could not understand the characters, which might as well have been Egyptian hieroglyphics. She pushed away the infantile flash cards and the child's toy that pronounced, "food" and "bathroom" when colorful pictures were pressed. Reaching her "plateau," she was relegated to a nursing home, where she communicated with facial expressions and just one word: *piru.* A nod of the head with "*piru*" for *yes*, a shake with *piru* for *no.* A crooked but real smile for me with "*Piru*!" for *You're here, Alina*!

That was when I moved to Mercury the first time, so I could see her more often. Evenings I'd drive back from the Blaineville nursing home, and, approaching Mt. Mercury, see the mountain bathed in crimson light, lit by the setting sun, red as a beating heart.

"Come on, Piru," an aide in a turquoise uniform said as she leaned into my mom's chair-back. "Lunchtime."

I overheard this one day as I approached from behind with a plastic bag of food and a thermos of coffee. I elbowed the aide aside and snapped, "She's *aphasic*." The girl looked at me as if that were possibly my mother's name. She had lank hair and a blank stare. I grabbed the chair handles and flung the bag of food over one. Whirling my mother toward the patio doors, I mumbled over my shoulder, "Her name is—" But the word "Lempi," the name that means "love" in Finnish, was a lump jammed in my throat.

But it wasn't until I walked in her room to see a male orderly cleaning Mom, her flaccid buttocks smeared, her poor naked backside exposed, only a pale membrane of skin covering the knobs of her spine, that I lost it. I knew that on the other side of my mother's fetal position, her eyes were squeezed shut and her hands were clenched, her good hand fisted tighter than the one in the permanent half-claw, her jagged nails digging into her flesh.

I crept in and took over, cleaned her myself, allowing the aide to get away from the most odious chore of his day, the one he has to perform with crushing frequency. I couldn't talk. Hot tears slipped down onto her angular hipbone. Back alone in the car, I heaved jagged sobs, and when I was done proceeded to hire a home care agency.

Less than a week later, against the advice of everyone—the social workers, nurses and doctors—I took my mother home. There she refused all her medications, from the stool softener to the blood pressure meds to the Coumadin, which was supposed to prevent blood clotting. She contracted pneumonia after two months and refused treatment. They brought in oxygen, morphine. She yanked the air mask off whenever the hospice nurse or I tried to stop the panting. She denied herself air, like forcing herself to drown, pushing herself underwater against all natural instinct.

"I mean, isn't that almost unbearably impossible?" I sit up, turn my red-eyed, teary face to Paavo.

"So much *sisu* she has had." His voice is quiet, "It must be very hard for her to leave you."

"I wasn't enough. I didn't do a good job."

"She has lost too much." Though the tears don't stop, I nod. I couldn't give her what she wanted most: her old life. Tears stream down my cheeks until Paavo hugs me—then I give in to quaking sobs. He rocks me from behind in a sitting hug. After a while he says, "You have had too much trouble in such short time. With your father gone so soon before."

I hold onto his arms and look through the blur of time and tears. I'm forgetting so much. I snuffle that my dad should've stopped drinking sooner, that one time my mother threatened to divorce him, and I, young and without siblings, panicked for weeks, imagining being left adrift somewhere in the empty sea between them.

"He has finally stopped the drinking, you said."

"Yes, too late, though." I remember sitting by his hospital bed while he slept, after his liver operation. Wishing in vain that he had a heart problem like the man in the bed next to him. The man who rolled into the ICU after him and left before him. Homeward with his boisterous family and the Mylar balloons, everyone inflated with relief. While my dad, Aatos, remained, orange with liver cancer, never to leave. Wishing that instead of cancer my dad had a broken heart, like mine.

I grow silent, returning with too much clarity to my mother's last day. Her hospital bed was in the family room with a view of the budding early-summer yard. As the pneumonia grew worse, each breath became a rusty wheeze. I put the mask on her, said I'd quit my job, take better care of her. "I'll take you on more walks, we'll get outside. We can sit in the backyard." She gently shook her head, closed her eyes. The bones of death were visible now: in her rounded forehead, prominent cheekbones, her sunken eyes and cheeks. I stroked her sparse hair.

The room was a mess: my neglected work papers mixed in with medical supplies, tubes, her swinging, wood-grain bed-table cluttered with uneaten food, a pink plastic kidney-shaped bowl, water pitcher and drinking cups, homecare instructions stained with coffee… As she starved herself of air, I promised, "I'll clean up!" I thought she tried to smile. We held hands. Without opening her eyes, she miraculously summoned a faint, raspy, "*Sisu*," before her wheezing grew too violent. I choked out, "I'll always love you," before her body fiercely shook—and then went still. She was gone.

I turn into Paavo's chest. He holds me as I cry until I'm spent. Before long, I feel myself falling into a deep, underwater sleep. As if reading my thoughts, he strokes my hair and soothes, "You are not alone."

~Halukas auttaja tulee käskemättä.~
~A willing helper comes without asking.~

The Russian Problem

Me and my silly jealousy. This bright Sunday morning after my cathartic night, after a peaceful sleep on Paavo's couch, I feel that he, at least in part, learned Reiki *for me.* And Meredith helped make it happen. Feeling lighter, relieved of a burden, I skip around Jukka's apartment, sweeping. He's locked in his bedroom-office and I know not to bother him.

After a quiet breakfast together, Paavo dropped me off. I hugged him tightly, with great affection. It felt right; the desire can wait. Humming a tune from last night, I excavate debris from behind the refrigerator (and vow to hear more music, for I've been depriving myself of this all-pervasive aspect of the culture here). When I rehash the night, I acknowledge that Reiki might not be the cure-all for my headaches; but I know with certainty that I need someone caring like Paavo by my side in this life. How ironic that I'd felt so threatened by his learning Reiki with Meredith, when I feel so changed by it!

I want to tell her about my session, about Paavo's loving care. I've left voicemails indicating that I plan to meet them in St. Petersburg. But I want to talk to her *now.* The time difference, her concern about cell phone charges, and my busy schedule have made communication virtually non-existent.

Sitting down, I call her. There's no answer. I leave a message, my crossed leg wiggling with impatience, then redial and redial. I can't get hold of her, so I call Steffen.

My heart nearly stops when he answers his cell phone and

tells me that Meredith has already left for Russia. She's in St. Petersburg as of the day before yesterday. Now my chest pounds so hard, I put my hand to it. *In St. Petersburg already?* How could I so lose track of time? Lose track of Mere?

I croak out, "*Alone*? You're not with her?" Though the answer's obvious.

"Unfortunately, yes. No." His voice is quiet and even.

"Yes no what? Where are you? Is her sister with her?"

"I'm here in California, Alina. Working on your house. Taking care of Lou. I'm afraid that Meredith was determined, and now she's completely on her own over there."

My blood rises. I stand and shout, "How can you be so calm when you're in the middle of an adoption and your wife is off in Siberia?"

"You know your geography. It appears she's about an hour away from you. Hardly the Gulag." He doesn't mention my use of the word "wife."

"I know, I know, but I'm trying to understand." She's alone in a foreign country. She doesn't speak the language or know the ways…he waits for me silently. "Steffen! I'm trying to stress the *magnitude of this.*"

"Alina. I'm all too well aware of the magnitude."

"But how could you let her go?"

"The question's actually how could I stop her?" In the quiet that follows I realize it's true. They'd been arguing about it since spring and now, a mere few months later, amazingly, it's happening. "If I could've stopped her I would have. I even offered to go in the end. She wouldn't have it, said since I wasn't fully 'on board' she didn't want me there. Said I'd be better off staying home with Lou." I wonder what time it is in California, whether he's stroking Lou's head at this moment. "Which is true," he says. He clears his throat. "She thinks it'll all go swimmingly because Sue's got it all sussed. What can I tell you? She'll be back in eight days with a new baby and I have nothing to say about it."

His matter-of-fact tone disguises underlying frustration, I think, or anger.

I relate to his lack of control, his concerns. "I'm sorry, Steffen. I know this is hard for you." My brain hurts, so many questions bombard it. I manage to add, "Thanks for all you've been doing on the house." Absorbing the news as real, I sit back down. "So, is there any news yet about the baby?" The baby. Just yesterday it seems I was holding a pink and squishy-faced newborn Lou.

Steffen tells me that she texted just yesterday, that she's fine, settled in a hotel, and has met her "roof," which he reminds me is the translator and facilitator, the go-between. "She's going to the baby house, as they call it, soon. Maybe today your time?"

"So she'll get the baby girl *today*?"

"Natalya," he says, then stops. I feel him with me, trying to adapt to it all. *Natalya*. Lovely. "It's possible. I'm having trouble getting hold of her now. The cell phone connection seems to be flakey. But it's like Meredith not to charge it."

I start to worry, "Have you Skyped her?"

"What's that?"

God, these people live in Silicon Valley, it's 2007—he should know what Skype is! But then, Mere is techno-challenged and wouldn't be traveling with a laptop, anyway. "I'll reach her," I say. "We'll take care of her." I try to console him. "It's a civilized country, we're close by, and…and I'm sure her sister has it all arranged." After a "*hmmm*" from him I become a cheerleader, "Just think, Steffen. A baby sister for Lou!"

After a pregnant pause he says, "I just hope she's all right."

*

By the next evening, I finally hear Meredith's real voice on her phone. Since talking to Steffen, I've done little but call, text, and email Meredith (doubtful that she'd check an internet café)—and research travel to St. Petersburg. When I hear her say, "Hello," sounding clear and close, as if she's next door, I jump up from

Jukka's patio chair with joy.

"Meredith, Meredith! It's so good to hear your voice!"

"Hi, Ali," she says simply and all I can think is: *she's so close.* The feeling that Russia is some foreign cold place vanishes, replaced briefly by memories of boating there from Vipuri—Vyborg—just a few beers on a boat-ride away, as I recall. Though when I went with my parents and some related Finns, I was drinking Coke.

I begin to ask about the baby when she cries, "It's falling through, Ali. I don't think I'm going to get Natalya." She explains that her roof, Bogdan, took her to the baby house—a small non-descript home—in a suburb of the city. She stood next to him at the front door, could hear children laughing inside, babies crying. The woman at the door, possibly in her 50s, narrowed her eyes and kept her mouth tight as Bogdan talked and talked.

"They wouldn't let us in. They wanted to meet my husband. But that wasn't supposed to happen! Sue arranged it so that they knew I couldn't bring him, that we have a son at home," she wails. "I miss Lou and I think he was excited about getting a baby sister."

"What about the roof? Can't he fix it? I suppose it's too late to pretend he's your husband?"

She sniffs, "I can't reach him now. I've been trying for hours. He, *they—someone* has half my money! I thought of trying to drag Steffen over here but that would be disastrous. If I knew Russian I'd pay my food and board cash to have someone stand in. That's all Bogdan said I need: a man. He claimed maybe any guy would do. But I don't trust him now because he asked for some outrageous amount of money to find me one."

Although I, too, immediately distrust this Bogdan character, I ask how much. I gasp when she tells me, as even I can't afford that, what with my house woes: my lapsed insurance policy, falling house prices.

She moans, "They've got half the money already! I owe my

sister so much."

"Do you have to pay her back?"

"No, but that's not the point."

"Of course not." I say. "Oh, Mere. Do you think he's right about showing up with a partner?"

"I don't know, Ali. All I know is I had my heart set on…I have pictures, even a video. After the fire, I didn't want to burden you with my life. She's so adorable and I just knew, I *knew* when I saw her… She looked like a dream."

"I'm coming over. I can help." Although I try to sound positive and in-charge, I can't see how my presence will do any good at all. But she needs company, and I feel compelled to act.

"It won't help unless you get a quick sex-change. Sue said they don't care for gays, you have to be careful, there's bigotry. Oh, Ali!" I hear her muffle her crying.

"But Sue. Your sister's gay."

She says her sister brought a male friend—they didn't even check the papers, even though they had some bogus marriage document. "And Sue said it was all set for me, the baby house knew that Steffen couldn't come. Not that he couldn't, he *wouldn't.* Anyway, somehow since it was the same place and they remembered Sue, they were good with it. Or so we thought."

"Mere, I love you. Hang on there. Don't give up your dream. You have helped me so much." My plan to tell her about Paavo and Reiki will have to wait. "Let me help you."

"Unless you know some random Russian guy in St. Petersburg who owes you a favor, I guess I'm S-O-L." Eventually, we hang up, but in the middle of the night I come up with the Best Idea Ever.

~*Kaveria ei jätetä.*~
~Leave no man behind.~

A Man

I pace Jukka's apartment, impatient for him to return from his morning swim. Hearing feet on the steps, I rush to open the door and am jolted by the sight Jukka followed by Paavo. Tucking my hair behind my ear, I greet them. Jukka walks past, then Paavo, smiling, says, "*Huomenta.*" Both of them damp-haired and ruddy cheeked, smelling of fresh salt water. I answer good morning. He says, "I have come to see how you are."

I glance at Jukka, but he busies himself pouring from the fresh pot of coffee I made. As Jukka sets out three cups, I tell Paavo that I'm feeling fine, really quite good. Although for once I really haven't been thinking about myself so much at all. "We have had quite some night together," Paavo announces, which causes Jukka to ogle us, then shake his head—in disbelief?—before sitting down to cut a loaf of bread.

I'd love to talk to Paavo more about the transformative Reiki treatment and my feelings, but not now. "I really want to thank you for Saturday night," I say, "but—" A snort from Jukka stops me mid-sentence.

"Man should thank the woman for this, I think," he says, chuckling. Always enjoying himself.

I grimace at him as we all sit at the table. "You don't know what you're talking about. What *we're* talking about. But never mind. I have something really important to tell you both." My leg wiggles until they finish fixing their coffees, stir milk, sugar, and butter the bread. I want their full attention. Finally, their eyes upon me, I quickly dump all the details of Meredith's Russian plight. When I finish my outpouring, breathless, I look at them expectantly. "We have to help her," I say with urgency. "We can't just sit here *tumput suorina!*" With our mittens straight. Mom used that phrase when I needed to get to my chores.

Paavo tells me that I'm a good friend to want to help her. I smile at him, avoiding my scowling cousin. "I'm glad you agree. But I don't think I can navigate Russian bureaucracy on my own." I explain that she has only about a week remaining there. Jukka says it's all nonsense and she cannot be helped. They have taken her money.

"But Bogdan, the roof, he's coming back. He's still in on the deal. We just need a man to pretend to be her husband…" and though I search the faces of both men, it's now Paavo I focus on. How could I think that pessimistic Jukka, the bigot when it comes to his Russian neighbors, would be of help?

Imploring Paavo with my face, I suggest that he and I make a short trip to St. Petersburg. His drawn face tells me he's thinking. "Well, I'm not the quick person like this. And not liking to be dishonest. Also, you know, I have much work to do." He licks a crumb off his thick lower lip.

"We have this weekend!" I step over to him, bending to enfold his seated figure from behind. Feeling his strong swimmer shoulders and his smooth cheek against mine, I say, "You won't have to take time off from work. We'll just leave Friday and come home on Sunday. Va-voom! Done!" I love the idea of working miracles for Meredith. With Paavo.

Jukka says flatly, "Not Alina." I let go, stand tall to face Jukka. He waves a piece of bread back and forth in front of Paavo, "She cannot go."

"I'm right here, Jukka, you can speak to me in the first person," though I'm pretty sure he doesn't know that grammatical phrase.

"OK then, you are the first person who cannot go."

Huh? What right does he have to say I can't go? "Excuse me? *Anteeksi*?" I use the Finnish word that means pardon me, but expresses none of the sarcasm I mean to imply.

"No problem," he says. "But you are forgetting the big group of Eskalas on this weekend. You have asked me arrange this and many people come from all parts of Finland to meet up with you." I slap my forehead, *shee-oot*! It's true, I've finally tired of traveling miles to sit in one house after another for hours on end. I'd requested a gathering to meet everyone on Dad's side, and Taimi had mentioned that they'd arranged a party.

"You guys have been great to do this for me, Jukka. Seriously, wonderful. But Meredith—"

His face reddening, Jukka blusters, "My sister and I are working hard for this to happen. You want to meet your father's people and they are not so easy to find. They are like *metsän väki*."

Paavo says, "Forest folks. Elfs or something."

"And now you want to run off to Russia on that day!"

I drop back onto the kitchen chair. "No. No way would I miss that for the world!" I need to learn about this Alina Eskala. This is my chance to discover if I have a close living relative. Someone with my name. Maybe a whole clan of close living relations. Family.

Paavo asks if we can go the weekend after, but I explain that I don't think Meredith can extend her stay because of money, her work, little Lou waiting. But maybe, maybe…I think of how I prevented Meredith from asking Paavo to the Reiki conference, how selfish and misguided I was. I hesitate, then say quietly, "Maybe you could go alone, Paavo?"

Jukka says flatly, "I'm not thinking this is good idea. You waste your time and money over there."

"But Paavo might be her only hope. At least he'll understand what's going on, we don't even speak Russian." Facing Paavo, I say, "I think you only have to show up at the baby house, the adoption place."

He runs his fingers through his short hair. "I like your friend Meredith very much and would like to help but this seems not right. They are not going to think some Finn is her husband."

"Why not? Lots of people inter-marry." Is he not thinking like me? *What of our relationship?* Returning to the matter at hand, "It's worth a try? Besides, it doesn't sound as if they're asking for papers, just a body. The whole thing's kind of under-the-table, but Meredith said the women there really seem to care for the kids. They want them safe. At least you understand some Russian..."

"I'm sorry to hear that she is there all on her alone. That I feel is not right. *Mutta*, but…" He shakes his head.

"But you could figure out what's going on, maybe get the money back. Or the baby… Just think about it, Paavo, OK?" I add that I'll pay for the trip, though I know it's not the sticking point.

Jukka pipes up again. "I'm knowing her idea is bad one from the go-get. Her man Steffen was right." He does his dismissive wave as he gets up to clear his plate. "Crazy stuff."

When Paavo reluctantly consents to make the weekend trip to St. Petersburg, I feel oddly ambivalent. Happy for Meredith, naturally, but something nags—the unforeseen, I suppose, the unknown. I hope this is not another blunder. Pushing away these negative premonitions, I call Meredith until I finally reach her on the hotel phone.

I quickly learn that nothing has changed but her mood, which is deteriorating. She despairs, "Bogdan promised to come, possibly with a guy to stand in, but I haven't seen him for two days. I can't believe I fell for this."

"Mere, fear not," I assure her. "I have a plan…you know how close we are here. It's a long story. The main thing is, you'll be able to show up with a "husband" to get your baby."

"Ali, close or not, I doubt you can help." Meredith sounds so defeated, so unlike herself. She says, "Sometimes your ideas..."

when the line crackles. The connection from her hotel room is poor—I briefly wonder if we'll be cut off by ex-KGB—when I quickly say," Trust me. Because of you, I'm *changed.*"

"What's that mean? You're coming here as a man?"

Ignoring her sardonic tone, I triumphantly announce, "Even better. *I'm sending a real man!*"

~*Ei kysyvä tieltä eksy.*~
~He who asks won't lose his way.~

Meet the Eskalas

*I*s Alina Eskala here? I face a yard full of people all somehow associated with me, feeling disconnected. I hesitate as I approach the spread of people across the mossy lawn, some at the laden food table, others in clusters holding paper cups, some alone surveying the scene as I do now. For some reason, I expect to recognize Alina by some familial resemblance to Dad, or by pheromones, instinct. Some close tie that will be palpable.

We're gathered in a verdant backyard near Joensuu, set with long tables of food and drink, folding chairs for fifty. Clouds threaten rain; as in New England, a downpour can spoil any summer event. I think about the constancy of summer sun in inland California, how accustomed I've become to its reliability.

Distant relations, too numerous to count, have quite literally come out of the woods to meet me. Taimi shows up beside me, saying that entire families have come, some from as far north as Oulu; with one small group journeying all the way from Rovamiemi in the Lapp province. Despite the Karelian influence, many of them, related by marriage or not, look typically Scandinavian. Others have Dad's Eastern features, slanted eyes and sky-high cheekbones. Their rounder Karelian faces smile at me more than the typical Finn, and I wonder if Jukka is right when he says that Karelians are "too much the talkers." As we weave through the crowd meeting them, shaking hands, I notice that, oddly, they *smell* like family.

The presence of so many gratifies and me, and for the

umpteenth time I'm humbled by their interest in meeting me. So why do I feel so off today? So foreign?

I need to meet everyone, and the nametags, Taimi's idea, help. On earlier occasions, being introduced to a *Pyry* or a *Marjatta* would just fly in one ear and out the other. Now I'm able to link the pronunciation to the spelling. I like the nature names: surnames *Virtanen* for "river" and *Lahti* for "lake." First names such as *Ilmari* for "bear," *Suvi* for summer, *Meri* for sea… Between introductions, I wonder if Meredith has connected with Paavo, who left by train for St. Petersburg early this morning. Then I'm back to searching for someone named "Alina."

As I sit to eat with a bunch of young people—teens and twenty-somethings I'd guess from the two metal-heads here—I hand around my notebook for them to sign. By now I have scores of names, email addresses and phone numbers…a large Finnish family, I suppose. But despite my smile and the friendly talk, I feel blue, unable to shake the feeling of being different. Or the thought that we might not find the phantom Alina Eskala. So far my queries about a Russian relative have only produced mystified faces and shrugs. I hope that Jukka and Taimi, circulating elsewhere, are discovering something (although I can't rely on any zeal from Jukka in this regard). Since my father's father had no brothers, the woman with my last name will be hard to track down.

The food, at least, is pure comfort. We eat off paper plates on our laps, dining on rich Karelian stew with beef, lamb and pork, thick sauce smothering my mashed potatoes. My plate sags from the soggy weight. I bite into the rye crust of a homemade meat pie, savoring the buttery rice and egg mixture that evokes rich memories of dinners with my parents and grandparents.

To build a new life here, I'll need a close family member: my Russian relative, about whom I've yet to learn anything, who must've known my grandparents. Or a partner. My mind skitters back to Paavo; doubts, like the dark clouds, grow. What if it doesn't work out with him? But it has to! We need to move forward more quickly, I'm feeling lost in limbo. Yes, I'll talk to him when he returns; he's showing signs of interest and I'm learning to love, to open my heart. Something I wasn't ready for with Steffen. The timing's right…when Paavo returns, I'll make my feelings for him clear.

I feel penitent for my brooding silence, when this whole affair was arranged for me. Over a low grumble of distant thunder, I take my address book from a young guy who looks like a flaxen-haired Eskimo—chopped bangs, with slits of blue eyes in a tan circle of face. Saami blood, possibly. "I just write my name down. Pekka Turi. You can find me on the Facebook."

"What's that?" Perhaps there's a Finnish encyclopedia of inhabitants…but why wouldn't we look for Alina there? I ask him, "Would my relative Alina Eskala be on it? She might be Russian, though."

Pekka laughs. "That's not mattering. How old she is?" When I tell him the year we suppose, he shakes his head. "You should be knowing that not so many old peoples is on it." *I should?* Maybe Jukka's mentioned this directory and Pekka's translation is weird…I mean, what's a *face-book*?

"How do you say 'Facebook' in Finnish?" I ask. The group laughs as if I've told a joke.

"You should come to ski in Lapland in winter," a beauty named Eevi says.

"I'd love to ski again!" I say with zest, now fueled by food, coffee, and such jolly companions. I do miss skiing, but taking the time to go to Tahoe has been too prohibitive in recent years. And I dislike the weekend mayhem there. "I used to ski *a lot*," I say, recalling with growing nostalgia my youth in New England—swooping down slopes in graceful arcs, wind and snow spray in my face, the swoosh of my skis as I waltzed on snow. But I'm back in my head again, distant with memories. I venture to the group, "My Finnish *pappa* here married a woman with half a pinky finger. From skiing." This evokes more laughter, and I begin to suspect they've spiked their coffee with vodka. "Frostbite, yo," Pekka says, as if this is the norm. Oh right, this is the Rovamiemi crowd. The Arctic Circle set. Probably not a full set of digits on any of them.

I begin to lighten up among this younger, English-speaking company, when Jukka barges over. He takes my plate and cup from me, sets them on the grass, and tugs me toward a weathered man hunched in a chair. We squat to talk. A fleshy bump over the corner of his lip gives his face the appearance of a perpetual grin, and impishly he tells Jukka that he's lost track of his age since turning one hundred. I watch his diluted blue eyes as he slowly tells us something I partly understand. Something about a woman in the woods. *In* the woods or *near* the woods? Not much of a clue, since just about everyone in Finland lives near forest. It's like saying the Finn lives near water!

I turn to my cousin with the newest theory I've concocted. "Do you think this woman is a great-aunt I never heard of? Lots of families have black sheep."

Jukka squints as raindrops slowly begin to fall. "I can't really say if she is good aunt or not and I don't ask 'bout sheep." He gives me a queer look. "But no good getting your hopes high up. We try to find this *mummu*, but remember she has gone…*kuin tuhka tuuleen*." That phrase, what's it mean, I ask. "Like ashes before the wind."

"Oh," I sigh. *Disappeared without a trace.*

~Sota ei päätä kuka on oikeassa, vain sen että kuka on jäljellä.~
~War does not determine who is right, only who remains.~

Sauna with Sirja

"No way I stay with you guys and Sirja." Jukka maneuvers the car through Helsinki, en route to Paavo's sister's apartment. I laugh at him. He probably doesn't want to be the only guy there, and I'd rather it be just Taimi, Paavo's sister, and me. I've yet to sauna co-ed, and unless Paavo is involved, no desire to.

Before he left to act as translator and protector for Meredith and her 'iffy' if not outright shady deal, the plan included Paavo, Jukka, and a meal. But with Paavo gone, Jukka bailed and the plan changed from dinner to a girls' sauna night at Sirja's.

"After yesterday's gathering, I'm happy to be in a small group tonight," I say. Taimi and Jukka are quiet. Oh no, did that sound ungracious? Am I becoming a blunt Finn? "That party was great, though, really. It's just I do need some 'time down.'" Jukka doesn't notice my use of his phrase. Maybe Finns are not so much blunt as economical with words, terse. To seem really polite, one must add words, explanations, *blah, blah, blah.*

"We know what you mean," Taimi turns from the passenger seat to smile at me.

Contemplating a girl's event à *trois*, I'm reminded of my caffeine spa with Meredith and Cleo. I almost laugh aloud at the thought of Troy coming upon the three of us wrestling in the yard, coated in coffee grounds. A wave of wistfulness passes over me, making me long for the easy intimacy of old friends.

I can only hope that all goes well in Russia and Mere will be here before the week is out, for I'd suggested in our final conversation that she come to Finland—offering again to foot the bill. (She told me Steffen's dad back home has been complaining that I need to reign in my purse strings.) Maybe I've been too liberal with my funds, but what good is money if you can't use it to help friends? The cost of living here is high, but I won't be going home soon, as I see it, and while Meredith is so close it's senseless not to get together. Her answer was vague, she wasn't sure it could be arranged, but she said if she did get Natalya and all went well, she'd think about a short stop-over. Hearing Meredith speak optimistically about getting her baby felt like a victory, and the thought of seeing her, the warmth I feel for Paavo, for Jukka and Taimi, and my new connections here put me in a cheerful, sanguine mood. What better step in my quest for Paavo than to meet his family!

"This is very hip place to live," Jukka tells me as he pulls to a stop in front of Sirja's building. We're in a gentrified factory district called *Punavuori,* on a street lined with cafés and nightclubs, filled with trendy young people. Why haven't we been here before? "Maybe you want to go out here after meeting Sirja. Maybe you gonna need a drink." He emits a low chortle.

I ignore it. "Looks like a fun place." It'd be great to go out for a post-sauna beer and possibly dance. To modern music. While Taimi gathers her things, I ask how well she knows Paavo's sister, who's close to forty. She says "not good," that she has only seen her once or twice, and I wonder why Jukka kept Taimi in tonight's plan. I could have visited Paavo's sister alone, I tell him.

His eyes meet mine in the rearview mirror. "You should have interpreter."

Taimi says in her soft voice, "You know Sirja speaks English very good."

"Not interpreter, then. What is the word—diplomat?" Taimi laughs, and I get my first uneasy feeling about Sirja.

After a brief introduction by Jukka and a brisk handshake

with our hostess, he splits, no doubt happy to have time to himself. Poor Jukka, being my tour guide and caretaker is his summer sentence for blowing his budget in the States. Soon I hope to be off his hands.

Sirja opens the door to her apartment, and Taimi introduces us. She has a sculpted Nordic face that might be beautiful if the corners of her mouth tilted upward. Her brittle white-blond hair has suffered the effects of too much bleach. With her ice chip eyes and Alpine cheekbones, she is both taller and more severe than Paavo. Little padding for warmth. In fact, she and Paavo barely look related.

"So you are the American Paavo has spoken of," Sirja says, appraising my jeans, rumpled shirt, and faded highlights with her sharp eyes. Next to her crisp white blouse and slacks, I feel like a slacker. But Taimi's not dressed for success, either, so I'm not overly discomfited. In fact, I light up when she mentions Paavo speaking of me.

Smiling, I say, "Yes, I've enjoyed getting to know your brother. Very much."

"I doubt that you know him very much," she says, turning her back to allow us to follow her in. "I have reserved the sauna. But we'll have to wait a bit."

We sit in silence in her modern living room of stark whites and blacks. The gleaming black and chrome coffee table before us is empty. "Hey, no coffee!" I joke. "That's a "first" for me here." I smile gamely at her.

"It's brewing," she says.

"Great!" I say too loudly. My voice echoes off the hardwood floors. Where Jukka's parents used color and textiles to create a warm and welcoming place, Sirja's modern Scandinavian décor feels cold, chilly.

Taimi clears her throat and says the apartment is nice. Sirja concurs. But I find that the Scandinavian couch quickly becomes uncomfortable, biting my ass. What do they have against *cushions* here? Would it make life too comfortable?

I wiggle to ease my sore butt. "What is it you do for a living, Sirja?" Taimi looks askance at me. Even I heard the squeak in my throat. I've lost control of my vocal chords.

She says she works as a publishing executive and then she stares at us. Well, at me. Brows raised.

"Me? Oh, I'm in software test," I say.

"I have heard that you do not work at all," she says, sipping some ice water.

"Well, it's true, while Paavo and Jukka visited I happened to be…" I get the feeling she's the 'I work therefore I am' type of person. *What do they tell you to say in an interview?* My mind searches wildly for the phrase. "Between jobs!" I smile as if I've just aced a test. Or landed an actual job.

"You seem quite happy about that."

"Oh, no. No." I shake my head. "But it did give me time off to be with your brother." I look from Taimi to Sirja, who rises abruptly to walk into the kitchen.

"Finally, she feeds us," Taimi whispers. "And you see her? *Kuin seipaan niellyt*! Like she has swallowed a spear." She giggles.

Hip bones jutting ahead of her, Sirja struts back like a model to place a tray before us. Her coffee is not Finnish. It's more chic, perhaps, a dark, bitter French roast, the kind I can only stomach with tons of cream and sugar, even then getting rumblings of discontent from my digestive tract. The *pulla* is stale and there is none of the elaborate spread I'm offered by most of my hosts. Mentally apologizing for her, I realize I've become quite spoiled (and possibly fat. My jeans seem to have shrunk since my arrival in Finland, which is odd because the drying "machine" Jukka owns is a low-energy contraption, a large metal closet where my clothes slowly air dry).

I feel sure that we'll all relax more in the sauna, knowing that it will be electric and probably mild, unlike saunas at the wood-burning *moekkis* we've visited, where the heat has blasted me out to plunge into nearby water within minutes.

After checking her watch, she waves her large mannish hands for us to follow, raised blue veins bulging, angry hands. "Time to go." We grab the offered towels and head down the elevator to the communal sauna, which Taimi explains has scheduled times for condo dwellers. Sirja, taking a phone call, leaves us to undress in the anteroom. I've relaxed already in many saunas, swimming afterward with the women. The sacred Finnish tradition, voices hushed as if in a church. I've laid low, where the heat is less scalding, and let their sporadic Finnish small-talk lull me.

As we disrobe, Taimi expresses surprise that I grew up with wood-fired saunas in both my parents' and grandparents' backyards. She says, "Well then you should know that this electronic one will not give you the true *löyly* of the sauna." It's a word I'd heard my mother and father use, but they always said it had no translation. My thesis research taught me that originally *löyly* meant "spirit, breath, or soul," and that the word, in variations remains a part of all Uralic languages from the Udmurts to the Khanty and Hungarian. The very spirit of life, the pleasurable endorphins flowing...that's how a good sauna feels.

After showering, towel-wrapped, we wait quietly for Sirja. I think now that *löyly* was the feeling I had as a child, the perfectness of taking sauna with my parents. The smell of damp wood during our sauna nights. Mom vigorously slapping my back and shoulders with the *vasta*, the spray of fragrant boughs of silver birch. I would sit below them on a cooler bench. "You have the strong back that can hold," my mother often said, and I always wondered what, other than my head, it would be required to hold.

If I whined about the heat, Dad would playfully splash me with spoonfuls of icy water from the long-handled spoon used to steam the rocks. Sometimes I snuck a squirt gun in to douse him back and my mother, caught in the crossfire, would shake her head laughing and say: *kuin kaksi marjaa. Like two berries.*

But I can still feel that smoothly worn, wood-handled spoon with its copper cup, how I'd pour an icy cupful, the cool rim of the copper touching my parched lips, then a cold stream slipping down my throat. Nothing was ever as pleasurably refreshing as that pure water.

The warmth, the talk in English, Finnish, and hybrid Finglish: life in the sauna was perfect. And then out into the brisk air dashing to the house, where mom made fresh coffee and laid out pastries. I smile at the thought of us, fully naked in summer, all of us on "Finn Hill" running through our wooded backyards, bare butts on display. It seems so much a part of me and yet so far away…

"You are smiling at something," Taimi's voice breaks through time.

"It's nothing, just some memories. Of my parents," I say, and perhaps there's a catch in my voice. But I'm learning to remember the good times without so much sadness. "Good ones," I add, as Sirja charges in.

"Hurry. *Nyt*! The sauna is hot."

An understatement, to say the least. The heat blasts me in the face when Sirja opens the door. Drawing a huge breath, I set my small sitting towel in between the others on the top bench. My prickling skin tells me that this electric sauna is nothing like the tepidly warm public versions in America. And I know it will only grow hotter.

After scooping water on the *kunis*, the rock-filled stove, to start the steam rising, Sirja begins speaking rapid Finnish. Taimi answers briefly, Sirja talks more, and I look from one to another, completely lost. Are they talking about me?

Taimi says in her soft voice, "Alina is not understanding. We should speak English."

"She should learn Finnish," she states, rubbing her back with a loofah. *She's right here*, I want to say. I'm trying to like Sirja but it's becoming hotter and harder. For my sake, my parents kept our sauna down to 175, 180 degrees Fahrenheit, but I sense Sirja has no such intention.

Taimi, paradoxically, tells Sirja something in Finnish and the two of them chuckle. When she sees my glare, she says, "I was just telling her bout when you have first been writing to Jukka. You have written something about also wanting to meet your buba's family. That was very puzzling to us. We tried to find such a word in English dictionaries. It's quite funny."

"But 'bup-bah' is grandfather."

"Yes, *mutta*, you must know there is no "b" in natural Finnish language. That word is spell "p-a-p-p-a." I squeeze cool water onto my chest from a wet sponge; I should've figured that out, since their soft "p" sounds more like a "b" to our ear.

I joke, "My dad tried to teach me Finnish. By the third lesson I asked him if there were any guns in the house."

"Yes, you have a violent gun culture in America," Sirja affirms.

"No, no, I was *kidding*. We didn't own guns." I shake my head so vigorously I see stars. Dripping sweat stings my eyes, and I hear myself saying, "Anyway, you actually have as bad a gun culture as ours." *Per capita.*

She snaps that Finland has many hunters. I say so do we, adding that Finland has "violent *human* deaths from guns, too."

"We have had to have a militia because of Russia." She ups the heat with a fling of water onto the *kiuas*. Steam burns my face.

I sound like an NRA member when I say, "And so did we. That's where it started, with a militia." Geesh, what a hole I'm digging for myself—me, the ultimate anti-gun advocate. "We got a militia to protect ourselves from the British."

She snorts, "And that was *when*?" Well, so it's been a few years since the Redcoats were coming. "Was that in the 1940s? The *20th century*?"

"No," I lower my head because the heat is too much, I'm

dying to move to the bottom bench, but that would be caving in. She's testing me in more ways than one. This is certainly no familial sauna night....if this woman's to be my sister-in-law, let's hope we move far, far away. I dunk the sponge in the bucket to wipe my face, saturate it again to squeeze water over my head. I'd like to pour the whole water bucket over me. Over Sirja, in fact.

But I don't relish Sirja's certain censure of any improper sauna conduct and just wish we could move on to more compatible topics. She says that she agrees with the stereotype that Americans tend to be ignorant and fat. "Fat? Not in Mercury, where I live. Lived." You'll never find a fitter, more flossed and toned crowd. All those runners and tennis players, hikers and bikers. She has no idea.

"Jukka says they are only fat above the waist," Taimi says, and when I shoot her a look she adds quietly, "the women are."

Sirja laughs saying fat in the head? They speak in Finnish and then Sirja laughs more—the two quite chummy—until I demand to know what they're saying. Taimi says, "Jukka says the American women look like boys but have such the large breasts." She folds her arms around her plush bosom. "He's not liking it."

Sirja tsks and nods at me, "Paavo has mentioned also so many big-breasted women where you live." *He did?* Did he like it, I wonder?

"Yeah, that definitely struck me when I moved to the Mercury Valley. Huge cars, huge houses, huge breasts! Then I realized that lots of them get implants." *So what did Paavo say?*

"That's unnatural," says Sirja. So Sirja and I actually have common ground—I agree with her!

"Yeah, it's like you look at these women and think most of them would really look better naturally." But I don't feel right putting them down for their personal choices. I say, with hope, "I'm sure Paavo didn't like it."

Sirja shrugs. "He's a man, who knows? But anyway, Finnish women are not so foolish to be doing this so much. No medical insurance would pay for this."

"It doesn't in my country either, I just live—*lived*—in a rich area."

"Rich and poor, we have avoided this dichotomy here." OK, not only does she know that word, now we're on to Finnish egalitarianism, no super rich, no poor…let's get back to our communal opinion on fake tits, already! And Paavo. So what did Paavo say? I know Steffen wasn't interested in over-sized chests, said it didn't meet with his aesthetic. Liked my medium padding just fine. But is Paavo a "breast man?" What do I know about his preferences in women? Or in anything, for that matter.

I assert that most men probably don't care for implants, either, when Sirja says, "I'm sure Paavo appreciates them. Maybe he likes what those women do for men. He seemed to enjoy the women there. But he likes Finnish women too." She adds, "The best." Finnish women are best or Paavo likes them best? And who knew Paavo was so interested in women? And their knockers?

She ladles on more water, more steam scalds me. My ass sweats. I self-flagellate with the *vasta*, the birch switch. "American women aren't so awful. I don't think they do it for the men. More for themselves." Recalling the sporty mom across the street with boy hips and bullet boobs, how they didn't make her less kind when it came to feeding me, I feel bad. And Cleo. It was just another one of her sundry beauty treatments, her quirky charm, "It's not really a crime, anyway. I mean, it's society, advertising, movies." I momentarily think of poor Maya, beset by food problems to stay so thin. "Besides, cosmetic procedures are only a few steps from coloring your hair, right?" *All is vanity*…Meredith used to say, quoting some poet. Maybe Shakespeare?

Sirja says, "I'm tired of speaking English. I have to do this with some clients at work and now, relaxing, we should speak Finnish."

"We should be quiet," Taimi says. "Sauna is quiet place."

I ignore the comment and insist to Sirja that I'm learning the language now with Jukka's help, and he's learning better English from me. "Finnish is just a difficult language, you know."

Sirja counters this with, "I'm sure you would like the whole world only to speak English. You would take away our culture, our *language*. You Americans want everyone speaking your language."

"If you're talking about English, I think the Brits might take issue with you." She splashes another scoop of water on the rocks. Scalding vapor assaults my face. In English, Sirja's name is phonetically "sear-ya." How fitting! Growing over-heated, I say, "*I* didn't invent the Internet. It's not my fault everyone's learning English by default."

Taimi inserts, not helpfully, "Jukka says Alina's parents is speaking Finnish."

Although I think she's trying to help me, my irritation grows. "*Are* speaking—*were* speaking it." *Spoke it*, damn it! "It's just, they tried to teach me but there was nowhere to use it." Except with really old people, who didn't interest me so much as a child, saving my own *mummu* and *pappa*, whose broken English was just fine with me. "I can count to ten and know the words for King, Queen, Jack, whatever." How lame, even Steffen knows those words, after our Sunday night card games with Mom and Dad.

"English is also a difficult language to learn, but as you see we know English, Swedish, German—"

"And none of those languages have over 2,000 forms for every noun!" You'd need a lifetime to learn Finnish—a lifetime in prison with nothing else to do. Even though I'm picking up enough to be friendly and semi-conversant when in deserving company, I get the feeling if I tried my Finnish with Sirja, I'd be corrected on every misuse, each error. It'd be like speaking French in Paris, a waste of time, too much condescension.

Wanting to tone it down, I lower myself to the bench below for relief, defeated by the high heat, and say, "I love the Finnish culture—many different cultures. I studied Anthropology—so of course I don't want them wiped out."

But she quickly challenges me, "So what do you know about *Suomi*? Most Americans have never even heard of our country. Until this Conan clown has come. You learn only if it's on the television, I suppose." She refers to a recent visit by a TV comedian, who made a comic splash by comparing his appearance to Tarja Halonen, Finland's president, a woman in her 60s.

"I love Conan O'Brien," says Taimi. "He's so funny."

"The self-deprecating humor of Finns is wonderful," I say.

"We don't all think our president is big joke." Sirja's English is deteriorating—maybe I'm getting to her.

Suffocating, I exclaim, "I need to pee!" and bolt out to a rush of cool air, closing the hellish heat behind me. Back against the door, I breathe.

When I return, I sit on the lowest bench, full of reconciliatory notions. "Sirja, you're right about many being ignorant in my country, but so many are not." I mean, look at us in full, will you? Glancing up, I see her face remains hard. Quiet Taimi, knees to chest, tucks herself deeper into the corner. Using my remaining drop of good will, I move to a more pleasant subject, surely one we agree on: Paavo. "Your brother's such a nice man, I'm really grateful that I've gotten to know— "

"Paavo!" She sniffs and slams down her loofah. "*Han on typerä.*" The hiss from the rocks might as well come from her spit. I recognize the phrase. *He is foolish.* "Now off on this silly trip to Petersburg for some silly American girlfriend."

Girlfriend? I slap down the birch whisk. "Sirja, you don't know your English well enough. Meredith is my *friend. My* girlfriend you might say. But you would say that she's Paavo's *friend. Not girlfriend.*" A not-so-friendly English lesson for her.

"My brother has many women interested in him. You and your friend Meri should stop chasing after him."

"Meredith is not chasing after him!" I grab the spoon and

blast water onto the rocks. "And neither am I." Taimi sucks air, leaving the breathless room even more oxygen-deprived.

"You are not fooling me."

Taimi unhelpfully pipes up, "Paavo is now with your friend Meri. Is this more sharing?"

"*Because* she's my friend." She needs help, he seemed like the solution. Why do I feel a sense of déjà vu?

I grab the *vasta* and slap myself all over. This Sirja is downright scary! How could Paavo be related to her? No wonder he never talks about her. I swish the birch boughs back and forth in wide swathes that hit her legs. But she sits tall lording over me, dwarfed on the bottom bench. Sirja returns to her rant against America and I'm growing sick of it. "I'm sure they think we are Russian. Or from outer planets or something. All the Americans think is the Finns are somewhere in Eastern Europe and they like to drink."

"If the shoe fits..." I glance up at Taimi for some desperately needed support.

She says, "So once and while we like to party. Who doesn't?"

But Sirja doesn't listen, just blathers on with her litany of "firsts and bests," tired information for me, as my dad saturated me with Finn facts from an early age. "We have the best education system in the world, first in woman's voting, woman President …"

"*We* might have a woman president. Or an African-American!" *Beat that!* "We have all kinds of candidates already for our election in '08."

"You will not elect these people," Sirja states and all I can think is: *damn*, she's right. I fume in the heat, think I might pass out. I ask Taimi what the temperature is in here and she tells me "only 80 degrees or so." Not bad, until I realize that's Celsius and I'm possibly boiling to death. My saunas at home had built-in showers…but the shower is in the anteroom and I not only cannot admit my lack of knowledge of Celsius, I can't back out like a beaten dog. That's what she wants.

When she finishes her polemic, she smirks. "American's know nothing of this." She follows this with, "How many people live here? You do not even know our population." Oh, so now this is this Geography class?

That's it! *What a bitch*! How do you say *that* in Finnish? "Five million plus," I say icily.

"And no immigrants, right? We are just the Finns, that's what you all think."

Fully combusting at her combative nature, her sense of superiority, her black-and-white views, her simplistic judgments of my complex and inestimably varied land, I rise in full-frontal nudity and shout into her face. "Immigrants?! You think you have immigrants? Try running a country of 250 million with people from all over the fucking world! What, so you have some Russians, some Eastern blockers, a few thousand Somalians and Asians and—oh yeah—those poor, drunk Swedes who got lost in the forest and ended up *here*!" I grab my sweaty towel and step to the door wanting out, wanting to flee home to my big, oversized, messed-up country.

"*Kuin Euroopan omistaja*!" I cry to her before exiting.

Taimi, who trotted out after me, says conspiratorially as I drench myself with an ice-cold shower, "That's really good! *Kyllä on*. She does act like someone who owns Europe!"

~Joka menneitä muistelee, sitä tikulla silmään.~
~A poke in the eye for those who dwell on the past.~

Hitler at McDonald's

Why didn't I think of Hitler in the sauna?" I spout to Jukka and Taimi, who stop eating their burgers on rye and glance around the crowded Helsinki McDonald's. I haven't eaten real food at McDonald's in years, preferring only their coffee, but tonight, having escaped Sirja, I'm devouring something called a McFeast burger. Though merely a hamburger with toppings, it tastes like a feast to me. Mouth full, I burp. "*That* would've pissed her off!"

"You are still wanting to argue with Sirja?" Taimi sips her soda with a glance at her brother. We called Jukka to rescue us early, and the first thing he said as we jumped in his car was, "Not such the long visit," with something sly sliding into his voice. "You did not have beer after sauna, I can tell," I suppose he saw sauna steam blowing out my ears.

Although a beer might've calmed me, I wanted food. In particular, I was consumed with an intense craving for greasy American fast food. Now, with my Mcfeast before me—including extra large fries and a shake—my tight-waisted jeans be damned—I glare at him. "Why did you do that? Leave me with that nut job?" I shake more salt on my French fries, long for a larger shake. Super size it! American style!

"You women want me in the sauna too? Anyway, she's going to be your sister-in-low, so you're thinking."

"I am not! And it's sister-in-*law*. Like a judge. And she's already sentenced me guilty. Of being American." I pause. "And like you she thinks I'm chasing after her brother. I can't believe she's related to Paavo. So critical!"

"You want to know Paavo's family, right?" He snorts. "*Kuin kaksi marjaa.*"

"What? I know that phrase…'like two berries.'" I throw a French fry at him. "For one thing, I'm not *chasing* anyone. Secondly, I'm nothing like her. She's so superior. So ethnocentric! Finland this, America that. All black and white." I think of the woman on my flight here who whispered across the aisle to some European, possibly a German, "Just so you know, I'm not *American*. I'm from Toronto."

"Yes," says Taimi. "I also don't like when people feel so much superior."

"Like Canadians," I say, now pricked by that minor barb, overheard in passing weeks ago.

"Like Norwegians," says Taimi.

I rant, "Canadians think they're perfect, harmless, blameless. So much easier to hate Americans, isn't it? I mean, what can you blame Canada for? Curling maybe. Seriously, is that even a sport?" I rise to slide on the grease-slicked floor, mimic pushing a broom on ice. "All that sweeping. My mom could've done it." Taimi giggles.

Jukka, who's finished his meal during my tirade, wipes his mouth. "I have never heard 'bout such a fuss in sauna. What have you been fighting on? Men are not talking so much." What didn't we fight about? Politics, gun control, Finland, the American character…my stomach roils all over again. I look at the empty carton of fries.

"POOPS!" Taimi pipes up. My head whips her way. Admittedly, I stooped low in the conversation, but I can't recall bringing up feces… "They have been talking long time about women's…fake preasts." Then the "b" and "p" mix-up comes to me: Ah, boobs.

Jukka laughs as I flush. I have to laugh too.

We toss our trash and get in Jukka's car to take Taimi home.

But Hitler. I didn't whisk out my ace card: Finland's pact with Hitler. *That* would've trumped any of Sirja's criticisms. But Jukka and Taimi let it drop when I mentioned him.

Yes, it was early in World War II when the woe-begotten Finns, vanquished by Russia, made an expedient pact, a treaty more *against* a people than *for* another. And yet. Stalin's treatment and murder of Finns and Karelians, the seizure of so much land was brutal. But was there no remorse in siding with the mass exterminator?

I know the Finns turned to the Germans, who were moving toward Russia, as a last resort to regain lands lost to the Soviets. This "Continuation War" against Russia began with German troops in Lapland, but the offensive took them deeper into Russian territory. From the backseat, I announce, "Next time I see her I'm going to say, 'At least we did not side with Hitler!'"

Jukka seriously speeds up, passing a miniscule car. "We have had to do that. No one is helping us to get our land back."

"We did not need to do that," Taimi says from the front. "And we tried to take more land than they had took." I lean forward to listen as she says, "There was some crazy Finnish—I don't know the word. Group of people want all the Finns and Karelians and that sort of folk in Soviet Union to be together again. This would be some kind of nationalism."

Jukka says it made sense. The people there were related to Finns.

"But that has made us the warriors! We are not that way. And this turns the world against us."

Jukka slams to a stop at a light. "The world is not helping us fight Soviets so we turn to Germany for short time."

"Yeah, whose leader happened to be *Hitler*," I say. I ask Taimi about the history and through her halting English learn that early in WWII, Finland tried to retake the territories lost to the Soviets in the Winter War. But they advanced farther, east of Lake Ladoga, occupying Eastern Karelia, which unlike Western Karelia, had never been part of Finland. This caused Great Britain to declare war on Finland. "What happened to Jews?" I ask.

"Nothing. We have had Finnish Jews fighting with us," says Jukka. "Our army has built a synagogue in the Eastern Front."

"There were the eight Jews," his sister says.

"That was early in the war." Jukka keeps his eyes on the road, his mouth set straight.

"Doesn't matter," Taimi says, informing me that from some five hundred Jewish refugees, eight were handed over to the Germans. No more because the Finnish Lutheran clergy and Social Democratic Party protested.

When he stops abruptly in front of Taimi's apartment building, Jukka turns to face me, "Lipponen has given that official apology. Was some five or so years back, I think. War is bad and we have treated the Russians, our enemy, the worst. But that is all over. And we have repaid all war debts. Only country!"

I pat him on the back, as his sister jumps out. "I know, I know. I was just looking for the other side, the whole picture. No sense being myopic about it, right?"

"I don't know this word but yes, it's right to know whole history," Taimi says through the car window. "Jukka thinks that Finland is best so he chooses not to see."

Wanting to assuage him, I soften the tone as I hop in the passenger seat. "I suppose I've been known to be that way. About other things."

"This is all old history," Jukka ends the discussion. "No one but the old people are thinking about this much anymore."

Taimi swings her purse at the car. "Maybe then it's time for you and Dad to let it be. Who cares anyway? Big deal—so you don't have some *moekki* on Lake Ladoga to run off to. We have plenty land here."

"*Yo, yo*," he speeds off. I wave back to her as he grouses, "It's not like I'm waking up every day wishing to live over there in middle of nowhere."

~Keskellä ei mitään, Jumalan selän takana, Korvessa
~In the middle of nowhere, A godforsaken place, In the sticks~

Middle of Nowhere

We speed on Jukka's motorbike to the middle of nowhere. If the Eskimos have infinite words for "snow," the Finns have produced a prodigious vocabulary—multiple phrases—that all boil down to the *middle of nowhere*. The world might think Finland is such a place and frankly, I think most Finns prefer it that way.

It's a long ride to the house of this old woman in Karelia, on the far Eastern edge of Finland. We pass through quaint towns with cobblestone squares and Finnish Orthodox onion spirals. Outside one emptying church, a gypsy woman sells flowers wearing the distinctive, square-hipped bustle and billowy white blouse. A long queue of Russian trucks spews diesel at the border, the idle drivers outside talking and smoking.

Then we're on to kilometers of country roads, through the dappled forests of Karelia in full summer fecundity, the birch leaves fluttering iridescent silver in the breeze. Clouds breeze through the bluest of skies. It must've been crushing for my father's father to lose this land, the nearby sea being his livelihood, the land in his blood. The air whooshes as we ride in and out of meadows dotted with purple lupine and forests of conifer and birch. Past lake upon lake.

The ride is flat. A great glacier sliced the land and stayed, melting, forming all manner of shallow rivers, lakes, and gulfs and filling the earth itself with water. The ground is full of moisture, spongy swampland, the Finnish name for the country, *Suomi*, "bog land." Fertile ground for forests, exceptional for mosquitoes, a slew of which are squashed on my helmet visor. I've even learned to let go on Jukka's motorcycle. While at first I'd hung tight to his torso, fighting the curves, now I lean into each slant and tilt as we fly down the road, feeling free and joyful.

My pocketed cell phone is on vibrate, though I doubt I'll hear from Meredith and Paavo, no doubt busy with Russian bureaucracy—if anything can even be effected on a Sunday. I yell to Jukka that Meredith last called from Paavo's phone to say her charger's lost, and the text we got from him said only that there were "complications."

"HA!" Jukka's helmet bobs. "I know that is going to be that way. I'm surprised they come back with baby. Just no money."

I lean back, feeling strange…for some reason ambivalent about Meredith's adoption. But I think that whatever complications arise can be overcome by the money sent and the relationship forged with Meredith's sister. And Paavo. I even imagine her coming here, beaming as she did when Lou was first born, with a tiny pink person bundled in a flannel blanket, a living treasure all her own. A little girl Lou will dote on, and Steffen will fall in love with—I know that much about him—and how, after all, things will work out for her. For them.

"No. I think things will be fine. The baby will be good for her and Steffen. It will cement their relationship."

His head half turns. "I can't hear most, but doesn't sound so good to be in cement."

Near noon we stop for our packed lunch. Sitting on our jackets, we eat ham and butter sandwiches on rye and drink a thermos of coffee with cream. Only the rustling leaves and a few songbirds break the silence…and despite the numberless charms of Northern California, I feel at the moment as if I'm in the most beatific place in the world.

I let the soft breeze brush away any gloomy thoughts. I'm quite alive and finally on my way to possibly meet, or at least learn about, my closest relative!

Surveying the serene scene, Jukka tells me he will never leave this land. I'm both surprised and not—he was so enamored of the U.S. "Oh yes, I will always be the traveler. *A* traveler." I smile at his correction, as we've been helping each other learn our respective languages. "And I love hip-hop, American pizza and Vin Diesel." I roll my eyes. "But leaving *Suomi* for good is not for me."

"It would be hard to move," I agree. I'm not sure I could, either. Permanently. I wonder if Paavo would ever consider moving? Not wanting to sound obvious, I start talking of their visit to the States. "I always thought you could live there but not so much Paavo." Why do I sound like a Finn speaking English now?

"That's the strange thing. Paavo doesn't have the…if sailing I would say, '*ankkuri*.'"

"Anchor?"

"Yes. His brother is married now. I think he is still feeling free." Yeah, and who would stick around for Sirja? "I think he's wanting change in his life. He talks of this, of using these new healing techniques. Once he said it's much better to do Reiki and such in California than anywhere else in world."

"Really?" I wonder if he said anything—or *anyone*—else would draw him there?

"He said the people are most open there."

I perk up, so right! "Yes, kooks or not, we have open minds about everything!"

Jukka lies back against a rock, sucking a long blade of grass. I ask him if I've interfered with his plans, specifically with his dating. "I'll be off your hands soon, hopefully." Once Paavo returns, I plan to find out exactly where we stand.

He says that before traveling, he broke up with a girlfriend of five years. "She was the one who broke off." He closes his eyes.

"Oh, sorry. That's hard." After a moment I say. "And now?"

"Now I take time off from women."

"But you've had months off. Don't you want to start dating again?"

"Ya, maybe. But I am careful with my heart." He sits up and points the blade at me. "Like you."

I stand and wipe crumbs from my lap. With a proud smile, I say, "I'm changing that. I've been careful with my heart for way too long."

He looks at me seriously. "*Mutta*, but..."

"But *what*?"

He pitches the grass aside and grabs his helmet. "*Eipä mitään*." It's nothing.

As we chut-chut down an overgrown path to a cottage, no more than a shack, set under the evergreens, Jukka declares, "This is truly godforsaken place."

~*Vanha ei kuule eikä näe mutta kaikki ne kuitenkin tietää.*~
~The elderly, even if deaf and blind, still know a lot.~

Alina

The old woman, Rauha Haapalainen, shows no surprise at seeing us, two strange people at her door at the end of this forlorn horse path. Jukka speaks to her, pointing at me. I smile and peer at her, searching for family resemblance to my father, to me. Although Rauha's skin is surprisingly smooth, her bulbous nose dominates her face and her eyes sink below an old-fashioned head kerchief. As Jukka introduces us, she grasps my hands in hers, bony, with a roadmap of raised veins. Like my father's fine-fingered scholarly hands.

Her eyes tear up—something I'm used to now—and a slow smile of recognition lights her face. In her lifetime, Finland has transformed from a dominated peasant culture to an independent, world-class country of innovation, yet her property comprises a house simple as a *moekki*, an outhouse, and a true, chimney-less *savusauna.*

As she leads us to sit at the simple table, she speaks a few slow words to Jukka. An old red dog with a fox-like face and bushy tail naps in a corner. All dogs I see here remind me of Coco, who's thriving in the care of the neighbors and Steffen, and according to him has calmed down. And what is Lou like? A few months bring such changes in the young!

Jukka sits across from me. "Can you ask if we are related?" I ask, pointing to the old woman and me.

"She said she is the sister-in-law of your grandfather's youngest sister." *Come again?* Not even close to a genealogy expert,

I ponder this connection while Rauha methodically prepares a snack with her back to us, pouring glasses of buttermilk from an Arabia pitcher, slicing into a loaf of bread and methodically spreading each piece with a thick layer of butter. Jukka whispers to me, "Looks like she's *heittaa lusikka nurkkaan*." And that means? "About to throw the spoon in the corner. Die." I swat his hand. We wait in silence, a true quiet never heard in California, nothing but the occasional trill of a bird or the sound of insects fuzzing, droning, smashing themselves on the screened door and windows.

With measured moves she serves us. A quiet awe overtakes me as I watch her. I've been rash and clumsy for so long, thoughtlessly buzzing through my life like those flies, only to get thwarted by the next screen. Or flyswatter. *The world teaches us, if nothing else, to move more slowly*. My father used to say that; I can almost hear his voice in this quiet place. Jukka says that Rauha told him her son checks on her and brings provisions weekly.

After eating in silence, she says something to Jukka. Trying to be patient but anxious to know, I say, "Does she know about the certificate, Jukka? Who it is? Where Alina Eskala is?"

Jukka nods, says as he chews, "Ya, she's going to take you there. To see her. Your aunt."

The bread drops from my fingers. I *do* have an aunt? And she's here?! This must be a second or third aunt removed! My father had no siblings. "An *aunt*? Named Alina Eskala?" Perhaps an aunt by marriage. But to whom? And why have I never heard of her? Did the family denounce her?

"She's not much the talker. You gonna go through woods with her to see your aunt or some-such." *Walk* there? She's *here*? Another *mummu* in the forest? So that date…it must be her birth certificate. But why is it Russian? Could she have been a step-sibling? But Dad was born in the U.S.! My brain fires questions faster than I can ask. As I start hammering Jukka with all these ideas, Rauha dons rubber boots and hands me a red plastic pail. I follow.

"Come on, Jukka!"

"No, she says you go alone. It's best. This is big deal for you. I'm gonna rest here now." Arms behind his head, he shuts his eyes as he settles his feet onto a tiny embroidered footstool. I smooth my hair, feel the jitter in my hands. Here's hoping my 69-year-old relation speaks some English…

We go berry picking! Obviously, Rauha's in no hurry here. My apparent urgency hasn't added a line to her brow, a wrinkle in her composure. With a few deep breaths, I try to follow her lead, go with the flow.

We walk on ancient moss through dense forest: granite boulders, thickets of berry bushes, clutches of mushrooms under the pine and aspen canopy. The boggy ground is soft underfoot. Deep down the earth surges with water, everywhere the sea feels palpable. The loamy air, redolent with piquant pine, is intoxicating.

Rauha instinctively knows each bush to head for as I follow her deeper and deeper into the woods, like a child in a fairytale. Finding bushes loaded with blueberries, she bends and swipes dozens of them into her bucket with a quick whisk of her hand. I pick with less dexterity; my bucket light when hers is full. Perhaps they are a gift for my relation.

We pass an interdiction sign, one of the many markers that delineate the beginning of "no-man's land," the ten-kilometer-wide gap of empty land that lines the entire border between Finland and Russia, and I wonder if we're straying into forbidden territory. Guard towers are visible in the distance, now manned, Jukka told me, by Finnish soldiers who keep the E.U. border safe.

Sunlight filters in and again I feel mesmerized by the hushed and sacred place, the spell of the primordial forest. In the close distance, light flickers in the leaves like twinkling fairies, reflecting nearby water. I feel the souls of my parents and grandparents shine down, recalling how *mummu* used to say that Russians are good people. Now that I know we are related to one, I understand. As we walk, questions churn inside my head. How many live so deep in the woods? Does Rauha's son also care for my 'aunt?' As the forest thickens and grows darker, my feet begin to drag through the bush…it's too quiet here. Too desolate. Something feels off.

Through a clearing, water glints—a lake, the coast?—and then around a bend we come upon a tiny chapel, an Eastern Orthodox onion-domed church. Out of nowhere, a church, the size of a small square house. Brick, enchanting, utterly alone here in the woods, like something from a picture book. A pristine, unused chapel standing intact, sun bouncing off its crimson and gold stained-glass windows.

Rauha leads me over to the closed chapel, picks up a broom from a corner crevice. Now we're going to *sweep*? I follow transfixed, growing impatient, as she walks behind the church to a small graveyard, just a smattering of aged graves, most of them simple crosses. The old woman sweeps away pine needles and fallen leaves from a small grave marker. I stand off. She beckons me over. I close my eyes for a moment, feel my heart sink.

I stare at the crooked marker and the patch of grass that delineates a tiny body. With her broom she clears the grave. Heavy-footed, I draw near to read the stone.

Alina Eskala, Tytär
Ritva ja Ilmari Eskala
24.12.33 — 24.12.33

My grandparents had a baby girl?! And the date—*1933*. My father had a *twin*! Who died. A baby. I drop down, staring, let down to the point of tears. I look to her face, dumbfounded. But she cannot tell me: she speaks, but her Finnish only confuses me more. I don't understand. "*Kakoset*," she says.

She places a handful of berries on the grave. After some time she gently takes my hand without words. Zombie-like, I follow. My poor grandparents…my dad. No one ever letting on.

Back at the cottage, Jukka is fast asleep, bare toes sticking out from a striped woven blanket. I shake him awake. He sits up on the cushioned bench that lines the wall. "Jukka, can you ask her?" I point out the door. "About the baby?" He rubs his eyes, squints at me. "There is now a baby? Where is this?"

I point in a general direction toward the cemetery, my fingers stained crimson from the berries. "In a grave. A little grave. Alina Eskala's."

Rauha goes about with deliberation fixing coffee and a plate of food while my internal questions buzz. I know I must be patient for a few more minutes…"Why didn't you tell me my aunt was dead?"

"This Rauha doesn't say. *Didn't* say. She's keeping all the cards close to her breast. She's a good poker player, for sure."

"She put berries on the grave."

"Sure, that is some old folksy thing." He explains that on certain days of the year the dead were remembered by bringing food gifts to cemeteries. Shaking his head, he says, "They are thinking on these days the dead are with us here. She is the old broad. No, brood." He shakes his head in frustration. "I'm not remembering the word. Old type."

Well, I can see she's *old*. "The old breed?"

He nods. "I'm gonna have bigger wocabulary than you, for sure."

After she sits, I fold and unfold my hands, waiting and watching as they talk. I have got to learn this language! Rauha chews slowly between bites of information. At first, Jukka's questions fly, are answered in time. As more coffee is consumed, the two Finns become more animated. Intent, I watch their faces. Finnish fires back and forth. Jukka, obviously interested, does not just go through the motions as he has with so many other visits.

Rather, he leans in closely while Rauha talks and motions with her hands on the table, in front of her, then off out the window. She launches into pink-faced monologues that last minutes at a time—the old gal's become a veritable talk-show host!

Each time I try to interrupt, Jukka's hand flies up. "I'm going to know the whole story first, and then you will hear." Only fair, I suppose, as he's been waiting on me here and there for weeks. Fidgety as I am, I observe him with appreciation—for his time, his patience. For trekking to all my relations' homes and translating for me. At last, after three cups of nervous coffee, he spills the tale…

*

My father's parents, my *mummu* and *pappa*, Ritva and Ilmari, who lived next to us in Massachusetts, who worked in the old woolen mill as weavers, came to the U.S. because of that little grave. And since America is where Dad met Mom, I suppose it's why I'm here at all.

Mummu and *Pappa* were a young married couple in their twenties, skiing from this very moekki. Old wood cross-country skis, narrow and long with cable bindings, crisscross the walls and as Jukka talks, I glance at them. It was Christmas Eve, *Joulua*, and they set out from *Pappa's moekki* here toward *Mummu's*, farther East, to celebrate with her parents as well. A journey of some fifteen kilometers, but the snow blew in swiftly off the Gulf. Fifteen kilometers of open field alternating with forest and blinding white blowing snow. The day grew dark early, of course, and *Mummu*, seven months pregnant, grew tired fighting the wind. In the flurrying storm, they became lost. She buckled and clutched her belly. *Pappa* said, "Hurry, don't be a baby," but after every few strides she stopped, doubled over. "Ilmari, he's coming now," she said of the baby. "That's not possible yet!" her husband yelled through the gale, and they pushed on until she fell.

He could do nothing but build a hasty shelter of pine boughs. The wind pelted snow, the frigid air bit. Ritva lay down on the bed of pine and saw through the branches nothing but furiously slashing snow. Her husband removed his woolen coat to cover her. She bunched up her knees. "Don't have the baby now," he pleaded. She stared at the whirling white sky through the wobbling branches, snow snapping at her face, stinging her lips, her stomach seizing more frequently...and then a face.

Above her appeared a grey fur army cap. She cried out as contractions stabbed again. A Russian voice, vodka on his breath. He'd been watching from a guard tower, one of many littered across Eastern Karelia, former Finnish land, ceded after the wars. Land the Soviets surveilled to keep their people in.

It was this soldier, large as a Slavic god who brought a thick wool blanket and canteens of water and vodka. It was he who pulled Aatos, my father, out of my mother's womb, wrapped him in rough wool, cutting the cord with an army blade. But he could not save the other baby, the smaller one, the girl. He took them all to a hospital in old Viipuri, now Vyborg, over *Pappa's* protests. And there the baby was named and pronounced dead. Alina Eskala.

Jukka says solemnly, "Your grandparents and father have lived but not this little *tytär*. She has died." After Rauha says something, he adds that my *mummu* had some frostbite. She thinks some fingers went missing. I slowly nod.

The couple left Finland when my father was ten months old, and never spoke about his twin sister, the one who didn't make it. Delivered by a stranger, given a Russian birth certificate. It finally sinks in—*my father's* Russian! Or at least, Russian-born.

"And so." Jukka, trying to translate for Rauha, says, "Your *mummu* always has seen the good side of Russians but your *pappa*...he was still mad." I shake my head. He says, "Rauha has met with your mother. She has come few times out here to grave."

"I can't believe *Pappa* held his grudge! The Russians saved his life! His life, his wife's, Dad's..."

Jukka shrugs. I recall my *mummu* saying always, in contrast to *Pappa's* grumbling, "Kind-hearted people in Roo-si-ya and *you know that.*" But beyond those words, no hint was ever dropped that could've let me know. And what vow had my father adopted to maintain this silence? Perhaps the past was just dead to him, as he was more American than Finn, and of course felt no connection to the people who'd brought him into the world one stormy, Christmas eve.

But he couldn't possibly blame them for his sister's death when they all could have perished. I put down my coffee cup with shaky fingers, trying to absorb this strange history. "That's the problem with prejudice. It has no reason, no sense." My head falls into my hands, wishing away the world's conflicts, born of fear of "otherness," rooted in land.

Before leaving, I retrace my steps to the graveyard, Jukka trailing far behind as if reluctant to come. In front of Alina's marker, Jukka out of sight, I lay a swig of blueberries on the swept grave. A chill seeps up through me from the forest floor. I shiver in the failing light, hug myself, tired and cold. I sink to my knees, submerge into the moist ground, mired in the bog. I wish it would swallow me whole. Tears trickle for the lost baby. And perhaps for me: I've come to the loneliest place on earth.

~Helposti saatu on helposti menetetty.~
~What is acquired easily is lost easily.~

Together Again

There is no baby, no Natalya. From taciturn Paavo, who returned earlier, we learned only this. "It has not gone the right way somehow. There is no child."

Getting Meredith to come to Finland wasn't easy. I had to persuade her over the phone, convince her to take the train to Helsinki, then fly back home at my expense. She didn't like the idea of the extra travel, but I told her it was the same distance from LA to San Diego, a two and a half hour trip. That otherwise we wouldn't get to see each other for who knows how long. And I told her of my sailing plan, how I need her with me to scatter my parents' ashes. I couldn't believe she agreed, but she said she couldn't spend another three days alone in St. Petersburg waiting for her scheduled flight. With a plaintive note in her voice, she added that after our reunion, maybe I'd want to come home to California, too.

My first view of her at the train station showed her looking diminished, the skin stretched taught across her pale face. Running up to her, I draw her in, twine my arms tight around her frame. "Oh, Mere." She falls into my arms and I sense that I'm literally holding her up. My eyes swell. What a blow she's taken. To come all the way over here, yearning for a baby, returning with nothing. I stand sturdy as I feel her quake. I let her cry, finally with some empathy, at last *feeling* her despair. "I'm so sorry that Paavo couldn't help," I say, and she sobs harder.

Jukka drives us in silence to his condo while I hold her hand in the backseat. As the two of us head inside, he mumbles something about errands and drives off. I fix her tea and a late lunch of salad and potato soup, food she barely touches.

I present her with gifts, which draw out a wan smile: chocolate-covered berries and a brightly woven scarf I purchased at the *tori*, the outdoor market in Helsinki. And though I can't make up for her collapsed adoption plans, I feel confident that I can help cheer her. Besides, there's a chance that this communal setback could bring Mere and Steffen closer.

I tell her how sorry I feel. Treading carefully, I say, "I'm sure there are modern ways you can have a baby. I remember Cleo talking about freezing her eggs, or something. You and Steffen will find a way. Maybe try another adoption?" I want to say, "through proper channels," but don't. In fact, finding the right words is too tricky; I wish she'd talk. I want to tell her to "*use her words*!" Gently pressing for more details on the trip, she fingers oily hair from her face. "It's all too messed up."

When I set down tea she asks for a beer. Meredith drinking beer in the middle of the day? "What, one week over there and you've started drinking?" I give her a friendly nudge.

"No, beer makes me sleepy. I just want to sleep. Besides, they don't all drink over there. I met some really wonderful people. The women at the baby house...what little I understood, I could see that they really love those kids. There never was a child for me, though. And they knew Bogdan was phony." She shakes her head. "And maybe..." She gulps her beer, looks at me. "Maybe I knew all along, in my heart..."

"Knew?"

"That it wasn't really real."

"*What*?"

Looking out the window, she says, "Was I just trying to force Steffen's hand?" She shakes her head. "Maybe I just wanted change. Ha! Well, I sure got it." She stabs a forkful of lettuce while I process this...she sounds resigned about the baby, practical. So she, too, was skeptical? But her *affect* is so sad. Could it be she's just missing Lou and Steffen? *Home*?

"You want to be back in California, don't you? In two days you'll see your boys. Everything will look better then."

"I had no idea how much I'd miss Lou. Two days feels like forever. I wish I could go home, but the flights were all booked, and the round-about ways too expensive." She guzzles more beer.

"And I thought you wanted to see me," I try to lighten the mood.

With a thin smile she says, "I did. And who can argue with a stubborn Finn?"

"Oh, I'm afraid I'm quite American."

"Anyway, let's talk about *you*. Here. Your life. Are you finding your family?" She asks for another beer.

If she wants distraction, I provide it with beer and anecdotes from my stay—the journeys to meet relations, my getting to know Jukka and his sister, my sauna with Sirja. I try to amuse. I don't talk about the grave in the forest now, but I tell her about Reiki with Paavo, how it cleared something in me, and while I think she'll perk up at this, her face becomes inscrutable, her gaze wanders. The beer. Meredith's no drinker. I should get her to bed.

I pull her up, telling her that Steffen has called periodically since I got here—with questions about money transfers, house decisions, sub-contractor problems. He sounds perpetually worried, about what remains unclear. Meredith? The house? Falling prices? The need to make decisions, especially about selling. But it all seems so remote, and I don't want to think about the house, Mercury, the fire. I've left it all in his capable hands, knowing it's unfair, wondering if I can afford to pay him more.

I support her as she walks, woozy with exhaustion and two beers, to Jukka's room. After I cover her with the blanket, I close the blinds. Sitting by her on the bed, I remind her that tomorrow's a big day for me. She must come sailing. I explain that I understand the timing's bad, but moping around Jukka's place all day makes no sense. "You're all packed for your flight the day after, and it'll take your mind off things. Being on the sea, in the fresh air. Now that's a tonic!"

She protests. "I'm really not in the mood, Ali. Can't you just go with Jukka and his sister?"

"And Paavo." She doesn't say anything. A thought fleets through my mind, then dissolves as I remind her why I need her there. "For me, for my parents. It's what they'd want…" I don't mention my other plan, the one involving Paavo. The timing's not right.

She relents. "OK, Ali, I'll let you work your outdoor magic on me."

Yes! *My cure* for *her pain*. "I know it's not Reiki, but it's the Finnish way. 'When in Helsinki.'"

"But only because of your ceremony." She takes my hand. "And because I've missed you so." I hug her and turn to go but she grasps my hand to stop me with an unexpected outburst, "Ali, let's just go home!"

I drop down on the bed. "To what, Meredith? You're the one with family."

"Maybe you should stop looking at what you don't have there."

Her mood swing takes me aback, I pull my hand away. "I could say the same to you." Inhaling, I back off. "I'm sorry. You've been through so much. Just rest. We'll talk later." I smooth the blanket over her reclining figure.

"But when *are* you coming home?"

"I don't know. So much depends on…" Why don't I want to say it? Is it like her adoption—maybe not *really real?* I've had my doubts, have wondered if this love is my big fantasy. But now more than ever I feel that Paavo would be the only reason to stay here. So much rides on his feelings. I tell her. "It depends on Paavo."

"No!" She sits up. I'm startled by her response. Eyes averted, she says, "I don't want you to stay here." *Because of Paavo?*

Upset, I say, "Don't worry, Mere, I'll always be there for you." And as I watch her familiar and earnest face, I feel how hard it would be to live so far away from my best friend. "If things work out, perhaps he'll be open to moving."

She drops onto her pillow. "Forget Paavo!" Then she closes her eyes. *Forget Paavo? What's that mean? Is my best friend jealous?* She's acting so oddly. Although I dismiss her peculiar words, blaming them on distress, travel fatigue and alcohol…I leave the room with a queasy feeling about our boating trip tomorrow.

~Kyllä jokainen on kippari kauniilla säällä.~
~Everyone is the skipper when weather is fair.~

Sailing

The day dawns with grey importance.

Despite the darkness that descends in late summer nights, I couldn't fall asleep on the sofa and when I did, I thrashed about with strange dreams. Jukka wakes grumpy, and slaps a plate of cold herring in front of us. I wrinkle my nose, having realized that the food served by his epicurean mother on my first day here was not the norm. How unfair to introduce me with such deviously delicious food, only to be fed herring, meat and potatoes from then on!

The sky alternates between sun and drizzle during the silent car ride to the harbor, and again I sit in back with Meredith. But she only stares out the window with no evident interest in the passing scenery. Sullen company or no, I'm determined to see my plans through.

If Steffen was a racy speedboat when it came to romance, Paavo has been like the boat we approach now, bobbing in the harbor, no wind in its sails. And if Taimi's right about the pace of Finnish men, I'd better speed things up American-style. What better place than on the sea to begin a new journey? And complete one that began long ago…

With my arm wrapped around Meredith's waist, I propel her onto the dock, surprised that her middle feels more substantial. Maybe she hasn't been starving on grey Russian meat and beets, after all. More likely it's the thick sweaters she borrowed from

Jukka to ward off the cool sea air. Jukka boards the boat with his coffee. Mere and I sit cross-legged on the pier dunking thick slices of *pulla* into our warm coffee, and my spirits lift. The fog of not knowing will vanish when Paavo hears my declaration. Gorgeous white fleecy clouds float by, allowing us moments of sweet sunshine.

"Taimi needs to be here." Jukka scowls as he hops alone about the sailboat deck. "Why she has to see this one woman for haircut *today*? It's crazy. There are so many these hair places for women, one in every corner Helsinki. But this one she waits half a year now yust when I'm needing the crew…" his voice drops below deck with him. I smile.

As I step aboard with my precious duffle bag, I hear, "*Moi,*" from the deep voice I've awaited. My head pivots so fast that Paavo, approaching the boat, illuminated by the eastern light, appears lit by stars. It feels like viewing hope in this often lonely land. I expected to feel nervous when I saw him, but instead I'm calm. And glad to see him.

He nods at Meredith, asks how she's doing. She mumbles an answer. Jumping on the boat he says to me, "You are looking quite healthy and happy, I think. That's the funny thing, now is first time I notice you do not hide your face behind glasses anymore."

"Did you forget that I got LASIK like you?" I punch his arm, "Now all I see are good things." He doesn't get it, so I explain, "Remember how you said, "All I see are bad things? About my yard?" He shakes his head. "Well, I do. Back then I thought you were saying—"

"I'm needing some help here, Paavo," Jukka calls out.

"Anyway, I see everything great now and life itself looks great! *You* look great!" My English vocabulary seems to be shrinking…I need another word. "Brilliant" is what Steffen would say, though probably not about Paavo.

"You are seeing through rosy-colored glasses. Meredith has

told me this expression in Russia, when I'm trying to console her." We look to her still seated on the dock, her face half blocked by the coffee mug.

"*Nyt!*" Jukka bellows from the stern and Paavo hops to his side. Jukka complains about sailing these busy shipping seas. "It's better sailing in Åland Islands, but I do this for my crazy cousin here. She doesn't even say why." *My cousin.* Again I smile. I haven't told them why I wish to voyage east in the Gulf of Finland instead of sailing toward Sweden.

"You'll know soon enough," I say, storing the duffle under the deck seat. "And let me help."

He proceeds to point around, spewing Finnish, evidently explaining to Paavo the intricacies of sailing. "You listen also, Alina," he blusters, apparently forgetting that I barely speak Finnish, let alone nautical language. Jukka peers skyward. "Your friend should listen also because weather is unpredictable." He glances at Meredith, still plunked in the same spot. "And channel is very busy." Since we've been together Jukka's English has much improved, so this omission of his articles tells me he's anxious, agitated.

Meredith takes the hint and climbs aboard, Paavo assisting with one arm. He says that sailing might not be good for her today. I interject, "We talked about that yesterday. She's had a rough journey, but she'll be fine once she gets home to her family. And I'll help as much as I can."

Paavo says, "You and Meredith both go home then?" Do I detect a note of disappointment in that question?

"Oh no. I mean, not right away. But eventually…depending." I feel an urgency to say the words I have in mind, to catch my private moment with Paavo, but jittery Jukka hustles about, muttering. "You have to be ready for some things today," he warns, stopping to pop open a bottle of beer. A bit early in the day. "Hair of the dog, eh?" I nod at his bottle. "*Ei ole koiraa karvoihin katsominen.* Don't judge dog by its hair," and I laugh at his play on words. "This is gonna make me feel easier."

As I rehearse my words for Paavo, Jukka addresses us in English. I only half-hear his instructions between the wind, the clanking of metal on masts, and the chatter in my head. "It is busy traffic out here and I am Captain. You must listen and see," he points to ropes and sails and while Paavo attends him, I can't help wondering how he'll react. Meredith will be proud of my newfound assertiveness, but Paavo's so traditional—I honestly don't know. What I am sure of is this: I can't wait for Life to happen. For love, a family of my own. The clock is ticking… I need to act. Maybe Meredith's pending departure for California has sparked my need to find out whether my path lies with Paavo here in Finland, or not.

"This is main sail, you must pull that rope tight," Jukka motions. "When we come about, I gonna say "yippee" so you look and stay out of way."

"Yippee! I love it!" Because we're all here, and the future's bright. "A sailing cheer!"

Jukka frowns. "Cause if we gonna turn boat round, the boom…" he swings his arm dramatically. Meredith listens intently, following his movements. My phone buzzes in my pocket. Steffen's number appears but I ignore it. Today, any house decision can wait.

Boating lesson over, Jukka orders us all to sit as we motor out of the harbor. I clear my throat to speak. "I have an announcement. Meredith already knows this—Mere, thank you so much for coming." To the others, I pronounce, "Once we're really underway, out to sea…I will be scattering my parents' ashes."

Jukka pauses, then swigs from his beer. Paavo stops coiling a rope. "You put out your mother's ashes in the sea?" I think I see approval on his face.

"Yes, both Mom and Dad. Together."

The rope drops from Paavo's hand with a thud. "How is this

possible? You have said your father is already somewhere in the ground."

"Well he's not. Anymore." I'd rather not go into the specifics of Edna, April, and the funeral home. "We had my father's urn disinterred. Um, dug up. So he could be with mom. So they could be here. Not buried somewhere with no one around." The motor chugs as I point under my seat, "Their ashes are in this bag."

Paavo's brows merge. I stiffen. I'd never noticed how thick with disapproval they could be. "You have dug him up? This is not something we do in Finland."

I feel like saying *get over it, it's my decision*, when Meredith says, "Alina did what she thought was right, and I support her. It's why I'm here today." She puts her arm around my shoulders but faces Jukka, not Paavo, as she says this.

Once in full sail, rushing downwind, I walk to the front of the boat, to be alone. I want to take a moment to feel the cold salt spray on my face, taste it on my tongue and give thought to where I am and what I'm about to do. Paavo's reaction was a bit severe, but what couple doesn't have differences of opinion? The blue water, the waves like so many welcoming hands, the wind tossing my hair buoy my spirits. I inhale the fresh, slightly salty air, its unique smell of sea and lake. The sun comes out to bless me.

When I step unsteadily toward the back of the boat—the seas have become choppier—Paavo sits staring emptily across the cockpit. Jukka, at the rear holds the wheel in one hand and a fresh beer in the other. His mood seems improved, he's whistling. Unless it's the wind in my ears.

Meredith, sitting on the same side as Paavo, clenches her stomach and half-stands to lean overboard. As I reach them, he slides toward her in solicitation. I rush over to her as she sits, suddenly flummoxed by Paavo's gesture, not even sure who I'm jealous of—I mean, she's *my* best friend. "Are you OK, Mere?"

"Just feeling a little nauseated," she says, with a glance Paavo's way. I'm understanding something but not. They're getting closer, all this travel together, his obvious fraternal concern for her…

I turn to him, "I was seasick my first time out, too. I think she'll be fine." I need to get on with it. Even if we're not alone, it's time I spoke up. And Meredith's presence might again be supportive. I take a breath. "Paavo," I begin. He doesn't look my way. "Paavo," I say more loudly, "I've, well, I've missed you." He looks at me inscrutably, and I think perhaps I sounded insincere; I haven't had time to miss him! "Well, both of you, of course," I nod to Meredith who looks stricken, her arms clasped around her stomach. "I'm so glad you're here. Because I have something to tell you."

She says, "Ali not—"

But I interrupt. "No, it's OK that you're here." Big breath. "I love you, Mere, and now it's time for me to tell Paavo."

Paavo says, "What is it you need to tell?"

"Well, what I just said, that I lo—" Meredith groans, turns to spit again.

"Meredith is feeling poorly. We should perhaps turn back," Paavo calls to Jukka who, unmindful, whistles away. Wind in the sails, he continues drinking at the helm.

"Mere, are you going to puke?" I ask, not sounding sympathetic.

"I'm all right. But Ali, maybe you should wait…"

"No. I've been waiting and not acting for too long." So again I look straight into Paavo's squinting eyes. "I think we might have a future, love-wise." His eyes widen. "That is, depending on how you feel…"

"How I feel?" Paavo acts incredulous. "Now it is Meredith we must worry how she feels!"

Poor Meredith, yellow at the gills, shakes and seems ready to heave. But I can't let this hold up the works. "I'm sorry Mere, but right now I've got to talk. Paavo, I've felt from the start—well, OK, not the first day or so when you were wearing those weird goggles—but from Yosemite at least, that we have this connection, and—"

"Ali, *please,* later."

"No, you should hear this, too, Mere. I think I love you. *Him.*" I turn to Paavo, whose questioning face was turned on Meredith. I say to him blindly, quickly, "You. That I love you."

He shifts back in his seat. "What is this talk of love? Such as Meredith says to everyone? This is how they speak in America. Well, I suppose I love you too."

Vexed by his tone, this misunderstanding, I say deliberately, as if to a dense student, "No. I am talking about *a man-and-woman* love."

Again a glance at Meredith before he answers. *What's with that?* "But you do not even know me." Meredith, green as the sea, turns her face away as if to give us some semblance of privacy. To save me from embarrassment?

My stomach sinks as we roll down a wave. Hot-faced, filling with shame but insistent, I struggle on, "Bridal Veil Falls, remember? At Yosemite?"

He presses his lips together as if searching his memory. "This is the Indian girl who has fallen in the waterfall?"

"Yes, but that's not the point. Our moment there, when you held my hand..." my voice trails off as I see his confused expression. My mind scrabbles for evidence. "You kissed me! At my party?"

He swipes the side of his nose. "Yes. You have kissed me then."

"You kissed back!" I accuse, the wind picks up, blowing my hair into my mouth.

"Well...I was drinking, I suppose. Maybe you are being blue-eyed. No, starry-eyed."

It's sinking in that he's arguing with me about my feelings, I've caught him off-guard. I back off, weakly continuing, "The swim at the lake." I block that disastrous night out to think of all our special moments. The boat lurches. I struggle for balance. "You opened me up with Reiki, we danced together…" He gapes at me. I grasp at visions tangled in time. "I smelled your *chair*."

"I'm not familiar with this expression."

"Ali, we've just returned from a long trip and everyone's tired." Meredith clutches her gut and leans over the side.

Ashamed, confused, now angry, I assert. "These were signs that you loved me."

Paavo says, "*En mina voi siksi muuttua*," an expression I vaguely recall…my parents said something like that whenever I nagged for some toy I could not have. He translates, "I can't change into that." Change into *what*?

Why is this going so wrong? My cell phone buzzes in my pocket and I have the urge to chuck it. As I wobble with the slanted boat, I try to understand. The sun burns too brightly, suddenly I need sunglasses out here. Stranded with no shades. I'm seeing everything clearly but it's all muddled. Meredith reaches out, but I brush away her arm.

I stumble across the cockpit to gain some distance. This boat is too small. I climb up onto the deck, grip the cold rail. Out of the corner of my eye, Jukka turns the wheel while up-ending a bottle for the last drops of beer.

Meredith calls to me through the wind, which has picked up. Storm clouds gather. I see her shakily step out of the cockpit across from me to throw up overboard. Although her back heaves up and down pathetically, I cannot help her because I'm deep undersea where things are opaque and blurry. My phone buzzes—or is it my head? Mechanically I take it out. Jukka disappears below deck calling something about going to the head as I hear Steffen say, "Alina, I need to talk to you. Alone." He'd mentioned needing money, applying to the bank.

"A loan? Fine." I say.

"Come again? I can't hear you well. Where are you?" I turn my back to stare out to sea. A large wooded island looms ahead off to our right, foreboding with dense dark forest. The sudden roar of a foghorn startles as the tip of a ship emerges from the far side of the island. "We're *sailing*. I can't deal with the house now." My spinning mind runs to joists, haunch piers—he'd mentioned a loft. He should talk to Jukka about this nautical-sounding stuff. But Jukka's gone for some reason. I check the unmanned steering wheel, or whatever he calls it.

"There's something you should know," Steffen says. Turning back, I catch a fleeting view of Paavo, who looks miserable. The sails slap too loudly, the horn blasts again. Although I can't hear what he says, the sound of Steffen's voice steadies my shaky legs, grounds me here on the water. Regaining my bearings, it dawns on me. My illusion a delusion. I almost laugh. "Steffen—"

"*Perkele*!" Jukka swears as he rushes up onto deck zipping his fly. "That is not good place for you! Get way!" He waves a frantic arm at me.

"I hate to tell you this," Steffen says. "It's about Meredith and Paavo." I don't comprehend. Then Paavo, by her side, leans into her and puts his hand on her back in a gentle gesture that hits me in the gut…I cry, "No!" Good lord! Meredith's eyes meet mine, she implores, "*Ali*!" Salt air stings my eyes, my nose. The bullhorn deafens. *Would Meredith betray me? Her stomach! Is she pregnant?*

Jukka hollers, "We need to turn round! The ship!" The phone slips from my hand and skitters…I twist to look for it. Did it slide overboard? Steffen's gone. My brain spins as Jukka rattles something to Paavo. He takes the wheel. Jukka darts over to frantically tug at a winch. A bullhorn blares out angry Finnish from the other ship. Meredith, distraught, mouths something to me.

Jukka shouts, "YIPPEE!" Yippee?! Incredulous, I turn. He yells, "Yippee! *Down! GO DOWN*!" An uproar of nylon sails flaps madly. Stricken, I see Meredith lurch toward me, zigzag across the cockpit, pleading. The loose boom swings toward her mid-section. *The baby.*

"Ali, it's not what—" Fast as an elf, I plunge, sliding feet first to kick her legs out from under her. Swiftly I rise to shove her shoulders clear. Too late, I duck. A hard flash of metal—the whipping boom—hammers me dead in the head with a raging THWACK!

~*Vahingosta viisastuu.*~
~An accident makes one wiser.~

Recovery

They say I flipped back and over into the chilly blue Baltic. Paavo saved me, swimming hard to reach me and keeping my unconscious body afloat until Jukka could tack back to us.

I dream of my mother's bedroom filled with smoke. My scalp burns, it itches. My parents come close but dissolve in the haze and then I'm holding a box of ashes, a weight I cannot bear. The urge to drop them is strong. I want to scratch my head, which has a scar of fire. I panic, the box falls, my hands fly to my head—I feel a string of hot, stinging bumps, ants marching…

I wake up and see Mom and Dad through caked eyes, out of focus. I reach out to them but something tugs at my arm—*ow*. I try to sit up, my arm is tubed, and the room comes slowly into focus. Meredith stands over me, behind her Paavo. I reach up to brush the ants off my head. Groping, I feel bumps…stitches? I feel stubble surrounding the line of fiery stitches, so I pat my head until my hand finds hair. I lie back, close my eyes. The boat. I didn't scatter my parents' ashes.

Someone squeezes my hand. I look up to see Paavo attempt a smile. When he walks off, I see that Jukka talks on his phone in the corner of the room. Meredith stands over me, troubled lines between her brows, "Ali. You saved me."

"Am I OK?" I croak.

She pours and hands me a plastic cup of water. "The doctors said you'd be fine but I didn't want to leave."

"What day is it?"

"Still today." She looks at a clock. "Almost midnight." She takes my hand, "Ali, promise me one thing. Stop making me visit you in the hospital. OK?" I smile weakly, recalling awakening to these same three in the Blaineville E.R. Then I remember: "You're pregnant, right?"

"Seasick, depressed, guilt-ridden, yes. But not pregnant." She sighs. "Ali, if you were trying to save my imaginary child but not me, I'm afraid you failed." Silence. "Can I ask why you always think I'm pregnant?"

"Once bit, twice shy?"

"But—" she stops herself.

Before she can respond, Jukka pockets his phone and comes to stand by me. "I'm very sorry, Alina. I have never had that happen. I was not the good skipper." He looks down at his feet. "You should be very angry for me. This is really, very bad thing."

But I don't feel angry with him, I'm obviously in a hospital but aside from my head, I feel all right. "Why so glum? Am I going to *die* or something?"

With typical practicality, Jukka says, "Not from this, I don't think so."

Meredith cries, "God, no! You weren't even close. You're going to be fine, they say you'll be leaving soon. But I guess they keep you here longer than back home."

I ask them to raise my bed, then I draw Jukka in to swing my arm around his neck. "Don't worry about it. We all made mistakes. Make mistakes." Paavo joins us bedside. But Jukka shakes his head, not to be reprieved so easily. "I have made big mess."

As I reflect aloud, "We're all in the same boat," Paavo says simultaneously, "*Olemme kaikki samassa veneessä.*" This causes a half-smile to appear on Jukka's forlorn face. He says that the phrase is the same in both languages. "You and Paavo are thinking the exact same thing." Well, that's a first! "Anyway, I am taking some learning from this. Now I stop the drinking."

I recall an A.A. adage from Dad: "You've 'hit rock bottom.'"

"Well, I'm thinking it's you have hit the rocks," he jokes. My hand flies to my head, the itching, and I ask for a mirror. After fishing one out of her bag, Meredith holds it for me. I bend and feel for the cut, the black stitches, tilting the mirror…and am shocked to see a good quarter of my scalp shaved around the wound. "Jesus. How many stitches are there?"

"Not so many."

Meredith says, "Ten, I think. I can't believe you put yourself in danger like that for me."

"I can't believe they had to shave half my head for ten lousy stitches!" A huge lump juts above my hairline and bright purple bruises extend down to my right eye. "Arghhh!" I fall back on my pillow.

Jukka says, "You look—" I gird myself for the harsh truth, the appraisal I'll take as an insult. "Goot!"

I smile. "*Not so bad* would've sufficed. Don't go overboard." We all laugh. Then a nurse or doctor comes in and shoos everyone out. But before they go, I say to Paavo. "You're the real hero here. You saved me from drowning." I stretch out my hand. "Thank you, *kiitos paljon.*"

He looks down. "*Kiitos kiitos.*" Thank you, thank you, the Finnish way of saying "you're welcome."

The medical woman interrupts. "You can see your friends later. I'll check you. Then you will rest."

*

When I awaken from what felt like a long sleep, I feel drowsily happy. Maybe it was a dream, I can't recall. I'm in bed in a lovely room lighted by bright windows. Whose house is this? Is this the house that Steffen built? Where is Steffen, Meredith?

As a new nurse pads in with a tray, I spy coffee and a pastry; my mouth waters. The bedside phone rings. The nurse nods to it and raises my bed. I pick up the receiver to hear Steffen's voice, clear and true. A barrage of questions I can't answer without caffeine. At the end, he says three sweet words, not those words—I can't expect him to ever say them again. But these sound as wonderful as any I've heard in my life: "You belong here."

After I hang up, I gobble the apple pastry and lie sipping my comfort drink. I see Meredith's hovering figure near my door. She wears a trench coat and her hippie woven backpack is slung across one shoulder—she's leaving. My heart sinks. She disappears from view. I point to the door.

The nurse looks concerned. I try to ask about my friend in Finnish. What's the word? *Aiti*? No, that's mother. I give up. I ask for "*sisar*," raise my arm to indicate a tall woman. The nurse says in perfect English, "Your friend has been waiting for you to wake up. I'll get her."

Meredith enters the room and pulls up a chair.

"So you and Paavo."

She takes a deep breath." What happened was a mistake."

"You slept with him. After I confided in you."

"No, no, Ali, please listen." I'm grateful for the tray table across my chest, it keeps her at bay. I don't want to sit near or hold hands. "It was like this. The adoption fell through and I was so depressed—no *despondent*—for a couple of days. We—"

"You and Paavo."

She clasps and unclasps her hands. "Yeah. We got drunk on this watery beer and had to stay the night at the hotel just before coming here. There was a single bed—he couldn't get a room. And my room was like cement, a cold brick. Some Soviet-era atrocity of a hotel. Paavo was going to sleep on the floor but we couldn't even get another flimsy blanket. And it was freezing that night." She stops to gauge my reaction.

My direct gaze causes her to avert her eyes. "We slept foot to head, but I guess he heard me sob. He held me and he was so…comforting. I really needed comforting." Her eyes water. She says quickly, "And you know, we were drunk—it just happened. The once." Slowly emphasizing each word, she says, "I am so sorry."

The hum of the machine I'm attached to thrums steadily. I take the news calmly, indifferently. Strange, but no jealousy piques me. I recall a moment on the boat, before I saw the move that betrayed the lovers—an epiphany about Paavo…

I brush pastry crumbs from my gown. "So I guess, biologically-speaking, you wouldn't be pregnant. Or wouldn't know yet." She shakes her head vigorously. "What about Steffen?"

"Of course I told him it's over."

Wait! What's over? Who's over? I jerk forward, the tubing pinches my arm. "You told Steffen it's over with Paavo?" I yank the tube loose. *Ouch!*

"Ali, No! No. I told him—as if I had to—that it's finally over between us. *Steffen and me.* I'm letting him go." She scoots forward, takes the sore arm I rub, tries to stroke it. I pull away. "Something I should've probably done a long time ago."

"Let me get this straight. You broke it off with Steffen to be with Paavo."

"Not exactly. More like I conceded that Steffen never really loved me, yes. But I'm not going to be with Paavo." She's not going to be with either man?

"What about Lou?!"

"Alina, Lou has two loving parents who spend tons of time with him. They happen to live apart. That's his reality and pretty much always has been. He's fine."

"So why can't you be with Paavo?" I demand. She should hurt. *She* should have a needle jabbed in her arm and ants marching on her head! "Paavo clearly likes you. *Loves you.*" Don't they all?

"Ali, listen. I'm not perfect. I haven't ever been able to tell you how I felt about Steffen, how I always felt like his 'rebound' girl. And then I got pregnant…did I want that? Yes, I've wanted a child ever since I can remember. I don't regret Lou. Did *he* want it? I thought he might be open to it at the time…it was pretty early in our relationship."

"Yeah, I know."

She takes in my sarcasm. "Anyway. Waiting so long for him to commit, to marry me…obviously I was deluding myself.

"You had to! Lou."

"For four years? I don't think so." Sighing, I sag into my slanted mattress. Illusions, delusions. We all have them. What's to distinguish them from dreams?

So much talking has made me tired. I need another cup of coffee. "Where's room service?" I wouldn't mind staying in this place a while, if they'd quit with the poking and prodding.

I give in as Meredith grasps my hand. "Alina, I honestly feel that no man is worth forfeiting our relationship. Remember that baboon thing? Or was it chimps? You said females who lose their grooming partners get depressed. You said it could be fatal or something."

I have to smile at her. "I guess you can see I'm going to need grooming help."

"Do you think you'll forgive me eventually? My flight's in a few hours and that's all I want to hear…that I can hope." Tears glide down her downy cheeks.

"Don't cry." I wipe at her tears. "Hey, have some *sisu*, will you?" Eyes glistening, she smiles and hugs me. "So. Where's Paavo?"

She looks away. "He's an amazing man, Ali. It was just a one-time mistake. If you want him…you probably don't. Anyway, I've told him that I can't see him. He's leaving."

"Leaving?"

"He's going camping in Lapland. And I need to get home. To *Lou*."

"Jesus, I'm not going to run up to the tundra for him!"

She looks shocked. "Well, I think *right now* he's out in the hall..."

"Then call him in."

When Paavo enters, looking sheepish, Meredith grabs her bag from the chair. "Don't go, Mere. I need to talk to both of you." So I tell them. I've been blind, silly, really. Of course I don't know Paavo. I decline saying that I had second thoughts even as I declared my love on the boat—the words came out but the feeling wasn't there. And talk about unappealing! The guy was arguing with me! I say aloud, "That mast knocked some sense into me, eh?"

Paavo says, "I think so."

Mere says, "Ali, we were the ones who acted foolish. We acted wrong."

"You acted on your true feelings, at least. Maybe you two should see if you have something together?"

"Something?" Paavo questions.

"Yeah, Paavo. Something *romantic.*"

"Meredith is thinking she cannot be with me."

"She can be with you if she wants to. If she thinks the two of you might have a future."

He looks down. "Well, this is early to say." *Dude! I feel like saying, Go for it!*

"Ali, why are you talking like this?

I gaze at the two of them, how perfect they seem for each other. "I don't know…maybe I know myself a little better. And maybe you two should get to know each other better, that's all. Paavo's never been interested in me."

"It's true," he nods. I shoot him an annoyed look.

Meredith jabs him. "He's very fond of you. He says you're like a sister to him."

"Ha, I'm like *his* sister is what he means!" His judgmental, annoying sister!

"Little bit, ya," he says, taking no notice of my tone.

"I've got to leave now," Meredith says firmly.

"Well, I just want you to know that whatever you two do, I'm good with it." I smile and feel genuinely happy to be relieved of the peculiar burden of questing after Paavo. "As for me, I am so, *so* ready to go home!"

"Home?" Mere asks.

"I have an intense longing to see my house." And the man who built it.

*

Goodbyes to my Finnish family in the following few weeks aren't so hard. I say "*Nakemiin,*" *see you later*, to them all. Only my farewell to Jukka causes tears to spring to my eyes. At the airport, I openly cry and laugh as we hug goodbye, and then look into his red-rimmed eyes to say that I'll come back.

My overwrought tirade to Sirja aside, I'm flying from Finland with love in my heart. This land, these people are in my blood; I can't stay away. Besides, I'm "leaving something behind." My cell phone lies at the bottom of the Baltic.

~Isoja kaloja kannattaa pyytää vaikkei saisikaan.~
~Big fish are worth fishing for even if you don't catch one.~

Mercury Rising

Looking out the large loft window opening, I gasp. The great oak is gone, but the spacious feel of the expanse is like a park, a baseball field. And without all the tall trees in the middle, revealed is the first rise of Mt. Mercury, a mix of tawny chaparral with patches of pine and oak. "Wow, I can see the mountain!" Previously the low house, so close to its base, allowed no view. But now, here in this new loft, I have a piece of the mountain.

"Beautiful, isn't it?" Steffen says, gazing with me out the un-paned window. On this late summer afternoon, the house and yard are empty of workers, though much work remains. The yard is cleared of debris, but it needs grass and landscaping. The new bedroom and bath, along with this loft are roofed, framed and sheet rocked, but little else. Fortunately, half of the house, which included the parlor, spare bedroom and only bath, survived the blaze and the plumbing, at the moment, is functional.

"I love it." The house now filled with light, so wide with space, the fresh scent of sawdust replacing the charred smell of burnt wood. My chest opens as if my heart is expanding.

When I bend to pick up a watercolor at my feet, Steffen holds me back from the un-paned window. The painting shows an envisioned backyard in pale pastels with shrubs and flowering plants. Trees border the yard more than fill it. An aqua lap pool stretches back from behind the sauna. The remaining old trees around the property's perimeter are showcased with plantings of pansies around their bases—purple and gold, white and baby pink.

The pictured yard is fenced with redwood. Pale wisteria like tapered clusters of grapes drape from a latticed trellis over the deck. I can almost smell their sweet scent. The effect feels Mediterranean.

I hold the painting toward him. "It's amazing, Steffen."

He moves in to point, "These are water-conserving plantings and—"

"But we need grass. A field for the kids."

"Kids?"

"The neighbors. And the fence is nice, but… "

"Alina, tread lightly. That's my design."

"I was thinking of no fencing, like free passage for the neighbors."

"The house isn't being sold with the neighbor kids attached." Arms crossed, he says, "It has to be fenced. Especially if the pool is built. Which you agreed to in Finland whether you recall it or not. Sometimes I doubted you were even listening to me on the phone. Too busy with other *pursuits.*"

This is our first encounter since I taxied home. As I hand over the painting, his eyes seem to reflect the blue of the sketched pool. Everything about the new house—this proposed yard, the loft, the larger master bedroom and second bath—delights me. While Steffen reappraises his watercolor, I watch his face, smell the sweat-salt of a workman, glad I dressed in white linen shorts and a sleeveless blouse cut to flatter my shoulders. Growing warm near him, I whip off my floppy hat. "It's gorgeous, Steffen. I mean it. I owe you."

"Hello! What's this?" Steffen rears back to look at my completely shaved head.

"My roots were showing?"

"Resolved your hair issues, I suppose. Quite a bold move."

"A bald one, for sure." Looking at him awash in bright light, I color, want to put the brimmed hat back on, hide in sunglasses. It's like staring at the sun.

"Going for the early Sinead O'Connor look?"

"Yeah, before she got herself to a nunnery, or whatever." That nunnery reference is so apt—I feel as though I've been in one for ages and being near Steffen, my hormones whipping into over-drive, I'm aching to revoke my vows. "I guess it'll be hard getting a date with this 'do.' But what the heck. I felt like a fresh start would do me good." As he continues to stare, the room grows hot—September, October, the hottest time of year approaches. I see that bemused grin he gets from teasing me.

"*Ei ole koiraa karvoihin katsominen,*" I admonish.

"Come again?"

I phoneticize it for him: "Ay oh-lee koir-aah kar-voi-hin kat-som-i-nen."

"Oddly, with Lou, the dog, and working with Dad on the house, I haven't had time to brush up on my Finnish. Afraid I'm not quite as fluent as you now seem to be."

"Judge not the dog by its hair, that's what it means. Pretty funny, eh? Like I haven't judged everyone. And everything." As I bend my knees to sit on the ledge of the gaping window opening, he jumps forward, holds tight onto my arm. "Don't worry," I carefully lower myself to sit on the sill. "I'm taking it slower these days. Not quite so klutzy." Despite my assertion, he sits next to me, and I feel a bit dizzy. *His touch.*

There's an awkward silence. "Alina, I have to be honest with you. I put a lot of time into this project, really got into it. It's been a labor of love, I suppose." *Of love*? For me? My heart speeds, pounds at my chest, I hold my breath. *Could he possibly still love me after all this time? After the way I broke up with him?* "I want to see it through. It's been good for me. And…" He ruffles his hair. "I guess it would be nice if you stayed here. For a while, at least."

I exhale. Of course he'd like a friend living here; me here to appreciate it, not just some strangers. I imagine working or studying in this loft, living in this soon-to-be charming cottage with its yard—where else would I be able to afford this in

California? But there are the issues of low housing prices, inadequate insurance money—which I didn't keep up after the death of my parents—loans and my recent laxity with money. Along with my plans to study rather than immediately go back to full-time work.

"I'm not even sure I can afford to stay here now, Steffen." Standing to pace, I notice several canvases leaning against a wall. More of Steffen's pictures? I step over to pull one out.

"What's this?" I hold up an oil painting of a mountain. I look at the familiar angles and shadows of Mt. Mercury at sunset. "You're painting again!"

"You'd be surprised how popular views of that mountain are. I've already sold one." I pick up another with thick strokes of army green, khaki, patches of deep forest green, camouflage colors. Army colors. I used to do battle with that mountain, this area. He takes the picture from me, replacing it in the stack. "That's not finished."

Instinctively, I hug him. "Don't be modest. They're fabulous." Inhaling his sexy salty sweat, I don't back off. "Better than fauxing, eh?" I say into his chest.

He puts his arms around me, our bodies close and warm. "So much better," he murmurs. My comfort becomes arousal… *mmmm*, how much better than the stiff embrace we performed upon my arrival here. Hugging him tighter, I feel vibrations. His cell phone rings.

Always the on-call dad, he picks up. "Not really a good time," then with a glance at me, he says, "The owner's here." The *owner*? Next thing I know he's bending over the loft railing to look out the spacious windows that flank the new front door. The high-ceilinged foyer flooded in light. "Oh." He presses the phone to his chest and says to me, "I'm afraid a friend's dropped by. A client. I've painted her something, as it happens, so—"

"So invite her in."

He hesitates. "Right."

When I turn around a few minutes later, a stunningly beautiful woman stands smiling next to Steffen. I swallow hard. Before me appear two perfect California sun-dolls personified. The woman is too faultless. Her auburn hair shines to her shoulders, absolutely straight in the current style, TV commercial straight, and her poochy lips glisten with gloss. She's dressed in a clingy black wrap dress that reveals a sizeable slit of cleavage. And though she's probably about my height, her steep heels make her an ideal fit for Steffen.

She's not his type, is my immediate reaction, but I can see that there's something between them. She stands so close. She grabs his hand and says with an eager squeeze, "Can I see it?"

"Well, um, perhaps we could take it downstairs—"

"No need, Steffen," I interrupt. "You know I love your painting."

"Right." Again with the "right" when everything feels so wrong. This woman is *so* wrong, some Mercurian coming on to him, a handsome single dad, easy prey. With that figure, I doubt she has kids.

"I'm sorry for interrupting," she extends her hand with a crystal smile to introduce herself as Kristen, politely averting her gaze from my shorn pate. My cranium hurts.

"Let's see the picture," I say curtly to Steffen, who leafs through his canvases by the wall. "So how did you two meet?" I ask Kristen. *Kristal Barbie.*

"At the park. I was there with my little Thatcher and he was there with Lou," she says. *Lou*, I don't like the sound of his name coming through her white teeth, the symmetry of her smile completely annoying. Someone should ban these playground meetings, it's unseemly for adults to use their kids to hook up. From the corner of my eye, I see Steffen redden. Kristen adds, "I'm divorced too."

"He's not divorced."

"Well, I know, but when a long-term relationship ends. You know." Geesh, he didn't waste any time.

"Right," I say. Right right right. She's too right, too flawless.

"Anyway, I've always wanted my portrait painted,"—I bet she has—"and when I found out Steffen's an artist, well." She bends down to join him at the canvases. How long can it take to find one human portrait in a range of damn mountains?

My gut churns. I'm backsliding—I don't want to feel this way again, making assumptions about this person, who currently leans into Steffen and whispers in his ear. If Steffen's with her she's probably very nice, possibly wonderful. I look at her perfect pear-shaped bottom, the thong lines barely visible under the tautly stretched fabric. No doubt great in bed. And an art lover, maybe quite an intellectual. She's a Venus genius, dammit! "Where's the freakin' picture?" I say, pulling on my hat, wishing my hair would instantaneously sprout.

"Got it." He holds the canvas frame up, the blank side with the wood cross-slats facing me. "I'm not sure if Kristin here would want you—"

"It's fine. I've got nothing to be ashamed of," that smile again. Beauty pageant material. He flips it around to show her lying on her side on a floor, head propped by one arm, under a window reflecting the greenery of treetops—completely naked. Long hair draped over one of her perky breasts, her top leg bent and draped over the other outstretched leg, a coy smile on her face. A perfect, unabashed, unblemished nude.

My brain tries to take it in, swirling, until I realize she's on *this* friggin' floor, my floor, with my green trees as backdrop. Then scanning her painted figure, my clear eyes see too much: she's nude everywhere, as in hairless! The small gap of crotch visible under the draped leg is bare as a baby's ass. I gasp. My hand flies to my mouth. My yard, her vagina—this is too much deforestation for one day!

I race from the room, feeling sick, slip down the newly

varnished stairs to lock myself in the old bathroom. Sitting bent over on the toilet lid, grasping my knees, I let the tears fall, hot and heavy, and try to stifle my sobs. What had I been thinking, anyway? That Steffen was waiting all summer—all these years—for me to come around? How can I still be so clueless?

Before long a knock rattles the bathroom door. "Alina?" Steffen says. "Are you all right?"

I snuffle quietly and clear my clogged throat. "Unh huh," I garble. Damn.

"You don't sound it."

I rise from the toilet but don't open the door. I sniff, "OK, so I'm not all right. I mean, what was that all about? Painting your naked girlfriend in my house? What, you think it's your studio? What else did you do in there? I mean, look at her! The hair, the bod, the…the *Venezuelan*!"

"If you want to talk about her crotch, I'm sure even you know they call it a Brazilian."

"Chilean, Uruguayan, whatever."

"Alina, painting a nude is no big deal. And plenty of women go to spas to wax—"

"I guess you're the expert on what plenty of women do! Besides, you know I'm not the spa type."

"Is that why you get your hair cut at the hospital?"

I slap my hand on the door. *Ouch!*

"Sorry, couldn't help myself. So what did you say? Let's not be judging the dog by its hair. Or lack—"

"She's no dog!" I try to piece this new Steffen together with the old one, the one I thought I knew. "It just seems. Weird. This is so *not you*."

"You'll be glad to know my pubic hairs are still intact, if that's what you're implying." After a pause, he says, "All kidding aside, Alina, won't you just open the door so we can talk?"

And those lips of hers! Looking in the mirror, I use my hand to push my lips out like a duck's. *Bee stung? More like hornet stung.*

Looks like she stuck her head in a hive—what, was she on a honey binge? I splash water on my face, check it in the mirror. Oh God. Elbows on the sink, I drop my head into my hands. This isn't the old me, it's a new feeling. And it hurts.

After a few deep breaths, I calm myself. I pat the stubbly, stubborn hair sprouting from my skull. My previously purple forehead bruises have healed to the mottled green and yellow look of dying leaves.

Steffen backs to the hallway wall behind him when I come out of the bathroom. In a defeated voice, I say, "Would you like me better if I had implants?" He stares, his mouth contorted. I sink down the wall behind me. "Or *hair*? Up here?" I pat my head, "but not down there?" I motion to my crotch, then my scalp. "If I moved my hair from here to here?" This jealous talk is crazy, I know. I have to stop.

Steffen slides to the floor across from me. "Banish the thought."

Sitting knees bent, I hide my face in my hands. "God, I'm sorry."

More gently, he says, "You know, she's really quite a lovely person." He lost me at "lovely."

"Yeah, I could see that." I raise my head, clear my throat. "Steffen, I'm really over that. I've *evolved*. Or am evolving. I'm through getting all worked up about all the pretty people and pretty houses and it's great that she named her kid after an ex-British Prime Minister and all but…" He waits. *This isn't about her. It's about you. And me.* "She's not for you." I stare at his work boots.

He scoots forward so that we sit toe-to-toe. "If you're so "evolved," as you put it, how is it you know after a five-minute meeting that she's not for me?"

I look up into his frank blue eyes. "Because *I* am."

*

When his mouth meets mine, my lips open wide and my whole body surges with electric pleasure. In the hallway, our tongues twist frantically, while his hands move from my shoulders to my hips and back up, stopping on my breasts, which he squeezes in his large heated hands. I groan. My body remembers this. I'm warm and pliable, he could mold me into anything. I grasp his neck and pull his thigh against me with my ankle. He nuzzles me, murmurs, "We left the bed in the spare room." I have a moment of lucidity as we walk there, wondering about protection, whether having sex now is the right thing to do…but as he takes my hand in his, my mother's words come to me: "Life is uncertain, so eat your dessert first."

Head bent, I fumble with the door handle. Steffen's lips gently brush the base of my neck. I tingle from his warm, moist breath, forget the door. From behind, he kisses me down the length of my shoulder blade, nudging away the fabric of my top. When his hands grope under my waistband and I feel the press of his hardness into my backside, I melt. I swivel to urge him against me. Our mouths grope and suck, tongues searching. I wrap a leg around him, he lifts the other and we slide into room.

On the bed, we strip madly. His hungry hands are everywhere. Moving down, he buries his nose briefly in my loins. I clutch his thick, silky hair. He kisses up my belly until our lips lock again. By then, I want all of him. The muscles and nerves between my legs contract and expand, breathing with a life of their own. I suck him in, swell around him. Rhythmically, I rise and fall. Slowly, he moves inside me. His thrusts make me draw him deeper with mounting waves of pleasure. Suddenly I arch and tighten, groan in bliss. He shakes with ferocity and fills me. His enveloping warmth feels like love.

Our lovemaking feels different now, deeper, because I am open, no longer afraid. I'm ready. Ready for whatever this all means.

~Isan hyvyys on korkeampi kuin vuoret.~
~Father's goodness is higher than the mountains.~

~Aidin hyvyys on pohjaton kuin meri.~
~Mother's goodness is deeper than the sea.~

Planting Birches

Now these are pheromones! After Steffen left yesterday, I chose to sleep in the sauna. He's been here, lying in the flannels of his sleeping bag, working on my house while I traipsed off to Finland after the wrong guy. Inhaling the musky sweat of Steffen in the bedding drugs me. I caress the soft cotton, snuggle deeper into the cozy bag, letting it swaddle me. When the sun rises, I grow warm thinking of our lovemaking.

Late in the morning, I pull the two boxes of ashes from my duffle bag, my mother's clean and smooth, my father's moldy and rough, the box covered with dirt and still damp from years underground. When Steffen arrives, he uses a flat blade to jimmy the top off of my father's pine box. Dipping my hand inside each urn, I feel them, my parents, bones and skin crushed to soft ash, a few hard shards.

In front of the house I ask, "What do you think of two birch trees flanking this front walkway?"

"Would look nice." He gives me a quixotic look. "You're talking about burying your parents' ashes here, Alina?" I tilt my head to the side to envision the willowy trees. "That's where they'll be, *forever.* I have to hope that you're not planning to have them dug up again?"

"No," I say. We're staying, all of us: Mom, Dad, and me.

We drive in Steffen's truck to the nursery, navigating first through Mercury. We pass the horse corral where Astro idles and

I smile. Steffen stops so I can jump out to stroke his rough mane. He lifts a hind leg, bats his child-like long lashes. I used to wear loneliness like a horse blanket, coarse and perhaps comfortable, but now I'm ready to fling it off. I'm eager to know my new home and its people.

At a rise in the freeway, the hills to the east roll in golden waves, those to the west ever green, I feel him turn toward me. "Can you afford it, staying here?"

"I think so." I don't mention that I'll need a roommate. "You know I want to study, possibly teach, like Dad. Maybe support myself doing part-time software testing."

"What would you study?"

"Well, I want to learn Finnish."

"Don't we all?"

"It gets better. I'd like a degree in something like...the Origins and Myths of the Finno-Ugric Peoples of the Volga Basin. You know, something useful." I catch his sideways smile.

As we walk through the bowered nursery, I garner the courage to say more. Away from the other shoppers, I pull him onto a stone bench behind a hedge of fragrant jasmine, a sweet spot. A fountain trickles nearby. I take his hands in mine. They're calloused. He's calloused because of me—and now maybe Meredith, though who could blame her? He's not the same easy-going, impetuous artist. He's careful, more subdued. But then, we're older. And he's a father.

"I want to stay in the house because of you. Because now I can't see myself anywhere else." His blue gaze is steady but unreadable. "I'm sorry," I say to the man I once spurned. "I'm sorry for the past. Maybe I figured out I loved you too late. You had Mere and Lou. Maybe I didn't want to admit it even to myself—who knows? I'm sure I belong in twenty years of therapy." I pause to think of all the things—so many!—that I want to say.

"Back then, I never really gave you a chance. I was so cavalier with your feelings. So… distrusting of their genuineness. But I was scared! I was afraid of getting pregnant. I was afraid of you and your—what you said you felt—love." I flail my arms. "Don't ask me why. I just blew it."

I look for a reaction but find none. Taking a deep breath, having doubts about how to word this, I continue. "So, if things with Meredith…if you decide to split up, there's always a place for you at the house. I'd like a roommate."

"You want me to help pay the bills." I see a twinkle in his eye.

"I'd prefer a roomie who didn't drive me crazy."

"Stop the sweet talk, already."

"Crazy with desire."

Since he smiles, I lean my head on his shoulder.

"What was it about Paavo?"

"I don't know, timing?"

"Then why'd you do it? Why'd you send Paavo—your *well-timed* love interest—alone to St. Petersburg?"

"It seemed like the only solution for Meredith at the time. But I know what you're asking."

"Maybe you wanted them to get together."

"I'm not sure I really cared. Maybe in my heart I already knew that he didn't love me? And that my feelings for him were somewhat contrived. He was a bit of a fantasy. But not in *that* way!" Oh, how could Steffen possibly love me after all the daft things I've done?

We choose amongst different trees, as he tells me that birches will need watering in the summer, they're not native to the climate. But they'll grow all right in my front northern exposure.

"Too un-PC of me?" The rest of the yard can be cacti, for all I care. I just need these to be birches. I tell him that the birch is sacred, the national tree of Finland, one that the Finnish epic, *Kalevala*, calls holy. I recall that flanking birches welcome visitors at *Juhannus*. (Though I think my next *Juhannus* party—if I ever attempt another—will be held at Ocean Beach.)

"How many gallons?" He holds up two hefty grown birch saplings. "Do you like these?"

"*Kyllä*."

"Goo-la?"

"*Keul-la*, it's more like the French. I make a deep, loud distinctly bovine noise, "GYOO" —just as a white-haired couple rounds the bend and pulls up short.

"These are somewhat heavy, Alina." He bends to drop the plant buckets. "And since I don't know French…what the hell are you braying?"

"*Yes*! They're perfect."

Back from the nursery, we dig a hole on either side of the front walk and place a sapling in each. I pour Dad's ashes in one. "Aatos means 'thought.' I'm his daughter, so I guess that's why I'm—or I *was*—always in my head."

"Not always," Steffen squeezes my arm.

I pour mom's ashes with the other tree. "The name Lempi means love." I let my tears be the first water the new tree receives. Together, Steffen and I add nutrient soil and move the clay-like earth over my parents' ashes. "Rest in peace now, Dad. With Mom. I love you both." Now, they are here, part of the living earth, together. With me.

Looping my arm around Steffen's waist, I say, "I'm so glad you knew them." More tears fill my eyes. "And I don't think I'd find a more wonderful place anywhere," the loveliness of the house stemming from the love he poured into it. "They'd like this. What you've done here." And I can tend to these trees, watch them grow, thrive from the tough stuff of my parents. "These birches will have *sisu*."

~Rakkauden tunne on kuin aurinko molemmin puolen.~
~To be in love is to feel the sun from both sides.~

Home

As I drive the winding road to buy bagels the next morning, I wonder where Steffen's been spending his nights. I'm not sure I want to know. I brake suddenly as a pair of wild turkeys crosses the road; the slanted sun illuminates their waddles day-glo orange. The small deciduous trees that line the road shine gold and vermillion against a sky bluer than the Baltic. A breeze hits, throwing a shimmer of tiny yellow leaves fluttering down like gold dust. The air is dense with change.

Once home, I sit in the crisp, fresh air on the deck my dad and Steffen built. Autumn, with the sweet smell of sycamore, on its way, my favorite time of year back East. Here, early fall is hotter than summer, but mornings can be cold, brisk, delicious. I hear the chuttering of squirrels and watch one loop along a far telephone wire, then slink up around a nearby elm. Drinking my hot creamy coffee and biting into a chewy bagel, I feel contented. Alone but not lonesome. The neighbor's house seems empty. I hope not for long…I want to see them all.

Steffen left after our planting yesterday without saying when he'd be back. But we're good, I can tell. Whatever happens, I've been honest with him, I've felt my feelings and expressed them. There's no controlling the outcome. Some things take time… I close my eyes and lean back, wrapped in my sweater. I tilt the baseball cap I've taken to wearing—after being asked twice, by total strangers, how the chemo is going.

When Steffen appears on the deck minutes—or an hour—

later, he kisses me on the neck. My entire body tingles with pleasure, I could make love with him here and now. The yard is still fully secluded by summer foliage, but soon enough the houses of neighbors on the next street over will be visible. I turn to draw him down, but he pulls back. "Keep your knickers on," he says.

"My knickers have been on for way too long." I go inside to pour him coffee, quickly smear a bagel. Sitting across from him on the deck, I ask about my dog, Coco, for it seems like the tenth time. Each time I hear that she's fine, growing, and staying with—*whom*? He tells me the kids next door are confused about who she belongs to—them, Lou, or me.

"It takes a village," I say. "But I haven't seen the neighbors."

"When Lou left with the dog, they were pretty bummed about both. So Marty and Becca packed them up for Disneyland or somewhere.

"And Lou? Have you been seeing him? And…Meredith?" The two would go together.

"It's a right zoo down there. Sue and Germaine are visiting with their wild twins, Lou's loving it, the dog's going bonkers. In fact, this morning even Paavo was there. Virtually." He raises his eyebrows at me.

"What?!" Then he explains that they were Skyping Paavo this morning. I say there is *no way*. Meredith doesn't even have wi-fi.

Turns out the new guy behind her is connected, and Germaine brought her laptop. Steffen says, "I even said hello to the bloke on my way out. All very civilized. But enough about that. Here." He places a small box, crushed velvet, royal purple, shabbily vintage, a tiny cube on the teak table between us. I fixate on it. His eyes are hazy. My heart hammers as peppy, happy mariachi music plays from the road, a passing car, its stereo on ear-splitting volume. The rising sun grows warm on my face. "Is that for me?" my voice squeaks.

Elbows on knees, leaning in, he takes my hands. "Alina, please, whatever you do, don't laugh. I've honestly felt something…something magical from the minute I met you—"

"You're the one I want!" a voice proclaims, and startled, we drop hands and turn to see Troy tromping through the back gate.

My heart on overdrive, I press it to calm the thumping. "Is he still coming around?"

"Sometimes." Steffen sits back, blows air out his cheeks. "I think he still feels invested."

The ever-dandy Troy trots across the lawn toward us in a dapper light-blue suit. At the bottom stair of the deck, he trills, "It's delightful to see you again, *Miss Eskala*. I didn't know you were back, or I certainly would've went to the store for flowers!" He sticks out his hand, "May I say you're looking lovely and I hope that all has been forgiven?"

I still hear Mexican music, a buoyant, dancing tune. You could do the polka. I bend forward to shake hands. "Yes, all is forgiven, Troy. Maybe not forgotten yet—but not to worry. Sorry I haven't had time to let you know."

His palms fly up. "Not a problem. But—" he checks out the situation. "It would appear that I'm *interloping* here?"

It would appear that my natural urge to offer him coffee has left me. "Sort of," I say, eyeing the box Steffen now holds. *Don't take it back!*

"Allow me to leave. Perhaps after asking just a few questions."

Steffen says, "Troy, this is a bad time." At which point the Mariachi music blares louder, then one after another three, then five, maybe six men appear at the gate. A backhoe or bobcat engine roars in the background.

"What the?" I look at Steffen.

He rubs his eyes. "What time is it? Forgot they were working today. The yard guys. Not sure what they're doing now… Dad handles the subs. Sprinkler system? Pool prep?"

"A pool? An excellent idea," Troy interjects. "Yes. A *must* for this property." Then he frowns. "Although it may add to the asking price…"

"Isn't this Saturday?" I ask. "Shouldn't they have the day off?"

"The guys here today *want* to work, Alina. *Venga*!" he waves in the men, who've remained paused at the gate's entrance. They pile in with their shovels and gear and one turns down the boxy, dust-covered radio in his arm.

"Miss Eskala, let's put this yard in shape for your new buyer!"

"New buyer?" I search Steffen's face.

"Well, Miss Eskala, Alina, I have a very interested party." I think the buttons on Troy's tight shirt might burst, he's so pink and puffed out, like one of those plucky tropical birds whose chest expands when courting a mate. I start to tell him that "it's too late," when he blurts, "*Me*!" and smiles to the far reaches of his expectant, chubby face.

My jaw drops. "You? What?"

"I'd like to buy the house!"

With a peek at the box and a wink—I think—at Steffen he says, "You might not know this, but Cleopatra only stayed with me the night of the, uh, *event* because she was interested in me. She doesn't even like the outdoors!" he chuckles, turns rosier. "I hope I am not taking the wind out of your sails when I say that I made a proposal to Cleopatra and that she has accepted it. My first offer!" *Is he talking about a house or a marriage?*

I'm trying to process this news: Troy and Cleo married? Wanting to live here? Can they afford it with his sense of non-reality? With her pharma sales, if that's what she still does? She'd explained in a letter I barely comprehended that Troy had "clicked" with Garth from the night they met, that somehow he had a natural way with him that put her often-agitated brother at ease. (She also alluded to sexual acrobatics—mental images I quickly erased.) But marriage? My house?

I gaze around and see the workers peeking from under the brims of baseball caps, cowboy hats. "It'd be too expensive, Troy.

But congrats to you and Cleo. Give her my best!" Thus dismissed, he proceeds to stand transfixed on the stair, evidently distracted now by the velvet box in Steffen's open hand. I wonder if he heard me.

Steffen says, "Excuse us, Troy." He leans toward me again. "Alina, as I was saying…"

"WHAT'S taking you so long?!" Cleo booms, striding toward us only to slow down at the sight of me. She's dressed in short shorts and a light, tight sweater but looks smaller than usual in flat sandals. "Oh," she gives an uneasy wave on slowly nearing us. "Hi?"

I step down to give her a hug. "Didn't you get my postcard, Cleo? We're good."

"Still." She looks to Troy. "I, uh, we…" She pauses, apologies not her strong suit, then comes out with, "Sorry about burning down your house."

"Yeah, well, mistakes were made all around."

"And we only burned half of it."

I smirk. "Right."

She scans the new bedroom addition, then cranes her neck up to the loft window that looks out on the yard. "Maybe we did you a favor."

"Har."

"The thing *is* is that Troy wants to live here but I'm not into this scene," she raises her arm to the vast property. You know me. And for Garth I think it's better if he stays in our—"

"Is he still in the car?" Troy interjects. "Let me go retrieve him."

"No!" I say immediately, rejoining Steffen on the deck. "Troy, Cleo, this is kind of a special moment and we need some priva—"

"O-M-G." Cleo spies the box that Steffen holds. She loops her arm around Troy's as he says something about Garth. "Shh," she says. "They want us to shut up." *Yes.* "And watch." *No!* My eyes race to the yard laborers nearby, back to Troy and Cleo—all these spectators! It's turning into a Hollywood scene...the audience, possibly applause...

At this I panic. "I'm sorry, guys. I'm not selling!" I grab the box and Steffen's hand and pull him down the steps past my open-mouthed friends. "Maybe you need time to learn what you *both* really want. Sometimes dreams take time!" I tug Steffen full-speed by the curious workmen. Panting, I shut the door inside the cool, dim sauna. Alone together, the cement floor firmly below my feet. I sigh with relief. "Whew!"

Steffen opens the velvet box to expose a tiny diamond ring. "Alina, at the extreme risk of coming off all rash like a rebounder—"

"*Yes*!" I scream and wring my arms around his beautiful neck. Yes yes yes! I slip the ring, too big, on my finger and pull him to the bench, onto the flannel bed. It smells like home. Excited with desire and a passionate yearning to be joined here and now, we make love, after all this time, in the sauna. Our lovemaking is a slow, long waltz that ends too quickly. Afterward, we both smile, blooming with love.

We lie on our sides on the bench, narrow for two, our sweat mingling. I hold my ring up to the draped sauna window to admire it, and Steffen tells me it was his grandmother's wedding ring. "It's a rather small diamond, but then I know you're not big on them." The stone is a murky dot in the delicate band; the gold setting envelops the stone like a volcano.

Giddy from just looking at it, I tease, "It's a good thing I got my eyes fixed or I might miss it. But then it's a diamond, why shout it, right?"

He smiles. "We could change it."

"Never. I love it." I look into his eyes, "I love *you*." He kisses me. Twisting the ring on my finger, I wonder if we made a baby. "What do you think of the name Mariel?" Steffen looks at me quizzically. "You know, from the Uralic people related to the

Finns…the Mari-El, the Khanty, the Udmurt."

"I like Mariel better than Udmurt." I laugh. Steffen, Mere, Lou, I'm marrying a family. All of a sudden, the world is perfect. I'm a member of more family than I dreamed of.

We sit up and slip into our clothes. I'm mentally keyed-up, excited. *Steffen*! This amazing man. Brimming with joy, I want to call Meredith, talk to Lou, Cleo, April back East. I want to tell the world. Jukka and Taimi—even Paavo. I want everyone to see my ring, to show it off.

I push aside the sauna curtain and see the yard workers toiling, shoveling as the day grows hot. "I'm glad we got to do that without onlookers."

"Have sex?"

I nudge him. "Your *proposal.* But now…I'm going to go tell them!"

Steffen stares at me in wonder. "Who? The men? Most of them only speak Spanish."

I stretch up my ringed hand. "I think they'll get it." I slap on my baseball cap and grasp his hand. "Let's go!"

He holds back, rakes through his tousled hair. "They might make a fuss."

"Wonderful," I say with a laugh, drawing him close. As we dance out the sauna, I fling my hat skyward to the glorious, peaking sun. "Let them cheer!"

~

ACKNOWLEDGMENTS

My thanks go to the faithful. First, writer and teacher Tom Parker, who in my mind remains my writing "mentor," whether he likes it or not. Readers of my early chapters—Tom, and writers Veronica Rossi, Harriet Chessman, and Wendy Tokunaga—provided encouragement and valuable feedback.

For developmental critiques and sorely needed confidence-building, I wholeheartedly thank Lyn Roberts and, above all, editor Vicky Mlyniec. Vicky, award-winning writer and editor of so many acclaimed authors, stands out in the field as a supportive and immensely talented professional. (Moreover, I suspect she possesses true *sisu*—a hidden Finn in her bloodline?)

Expert Lucinda Campbell kindly saved me the pain of converting the novel to e-book formats (several times), providing outstanding service for so little money that it feels criminal. Graphic artist Tracey Kirkman deserves a nod for fixing my back cover *gratis*.

To all of my Finnish relatives, especially Kari, Hannele, and Antti Valkonen, *kiitos paljon*! I promise to stop bothering you for a while. Additional thanks go to those friends of mine—you know who you are—who've been enthusiastic from the start. I'm filled with gratitude.

Last, I want to express appreciation to Eva, Chris, and Matthew, the three most beautiful young souls in my world. And to Mark, my *hengenheimolainen,* my first reader and first in all else, I thank you for the constancy of your love. Without that—without *you*—this book would not have been written.

ABOUT THE AUTHOR

Ellie Alanko is an award-winning author who enjoys writing about her Finnish heritage after too many years writing quasi-fiction—computer software manuals. She welcomes reviews and comments.

You can contact her on Facebook under Ellie Alanko and From-Finland-with-Love-a-Novel. She lives with her family in Northern California.

Made in the USA
San Bernardino, CA
06 January 2014